EARTH*BABY*

EARTH*BABY*

PETER SUCH

Ekstasis Editions

National Library of Canada Cataloguing in Publication

Such, Peter
    Earthbaby/ Peter Such.

ISBN 1-894800-57-5

    I.†Title.

PS8587.E695C64 2005   C814'.6   C2005-906279-1

Published in 2005 by:
Ekstasis Editions Canada Ltd.   Ekstasis Editions
Box 8474, Main Postal Outlet   Box 571
Victoria, B.C. V8W 3S1   Banff, Alberta ToL oCo

 **Canada Council Conseil des Arts
for the Arts du Canada**

 BRITISH
COLUMBIA
ARTS COUNCIL

Earthbaby has been published with the assistance of grants from the
Canada Council for the Arts and the British Columbia Arts Board
administered by the Cultural Services Branch of British Columbia.

Printed in Canada.

To Joyce – Warm wife and insightful editor
and to my daughters Julia and Zoe
none of whom will ever abide the future here presented

EARTHBABY

SOCIAL DYNAMICS RESEARCH PROJECT: EARTHBABY
(JOURNAL OF DR. LILLITH SHAWNADITHIT)

Paranoid as I am these days after Jock's death, I keep going over and over in my mind how best to keep these records confidential. One thought I had was really hair-brained. What if, I said to myself, I actually *write* this record — by hand I mean. You know, in little notebooks. No one on board will be able to read it, not even Alexandra, since she told me holography is one of the rare subjects she has never studied. Except for Clarke, the others are all younger than me; so I'm sure they weren't subjected by a reactionary Grandmother, as I was, to learning a skill about as relevant as embroidery. I laughed to myself imagining her wagging her finger with a gesture of "I told you, you'd find it useful one day."

In a collectibles store, I found a package of ancient Bik biros that actually still worked. But when I tried to use one I realized I'd lost the hang of it. It was so painful and so slow trying to etch out each letter of each word like that. Soon I gave up, my fingers cramped, wrist aching. Then I thought, well at least I'm from the generation that learned how to use a keyboard, to type, I mean. So I hunted around for one of those Little Red Schoolroom laptops that students used to use before the teacher lobby broke down and accepted the constant murmuration of classrooms of students using voice activators.

I've often thought how odd it is that typed information can be read silently much faster than if you read it out loud; but, on the other hand, no matter what you use to get it down on paper, you can't write or type it or feed it in vocally any faster than you can speak.

So now I type on this little laptop (in the hidden-text mode, with privacy-code — my ultimate solution).

This first evening I am strapped to my berth in the super shuttle. We have been catapulted successfully out of Earth orbit by the energy transfer of rounding the moon into a deep space trajectory half way toward Mars where Earthbaby rides waiting for us. I can feel how self-conscious I am, knowing these records are going to be poured over by a host of researchers and historians, continuously reinterpreted according to the fashion of their age, and their own predispositions.

Start with the launch.

Scared? You bet. I always hate losing consciousness, even if only momentarily. And that sense of total helplessness, being entirely in someone else's hands... Alexandra was the first to come to life. While we others were stirring into full consciousness, she was already sitting up, alert, on her launch couch. Actually I was quite impressed by the way this middle-aged body of mine performed. Even better than Clarke's and Grainger's I suspect. As for young Adam, he later told me he was so struck with terror or with making a false move he just lay there paralysed.

For a moment, elated the actual launch was over with, I momentarily forgot about Jock — about his being dead, I mean. In my mind was the image of his pleased half-shy smile at how successful he would have felt with Earthbaby finally completed, and we — its first crew — well on our way. The same smile he'd have on his face... what the hell, I may as well say it since I have the option to edit it out any time I want with this thing... the same smile he'd have on his face, looking down at me after I'd had a screaming come when we were love-making.

But, of course as always, there follows the rush of bitter black reality. Months now, and every morning I still wake up despairing, heart-sick... though by the time I clean my teeth — at least these last few weeks — I feel the anguish being taken over by anger, a hot fury rising up from my groin, from there where our love was planted.

Those bastards. One day, Jock, they'll answer for all this.

There. I'm doing it. Writing to you as if... Shit! I know that's a stupid thing to do. I know you're dead. Still, I should be easier on myself. As long as I keep it a harmless fantasy, won't it be all right? I mean, wouldn't I allow that, maybe even encourage it, in one of my own therapy patients? One thing I'm glad about is the secrecy we had. That only Tremaine knew about us.

I guess people can be amazingly blind to the soap opera around them if the characters don't fit into the conventional mold. I mean, look at me. Not bad for my age, but not exactly Marilyn Maddona Mona Lisa. And Jock could have had his pick like Tremaine does if he had wanted to.

All right. Enough of this. Back on flightpath, please!

Alex was really sweet to me. What a paragon she is. "Come on," she said, taking my hand in hers, smiling as if this was all just simulation play, adroitly negotiating my floating body towards the port window, my palm oozing fear-sweat onto hers, a tiny droplet suspended like a dustmote in the sunbeam filtered by the isinglass. I hope Tremaine saw us.

Tense as I was, it was nevertheless very impressive to see the tracking satellite glide close by, a metal pterodactyl, clumsy yet so graceful. In fact I found I was crying when we looked back at the earth, shoulders of its dark side spangled with lights of cities; and the blue of its atmosphere was the colour Van Gogh uses to evoke starry skies and old church windows.

Then she went over to Adam, who was still lying there just staring into — quite literally — space. She floated him back and positioned him beside me, making a little chuckle when Adam couldn't stop himself twisting upside down.

"What's so funny?" he said jovially, making a brave attempt to make light of his anxiety, wiping his forehead and clownishly veering off balance again so she had to straighten him out.

"You remind me of two goldfish banging their noses on the side of the bowl."

Adam was transfixed once he got a good look at the receding planet. "My God! Look at that will you? Just look at that!"

"How you doing?" I said, noticing him trying to control his tendency to hyperventilate. He's one of those sinewy types, cerebral and awkward from lack of body awareness, the kind who get vaso-vagal attacks. I didn't fancy going the rest of the journey in a cabin full of free-floating upchuck, thank you.

"Fine Lilly. Just letting the rest of the world go by, you know."

I had to admire his attempt at bravado. Somehow, Alexandra has that kind of influence on men. They don't tend to behave like such god-awful wimps all the time. Taking my hint, though, she took him by the ankles and maneuvered him back to his launch-couch. I made my own way back, my last sight of the earth making me think how picayune it looked receding into space. ᘰ

ndrew Tremaine — still, goddam it, civilian head of NASA — waits for the producer's signal. What more could a man want than to see the fruition of his life's work scintillate over a billion TV screens? On a wall-sized monitor he scrutinizes the supershuttle's vapour trail uncoiling across green continents. No problem. At least the fucking thing is up there. What happens once it gets to Earthbaby is anyone's guess.

So here he is, probably for the last time, earthbound as usual, sitting beside Bill Edgely, last of the old-time anchormen. How many times have they done this at the start of a launch? An assistant dabs shine off Bill's dark forehead with a powder pad. Edgely grins. "Thirty seconds, Andy."

"Okay Bill. You going to lead me in?"

"Sure. You're doing great as usual, Andy boy. Listen. Want to stink this up a little? Some comments on the future of NASA once you're gone?"

Tremaine's heart tightens. "I want to mention Jock, naturally. And also take a few shots at that bastard Foreman."

"So go for it, man!"

Through his headphones, Tremaine hears Captain Clarke's voice crackling down from the super shuttle cockpit: "Booster jettison confirmed, NASA."

And there he sees it go — spent propulsion cylinder reeling away, the shuttle continuing spacewards straight and silent. How romantic it all looks when the screen is framing it, gleaming silver against the blue arc of the atmosphere. In a few moments, though, it will enter the deep black contrast of space where there's no up, no down, no human turmoil. No second chances allowed.

The producer signals, points at Bill Edgely. They are on — his own face white and work-drawn, set against Bill's black and mobile one.

Edgely assumes his familiar role, dated now, in contrast to the hipsters on news-games videos, but still treasured by that economically potent golden oldies segment merchandisers are always aiming at.

"Back on earth here again with Andrew Tremaine, Chief

Administrator of NASA. How does it look, so far, Mr. Tremaine?"

"You could see the booster drift off there a moment ago, Bill. It all looked good. Very soon now we'll lose our video contact for a minute or so until the next tracking satellite swings round on it."

"Yes. You can see the shuttle dwindling on the right of your screen, viewers.... In the meantime, while we wait for our next pictures of the super-shuttle's epic journey, let's learn a little about its crew. Five diverse people on their way to be colonists of the first self-supporting deep-space habitat."

"Each of the crew members chosen to live on Earthbaby, Bill, was selected by a three member committee representing the three partners in this enterprise...."

"Those three partners are, of course, yourself — representing NASA.... And I see you have chosen two famous female astronauts. There. Now you can see their pictures."

"Yes. Dr. Lilly Shawnadithit, social dynamics officer and, on the right, Dr. Alexandra Adachi, communications."

"Then, the major financial contributor from the start of the Earthbaby project, Agriminco corporation...."

"Right, Bill. Their two selections are more in the technical line: Co-pilot Grainger Prashad and botanist Dr. Adam Rutenberg."

"Finally, Bill, in these very difficult last stages of the venture, Colonel Clarke Grantham, appointed by the Pentagon Corporation under CEO General Foreman,..."

"Our country's military corporation, which, we all know from the turmoil in the media, recently replaced the original Eurosoviet sponsors."

"Exactly."

"As noted, Colonel Clarke Grantham is shuttle pilot and mission commander."

As Edgely speaks, the crew's five faces are replaced on-screen by the super-shuttle in extreme close-up.

"Here we have the super shuttle again. See any problems?"

Tremaine hunts for damage as the craft turns gracefully like an ancient whale in the ocean. An edge of the sun brushes like a hand over its gleaming grapho-plaque skin. The spacebride...and not a scratch on her. Thank God, he thinks. Looks like she's delivering them all safely.

"All clear so far, Bill. Now you can see the port window coming into view!"

"Amazing shot! I can actually see their faces!"

Yes…Lillith's face…and Alexandra's…clustering there, as they said they would, his chosen ones…the hope….

Quickly the image of the craft dwindles and fades as the tracker's zooming telephotos begin to lose it in the black of space.

"I guess, folks, that's the last we'll see of this fantastic craft and it's amazing crew for some time. And surely, back here on earth, Mr.Tremaine, you must feel a great sense of pride in what everyone recognizes is your greatest triumph, fought for so long and hard through so many difficulties and delays…."

"My one regret is that Jock Sparling is not here to share it with me."

"I understand you and NASA have officially dedicated this launch to Jock Sparling's memory. It must have been quite a shock to you and, of course, the original Eurosoviet contingent with whom he was working so closely…."

"There are always battles to be fought."

"Speaking of which, there's been some talk that under General Foreman's leadership the Pentagon, having replaced the Eurosoviets as the third partner, may intend to use the Earthbaby Space Habitat for purposes other than originally intended. Any comments, Mr. Tremaine?"

Tremaine takes a deep breath. Let the bastards have it.

"As you know, Bill, like yourself, I'm due to retire in a few months: but I can say this. It will be over my dead body that Earthbaby's mission will be diverted from Jock Sparling's vision of humans taking the first step to becoming a unified multi-planetary species. While I have anything to say about it, I will vigorously oppose any attempt to involve Earthbaby in either domestic or international military chess games."

"Clearly, then, you are looking with some trepidation toward the outcome of the forthcoming presidential election?"

"It would certainly be naive of me not to do so. General Foreman's policy slogan: *Army Aiding Industry Aiding Army* signals the end for NASA, or for that matter, any other independent scientific or space research programmes not dedicated to military use. NASA will simply be privatized, like the Pentagon itself. Then, I suspect, the two will be merged under the Lifeist Christian Soldier syndicate in a share buy-out engineered exactly the same way as their buy-out of the Pentagon itself a few years ago."

There goes the producer signaling frantically from the control booth. Tremaine watches Edgely hesitate, wanting to continue, but afraid of having what has just been said cut out by the five second tape delay if he goes on with it.

"Thank you, Andrew Tremaine, for your great service to our nation. Let us fervently hope that your vision of all humanity living in space in peace and harmony will be realized. And now, back to New York, where I will be talking to General Foreman himself, catching perhaps a response to what Andrew Tremaine has had to say today."

The producer counts his ten seconds for the fade-out as Tremaine watches the programme signature scroll over his and Edgely's faces on the monitor. Bill takes off his headset and he follows suit.

"You were great, man," Edgely says, offering him a coffee, looking around to make sure they have privacy. "This upcoming election special's probably my last gig too, did you know that? Before I go I'm gonna get the knife into that bastard Foreman."

"Wish I could say it might make a difference. Foreman will win even if he has to rig every computer voting machine on the continent. That's too bad you're going, Bill. You're about the last island of sanity in the media mess."

Edgely extends his hand. "Hey, we may be silverbacks, but we got a sting or two left before the used parts factory gets us, man."

Tremaine takes his hand, feels something in Edgely's palm pass into his as Bill, giving him an old-style bearhug, drops his voice low, murmurs in his ear, "The number, man. Memorize, destroy immediately, password is SHUTTLE. Urgent. Real urgent."

Tremaine whispers back, "The Society? Through you?"

A quick affirming grin; then Edgely, charming and public again as his producer comes forward, backs away, waves goodbye with, "Any time, Brother. Be seein' you."

Tremaine, left alone and alert makes straight for the washroom. He goes into a booth and hunches over, suspicious of cameras. He fixes the number in his mind quickly, rips it into microshreds and flushes it down with his own body stream.

So far, so good. Anyone could see he was more sympathetic to Tribals than to Privates, but up to now The Society's contact with him has only been subtle and oblique, especially after Jock's death: little slogans on his computer with ten second decays, people in stores saying hello out of the blue and sympathizing with him over things they shouldn't have known about. Obviously all that has been a kind of testing to see if he would report any of it. Urgent. That's what Bill said. Meaning he should call the number right away? In the middle of a launch? He should be back in Central Control right now, in fact. Tonight, then. On an unbugged phone....

Tremaine makes his way into the high-domed amphitheatre room from the back. The vast dim space reminds him of an old-style movie theatre. As he sidetracks the visitor's section, Foreman's face flashes onto the big wall screen, being interviewed by Edgely. The rows of spectator seats, at launch times normally filled with an excited jabbering crowd of the control room crew's family and friends, are strangely quiet.

Jesus! Every one of them is filled with Foreman's men, silent, gum-chewing. All of them are uniformed in that ridiculous padded-shoulders look of fifty years ago: suit, shirt with priest's round collar, topped with an old-style baseball cap emblazoned with the Lifeist cross. 'Lifeguards'! How could they have the nerve to call themselves that? What a bastardization of the language! The usual lively crowd has been excluded: probably by being refused visitor permits.... Damn it! Something else that must have gone by his desk in the last few days when he wasn't looking... All these little ways Foreman's lackeys keep people on the defensive... forcing them to react to the Lifeguards' unremitting obsession to control every little corner of the world around them: what's taught in schools, is seen on the media, is allowed on the streets — a reactive fundamentalism deadening as any in the Sword of Sadahm Crescent.

And Jock, the uncontrollable, reacting to them all too powerfully, too well.... At least Lilly is up there now. For Jock's sake he has managed to make sure of that.

Foreman's doughnut munchers stare at Tremaine coldly as he descends the aisle, towards the apparent confusion of the technical cockpit area. In the middle of that hive of flickering screens is his traditional seat, side-by-side with Jock's on the little raised podium over ranks of technicians and scientists monitoring the supershuttle's systems.

At this moment, on the large screen, Foreman has his mouth

open, looking rather stupid. Edgely is going after him. Down on the floor, Tremaine moves through the maze of control desks and over to the few steps leading to the podium. He looks up to where Jock has sat so many times....

And what's this? In the chair next to his — Jock's chair, for God's sake! Yes. Someone has had the gall to sit in Jock's chair! Okay, buddy. Someone is going to get hell for this!

An arm grips his above his elbow. He turns....

"James! What the hell is going on here, you know I gave specific..."

In the dim light, James' face is a pale blob. Without his glasses on, Tremaine knows he won't be able to read his features.

"I'm sorry, Andrew. I was just about to go up and get him out of there."

"Who the hell is it?"

"Regio Powers. President of Agriminco. I think he went up there quite innocently. His henches hoisted him onto it."

Tremaine looks at the semi-circle of steroiders at the podium's base standing by the President's elaborate empty Carechair.

"Is he a genuine crip or just a prostheticant?"

"Genuine, I think. Look at his henches."

True. None of them are wearing crip gear, not even neck cages. So this is how fashion-fads start: homage to power, desire to share in it, a touch of mockery through exaggeration. Well, here's one of its major inspirations. And after all, compared to Foreman, Powers and Agriminco have carried out their contract agreement fairly responsibly. The old fart probably has a genuine interest in the Earthbaby venture.

"Shit!" he tells James. "Let the old boy stay. I hear his brains are notchy any way. Fuck. What a comedown from the old days when Jock and I..."

On the big screen, Tremaine sees Foreman trying to divert Edgely's straight-on attack by falling back on one of his usual platitudes: "The success of this venture is exactly the kind of thing the Pentagon Corp's social service role can help accomplish..."

Tremaine, barely acknowledging James' introduction to Regio Powers, slides into his seat with a curt, "If you'll excuse me, I'm rather busy here." James stands, leaning over, on the other side of him. The Agriminco president continues watching Foreman being made a fool of. Tremaine slips on his glasses.

"I thought you might have taken the opportunity to publicly announce your early retirement just now," James says.

"Just think," Tremaine says to James, "if Foreman himself were here — instead of you standing in for him — I could reach up and strangle you, and all my troubles would be over."

"I'm just thinking of your welfare, that's all, Andrew. I've seen you popping those stripping pills."

He has a certain likeable quality, James, the thin looks of a sensitive opera-going type, with a nice wit of his own and often — like now — an apparent empathy, unlike his crude Pentagon colleagues. Maybe James has a *genuine* liking for him.

Hold on…. Listen to your paranoia. That concerned demeanor of his is just one of a front man's manipulative devices, calculated to gain trust. But boy, James does seem agitated today, the way he's holding on to the console, whipping his head around every few seconds to stare at me….

Edgely continues to make Foreman uncomfortable. "The world's press has been uniform in condemning as a threat to world peace the input of the Pentagon into what was to have been an international collaboration. Just what are the Corporation's intentions in regard to Earthbaby?"

"Intelligence information led us to believe the original NASA concept was a subterfuge, by certain leftist Tribals in the organization, to reduce our Nation's distinct leadership in space minerals exploitation."

"General Foreman. There are rumours that should you be elected, you intend to use Earthbaby as a military base."

"Our aim is peace through strength and security, in the tradition of Miles Standish, protector of the Plymouth colony."

"Can we get clarification here? Will there be nuclear weapons on the station?"

Foreman goes into a rant: "Without a large injection of discipline and efficiency, this project would have foundered and our national security would have been…"

Tremaine puts on earphones, cutting Foreman's voice off, concentrating on re-establishing himself in the present configuration of systems lights before him. Through the phones, he recognizes a couple of familiar voices from the control room. A poignant rush tightens his chest remembering earlier launches with Jock and the others by his side, the elation, the zest.... Truth is, ever since privatization of the military and its take-over by Lifeists, boundaries of acceptable right-wing philosophies have been pushed steadily towards Neo-Fascism. These last few years have been a kind of guerrilla warfare, warfare conducted in boardrooms and corridors of affable threat.

On the large screen, he sees the General's bland face grow gruff and angry. Go for him, Edgely. He takes the earphones off, only just in time to hear Edgely closing out the interview. That face, seamed and polished with over forty years of thought and work, fills the room benignly for a moment, then disappears. I may never see him again, Tremaine thinks, unless....

James suddenly breaks his silence.

"Well, Andrew, you and Edgely sure gave it to the General this time."

"No more than you guys deserve, James."

"All that aside, Andrew, I speak as a friend when I say it must give you some satisfaction to know you're ending your career on such a high note."

James' tone is so complimentary, Tremaine almost falls for having a rush of liking for him. Wait. Think of what they probably did to Jock.

Polite as ever, controlled, "Thank you, James," he responds.

"Listen, Andrew..." (This new urgent tone in James' voice not heard before. What's happening with him?) "...The election's only two weeks away now. We know Foreman's going to win one way or another. You've done what you wanted as far as you could. Why not bow out now, gracefully, full of honours, in a blaze of glory?"

Tremaine steels himself. "You mean, like Jock did?"

Shit! Now he's let something slip. Take care. Take care. Pay no attention to Jame's face wilting and crumbling....

"I want you to know, Andrew, I thought very highly of Jock."

In the eerie glow of the huge room, surrounded by banked rows of menacing uniforms, console doppling, voices crackling in his earphones, Tremaine feels cut off, floating like the spacecraft in an empty black. Some people *do* break down. Some people *do* defect to the other side. Something serious happens that disgusts them...like murdering Jock?...and then...? Wave of paranoia again. Mustn't let on he knows anything about Jock's murder. Or that The Society has been working on it for months, trying to make a case against Foreman that will stick....That's what all this with Edgely and the society is to do with no doubt.... Christ! What if James knew I had the connecting phone number in my pocket only five minutes ago?

"I'm sure Jock would have greatly appreciated your remarks, James. If you don't mind, I've got things to attend to here."

Turning on his swivel chair deliberately away from James, Tremaine notices the president of Agriminco, gesturing to his henches. Good. He's leaving.

But seeing Tremaine looking at him, Powers raises his hand in triumph.

"Brilliantly done. Another giant step for mankind."

"Step one, anyway. A launch is always a tense time. Glad you could be here."

All these platitudes. How many times has he said that and never meant it?

Powers seems to be still elated. His henches start to carry him away, but he stops them. There's more he wants to say. Judo-chopping the chair-arm, continuing the motion with every word, he proclaims: "Capital! Capital! Focused capital! Concentrated capital! That's what gets things done. You're a scientist, Tremaine. You know about critical mass. None of this so-called democratic diffusion of money. A critical mass of capital and power — that's what you need."

Astounded, Tremaine says nothing as Regio Powers is carried off. Jock's chair, empty at last. Tremaine tries to concentrate again, switching to the shuttle audio.

Enhanced by the vox-coder, Clarke's voice from the shuttle comes through flat but clear. "Thirty seconds and away we go!"

A good steady pilot, Clarke, even if he is the Pentagon pick. Wait! What's happening? A flash of lights on the console out of phase. His peripheral vision has caught it. An anomaly on the countdown sequence for shuttle engine ignition — crucial for the acceleration which will boost the craft on tangent out of earth orbit.

"Control? What's going on?"

"A pre-ignite on stabilizing nozzle. We're trying to catch it, Mr. Tremaine."

Then, Clarke's voice, still calm, "Hey NASA! Get this spin will you?"

For the first time, he hears co-pilot Grainger, Agriminco's asteroid man: "Gyro stable hitting red, Clarke."

Tremaine is now alert, totally occupied, as if he is Clarke, is co-pilot Grainger, is Lillith, Alex, Adam, even the trembling engines of the craft itself. Nevertheless, he becomes conscious of James clutching the arms of Jock's chair as he stands behind it. Tremaine has time for a fleeting thought only: My God he's as involved in this as much as I am…Five seconds, ten, fifteen….

NASA isn't getting it. He hears Grainger, tense this time: "Override it, Clarke."

"Overriding might kick us off trajectory. Let NASA get it, Grainger."

He's right of course. The wise decision, but what if…? Those damn retro-nozzles have limited capacity. If this spin mode gets going much faster…. He checks the dopple of lights…. Damn it!

Clarke's voice now panicky: "Jesus guys! Catch this spin for Christ's sake!"

Clarke's hands would be over the panel waiting to dart down…seconds, only seconds, and the damn thing is spinning around enough, even in zero-gravity, that you would feel it, would know that little window was closing on you, closing….

Then Grainger. No pretense now, yelling, on the edge of hysteria. "I'm taking it, Clarke, goddamn it. I'm taking it!"

"Let him take it!" Tremaine yells into the communicator.

Grainger. Younger, faster. A better chance.

Clarke cuts in: "I'm also overriding on the velocity program NASA. Cutting with retros. Reprogramme at 6,000. On signal. Now!"

"Good man!" Tremaine mutters, realizing how Clarke is backing up Grainger's actions. He watches console lights flicker as the laser umbilicous readjusts attitude and vector, smoothing out the two pilots' crude manual overrides.

"Come on, come on," Tremaine almost shouts as he watches them try to grapple with a violent port skew.

Too much…easy…easy…. It's as if the sticks and buttons are under his own fingers. But his own reflexes are that much slower than Grainger's, his eyes recognize the next necessary moves only in the instant that Grainger is actually applying them.

Gradually the reds give way to yellows, blues, and greens, each flicker a knot untightening in his stomach until finally Tremaine knows they are going to win and the console dopples down to its previous equilibrium. Tremaine breathes with relief, a slight tick of angina pain registering down his left arm from his still thumping heart. Shit! More stripping pills. More wooziness and irritability.

He presses "M" on his keyboard. "Monitoring? I want a search and report on that anomaly right away."

He turns to James. "You look a bit green, there, old boy. Lucky we had someone self-motivating like that Agriminco chap, Grainger, up there. If it had been all your Pentagon boys it would have been kiss goodbye while they waited for orders."

James has a feverish sweat on his forehead. He stares at Tremaine as if he hasn't heard.

"Are you all right James?"

James takes a deep breath, leans forward and grabs the arms of Tremaine's chair, swivelling it so they face each other.

"Listen Andrew. You've got to resign. Right now. Right now."

The intensity of James' look is startling.

"What the hell's the matter with you? Are you ill?"

"There's no stopping Foreman, Andrew, and you know it. No stopping him, Andrew. You must quit now."

Years of compromise and studied politeness gather like a knot in Tremaine's throat. He's surprised how angry his own voice sounds.

"Sure, James. Roll over like a dead dog while Foreman's Lifeguards convert Earthbaby into a fascist dugout bristling with missiles? Fuck off, James."

James staggers to his feet, looking nauseous.

"You asshole. You're so pigheaded. You won't listen to anybody who…"

Then he stops, gazes up, conscious he's being observed by those rows of Foreman's Lifeguards beginning to file out of the visitors' seats now the show is over. He rises.

"I'm going to be sick," he says, rushing away, staggering blindly out the lower exit.

Tremaine gets up to follow him. Then sits down again, watching the console. Everyone's nerves are shot, all right, including his own. That's the trouble with getting older. When you're young, you think that experience will make you calmer. But experience only pushes the agitation back a notch so others can't see it the way they can when you're first-timing things. His hands are shaking. He looks over to Jock's empty chair.

All these people, and not one he can talk to….

SOCIAL DYNAMICS RESEARCH PROJECT; EARTHBABY.
(JOURNAL OF LILLITH SHAWNADITHIT)

How picayune…. Yes. Applying also to what I'm about to write about now. God I get tired dealing with the predictable ups and downs of people's delicate egos. It looks like we're in for a dilly of a leadership contest between Clark and Grainger. I don't have much of an idea, technically, about what went on during the emergency except we could all hear the communications quite clearly. Those guys are trained to act and talk like robots, so you know something pretty serious is up when their voices lose it. I won't go through it all. NASA has all the tapes and data, and they'll be able to make a better judgement than I whether Grainger was right to supersede Clarke's authority. Who knows? Maybe Clarke could make a case that there was still time, albeit short, for the override decision to come from himself or NASA. Personally, I'm glad we're all here and that Grainger's decision, right or not, had the value of successfully saving us!

Once it was all over, and we were out of the spin and back on trajectory, I tuned my eyes and ears up to see what might happen between them. Clarke could have cited Grainger for pre-empting him, going off half-cocked with panic, that sort of thing. I was surprised, and rather glad about it too, for I do like Clarke personally, maybe because he's more in my age-group than anything…surprised when he reaches out to Grainger, shakes hands with him and says, "Well, Buddy, we made it."

Spontaneous cheers broke out from the rest of us which I found myself joining in on. Oh that was clever of you, Clarke. At the same time as recognizing Grainger's contribution, it confirms you in your position of authority: a wise praise-giver to a lesser subordinate.

But I know Grainger is going to be on his tail. He has that young knight-errant quality, one of those bright talented young buccaneers who make their way up in corporations with a single-minded self-serving ambition. Clarke, in the face of that, trained in military loyalty codes and habits of self-subjugation to authority or group welfare, could have a hard time competing.

If this develops, we all could have a hard time of it…. ❧

H ead in hands, eyes closed for a moment, Tremaine reminds himself, don't act in panic.

A run-in with James is nothing to worry about. The main thing right now is Edgely giving him the Society's phone number. Urgent. Damn! Why can't they all just go away and leave him in peace. There's only so much a man can do, after all, and fighting the good fight against the cultural tide all these years....

How old was he? Ten? Squatting on the floor, with one hand gripping the arm of his grandfather's wheelchair, watching the twenty year anniversary rerun of the first moon landing all in black and white. Werner Von Braun, then head of NASA in 1968 had come on, all friendly and chatty.

"My God!" his grandfather had said. "You see that man, Andrew? He's the man who invented the rocket bombs which blew up the women and children of London, forty-five years ago. He dropped a rocket bomb on me when I was no older than you are now. You know something, son. That old war ain't over yet." And he had lurched his chair forward to turn the hated face off, cutting the image dead.

Fifty years ago, his life was set. And that war of his grandfather's still not won.

"I'm taking a break," he announces over the intercom.

He heads for the cafeteria. Not the executive one. He wants to go to the one with mechanics, secretaries, warehousemen... ordinary people doing their best at the things they've fallen into, stumbling through their lives without taking more than their fair share... those are the people he wants around him now, people like his Grandad who worked from his chair drafting up plans for airframes at Avro on the ill-fated Arrow, his Grandma in the shipping department, up there in Cold City, as they used to call Toronto before the warming, on the shore of Lake Ontario in what used to be Canada.

As he strides quickly through echoing corridors, past security checks, he becomes conscious of being followed. Big deal.

In the cafeteria he searches through the sea of faces looking for a comforting island. Ah! Janet. A pleasant bright woman, drop-out from astronaut training, someone he'd helped now and then. She was once a member of Jock's old staff, working now under the new penta-gon masters.

Many eyes on him, but few greetings as he brushes through a thicket of plastic chairs. She sees him coming, turns her face away and reaches for her handbag.

"Do you have to go?" he says, sliding into a chair beside her. Since the last time he's seen her she's had a holocaust haircut, and across her neck is a throat-slash transfer, a bare nipple showing through the rips of her rape-victim blouse is metallicised. At least she hasn't picked up on the prostheticant fad.

"I didn't know you were a fashion freak, Janet? What's been hap-pening?"

Janet's face goes blank.

"What's happening is survival, Andy. I've got to get going, okay?"

The fact she ends with a slight question in her tone gets his anten-nae alert again.

"Can't you talk to me?"

Distressed, Janet begins moving away.

"I can't talk to you ever."

In her haste she crashes over one of the chairs. He's suddenly the centre of every one's attention. Left alone, Tremaine senses the pool of silence around him.

So. Suspicion about Jock's death is probably tribal knowledge throughout the centre. If you step out of line, then…

What had he said to Edgely? "Over my dead…"

And then there was James' strange behaviour. And Edgely saying, "urgent…"

Two Lifeguards are framing the door where he came in, their stu-pid baseball caps like bird beaks about to peck each other. All right. Don't panic, he says to himself, that's the thing. There's another exit at the back of the cafeteria.

No-one there. I'll go that way. They'll expect me to return to con-trol. But I'll head for the roof, take my private 'copter… Do the unex-pected thing. Keep them off balance.

So far so good. Knowing his way around the blind alleys of the complex helps him keep the security people confused as to where he's going. He makes it to the small private elevator going up to the roofpad and operates it with his key. Two Lifeguards holding radios in their hands turn into the corridor as he steps in. Damn. But what can they do?

At the top the elevator opens onto the vestibule of the helicopter pad. Real daylight shocks his eyes. And the real heat of the day, damp and perfumed, pats his face. On the wall across from him is another Foreman poster with his catchline, 'It will be done' under his picture. A few miles away, under the haze, is San Juan where only the old folks speak Spanish any more, and where, every day, he's seen this same poster — laser projected as a hologram across the highway.

He hustles straight out onto the tarmac, passing a security man with his radio to his ear. Quickly he climbs in and presses the start-up button, skipping a cockpit check. His heart calms as he undoes his jacket and locks into the seat. The rotors spin then catch fire. He watches for the hydraulics to reach operating pressure, glancing out the window at the same time to see James, with two Lifeguards, running out to him, James waving his arms frantically.

Quickly Tremaine pulls down the harness and feathers the blades, causing a burst of air to ripple their clothes and blow off the Lifeguards caps as he increases the revs. Afraid to come closer James and the Lifeguards stand there, mouths open as he slides the copter over their heads. Too bad, guys. And don't expect to find me at home, either.

He keeps within the protected zone surrounding the laser umbilicus that connects with Earthbaby. That way he'll be invisible to radar. To stay in that zone as long as possible is the idea, which means going for maximum height at this time of day, if he remembers the co-ordinates right, maybe even above the cirro-stratus cloud streaks. There's no feeling quite like this, free and alone, rising gently to a hawk's eye view. And besides, staying in the zone means they can't monitor his communications. He'll call the Society's number, and find out what's going on.

Below him, the ragged peninsula with its hodge-podge of buildings and blasted tropic meadows juts into the Caribbean. Offshore, a band of dark reefs holds back the deeper blue, itself spotted with green paint spots of the Virgin Islands. He continues climbing. What's the ceiling on this bird anyway? Copters in general tend to run out of dense enough air around what? — thirteen, fourteen thousand feet these days?

Seven thousand. From up here it all looks very neat. The sprawl of the mighty ocean floods over the continental shelf changing colour from indigo to blue to turquoise, its green fingers clawing into the soft mud of the coast itself. And the island chains seem so fragile, little Noah's arks adrift on the massive flood.

Higher. He activates the phone, speaking the number into the vox-coder. "Eliciting response," the sexy digital voice informs him. "Still eliciting." Up here, how can you see what is going on over those reefs? That's the problem, having this detached perspective. Maybe there's still electric fish swimming multi-coloured and fantastic, like thoughts of the great brain corals brooding in the deeps. Surely there must be some well-kept secret place where the Great Die-Off didn't happen. No. Everything's known now. Every inch observed and cal-culated. The world has become one huge security system, everywhere regulated, everything recorded.

"Connected," the voice says.

"Hello?"

"Hello! The word is SHUTTLE," Tremaine says, noting his alti-tude is approaching twelve thousand and an oxygen light has started blinking.

"Tremaine? Hold on."

Bleeps and bloops. They're transferring him around. Suddenly, Edgely!

"Jesus Christ brother! Are you okay there? Where the hell are you?"

"In my copter, right over NASA. They can't hear me."

"Shit! We was stressed they'd ashed you already. You gotta phase outta there tonight. Set down on one of the Virgins. "

"You mean they were really intending…?" Paranoia confirmed. A bitter metallic taste comes into his mouth. Half terror, half anger. Those fucking bastards!

Tremaine checks his watch. "Two hours to sunset. I don't think I can float here that long. They'll organize a search, figure where I am…unless I can…"

Close to the clouds. A jerk, and the cabin lurches. Tremaine straightens the harness. What the hell! "Fuck! Hold on, Bill. I got trou-ble here."

Again the copter shudders and twists on its axis, momentarily recovers, then drops and twists again. Tremaine's hands leap to adjust the tailrotor as a bunch of lights and beeps spring out of the control deck. But it's futile.

"Tail-rotor gone!" he yells as he hears a great thump from the disintegrating blades and the cabin spins uselessly around the axle of the straining main rotor. Instinctively he cuts power. The copter drops sickeningly, but its spin slows and stops as the rotors start feathering through the atmosphere.

He changes the rotors' attitudes slightly, noting how they are beginning to parachute his fall. He's become a powerless gyro, rather than a plunging stone, gaining himself a few precious seconds. "Those bastards!" He yells into the phone. "Those bastards sabotaged the tail rotor."

"Hang on, Brother! Hang on! We're with you! We're with you!"

Small comfort, Tremaine thinks. He slips the copter slightly sideways so it glides out over the sea towards the Virgins. It might make it there. So what? He's still at ten thousand. He's still in control.

Tremaine looks up into the sky, away from the drowning sea.

But it makes no difference.

It is the same blue.

SOCIAL DYNAMICS RESEARCH PROJECT: EARTHBABY
(JOURNAL OF LILLITH SHAWNADITHIT)

Amazing how fast you can get used to things. The flexibility of human consciousness will never cease to amaze me. It all goes back to good old Cro-Magnon, 50,000 years ago I guess. I mean, when your previous existence has consisted of running naked through tropical jungles eating oranges, what's so different in degree from suddenly being forced to hunt woolly mammoths at the edge of a glacier to finding yourself hurtling into solar orbit midway between earth and mars encased in a graphoplaque projectile? Piece of cake, right?

In the course of our journey to Earthbaby, I find myself calling on my past experience of scuba diving as a means of adjusting psychologically to zero gravity conditions inside the shuttle; and, for our passage through space, I click into the memory of flying in a jet through the black of a moonless night with stars twinkling and no sight of the earth below. This is not so successful, however; for no matter where you locate yourself in the cabin, there is the incredible blaze of the sun, even though it is dulled through auto-shade portholes.

We forget that, on earth, we are surrounded by a blue envelope of illuminated gases, that we spend our daylight hours inside a huge fluorescent light-bulb. Being on the "dark" side of the supershuttle, doesn't exactly have the same effect as being on the "dark" side of the earth either. As I said, the sun cannot be escaped from. In one respect, being in space is being in eternal daylight. At the same time, because there's no molecular matter close at hand to reflect it (except the bits and pieces of your own body passing before your eyes) the sun's light travels invisibly through the great black maw of the universe; so, one also lives in a kind of eternal darkness.

I know this is all very simplistic stuff, but to actually EXPERIENCE it as a basic ongoing phenomenon, realizing that what we think of as our earth experience with equal light and dark is actually only a special case, is quite an adjustment. Of course, even on our planet polar peoples have quite a different awareness of the vagaries of solar illumination than tropic peoples who never experience those long summer days and unending winter nights. I'm excited about this aspect. It's something Jock and I used to discuss many times: how psychological adjustment to macro-environmental changes might develop space cultures in tune with an entirely different cosmological consciousness.

I'm going on about this, in this rather blundering manner, because, of course, having somewhat adjusted to travelling in the supershuttle, I realize that a few days from now, we "spacelings" will have a more long-term adjustment to actually living on Earthbaby itself. What a unique chance I have to be a researcher and at the same time a subject — a classical feminist academic posture! Up to now, my own research in psycho-simulacra has only offered this opportunity rarely — the six months I spent living with the Bedouins during the Saharan Astro-Turf-Oasis Project for example.

I'm going to be interested in seeing how this works out. I had many discussions with Jock over the basic attitudes the engineers took in constructing Earthbaby. But by then there wasn't much that could be done. It was a mistake, I believe, to attempt to create a simulacrum of Earth habitation, especially since most of that environment is itself completely artificial — think of those stupid picture windows they've put into our cabins, just like the ones on earth, with all those hokey changing holograms of mountains and beaches.

Stacking people up in those seamless, slippery-walled American Standard Privacy modules is largely responsible, in my thinking, for the alienated, cynical, fad-ridden society we've inherited from the twentieth century. No wonder they all want to join up to be Privates in the privatized army, or Lifeguards for the Lifeists. No wonder they're all going to vote for General Foreman.

The deeply conditioned other-human avoidance patterns of Trans American urban-technological culture, patterns which have led the world to its present sorry state, will tend to remain operative as Earthbaby develops into a full-fledged community, especially when you add to the equation the patriarchal hierarchy the Privates imposed on this project. In its beginnings you find its ends. I'm convinced the plan for this station is to create a garrison, not only physical, but also mental, against the creative changes going on in the Eurosoviet that might threaten our Trans-American cultural baggage. As I see it, my real job, as a closet Tribal supporter, is to undermine the tendencies of the Privates and the Lifeguards whenever possible.

The rest of our journey after the spin crisis has been uneventful, except that refining our somewhat dislocated trajectory took up considerable time, the on-board computer having to be re-associated with NASA analogues, all of it passing up and down the laser umbilicus like blood and oxygen from placenta to foetus as Alexandra put it. As communications expert, she soon became the major player in this exercise, Clarke and Grainger devolving the entire operation into her hands.

And what a fascinating study she is, this almond-eyed outcome of a vast and varied gene pool — oriental, polynesian, european, one of those trans-national refugee orphans from the Japanese de-technologization days. Every time she turns, she is one or the other. But it's not her physical looks I'm talking about, it's the expression frequently on her face. I've seen this look before — a look of almost religious serenity — in the faces of those whose egos dissolve utterly into their creative enterprise, who become one with the elegant and fascinating dances of abstract possibilities. Jock, you had this look. To you, as to Alex, those symbols and equations existed as more than just a kind of language, didn't they? They were live things, combining and recombining like those complex genetic molecules which Adam himself has made his special study.

While I watched Alex, so did he. In his admiring look was the recognition of a commonality between them.

A natural pair bond.

So Jock. Here we go. Seeds. Seeding the universe….

Goodnight. ∽

One thousand feet. All the life that's left to him. Given the autogyro effect of spinning rotor blades, Tremaine's brain, as if working independently of it all, calculates his impact speed at about eighty miles an hour. Into water, strapped in his seat, the plexiglass cabin bubble taking the shock, he won't be killed instantly. Stunned, he'll drown moments after.

Two hundred feet. My last chance. He shoves the rotorblades into gear, throttle rammed wide open. The inertia of the cabin is enough to give the blades a temporary bite into the air, slowing his fall, before setting the copter twisting wildly. And that's the way, with a great roar and splash, it hits the waves and submerges…

The jolt beats at some dark spot in his head, a mailed fist on a castle door. Vaguely he comes to, conscious that the cabin has not shattered, a dense froth churned by the rotors all over it. Is it sinking?

Mouthpain where his teeth have jarred together. Duller pain creeping up hips and back. It's dead quiet, water seeping over his feet through vents. Shit! I'm alive! Elated as his brain wakes fully, quick terror following, hope as he feels the copter and its trapped air begin rising, rising… until… Sun!

But then he's on his back as it keels crazily over, settling. Out! I've got to get out!

He releases the seatbelt but can't open the hatch. Too much water pressure. He unlatches the window flap. Just wide enough to squeeze through. Free! I'm free! He swims ignoring agony in his pelvis, kicks onto his back just in time to see the copter, with one rotor tip sticking up like a handwave, submerge belching.

On his back, still driven by adrenalin, he shrugs out of his jacket, more pain shocking him into bright consciousness. His shoes next. At least all his limbs are working so far. He loosens his belt and manages to kick his pants away with a couple of backstrokes. Again he floats, closing eyes against the evening sun, devouring its warmth, aware, from the trembling of his suddenly chilled body, that he's in shock.

So what's next? Will Foreman's men come? Edgely's? Fat chance! And what if there's no-one? How many hours will this old body hold onto life once the sun goes down? What about sharks? Take it easy.

Give yourself a minute to recover.

Two things they hadn't counted on. One, that I'd leave in day-light, rather than after the launch checkout. Two, that I'd take the chopper up to the limit, giving me time to get over the sea. First stage of hysteria, this chuckling, this crazy feeling of pride that you've cheated them. Close your eyes, old man. Imagine you're on vacation. Relax.

Tremaine's head bumps into flotsam from the sunken copter. Papers stick to him. A pop can by his ear, and...ah, the seat cushion! He grabs onto it and shoves it under his head, lifting himself clear enough of the waves to take deep unhampered breaths. Rising on a crest, he scans the horizon for sight of land. There. A smudge of something? Or just a far mist. Everything around here's so low-lying you couldn't see it anyway.

Up on the swell again and he takes another look. Now that, that small speck coming in from the west, that makes his heart thump. Again he sees it, closer, hears it now. A search copter.

He watches it quartering the search segment, buzzing, black, methodical. He makes up his mind. The cushion has a strap on it. Tempting to think he might be plucked out, but they won't want to fuck up his death a second time, thankyou. No. He'll take his chances with the sea. Kicking slowly, he makes his way into the oil-slick where the copter went down, feeling it gum up his hair.

As the copter's noise comes closer, he takes a deep breath, puts the cushion over his face and lets himself sink under it, holding on to the strap. They're here. They're hovering over the slick, checking the debris. The water ripples under the airflow. Still there. Still there. He lets out his breath slowly, unable to hold it longer, then comes up under the cushion, easing up one corner of it, taking in a breath with a mouthful of foul water, going under again, hoping they haven't noticed, this time staying till almost unconscious, his heart hammering in panic, then rising again, gasping under the cushion as he hears the loud plop of a bouy. He realizes the copter has risen, is departing, maybe to call in the coastguard to see if the copter can be fished up, or maybe to mark his last resting place, some kind of superstition on their part demanding they leave this floating gravemarker for good measure so he will not haunt them.

The searchplane veers off back to base, seeing no signs of life. They'll report him dead as a doornail, gone to the bottom. An accident, of course. How tragic. In his finest hour, the director of

NASA.... Now what? If a coastguard comes, spots him, her crew will be less likely to be in on the plot, right? Then his miraculous survival couldn't be kept under wraps. But Foreman would make sure he was quickly spirited off to some military hospital, at the mercy of a quick hypodermic, dead of his unfortunate wounds suffered in the crash....

A sudden flurry near him makes him start. Flying fish darting out of the water. What's behind them? He shudders, expecting the nudge of some terrible body. But since the Die-Off marine life has become scarce, sharks included. Besides they don't like dirty water. He stays in the slick, comforted by the thought, till his nerves begin to settle again. How much can a guy take of this?

Then he hears the sound of another motor. A boat this time. He lifts his head. There it is. A tuna rig with a flying bridge. A guy up there eyeballing the surface. Perhaps they're just curiosity seekers. They've seen the crash, maybe. Certainly seen the search copter.

My chance. He lifts himself up and waves. Do they see him? He shouts. Yes. Their bow-wave drops and they idle over. He can see two men on board, the one on the bridge waving, excited to see him. At the square stern as it drifts towards him a muscular young black guy slips out of white pants and dives in, swimming to him, human, holding him up, clutching him under the armpits.

"Just float now, man. You'll be okay. Sure thing. We gotta get you outta here. Old BIll sure gonna be glad to see you."

Bill! Jesus! Tremaine's mouth trembles trying to make words. A wave of utter exhaustion and vicious back-pain makes him scream as they haul him over the gunwale onto the deck like a landed, gasping fish. Before he passes out, he manages to say, "I'm real glad to see you."

*   *   *

Tremaine comes into full consciousness on an eviscerated sofa in the back of Neil's garage, surrounded by dismembered motorbikes from a forgotten era. He knows it's Neil's garage, from overhearing their patois between fainting spells while being carried in a blanket from boat to small pickup for an agonizing ride over cobbled streets. Neil's garage. Strange to know that detail, but have no idea what town, what Island. In the Caribbean Protectorate, though. He could be sure of that.

Sure, too, that the damage to his back was more than your average strain. A herniated disc, most likely, because pain has been radiating down his sciatic nerve, stabbing behind his knee, cramping his calf muscle, leaving his left foot without feeling. Thank God adrenalin in his system kept him going those minutes in the sea. By lying on his side, left leg drawn up, he can just stand the agonizing spasms which keep him constantly nauseous, and his face drenched with sweat. But at least he's no longer blacking out and there's an odd relief at knowing it's not his heart, or internal bleeding, or something incurable like that, but merely something mechanical, fixable, like any old piece of this machinery strewn around him.

"Hey man, how you doin' now? You want a drink? We got a cola here, you see? You put this straw in your mouth now and you feel stronger."

"Thanks. Thank you. But I have to pee. And I can't move."

"Oh shit there man. It is real painful, I can see that. We gettin' you someting for it pretty soon. I get a bottle for you, so you don't have to move at all."

He still has on his undershorts, damp and salty from the sea. He can't even move enough to free himself. They do it for him, holding the shrivelled white worm of his penis, directing it into the bottle neck. His bladder lets go with an enormous sense of relief. Another good thing: the fact he's not incontinent means there's damage to only one of his vertebrae, not a bunch of them. He drags gratefully on the cola, his system craving the instant energy. Another black hand appears in front of his eyes, holding pills in its pink palm.

"You better take this now. We gotta move you soon."

"Can't I just stay here?"

"Yeah man. It's much too dangerous. Too many people with too much mouth."

"Oh shit."

"You better take it."

He swallows it down, has barely time to register the thought the pills are knocking him out, pentathol probably, when he sinks into grateful oblivion, into the sofa, into the deep black sea.

*   *   *

This is really not worth it, he thinks to himself. Why didn't I just die in the sea? He tries to brace himself with his good right leg against the front seat, every bump and lurch of the old car agonizing. Taking more of those pills isn't the answer. They might do permanent damage to his liver, kidneys, god knows what. This would be the fourth dose. His heart might just pack it in. Hang on. It all must end.

And it does. They carry him out of the car on a blanket into the fresh night air. He can't see, but he hears their feet crunch on shingle and they place him into a rubber zodiac.

This is all right, he thinks. At least by comparison. He rests his head on the airfilled gunwhale, his eyes fixing automatically on Arcturus, riding high in the northern sky, imagining, indeed, that he can see a glint of earthbaby. Lillith, Alexandra.... They'll tell them the news, won't they? They'll think I'm dead. I wish, I wish....

At last they manage to transfer him onto a large cruiser anchored without lights a few miles offshore. I'll be okay now, he says to himself, not even able to twist his head to see what hands are tending him, are carefully easing him onto a soft bunkbed. Naked, washed, warm, a heating pad and anti-inflammatories offering enough relief, secure in the little room with moonlight drifting through the portholes, child in rocking cradle, he actually, by himself, falls fast asleep.

At anchor. But where? A slight shift in his position makes him gasp. But if he stays still in the fetal position, agony is reduced to dull ache. He has to pee again.

Groping for the edge of the bed, he feels the hard metal of a flat bedpan. Very thoughtful. What's the cure for this thing? Isn't it to stay absolutely still lying down? Jock had this once. For nearly three weeks, strapped to a board, he insisted on being carried around the Centre, demanding to be propped up like some live mummy against the wall at conferences, then yelling, "Bearers! Away!" when he wanted to be shifted. As for sex, Jock had joked, that was no problem. He just lay there and took it like a man.

A strange hilarity wells up in Tremaine as the muted sound of the filling flask rises in note. I'm alive, By God! I've really cheated those bastards. And I bet, Jock, you were up there looking out for me. He's surprised to find tears streaming down his face, a sob in the back of his throat. Just then the cabin door swings open, brightening the room.

It's Perlita who comes in first and moves to the window. He recognizes her from the evening before, the one whose firm hands had given his back so much comfort. As she opens the blinds, light surfs through curls of her dark hair, inappropriately long and wavy, some sort of varied Caribbean heritage. Behind her enters an athletic young medic wearing a Dragon-brand, yellow J-cloth astro-suit, ballooning from the pressure of its built-in cooling unit. Tapping his crotch, where the switch and vent of this year's model has been sexily placed, he turns it off.

"Good morning, Mr. Andrews," Perlita says. "How are you, Mr. Andrews?" (In case he didn't remember, deliberately stressing his false name, concocted last night.) She gives him a cheerful, conspiratorial smile, while placing her hand on his shoulder and smoothing the covers. "I've brought the good Doctor Singh from St. Kitts to have a look at you."

All the while, this handsome young Punjabi, his parents probably escapees from the Sword of Saddam revolution in the Muslim Crescent, is rapidly assembling a portable cat-scan ultra-sound unit.

"I'm a back specialist, Mr. Andrews. You'd be surprised how

many people slip on the decks of their boats, fall down companion-ways, tumble from masts, heave up heavy anchors without bending their knees. Believe me, you shouldn't feel embarrassed. This sort of thing happens all the time. These days, fortunately, help is at hand with all our new advances in treatment technology. We'll have you back on your feet in a week or two, I guarantee. You can just stay right as you are and we'll get this thing on you….First, let me do a little scratch test…."

Tremaine jumps a little as he pricks the sole of his right foot, conscious of feeling only a slight pressure in his other one. "I guess the old nerve's damaged, Doctor."

"It'll probably come back. If not, the muscles will still work. Your foot will just feel a bit numb, that's all. That's about the worst. I can see from the scan that your L-five/S-one disc has herniated, facet joint inflammation on neighbouring vertebrae…. These days we just dissolve the viscous leak in a matter of minutes with one injection, then replace the disc tissue with a self-congealing polymer, and you do the rest by staying in bed for a few days, gradually increasing your mobility till you're back to normal."

"I don't have to be strapped to a board?"

"Not unless that's the sort of thing you like," he jokes, checking a large syringe. "Close your eyes, old chap, hold tight." His tone of voice implying: naturally, you'll be at least as manly as an English schoolboy. "This will be over with in a moment."

It isn't of course. Doctors always lie like that. But you believe them enough to allow it to happen, and indeed, after the dizziness and shock and burning pain of a few minutes, you are again ready, for you may as well get it over with all at once and the last needle is sickeningly plunged into your shaken body, explodes in an irrepressible cry, is mercifully withdrawn, and you are left lying, beached like a wreck on your bed.

"Admirable. Absolutely admirable, Mr. Andrews," says the young Doctor.

Sincere or not, Tremaine feels it's genuinely offered as a tribute to his suffering and accepts it with thanks as Singh rapidly compresses his complex gear into a small package, inflates his suit, dons an Australian desert hat with cork bobs swinging from its brim, and leaves.

"Now don't you move for at least an hour while that stuff starts to set in there, like he said," Perlita warns him. He admires the set of her head with its wonderfully mixed features, her skin not black, not bronze, but amber — that was the word for it — and between the deep jar of her eyes as she bends her face over him he notices a spray of freckles across the bridge of her nose. What astounding types human beings come in these days. Every year, it seems, brings new wonders of them as the great mixing goes on ever faster. How boring to be himself, with this white skin made even more useless since the ozone disappeared.

Then it is that Perlita, holding his hand, comforting him as more painkillers take effect, strokes his hair, humming softly as he drifts off. He feels the boat weigh anchor and start up. Her hum and the soft rumble of the motor blend together. His last waking thought is how pleasing the fragrance of Perlita: musk and frangipani....

*   *   *

He has slept all day, eaten, slept again. Toward evening has had to ask Perlita to virtually carry him, staggering, to the toilet as his bowels finally unloosen from days of tension. Now he's discovering other aches and bruises throughout his body that the painblock of his injured back has hitherto concealed. In the bathroom mirror his face looks puffed and drained, a grey stubble on his cheeks and chin.

"I look like an old derelict," he tells her.

"Listen to this guy. People would kill to have your distinguished white hair and those blue eyes."

He grins at her cheerfulness as she helps him on to the bed again.

A few minutes later, Perlita brings an electric razor with a hand mirror. Still lying down, he manages to clean up the stubble. She puts a brush through his hair, taking out his usual parting.

"There. You look good."

"The boat's stopped," he comments. "What's happening?"

"Someone's coming to see you."

It's Bill Edgely. He slips on board from a zodiac and hustles in to Tremaine full of worry and bravado.

"Jesus I figgered you was fizzed in that mixmaster, brother. Some fuckin' splashdown, man!"

"Pure luck, Bill. If it hadn't been for you getting that tuna rig out, I'd be sharkfood."

"Very synchro...."

"Does everyone know about it out there?"

"Yeah. We Tribals are making mileage on you crashing. Too collateral with Jock's hit, right? But without forensic this soon before the election, Foreman's not getting much image decay."

"You've got evidence, Bill. Get me on some TV show. We'll get the bastard."

Edgely turns to Perlita and his two companions, obviously henches he's brought with him.

"Has this brother got the Rambos or what? He wants to jump without a parachute again."

"It could swing a few votes in the election."

Edgely gets serious. "Look Andy, we've thought this through. After our shuttle-launch interview, everyone in vacuum-land knows you have it in for Foreman over his Earthbaby take-over. Suppose we media splash you. You do damage, but how much? Where's your exhibit-one to show you were set up: some uncollaborated jive how this underground organization warns you Foreman's planning to ash you just before it happens? Foreman will know you're alive, and the Lifeguards will track your spore for sure. Because you know stuff. You're a treasure trove, man. Let these fucking Privates get you, and you will be *buried* treasure, brother."

"I don't care. I'm on borrowed time anyway. If it might make the difference in the election, I think we should do it."

"It'll still be a dump-site. Half the computer polls are jiggered his way. And if that don't work, our deepthroats tell us Foreman's intending a coup."

"I should have suspected as much. Look at how he lobbied to ram the Competing Armies Law through Congress after his Lifeists bought out the Pentagon. What this guy likes is a monopoly."

"That's why he wanted you and Jock out of there. The mistake we Tribals made was underestimating this character right from the start."

"Well, he seemed so fucking laughable."

"It was the Tribals' own fault. All that internecine warfare with those turn-of-the-century style sex-splitters. He slid right in there down the middle."

"That's what they said about Hitler, about Stalin, about Cromwell.... Truth is, Bill, the last few years, support for the Multi-Racials, the Greenies, and even the Consensualists has been eroding to the Privates."

"Right. All those new-age identity-addict wankers panting for big daddy with all the easy answers as to why they're so fucked up. Did you read that profile of Foreman in SELF magazine? 'The able man for every man,' for God's sake!"

"Talk about edifying the banal! Not to mention sexist lingo," Perlita cuts in.

"Anyway, better you stay alive by staying dead for now."

"I never thought I was that valuable a commodity."

"If we figure right, Earthbaby is potentially Foreman's main terror weapon. The big eye in the sky. Add a few neutron bombs, a little heavy lasering, none of it stoppable, and he can scorch anywhere in the world he wants to."

"So. What do you want me to do?"

Edgely goes thoughtful. He kneads his brow, muting the headache Tremaine knows he must have there. "I'll give it to you straight, Man. I like you. We could use you. But if you want out…and I understand why you might, God knows… then we just drop you off and say goodbye."

This is what Tremaine has been waiting for. This offer. This choice. He has scores to settle.

"What the fuck, Bill. I'm living on borrowed time anyway. What have I got to lose? I'm with you."

Edgely grabs Tremaine's head in both hands and plants a kiss on his forehead. "Yo! Okay! I said to myself when I heard you survived, this is good fortune, this is turning the tide. Now we get to wage war with those fucking Privates. And you know something? We ain't totally helpless here. Foreman's going to have a little jolt when he sees what's going to be coming out of the Eurosoviets today."

"What's that?"

"Oh, just a little something to let him know he doesn't have a complete monopoly up in space there. So lie back. Take it easy. Tell Perlita everything you can think of: facilities layouts, computer and communications systems…. After the election, we'll start you up."

"I'd like to at least let my daughter in San Francisco know where I've got hidden bank accounts."

"We'll fix the accounts. Better hold off on letting her know you're still around, though. We'll talk about it. In the meantime, you take care of this brother, Perlita."

"It's my pleasure."

When they've all gone, Tremaine lies, gathering strength. What was that bit about Foreman not having a monopoly in space? Could they have a competing scheme of some kind? That would be nice. To work on a smaller, more efficient type of Earthbaby. One like Jock had spoken about: it would be mobile. A kind of space trailer. He closes his eyes, feeling the boat start up.

What skin is this I'm wearing? It feels like someone else's. Like someone I used to know, many years ago....

It strikes him his past life exists now only as a filed away memory, just like that space campervan prototype design of Jock's, for instance, on the NASA central computer. Once, his life, like that prototype, was studied and applauded; but now, like that design, it has been assigned from "current" down into "filed" and from there into one of the archive slots in deep memory. It could be recalled, yes. But only with great effort, if at all. Many things got lost in that vast brain machine as the vicissitudes of modernization and viruses and electronic accidents took their toll. One has to remember the pathcode, the ancient directory name, the folder, the file number, the call number to re-energize it or bring it into any kind of existence. Otherwise it remains, like his past life, as some forgotten ghost, an echo, or a backup file.

It was an appropriate analogy, all right. Particularly for these last — how many years? — fifteen! Good God! That long? How we imitate our technology. Look at those identity-addicts, cocooned into their home-entertainment centres, in their singles habitats — no wonder the Privates have managed to make such inroads. "Living like that," Jock had said, "is society's idea for training to live in space. God forbid Earthbaby should turn out that way."

Nevertheless, in large measure it had, despite Lillith's efforts, bless her. And those computers had become his own mistresses ever since he vaulted himself from the head of Goddard Space Research into the Directorship of NASA's new complex in Puerto Rico.

A mountain climbed with no small cost. When Barbara had congenially left him, taking Alice with her to California he'd felt some relief. For already the single-channeling of his existence and its obsessive qualities of managing and control had begun to set into a mold which Barbara's departure merely hardened. From then on he'd become the perfect corporation executive: nice, warm, superficial, stressed and obsessive.

Not a particularly bleak existence either. Not on the surface, at least. For the most part he was able to take his pick among the ambitious young women — nice, warm, superficial persons of brilliance and beauty themselves — whose favours were part of the price of their own upward mobility, though both he and they kidded themselves it had nothing to do with it.

Once he'd been jarred by a rather literary young woman attached to the media relations unit who'd commented: "While the rest of us swim, Andrew, you go water-skiing through life. One day you will fall, and maybe you will drown." How prophetic! But he hadn't drowned.

Lucky. Just lucky.

SOCIAL DYNAMICS REASEARCH PROJECT
(JOURNAL OF LILLITH SHAWNADITHIT)

Now here's the odd thing. You'd have thought NASA would send us up some of the stuff going out on the public networks on the course of our journey, celebratory remarks made by bigwigs and all that. But NASA chose to stay locked onto official channel right until we docked at Earthbaby. Not only were these communications exceptionally terse, as they have been throughout the flight (I put that down to the necessities arising from our readjustments), but also *there wasn't one word from Tremaine. Not one.*

I didn't want to be the first to mention it in case it might reveal my anxiety. I was relieved, then, when, in sight of Earthbaby, a pinprick on the far horizon but growing rapidly in size despite our deceleration, we established communication with NASA. James came on to say that we hadn't heard from Tremaine because he had unfortunately collapsed with exhaustion following the spin crisis. They had not wanted to mention this to us given the stress we had been under until now.

I didn't know what to think. Alex, sensing my worry, murmured, "There's nothing we can do. I'm sure he's going to be okay."

The news also put a bit of a pall on the celebration we might have felt over our rendezvous with Earthbaby. Everything else aside, there was something magical about coming up on it, a delicate gleaming, almost transparent presence. I thought again about scuba diving, about how, in the near-dead sea you would suddenly encounter one of those incredible jellyfish lifeforms that used to be so numerous in the old days; or, again, what it must have been like to be a knight errant suddenly finding the fabled fairy castle after your long journey across the wastes of desert and mountains. There's something both loving and deadly about the way those magnetic grabs extended to enfold us, gently and irresistibly easing our craft into the slowly revolving dark entranceway of the station. The spacebride, delivered, into Bluebeard's Castle?

Because of our excessive retro-nozzle use over the spin crisis, NASA wanted us to hasten the shuttle return with the last of the construction crew still on Earthbaby when we arrived. We volunteered to help them unload the cargo hold, but they insisted. NASA wanted us to detoxify as quickly as possible so we could familiarize ourselves with Central Control and start up the return launch programmes. I had wanted to interview these workers, but our excessive time getting through the detox chamber (because Adam forgot to put his watch down the sterilizing chute!) left a rather tight window for their return in the supershuttle. I did notice one of them had a hint of the characteristic gait first described by Vassiley Leschuk in the nineteen nineties before transformational proportional gravity fields were developed for station living areas. I assume he must have spent considerable time on the outer edges at technical tasks.

The control centre inside was familiar to us all from the simulations. While Clarke and the tireless Alexandra sped through the shuttle deployment check, I went along with Adam and Grainger to the observatory. There, Grainger was in his bailiwick where he'd be hunting for, and spectroscopically analyzing, asteroids suitable for the mining development which is one of Agriminco's main objectives.

Adam's project space, which we visited next, is eerily factory-like — metallic furrows of its hydroponic seedbeds ranging row after row. Although his main project is to develop algal strains capable of producing vast mountains of protein through the use of the sevenfold solar energy space agriculture offers, his own pet project is creating a self-perpetuating biosphere. These two things together should be able to provide Earthbaby's oxygen needs in a few months, tying into the present atmosphere generation system.

As we went along, returning to control in time for the shuttle deployment, I couldn't help noticing the network of monitoring cameras everywhere. I didn't say anything. The others would come to an awareness of them soon enough. I found it fascinating that I alone, on the station, had the capacity, in this little room I now inhabit, to observe anywhere and everywhere I wanted, including reviewing any moment in time I desired. The inbuilt programmes were such I could simply order a search throughout the system for any "incidents" involving, let's say, two people in conversation, that might have taken place the previous day in any sector I chose. I could then hear what was said, zoom in on the data to catch reactions....the works. The crew had been informed that the system was in place as an archival and research facility. Each could maintain privacy in their own cabins, by flicking on a privacy switch. Otherwise, every move and mutter would be noted and stored.

Actually, I'm going to try it out right now for the first time, rerunning a piece of tape from the moments after the launch once I've finished this next paragraph.

Right now, however, I feel like an old lady in a new cabin. Besides the picture window giving a sense of depth — I must find out how to turn that damn thing off — there's a hell of a lot of glass in this place. An old decorator trick to give the illusion of a larger area. When I stand in a certain spot, just off the end of the bunkbed, I can see myself reflected from all directions, my images overlapping like an old cubist painting. After a while, you can lose track of the original image, the one that generates the other images in the other mirrors. I'm not sure the kaleidoscopic effect is good for serenity, to be blunt. One can literally lose oneself. I might send in a report on this. Personally, I find taping sheets of paper over one mirror immediately brings the place under control, grounds it, and I am able to sit and just be, far more comfortably. Ah. There's the window control. Now it, too, is off, and I am real again, except I would rather be able to see the stars. ◠◡

SOCIAL DYNAMICS RESEARCH PROJECT: EARTHBABY
JOURNAL OF LILLITH SHAWNADITHIT

I woke this morning with the feeling I was no longer watching the universe. *The universe was watching me.* Imagine how this sense of caged paranoia was heightened, then, when the morning briefing with NASA made no mention of Tremaine, but consisted almost entirely of a terse announcement that a rocket-launch had taken place from inside the Euro-Soviet. It had penetrated deep space in three stages and had then ejected a space capsule. NASA was attempting to sound calm about this, commenting that it was probably nothing to worry about — that it would turn out to be some token spit into the wind. The Eurosoviets may have been cut out of fathering the Earthbaby project, but they wanted to show they could still get it up — ha ha ha.

All day, Grainger and Alex worked in the observatory tracking the capsule's progress. They put a feed into Central Control where we could all watch it, first as a blip on a graph, and later, frighteningly, as an actual object, pinhead size, but hourly enlarging like a a time-lapse photo of an expanding mushroom ball.

"It's heading our way, all right," said Clarke.

This information was all shuffled back down the laser umbilicus to NASA, so their specialists could continue with analysis. They decided the capsule was one of the Eurosoviet's famous multi-purpose maneuverable satellites; beyond that, they had no idea of its purpose. Their reassurances starting to ring hollow, our imaginations, mine anyway, began conjuring up a wide range of best case to worst case scenarios.

Clarke, who knows about such things, expressed surprise how accurately the satellite was being kept on course.

"Their telemetry is way improved. I'm amazed how they're homing that thing in on us."

Indeed, we could even see little bursts of correction fluid spurt from the ever-enlarging spaceball, then disperse to form ghostly nebulae.

Glumly we all sat over the remains of our first breakfast, Grainger crunching his plate into little bits, piling them into an untidy-looking tower before dipping them into his coffee and eating them like cookies. Alexandra, who had drunk her fruit juice, nibbled on her cup in a descending spiral pattern, leaving little perfect toothmarks until only the bottom disk remained, which she popped into the recycler.

At last, Adam, innocent and naive, expressed what we all were fearing. "What if this thing is sent up here to nuke us? Can't we do something?"

"We can always blast it to kingdom come. That is, if we had any weapons to blast it with," Grainger said significantly, looking over at Clarke.

"Even if we did," Clarke added evenly, "that's a rather drastic measure considering the delicacy of world diplomacy right now."

Since what follows is self-explanatory, at this point I'm going to go into archive transcribe mode, stripping the event data off the recording system.

EARTHBABY ARCHIVE: 30/04/2039:
0910HRS-0915HRS: CENTRAL CONTROL.

GRAINGER: I didn't say I *would* blast it. I merely mentioned the obvious.

CLARK (conciliatory, paternally, wishing to avoid the issue): It's going to be twenty-four hours before this thing gets anywhere near here, so there's no cause for immediate alarm. NASA and the diplomacy boys are obviously working on it. Besides, they might have the telemetry to come close to us, but I doubt if they can manage anything more than that, certainly not a synched orbit or actual contact. Probably, it will just turn out to be observational.

LILLITH: Why would they go to all that effort just to look at us?

ADAM: Just to make sure we stay honest, I guess.

LILLITH (pretending innocence): Meaning what?

ADAM hesitates while GRAINGER looks up into the softlite ceiling panels, exaggeratedly twiddling his thumbs and whistling.

CLARKE: What are you getting at Grainger?

GRAINGER: As the Foreman appointee I would think you might know more than the rest of us on this score.

CLARKE: I don't know what you're talking about.

ALEX (rising to take a look at the monitor): Weapons. We're wondering whether Foreman is going to send missiles up as soon as he gets the chance.

GRAINGER: So, Clarke. Tell them. Is Foreman going to sneak

The last part he said. That was a mistake. He wishes he could undo it like a phrase on a computer.

Perlita is slipping on her ankle boots, looking out on the declining sun.

"This is where I live. No matter what else. I have to do this."

"I'm sorry, Perlita. I panicked."

He can't express the sudden heartburst of feeling he has for her. The next moment though, she has sensed it, maybe seen it quicken in his face, and she has come to him, holding him as he rises to meet her, clasping him tight with her solid live body, kissing him.

"Take care. Good God, take care," he says.

When she's gone he sits for ages, watching the sun set. How has he washed up on this particular shore: on this shore alive with ghosts of Caribs, Arawaks, East Africans, most of them worked and bullied to their deaths? What strange quirks of time and circumstance have brought him to this one particular place on earth where caves in fern-lined gullies yield sulamar and precious amber?

Under parasols of these very palms, native loves and foreign treacheries — Spanish, English, French — went on for centuries. Between Columbus and Perlita's grandfather, came that whole vast range of exiles: flotsam of the human shipwreck, dying of overwork, war and yellow fever.

Perlita's grandfather. Tremaine could not imagine how he must have felt, saved from Dachau concentration camp, by some fluke of time and circumstance and American-Jewish money. How incredible, after all that suffering, for him and his three hundred brethren to suddenly find themselves here, in Paradise, because of mad Dictator Trujillo's paranoid desire to lighten up the colour of his Island people's skin.

In a life-boat through the surge of the outer surf, wading at the end, he and his companions came straight up this golden beach, Perlita told him, to where a crowd of women waited: among them was Perlita's Grandmother. Calmly she had accepted the inevitable: she would bond with him or with another of his band, for Trujillo had put all the black men of her own lost tribe to death.

Another reality, that's what Perlita's grandfather stumbled into, some golden warp of time. Just the way he, himself, has. It is almost like that parallel universe young physicists are always talking about as a replacement for old time religion, that place where the mythical

Regulators are supposed to come from. But this island is an alternate reality where one plays for keeps. And isn't that why Perlita kissed him? It was just in case, one human to another, in case there came to be an end....

Whatever manifests this thing called life, please hold her in your hand.

The quick tropic sunset falls, bleeding into the sea.

*   *   *

For a while Tremaine thinks he can just sit there in the moonless dark, waiting for her to come home, in some kind of suspended animation. He can hear the gasp and sigh of the surf, a boat motor, the scurrying of some animal below the floor, the squeak and rustle of geckos scrapping in the rafters. Out to sea he can barely discern far lights: two whites. They must be coming in to harbour. Then a red goes to his left, a green the other way. Some things like ships' lights never change.

There's Arcturus glimmering again. Earthbaby would still be on a sightline close by it. If he had a powerful enough telescope he could see it. Would they be watching the election on TV? If they've told the crew about his "death," both Lilly and Alex would still be pretty shook up. They'd put two and two together. They'd know it was no accident.

He goes to the back and looks up the cliff path. She won't turn up until the polling stations are closed. In fact, some time after that. How many votes from here would count for the electoral college? Too bad it didn't still work on a population proportion basis instead of on the basis of Gross National Product. Considering the standard of living, the GNP from this island must be pretty picayune. That means one vote from here is probably only worth a seventh of a vote in the heartland. In such things is the triumph of capitalism over democracy made clear. The next step will be to give votes out like share units. One each to the poor and a million or so to the rich.

Finally, Tremaine can stand his silent vigil no longer. He goes inside and turns on the TV in Perlita's bedroom. He can smell her there. A set of silver bangles lies on the side table. She left them off so they wouldn't jingle. A hair comb on the dressing table. He pulls a long dark hair from it, turning to see it against the lamplight. How fine and wonderful she is.

On TV, Edgely, sharp-witted and cynical, is doing the anchoring of his life. Every one knows this is the last show he will ever do; so they're letting him get away with everything. It's live, too, and so they have an excuse to keep it rolling, no matter what he says. They're exercising some damage control, of course. For one thing, they're not letting him near Foreman, giving those interviews to everyone else. But he's intercutting and commenting satirically on every one. "Thank you for that insightful interview, Barry. Now we know even less about the General's policies than we did before. And now here's more numerology from the fuzzy logic bowels of the election central computer. Add those figures up and you'll see there must have been a few dogs and cats added to the voter list...."

He turns her leather stool and sits on it, watching for a while. Cut to commercial. Another army one. Then Agriminco: 'focused capital, to farm the future in the stars' with a shot of the shuttle and Earthbaby; then an observatory telescope tracking — at the controls a diapered baby, finger resolutely pushing a button on the control panel.

Over the sound, Tremaine, alert, thinks he hears a rattle of gunfire from out to sea. Yes. Again. He goes out to look. Red and green shiplights close to each other, white ones approaching. More gunfire. A dimly heard shout. The lights rock, huddled still. Some poor bastard has been ashed out there. Pray it isn't somehow her. She went inland.

He goes out and climbs the cliff rising steeply behind the house, realizing its shelter might have kept away any sound from that direction. He stands under the deep shadow of a flamboyant tree, a thin moon beginning to creep over the horizon, sharpening the outline of the ridge where she has gone to be with those whose livelihood is hacking down bananas or lining out ten thousand coffee beans in intricate squares to dry in the sun.

A breeze starts up, rattling the ribbed fronds of nearby palms like skeletons of hung men. A flock of raucous mynah birds stirs in tangled branches over him. A shadow crosses close. A rat? A mongoose? He goes back in, takes the revolver from under the bed, almost misfires it when a lizard darts out from there. He sits on Perlita's stool again, feeling how her hips have molded it over the years. Holding her gun in his hand, imagining her palm print on its stock, he sits on her stool and wills her to return unharmed.

When she does come, she shouts to warn him at the door.

"Oh my God! You're back, you're safe!"

In his excitement he still holds the gun. She takes it from him, looks at it and laughs. "It's not loaded."

She flings it onto the sofa. "It was easy, Andrew. No violence at all. Those young draftees they sent in there just needed an excuse they could give their officers for allowing us through. So we made an arrangement with them to make it look like they were ambushed. Tied a couple up and left them there. Let the others wait around and smoke till the voting was over. Then they ran back to base to get help to recapture their buddies we would leave conveniently on the side of the road."

She's very happy, still excited. Arms round his neck, she squeezes him. Under her armpits she's damp with sweat, her sweet musk smell is catching in his throat. He feels her muscular body shift and mold to him, so easy and used to itself now she is in her mid-thirties. This has been good for her. She's proud and wanting to celebrate.

She spins away from him, goes to the bureau and begins emptying her revolver, the bullets falling thwock, thwock, into the drawer. They rattle as she slides it closed.

"So my faithful Andrew, tell me what's been happening."

This is a side of her he's never seen before — folk guerrilla, lusty as a Carmen with her brigands in the mountains.

"Every one of the protectorates has gone against the bastard — in terms of popular support. Of course, he's way ahead on GNP's for the presidency."

Perlita swings the carpet bag off her shoulders.

"And it's all because of people like you, Perlita. Think of the thousands of busses that had to get through tonight."

She takes a deep, satisfied breath. "Yes. Small victories. But good ones."

She hangs up her hat.

"And what about in the heartland?"

"He's making it of course. But not by a hell of a lot, considering the fix is in. Riots in Washington, L.A., and of course Toronto."

She kicks off her ankle boots.

She looks directly at him, barefoot, hands on her hips now sliding down to the hem of her dress. "I'm hot, you know."

"I'll get you a drink."

Crossing her arms she lifts her dress from the bottom, sliding it up over her head. He cannot move, watching her.

She settles her hair with a toss of her head, her eyes dancing, brassiere and panties vivid white against her skin. "Water would be nice."

When he comes back from the kitchen, she is standing stocky and naked, her nipples dark and erected. She takes the glass and gulps it, handing it to him to share.

"I'm going to see the last of it in the bedroom, will you come with me?"

Mutely he stumbles after her. The broadcast is ending. Foreman has won. A travesty. Edgely, signing off, quotes the Greenies spokesman: "a technical knockout, a computer showdown of garbage in/garbage out…resulting in garbage in." Over the chanting roar of his supporters, Foreman begins his speech. Perlita has scrambled onto the bed behind him, sitting yoga-like, massaging the muscles of his shoulders.

"So now there's nothing left to celebrate, except the life that's left to us."

Tremaine doesn't hear Foreman's words. He imagines them spurting out of his small tight mouth like bullets, pellets of rage that lodge one by one in his heart. "I hate that bastard. How I hate that devil and all his kind."

She's pressed tight against his back, her beautiful dark hands inside his shirt, gently rousing him as his blood begins to race in anger and exultation.

"We are alive, and he is a dead man," she whispers, kissing him.

"…*There will be no more violence on the streets of this nation. We are extending our Pentagon Social Service policy to assist the operations of security officers and private police forces to achieve peace and order….*"

Carefully he allows Perlita to ease him down flat on his back on the bed.

"That bastard killed Jock, and tried to kill me. A murderer for President."

Perlita begins undressing him. "Look how alive you are, Andrew. How alive."

"…*In consequence we intend to institute a National Service Draft, beginning in some cases at school-leaving age of sixteen and over, to channel the energies of our young people into socially meaningful activities…*"

The touch of her hand makes him gasp with pleasure. Her mouth is enough to start him babbling. "Turn it off," he manages to say.

She kneels astride him in the flickering light. "No. Let him see us."

The sea anemone of her body begins to enfold him.

"*...administration is determined to deal with our enemies at home as firmly and decisively as our enemies abroad...*"

Then he is tangled with her in the sweet struggle of their two bodies, uncertain who is who until the great exchange completes itself, and they lie mated, collapsing into mutual pleasure.

Perlita taps the TV switch control on the headboard. There is nothing then but each other. Nothing but the far sound of the ocean surf forevering....

SOCIAL DYNAMICS RESEARCH PROJECT; EARTHBABY
(JOURNAL OF LILLITH SHAWNADITHIT)

I meant to make this journal a regular evening routine. The events of the past week or so, however, coupled with the ongoing problem of the Eurosoviet satellite, have been so harrowing, and my own involvement so exhausting emotionally, I've been putting it off.

Now I can see the advantages, at least for the work at hand, of the classic disinterested attitudes of those old-time objectivists who did their research at one remove from their subjects, at least pretending a certain neutrality in what went on. Even tonight, with classic avoidance, I spent two whole hours playing some mindless computer game, telling myself that if I won it then I would begin. I didn't win, but finally pulled on some vestigial remains of the old guilt complex my grandmother had instilled in me as a child (the devil makes use of idle hands!) coupled it with a self-affirmation session (you're the only one in the world who can do this, which is why you were picked to do it!) and finally, most effective but most heart-wrenching of all, *I owe it to Jock Sparling and Andrew Tremaine.*

Christ you guys! What Karma was it brought me to be your lover, your chronicler, your epitaph writer?

Ever since the double blow of NASA finally fessing up about Tremaine's so-called accidental death and then Foreman winning the election, I've found myself in some kind of mindless lassitude. What the hell does it all matter any more? And who gives a shit about the petty ego squabbles on board this floating crap-game anyway? Certainly not the Foreman crowd, who are quite likely going to rearrange our assignment up here as quickly as possible. I know Tremaine was hoping to keep us away from their interference.

In all this, I think I am merely expressing the emotional climate of the whole crew. I was so stunned when James came on to tell us about Tremaine, I really didn't manage to catch the others' reactions. Even playing back the observation tapes isn't much help. The way people's faces were angled towards the main communication screen makes it impossible to do eye-blink and muscle-group movement analysis.

I can, however, imagine the complex reactions there must have been in the other members of the crew besides Alex and myself who didn't have our close connection to Andrew. I missed observing them because my own eyes were riveted to the screen, listening to James stumble through the announcement. If only I had a tape of it to analyze. I was sure he was lying about the facts (the helicopter crash was supposed to be due to an apparent heart attack while at the controls) but his emotion of sorrow struck me as authentic.

As I mentioned earlier on in these notes, NASA had been only supplying us with official communications without any clips from the regular public broadcasts. In order for us to follow the elections the next evening, however, I guess they decided to come clean with what had happened, before some stray remark by Edgely or someone else in the uncensored snippets made us aware of it and gave their game away. Considering what Edgely did make of it, it was a wise move on their part.

The first response to what James said was absolute silence. I could see Grainger glance up for a moment to one of the observation cameras. It's at times like that those stupid things get in the way. Who the hell was really going to express what was in their heart knowing the record of it could be used by Foreman and his Privates to damn them later? Fear, I thought. Even way up here it touches all of us, puts us in their power.

Then Alex and I rose simultaneously to hug and comfort each other. From observing the tape, it appears Clarke remained seated, head down, hands clasped in his lap. I could almost swear he was praying. Adam, squirming in his seat, bewildered, looking about, wasn't sure what to do.

Grainger, on the other hand, was quick to be by Alex's side, murmuring "God, you guys, that's awful. I'm sorry. Real sorry." On the tape, his hand pats and caresses Alex's shoulder. Adam, with a look of, *Get your hands off her, Buddy,* then comes over awkwardly hugging me on the only available side of the comfort group left.

"This mission is jinxed," he says a couple of times.

Later, at suppertime, Clarke made a very decent announcement about how distressed he was, and how sympathetic towards our feelings, then called for two minutes of silence. That broke me and I had to leave the table in sniffles. In a few minutes, Clarke knocked on my door solicitously. I let him come in.

"I know somewhat how you must feel, what with Jock and now

this. It's terrible being alone. But I want you to know, I'm on your side."

"Thank you, Clarke. That's very nice of you."

On my side? What did he mean by that? I know his wife died of cancer a few years ago. Sharing the feeling? A conventional platitude coming from a team player? Or did he mean, somehow, us against them, the other three, that is, who were half a generation down from us? 'It's terrible being alone' being one of their old slogans, I don't dare to think he means he's actually a secret Tribal like myself.

The election itself inspired muted reactions, especially when the outcome became so obvious. Even snickers at some of Edgeley's remarks were suppressed and turned into coughs and nose-blowings. The next day I said to myself, *this is it*, and got Clarke's permission to disable the central control cameras and recorders.

"A safe house," Grainger remarked.

And just in time too. The next day, a state of the union address by the newly elected Foreman, assuming office forthwith as had been the custom for the last two elections, was piped in by NASA. It included a Social Service draft after age sixteen and a communications rationing decree called "the truth in media" pronouncement, as well as a shitload of other stuff about expansion of the Social Service cadres of the Lifeist Christian Army and so on.

"So much for free speech. Your boys don't mess around, do they Clarke?" Grainger sneered, trying to make some braggadocio points for Alex's sake.

Clarke, nonplussed, tried to back out of it. "I belonged to the old army."

"If you didn't like it, you could have quit when it became privatized."

Unthinking, I rushed to Clarke's defense. "The morals of your own outfit are hardly anything to write home about, Grainger. Take away the religious rhetoric and where's the difference? Everyone knows Foreman's a bedmate of Agriminco, if not an outright puppet."

I'm ashamed to say it slipped out. I relished this chance to give Grainger a little comeuppance.

"I'd say that all of us," Adam began, swallowing nervously, "except perhaps Alex and Lilly here, have had to make some compromises along the way in order to do what we were cut out for."

Alex realized she was the only one who hadn't said anything.

Every one was looking at her expectantly.

"Personally," she said, "I'd just like to salvage something of Andrew Tremaine's and Jock Sparling's vision for Earthbaby, however that might be accomplished right now."

"Bravo!" Adam exclaimed, flushed with admiration for her.

But Grainger wouldn't let up his attack on Clarke: "It makes it damn difficult to get on with what Alex and all of us want when Foreman's boys at NASA are screwing us up so royally with this satellite business. For God's sake Clarke, first my observatory was all tied up tracking the thing, and now we have to sit here in shield mode while that damn thing goes round the universe with us."

"I know we're all frustrated, unable to get started with our projects, but until NASA sorts this thing through there's nothing we can do but just tough it out."

Alex looks up at that. "I think there must be something we can do besides sit here and quarrel about it."

"Roll back the shields, for one thing," Adam chimes in. "They're only designed to deflect minor meteorites. If they really want to give us a shot…."

(Adam, of course, is peeved because his "orchard" — as he refers to it — isn't getting enough solar radiation.)

"I'm unwilling to directly countermand a specific NASA order, to be blunt."

"That's the difference, Clarke, between you and me," said Grainger, getting in his best shot.

Personally, I could have killed him. I hate that kind of adventurist arrogance. I looked at Alex, though, and saw she was smiling at him. Even Adam looked supportive.

Oh what fools we mortals be. ᴄᴠ

F oreman hasn't wasted much time, Tremaine muses. He's sipping coffee sitting on the edge of the bed watching the news channel. What little was left in the media mess of any pretense of independent news gathering has been thoroughly eliminated. Here's another announcement of another decree. The General has instituted a plan to eliminate "microwave pollution" by bringing in regulations designed to restrict communicator usage to a few hours each day in each zone. This will enable the de-activation of two thirds of the continent's microwave relay towers. Foreman knows his business all right. This means each zone will be information deprived and interzonal connections will be minimized and monitored.

"Hey, Perlita. Did you hear the latest?"

"I already know about it," she says. "In fact it's really screwing us up."

Tremaine pushes the off button and listens to the sigh of dying electrons hissing behind the screen. There's another noise. A jeep growling up the path. Perlita doesn't have to say anything. He slips into his sandals and eases quickly out the back door and down the cliff to the beach, leaving her free to deal with it.

Alone on the beach, Tremaine gives in to inertia, covered head to toe with ultima sunblock, the hot sands a comforting heating pad for his healing back muscles. If only he'd been living like this for the past twenty years, how he would have thrived, how much younger he would have looked and felt. And that's the strange thing, there's no consciousness in him of any shock of adjustment. It's as if all that work, stress, struggle and prestige was merely a passing phase on the way to the real life waiting for him, the real life which is simply this one.

Every morning he is amazed to wake with Perlita beside him. What a privilege to run his hand over her lovely haunches, to rest it in the hollow of her hip while he drifts with her into and out of a sun-dappled doze, the two of them mated like spoons together. How easy it would be not to bother with anything ever again, just drift along through space and time until a last sunset lifted his heart out of his mouth forever.

He gets up and strolls the tidemark, elated to see some kelp and other organic sea-wrack there among the nylon hawsers and bits and pieces of unidentifiable plastic debris. Maybe the die-off would turn around one day. Maybe Gaia would heal herself. He can hardly believe it when he sees a nautilus shell. It must have somehow made its way up from the deeps of the ocean trench that ran right by the islands here, probably escaping some catastrophe to die close enough to the surface for the upwelling waters to carry it onto the beach.

He holds it in his hands like a delicate piece of porcelain. Intellectually, he understands the mathematical functions on which its multi-chambered proportions are based, but he finds himself over-whelmed with the sheer magic of its very existence. He looks over to the toss of palm trees bordering the sands, the great scoop of the bay itself with its headlands jutting into the horizon, and is struck breath-less with the amazing forms of things.

Then there's a shout and he sees Perlita waving to him to come home. He carries the shell back up to the house, offering it to Perlita like an eager child. She places it on the windowsill, her face suddenly sad and tired. A moment later she is joking about how he is commit-ting an ecological sin by depriving the beach of its store of calcium carbonate. But her mood seems forced somehow.

He knows something is up when she sits him formally at the din-ing table.

His voice is anxious. "So what's up?"

"The jeep was just a news drop," Perlita tells him. "Edgely nearly bought it. They bombed his studio party right after the newscast. Luckily he'd just dropped in for a few minutes and was already off into hiding when it happened. Several innocent people maimed and dead, though."

"So where's Edgely now?" Andrew asks her.

"Safe," is all she says.

"And what about Earthbaby? Did the Eurosoviets get anything up there?"

"Yes. They've got it in synch orbit, so they can keep a close eye on things."

"What was it? One of their general purpose manoeuvrables?"

"Some adaptation or other. Apparently we're expecting news on that soon."

From now on, all the news is being brought to Perlita by word of mouth because jamming and monitoring of communications channels, even through the Eurosoviets, has made previous methods temporarily insecure.

Perlita tells Tremaine that guerrilla warfare is breaking out all over the Americas, but little news of it is reaching the general public.

"Standard technique," Tremaine comments. "Every one of those resistance movements think they're going it alone."

"That's one of our jobs: getting out the truth."

"Yes. But everyone's so bamboozled all the time, no-one has any idea what the truth is any more. You could be lying to them like any one else."

Perlita goes on to tell him that selective assassinations, especially of opposition candidates in the most recalcitrant protectorates, have been sudden and swift. Obviously, Foreman and his cronies had the whole operation pre-planned. Also clearly pre-arranged is the massive increase in his so-called Social Service cadres, many of which have moved onto this island. (So much for his dream of an untouched paradise.) There's a special bureau of the Social Service cadres devoted to searching out followers of the so-called 'meta-consciousness' movement throughout the protectorates.

"Why the hell would Foreman bother with all that harmless gobbledegook?" Tremaine was vaguely aware the meta-consciousness movement had grown out of the old alien abduction believers, and the archetypal X-files series about which there had been a spate of Ph.D. theses. In some arcane way it was connected somehow to the 'regulator' fad among some young computer nerds.

Perlita shrugs: "He's obviously into belief conformity."

"So is that everything, Perlita? Why do I think there's more."

"Because there is more. Things are changing, now, obviously."

She forces herself to look bright and perky. "I have a surprise for you. The courier just delivered these things for you."

It's a set of identity papers. Using his own travel fiche's hologram cunningly altered electronically, it includes his own fingerprint and DNA analysis under the new identity: Herman Pantone.

"I take it this is a signal for me to start living in the so-called real world again?"

"We're not casting you adrift. It's more a precaution in case things go wrong on our journey."

"Journey?" So there is an end to his stay in paradise after all.

Besides the citizenship fiche, there's a bank credit card, a RotoMasoLioniclub identity badge, Connecticut driver's license, and two 'Special Customer' citation awards from stores in New Haven.

"You've become my uncle from the United States, retired, here on vacation."

"This is a lot of work. By the way, who's financing this?"

She laughs. "The same experts took the liberty of purloining your current bank accounts using your own cards, in such a way it looks like you did the transactions the day before you died. The rest of your estate, of course, has gone to your heirs as per your will."

"Your uncle, eh? Sounds pretty incestuous to me."

"Only by marriage of course. I actually do have relatives there."

"About my estate. See if you can get that daughter of mine safe somewhere in Europe will you?"

"We can sort this out later, all right? There's more I want you to see in the bedroom."

He notices an edge in her voice, but follows her in. She swings open a closet and points.

"Special delivery. Tourist clothes."

He slips a lightweight fibre optic jacket off the hangar. It irridesces with little pinpricks of purple and green.

"It's a bit loud and a bit dated for me. Aha! New Haven label! Very clever."

He goes to put it back on the hanger but she stops him.

"Change into it. And put the rest in this flightbag."

"Why?"

"I'm taking you somewhere."

"Right now?"

"Soon. We should leave in an hour. It's quite a trip and they're expecting us."

She stands in front of him, looking down at the floor, her voice tone clearly shifted into a more formal, professional mode.

"What's up? Is everything okay?"

She brightens, her eyes dancing again. "Of course. Come on. You'll enjoy it."

Making an effort. Whatever it is, he won't bug her about it. After all, she does lead a pretty complicated and hectic life under this calm surface of tropical island bliss.

She watches him begin to undress, goes to walk out of the bedroom, but turns at the door. He stops and looks up at her, astonished at the turmoil in her face. Then she rushes over and clasps him, pushing him backwards over the bed. She takes him frantically, surprising him with her intensity, her coming followed by a gush of tears as his own violent discharges jerk his body into sudden stillness.

Instead of quietly lying with him in the aftermath as usual she tears herself away and gets up. Dazed, he observes her smoothing down her bunched-up skirt, breathing hard to regain her equilibrium. Seeing him watching her, she tries to joke about her legs feeling weak and does up the buttons of her blouse. She throws his clothes on top of him.

"All right. All right. I'll get going."

Still in a daze, he dresses, swallows a quick glass of water, hefts the flightbag over his shoulder, tilts the lurid straw hat onto his head as they emerge together into an intense sun.

Down the winding road to the village they go arm in arm, her fingers affectionately squeezing his until they approach the first mildewed cottages. She separates from him, warning him to be formal.

It feels so unnatural to be apart from her that he lapses into silence, although Perlita continues to chatter, pointing out the laboriously constructed checkerboard squares of coffee beans, set out one by one to dry on the convenient tarmac shoulders of the road.

"Can I inquire where we're going?" he finally interrupts.

"I'd rather you didn't know until we got there, just in case we don't get there."

A simple statement, eminently sensible. But it asserts and emphasizes her basic separateness from him. This necessary secrecy formalizes their relationship, reminds him again of the real life in which she's embedded, around which, so far at least, he himself is merely tangential. How many times, he wonders, has she had to do this sort of thing before? And maybe that's what this is about, some kind of conflict generating inside her.

He sees a group of children in a yard playing with a litter of white pups. Then he notices they aren't pups at all, but pigs. The whole village, in fact, seems filled with the little white squealers, running in and out of the see-through stick huts, romping with infants and toddlers and sitting on young girls' laps like sleeping babies.

"I guess they treat their pigs like family pets," he says.

"Yes." Then she adds, "But they all get eaten soon enough."

"There's no free lunch," he quips.

He might have said, *All good things come to an end.* His throat is beginning to tighten with the realization this lovely idyll with Perlita is coming to its end.

In every yard are tables set out between a banana and a coconut tree. Over and over, on rickety chairs placed in their shade, is a mother combing and braiding a daughter's hair. Proud of their muscles, several young men saunter about with machetes, palm fronds over their shoulders. Soon will come the rains, of course, and the roofs will need thatching. All poor, by anyone's standards, he thinks. But all equal too. No one with more than their share.

On the harbour wall, fishermen repair tattered nets in the shade of grimy cargo sheds. Nothing changes much, here. Gulls perch on the upturned hull of an old freighter squandered on the coral shore. Perlita begins to be greeted now. They want to chat with her, but she answers in a strange patois he cannot fathom and hustles him on by.

Alone again on the new coast road beyond the village, she takes his hand again. Beside the road is a tiny stone church gone to ruin. The new tarmac has bisected its graveyard.

"Not far now. Just to the fork"

Beyond the church a black river of asphalt flows down from the white fortress of a tourist enclave. Rounding the curve, they see a jeep parked on the shoulder. Bulky and bright-shirted, a nervous mestizo of middle-aged handsomeness, his dark curls streaked with eminent grey, descends with a heavy crunch to the gravel and greets them. He runs the car rental concession at the hotel.

A quick repartee between him and Perlita in the patois and he gives her the keys. Andrew climbs into the passenger seat and they drive off immediately, leaving their friend angling into his top pocket for a pack of fumaros.

Andrew makes himself as comfortable as he can with his feet on the dashboard. They hum along in the neat little Javanese buggy past the tourist beach with its guarded gateways and climb the rocky cliffs which harbour it. With relief, they enter the pungent shade of the green forest.

He's hungry. Perlita refuses to stop, but directs him to discover the hamper in the back seat. She seems more relaxed now, and they share the picnic hilariously as she drives adroitly with one hand while he changes gears for her up and down the slopes.

Coming into the precincts of an impoverished and gloomy forest village she slows down. Some young men heckle her, causing her to stare ahead grimly. "They think it's the usual situation between you and me, what with this hotel jeep." Carefully she steers around a group of women and children waiting to draw water from a communal standpipe. They too stare at her until she turns onto a sideroad.

Now the road crumbles into a cart track, washboarded and narrow. They leave behind an abandoned plantation, palm trees overgrown with lianas, their crowns victims of brown die-back. Perlita has gone back into herself again, refusing a sip from the wine bottle, concentrating on driving as fast as she can.

Cowbirds and vultures are picking their way through the dead fields as Perlita sets the jeep into four-wheel drive at the bottom of the sharp incline. The turbo motor sets into a different whine, enough for a tied goat to snicker and jump to the end of his cruel rope as the pebbles thrown up under the fenders clatter around the axles.

Now Andrew has to set himself because of the pain beginning in his constricted back. It looks like a hard road ahead and it is.

At last they come jouncing to the top of the rise and they roll onto the top of a flat escarpment. It's a beautiful panorama, one which must have delighted the officers of the doomed colonial outpost from the eighteenth century, the ruins of which rise from a nettled clearing. Tremaine is surprised to see thorn and thistles growing there.

"They all died of yellow fever. The thistles came out of their mattress stuffing."

Her first words in nearly half an hour.

"Are you getting a bit tired, Perlita?"

"I'm fine."

She points out a few other landmarks.

Below, like a scene from China, rice-paddies spread through the valley. As they descend, driving gets easier. A relief not to have turbo noise and constant bouncing. They are on no road now, only a raised quilting of dikes between polders.

His back is beginning to lock up so he moves to the back seat and stretches out. They pass below a high guard-line of vaneless old windmills in the windcatch of the valley. Their modern counterparts glitter as they turn, making a gentle hum. He stops himself from trying to engage her attention, though he wants to share this all with her.

Suddenly he's thinking of Earthbaby. Of Lily and Alex. How are they making out? And what will that bastard Foreman get up to now he has control of things? He's not through with that character yet. And, Herman Pantalone aside, he thinks, I guess I'm not through with being Andrew Tremaine yet either.

Another four wheel grind finds them back in the forest again, this time following a lush shallow streambed. Tiny monkeys dash away like squirrels, chittering. Then suddenly there are six or eight of them, hand to tail in a chain, leaping and bridging the treetops across the stream. At the pool of a small waterfall Perlita stops.

They sit there silently, gurgling water laving hot rubber tire knobs, the forest runoff gushing directly ahead of them emptying, emptying, filling eyes and ears like a mantra. When she doesn't stir, he asks her, "Are we lost?"

Perlita doesn't reply and doesn't move. For a moment, he sits mystified, then scrambles forward into the seat beside her. She turns to him, her face damp from the spray, her eyes blank.

"I love you," he yells over the white noise. "I love you."

"Don't say that. Don't say that." Yet she is kissing him again wildly, teeth bruising his lips, her hands pulling his own onto her erected breasts.

He hugs her tight, tight, but she doesn't soften. She cries out, and when he releases her she clambers down from the jeep into the stream. She thrashes right up to the waterfall, head thrown back in its downpour, gasping as it batters her face.

Hypnotized he watches her, sensing molecules of his own mind and body are splattering into a million shiny drops cascading into rushing water. In a few minutes she turns, calm, climbs into the driver's seat, starts the motor and skids the jeep expertly up the bank, crashing through undergrowth onto a well-worn muddy path.

A short way through a strand of sinuous trees and they break out onto an upland meadow, dotted with giant cottonwoods. Some great thing crashes away from them into the underbrush, startling him.

"Wild boars still roam here," she says, stopping again. "They're nearly extinct now. Occasionally they have trouble finding mates; so you hear stories of how they call domestic pigs into the woods and mate with them."

"You are going to tell me what's wrong, aren't you, Perlita?"

"When we get where we're going, which is very soon now, we have to behave like we did on the road through the village."

"I suppose I can understand that, but surely that's not all..."

"There are reasons. How difficult this is. You see...where we are going..."

Now it dawns on him. How could he be so self-involved and stupid? A woman like her. She wouldn't just be conveniently alone, conveniently unattached....

"So there's someone waiting for you there. Naturally."

She nods. Then she looks at him with a rueful grin.

"Worse than that. You aren't coming back to my house again. My job was simply to get you well and test you out. Things are never simple."

She holds both his hands, trying to make him feel better.

He forces himself to say, "Okay. Don't worry."

Then she honks the horn four times, the sound echoing over the savannah. On every horizon the crags jut up like broken teeth. They are in the mouth of an old volcano. She begins to drive slowly forward onto the peaty turf, patterned in patches like a waffle iron in metre squares.

"Is there an archaeological dig going on here?"

"Yes. In a manner of speaking. It's a very old habitation site, one of the last stands of the Arawaks when the Spanish set out to slaughter them all."

"Oh yes. Our famous friend Columbus. The original Yankee entrepreneur."

Down the last slope, into a wooded gully, and he sees the camp. A group of very fit young people come out to meet them, men and women, browned and tough as the high sierra around them.

Behind them, grinning with welcome, is a familiar face.

Squeezing Tremaine's hand, Perlita leaps down and walks towards him. He hugs her tight and kisses her passionately. Then he strides up to the jeep.

"Jeesus, Man. You sure look like you been on a good vacation. How you doin' brother? Yeah. How you doin' old sport?"

The crew's paranoia and frustration at being shadowed by the Eurosoviet satellite, took an extra turn when, the day before yesterday, Alex and Grainger, who have been sharing the tracking task, reported that the satellite was gingerly being shifted slightly in its attitude and orbital relationship to Earthbaby. Probably, the Eurosoviets had been waiting for a favourable point in our mutual rotation around the solar system to relocate the satellite, or, indeed, as we all immediately feared, to veer it off a sufficient distance so that, inevitably, in the near future, we would come into a vari-speed collision with it, one with enough impact mass to do us serious damage. In hindsight, of course, I'm pretty certain they wanted to do nothing of the kind.

Clarke immediately reported the shift to NASA, who began their own monitoring of our tracking system. After a few hours, James came on the screen, looking extremely worried and haggard. "My orders are to convey to you," he said, "the following instructions, approved by President Foreman, in light of what we perceive to be the very real danger posed to Earthbaby and you, the crew."

Again I had the impression, from the cautious phrasing he was using, and the way he blinked and swallowed, that part of what he was saying was a lie. Not a bad conclusion in the light of later events.

The idea was that we were to take evasive action and remove the satellite by pushing it out of orbit by using the sun-buggy, the experimental craft Grainger and Alex had been trained to pilot for asteroid exploration in a later stage of the Earthbaby project.

Grainger, asserting his independence from arbitrary authority, protested. He was damned if he was going to go out there until he had direct orders from his own outfit, Agriminco, thank you very much. Clarke conveyed this to NASA and very soon James reappeared on the screen to announce there was a communiclip coming for Grainger direct from Agriminco headquarters. It was the company president himself, chatting from his care-chair. Grainger almost burst with self-importance at this.

"Just thought I'd better confirm these orders, Mr. President, sir."

(Obviously the approved style of address at Agriminco)

"We need this done, colonel. And you're the man." (Judo-chop, judo-chop) "Quickly and efficiently." (final judo-chop)

"Yes sir. Yes sir."

The message pleased Grainger immensely, and he was gung ho to move on it. Alex, now it was a few hours after the satellite's first movements, expressed some puzzlement at the way the satellite's orbital variance was proceeding if its intention was to be destructive. Her observation, added to my suspicions about the truth of James' warning, made me express doubts about the wisdom of destroying the Eurosoviet's property until we had more to go on.

Grainger. "I think NASA might be over-reacting here, as Alex suggests."

"I tend to agree," Clarke said, surprising us. "I don't think we should rush into this until we have confirmation there's a real danger. What if the Eurosoviets are simply planning to bring the thing home?"

"Oh, come on Clarke," scoffed Grainger. "NASA and the intelligence boys must have gone into this. Don't you think they know what's up?"

"If NASA knows something we don't, why don't they come out and tell us instead of mouthing these vague ideas about there being some danger to us and the station?" Alex asked.

"What other evidence can they have?" I interjected. "They don't know any more than we do about the satellite's actual movements. What if Clarke is right and they're soon going to be heading home?"

"Let's ask NASA for a delay or a reconfirmation now the satellite's shift pattern is more apparent," Adam said, playing up to Alex.

"I agree," Alex cut in, pleasing Adam no end.

She referred again to her calculations. "Looks like it's slipping under our dark side now."

But NASA was adamant that the satellite be removed. This was despite James' initial response to Clarke's query, which, I am certain, seemed to welcome our hesitation as a means for him to delay the initiation of the satellite's disposal. My instinct here was further confirmed when James came on the last time with the final orders that we should proceed immediately. I was certain he was delivering the order under considerable duress.

"Well. There it is," Clarke said. "I guess you and Alex are it. We'll proceed with it tomorrow."

I suspect, like most of us, Clarke hoped that "tomorrow" would see the satellite either departed, or at least preparing to do so.

Before we retired, Alex began working out a flight-path for the sun-buggy that would conceal it from the satellite's observation system, using the powerful main computers in Central. Meanwhile Grainger and I hustled down to the launching bay to check the vehicle out. Normally, the buggy, when launched, gains motive power from the array of solar panels that unfold from it like a butterfly emerging from its chrysalis. Gradually it would accelerate across open space, utilizing the photon power of the solar wind to hop from asteroid to asteroid. This time, though, it would be using its hydrogen emission tanks for greater mobility and impact, keeping the solar arrays folded in tight to avoid impact damage.

There wasn't much for me to do but echo Grainger's checklist as a back-up through the systems-testing which the on-board computer was doing anyhow. This is how we humans keep ourselves relevant these days, with these kinds of deadly boring monitoring tasks. Activating the airlock, I let Grainger through to the cockpit itself after the check and he decided to remain there for a while, familiarizing himself with the controls until such time as Alex came down to join him.

First come, first served, I thought, watching him settle into the main pilot seat. It was pretty obvious who was going to actually fly this baby. Well, it was an Agriminco contribution, and Grainger was set on impressing Alex with his skills.

Waiting for Alex, I moseyed around in this underside area that I'd never seen before, even in simulation, and came across a locked bulkhead. That puzzled me. There'd been a certain vagueness about this area because of its high-tech systems, but I didn't remember there being anything classified. The previous technical crew who left when we arrived must have sealed it. I noticed it was a two-card entry format, probably a danger-radiation or similar area.

Alex appeared with her freshly prepared navigation module.

"Looks like you're going to be the passenger on this one," I said, nodding in Grainger's direction.

"Maybe I'll learn something. He's really tops at this sort of thing, so I've heard."

I almost said, "heard from whom?" but restrained myself, watching her clamber through the lock to join Grainger like two teenagers heading off in Daddy's new hover.

Well. Let's hope things will settle into normal routine around here some time in the near future. None of us ever expected the situations that have cropped up. I understand now that one of our main problems is going to be figuring out what is really going on. My own instinct is we are being lied to. The question is, how much.... Perhaps tomorrow will tell. ❧

L ying alone in the cool, screened lean-to attached to the side of the computer shed, Tremaine listens to faint sounds etching themselves on the midnight marble of the upland plateau. He tries to figure them out: marauding bats vacuuming up clouds of fireflies, marmots nosing in the bunchgrass, a flock of mynah birds rustling in the nearby thorn tree; further off, he thinks, there's a grunt from wild peccaries foraging in the forests around the old crater's rim. No frogs. He'd hoped that maybe here, as in some small pockets around the world, a few amphibians might have survived. Then he remembers that frogs never bred on these islands in the first place until the poisonous cane toads practically took over in the twentieth century. So it's natural, then, for those comforting bassoon croaks not to be heard here.

There are other noises, too, coming from the tents where the young crew members are mostly coupled up in their various ways, as would be Perlita and Edgely. Now he regrets not following up the friendly advances of the lean English woman, Lesley, seventy if she was a day, but tight skinned and slim like a teenager, who sat next to him at the communal dining table. Bill introduced him to the gathering, jarringly, as Herman Pantone, keeping his real identity secret; but he could tell that at least Lesley knew who he was. Considering the appearances on TV he'd made, that's another thing he should talk to Edgely about: some sort of disguise if he was ever to walk about in the real world. For Edgely, that must be a real problem.

What a good cover for the operation of a Society cell this archaeological dig is: a light-plane airstrip, comings and goings of equipment and supplies, an assemblage of temporary shelters for communications and computer equipment — all perfectly natural to the enterprise, along with the legitimate qualifications of its personnel.... The big blond Hebridean Scot, Donald Grey, the dig's supervisor, was a case in point.

Tremaine had actually read one of his books, a creative crossover between fiction and science that had dealt with the world view blending of Native Caribbean, African and East Indian indentured labour groups and European colonists in the West Indies. *Rage and Order*, that was the title. The Eco-femocrats had been ambivalent about it since it dared to concentrate on the point of view of females and discuss issues of race and colour, something white male writers had been timorous about doing since the end of the twentieth century because of charges of cultural appropriation. Grey had responded with the witty remark that under the skin everyone shared the same "grey matter" and there were many paths to truth, as there were many truths to discover.

Tremaine had liked Grey immediately, with his cro-magnon massive brows knitted over extremely shy, almost albino blue eyes and the little nervous tick in his neck muscle. He could see, when his face lit up with boyish delight at some witticism or other, why the crew universally adored him, especially the "lesbian tent," as Lesley casually referred to them, who treated him rather like top-class women riders treated their stallion mounts — with a mixture of petting and calm control.

Beginning to slip into sleep, Tremaine realizes how he yearns for the warm scent of Perlita lying beside him. A light scuffle over his head rouses him with a little gasp of panic. There's a thick thud as a gecko falls off the rafter and lands on the floor. Damn things. Fighting over banana skins. Vivaporous aren't they? Doesn't that mean they're actually all clones of each other? Hell, the species that do survive; why are they the most unattractive ones? Just don't shit on my face, you damn lizards. That's all I ask. That's all.

*   *   *

When the sun comes up sudden and brilliant, he wants to turn over and sleep some more; but it marches into every corner of the room, its heat gathering so he has to cast the sheet back and lie there naked and bemused.

He hears the camp bustle beginning and is just deciding to get up when Perlita comes to the screen door.

"Can I come in?" she asks, her hands and face pressed against the mesh.

"So how are you, this morning?"

"Not bad," he says, trying not to sound resentful.

She closes the main door behind her, darkening the room. He can still see her wide coaxing grin as she comes to him and sits on the bedside, her hand affectionately on his bare thigh.

"Come on, eh? We gotta be cool about this, right?"

He winces a little at the way her speech pattern has shifted. Under

Edgely's influence no doubt.

"That's all very well for you to say. You've got an emotional safety net with Edgely. What have I got?"

"Sure, sure. I know that. I'm sorry. Real sorry. I thought I was just giving you some real nice treatment."

"That's it? That's all?"

She twists uncomfortably, kneeding the flesh of his buttocks with her strong hands down the nerve-path of his injury.

"You know that's not so."

Fuck, he thinks to himself, how many times have I been on the opposite side of a scene like this? There's a come-uppance for you, there's an atonement. But she genuinely has suffered over this, he can tell from the shamed tilt of her head.

"Edgely and I don't have anything formal. In fact, we don't go for this possessive, exclusive kind of thing. We just love each other when we get the chance."

He laughs, angry, but also mollified.

"You should have told me right off."

"You're right."

"For Christ's sake Perlita. I'm too old to suffer from this kind of heartbreak. I want to live with you and love you."

Even as he says it, he realizes how melodramatic he sounds, realizes, objectively, what any therapist might say about his feelings and their long-term authenticity given the state of his life at the moment.

Her hand has stopped caressing him.

"I'm sorry to make you unhappy. I just wanted joy for you."

He strokes her hair. "Don't listen to me. I want you to be happy too. I truly do."

She grins at him, running her brown fingers through the white thatch of his chest, then down his belly to make him gasp. She kisses him while squeezing with one hand to make him hard. Then she moves her puckering kisses down, down.

He barely has time to think what is happening before he explodes devastatingly into this other sensitive softness of her, registering, before his eyes cloud over, the green flash on a rafter of a jealous gecko peeking.

*   *   *

Lesley turns out to be an expert on architectural reconstruction. Using computer imaging, it was she who was able to figure out the complete details of the wooden raftering and roofing of the Parthenon when it was reconstructed in the World Heritage Campaign of the Christian year 2000. It was one of her early triumphs, followed later by her brilliant concept of hologrammatic enhancement of ancient ruins whereby actual reconstruction of ancient sites, expensive and potentially destructive, was replaced by hologrammatic projections, right at the site, of the missing architectural pieces, thereby giving the visitor the full experience of the ancient exteriors and interiors.

This morning, Tremaine notices, she looks especially youthful with her body held in a dancer's chest lift, the slight looseness of her abdomen checked with a wide star-wars belt, her eyes brilliant in their nests of artful eye-shadow and tinted lashes. Tremaine looks closely for the signs of face-lift but finds none. What a shame hormone therapy doesn't work like that for men. The lines under his own eyes, at ten years younger than she, are far more pronounced.

Before Edgely convenes a meeting between them, Tremaine watches her in conference with the "lesbian tent," as she'd called it last evening. The way they joke with her and handle her familiarly makes him wonder. Edgely, noticing him looking at them, puts his big hand on the back of his neck and squeezes the tense trapezius there.

"She's English."

He says it with a kind of joyous chuckle at the wonderful diversity of human experience and Tremaine, flooded with liking for him, a strong coffee jag beginning to reach his own pleasure centres, involuntarily hugs him, pats his dark grinning face in playful punishment. "Racist, sexist."

"She's all yours, Andy. You can have her all day to yourself."

Breaking free, Lesley comes over holding a small vial of fibre-optic program disks. Perlita drives up in the hotel jeep, remains in it, obviously waiting for Bill. He begins to saunter over there, laughing to himself.

Lesley takes his arm and propels him toward the computer hut.

"So what's up?" Tremaine asks the world in general.

"We're going for a walk together, a long walk."

"Don't force him now," Edgely yells. Then, more seriously, "You don't have to do anything you don't want, right. But anything we can learn about NASA and Earthbaby could be very valuable to us sometime later on."

"Any news from the satellite yet?"

"Earthbaby's been shielded, apparently. That's all we've been told."

"Fat lot of good that'll do them. NASA must be in confusion. I wonder if James is in charge?"

Lesley, getting proprietorial, pulls him over the threshold.

"See you later, Billy boy, and you, Perlita," she calls out.

Perlita waves, throwing a kiss. Edgely walks backwards towards the jeep with his hands open in a gesture of mock helplessness. Then Lesley has Tremaine inside, totally dark as she closes the door.

The way she is with him he would normally have said to himself, the hell with it, and kissed her. But his lingering heartache for Perlita, especially knowing she is going back to the house of her grandfather without him, to the place where his life has made such an incredible turn, numbs his instincts for adventure; and after a moment or two, the expectancy between them dwindled, Lesley lets go of him and switches on the lights.

The room itself is a surprise to him since it is lined completely, floor to ceiling, with copper sheeting. He sees the two of them warmly reflected in it along with the equipment and furniture in a multiple of images.

"This is like being inside a kaleidoscope," he says.

"It's an old way of cutting out any kind of electrical interference, or electrical bugging. Saves several feet of lead and concrete."

She throws a heavy bolt across the door, sealing them in.

"What's that for?"

"So no one barging in will get a shock."

"A shock?"

She goes to a circuit breaker. "Hang on. You might feel a little tiny shiver. This is 20,000 volts."

He's going to scream in protest, but she throws the breaker and he feels nothing. Of course. They, and everything in the room, are simply part of the force field, a little universe, cut off unless somehow grounded into the larger universe outside, rather like a pool of insulated anti-matter.

"That is weird. It makes me very tentative about touching anything."

"You think that's weird. Wait till we take our little walk."

She's been fiddling with the computers, inserting the fibre-optic sticks, and now the big screen flares into life.

He stares at it, struck with some sense of familiarity as the image there spins and skews.

"Recognize anything?"

He sits down. Of course! It's the landing pad on top of the NASA complex in Puerto Rico.

"How the hell did you get this?"

"It's a combination of blown-up satellite pictures and imaging from verbal descriptions and hand maps we've gleaned from some of the staff over the years. I want you to guide us in, if that's all right with you, and add any little details you want. I'll stop the programme and feed them in through my imager here."

"You mean you want me to take you on a guided tour of the complex, so you'll be able to reconstruct it — like some real estate ad?"

"There are a few areas, still sketchy, that you can help flesh out for me."

"I see."

Her demeanour is quite calm now, none of her previous jokiness.

"You have to understand, Lesley, that all my instincts are conditioned to maintain secrecy about sensitive areas of the complex."

"Exactly. And as Edgely said, you don't have to do any of this. It would be lovely, though, if you could. I've been working on this simulation for months, so naturally I'd like to know how good it is."

"So you've pretty well got all of it, have you?"

"Why don't you just go through it with me and see for yourself?"

On the screen his own heli-pad is clarifying as if he's seeing it himself. Shit. This is eerie, but very compelling. He could just say forget it to her. But why should he? He's on their side now. They saved his life. And if he can do anything to get those bastards…."

"No problem, Lesley. I was just expressing how conditioned I've been."

Her eyes sparkle at him. "I knew you wouldn't let us down. How's this look?"

"Fantastic. You're amazing, I must say. Ah yes. At this point in the descent, you'd be able to read the security hologram which stays green as you approach and the sensors confirm your validity. They do an automatic inventory by reading off all your model and serial numbers and security codes. "

"Now we're touching down, and things will get vaguer. Is this okay doing it like this? Would you rather we started somewhere else?"

"No. No. Fine."

And so they continue hour after hour, the process so enthralling in and of itself that Tremaine hardly notices the time or the expenditure of his energy until he has led her through the complex towards the main control room. He begins to fill in the blank consoles by describing the controls on his and on Jock's monitoring stations. There, he stumbles, suddenly conscious he has been breeching pages of security secrets, his old instincts jarring him. Wait! his conditioned inner voice tells him.

"Wait!" he says. "I have to think about this a minute. This is triple A classified stuff I'm into now."

"It's all right. No harm can come to you now you're here, Andy. This is fantastically valuable to us should we have to try stopping a shuttle run loaded with nukes."

Her voice is very assuring. Very thrilling to him. These guys are clever, all right. They must have got hold of his psychological profile, or figured it out for themselves. Well disguised as it may be, the truth is he is one of those men whose validation can only come completely through women. Praise from men, however heartfelt, doesn't mean near as much, no matter what their position or importance. Is this the reason for Perlita? And now, after her nurse/mistress role has been completed, is Lesley the next — the mother/teacher — still intensely linked with the prospect of deep emotional and physical reward for good performance? The thought gives him a little shiver. Will he have to put up the same kind of paranoic shield with the Tribals and their Society as he did with the Foreman crowd?

"The point is, I guess…if this were common knowledge, so to speak…should it get in the wrong hands…. Once I tell you, if you see what I mean, then it's beyond my control, isn't it? It goes beyond just trusting you guys. The very space station itself could be endangered."

"How so?

He almost goes on to tell her about the laser umbilicus, how it holds all the life-support information, and will continue to do so for years until the expansion programme for Earthbaby evolves to the point where the beam is no longer necessary.

"Nothing specific, Lesley. I just want to get used to the idea of this for a minute, okay?"

"Of course. I know how shaky this must make you feel. I must say, Andrew, I do regard you as a real hero, not just for your physical bravery in this miraculous escape of yours, but also for how you tried so hard for so long to keep your ideals alive under terrible circumstances. And I can quite see how you feel right now. Why don't we take a little break?"

Her sincerity seems so intense, and his admiration for her is so profound as she gently caresses his wrist with her speckled lean hand he has to take several breaths, something rising in his throat and threatening to choke him. As he stands, the copper reflections dart and shift, dizzying him so he stumbles. She reaches over to steady him.

"Come outside," she says. "I've been driving you far too hard. Godlike as I happen to think you are," she teases him, "I have to remember you're only really human underneath."

Yes. Being motherly with him, now. Fuck this paranoia. How I'd love to just let myself go, he thinks, and simply fall right into it, just as I did with Perlita. And what could I possibly lose? What possibly? James, for instance. I should have trusted him at the end there.

Lesley throws the breaker to cut the electric field, then pulls the bolt. Outside, he strolls with her, in the bright high air of the plateau, towards the gently flapping shade of the refreshment tent. Their arms are around each other easily, like old friends. Enraptured with the slightness of her body and the tone and accent of her voice, Tremaine is amazed how lighthearted he feels, even when he crosses over the tracks of Perlita's jeep, going away from him over the grassland to the forest horizon.

In the tent they have actual glasses. He chinks his to hers.

"To life."

"L'Chaim," she replies, relishing, like him, the very moment.

"This is amazing," he says, gesturing to embrace the whole world around him. He drinks the chilled guava. "Truly amazing."

SOCIAL DYNAMICS RESEARCH PROJECT
JOURNAL OF LILLITH SHAWNADITHIT

I hardly know why I'm bothering to write this tonight. Not so much for the record, I suspect, but for the need to try and gain some balance in my mind, some reflection, so I can see where we might go from here. It's amazing how we psychologically protect ourselves, not giving credence to evil even when it reveals itself starkly and confronts us, and even then, sometimes, responding to it too late, like those poor holocaust victims of the mid-twentieth century, or, just as bad, the peaceable tribals of North America, one of whom I am named after, wiped out by the vicious European buccaneers of the century before that.

Now the election is over, and Foreman's triumph is complete, there's no need for the Privates to hide their real agenda any more. And now we've been duped into becoming their accomplices, even to murder.

Again the satellite had shifted further under our dark side. I would have commented about my discovery of the locked bay, but didn't want to confuse the issue what with the excitement of what was happening. We were all extremely nervous, but in some ways the operation, I decided, would prove to be a good bonding exercise. How wrong I was!

I went down to check out Grainger and Alex's launching. Alex sat quite comfortably in the co-pilot seat, letting Grainger do his thing. Then I saw her slip in the navigation module and set the analog with the Earthbaby computer. Soon after that, with a wave of the hand to me, they drifted elegantly away, slipping into the shadow side almost immediately on the complex spiral path Alex had computed.

I returned to central and there the remaining three of us watched on the screen, fascinated, as the operation got under way. At a crucial point, the buggy had to expose itself and the response from the satellite was almost immediate. It didn't fail to impress me when I thought of all those messages streaming back to the microwave clutter of earth space then returning to prompt the evasive movements we saw taking place as the satellite tried to avoid the buggy's rush.

"I can't believe that telemetry," Clarke muttered, repeating what he had said when the satellite had managed to catch up and shadow us so beautifully when it first arrived.

Perhaps Alex was right about Grainger's abilities because the buggy had the advantage at every turn. Once it had engaged, there was a frantic burst of gas from the satellite which slowed, but did not stop, the inevitable. Gradually the satellite was pushed out of orbit into space, the buggy only letting go after a burst of acceleration which sent the satellite spinning hopelessly, its nozzles merely spewing out ineffectually as it accelerated logarithmically dwindling into the black.

Now here's the horrible part. As we were all, despite ourselves, cheering the success of the operation, and watching the buggy make an abrupt turn, we suddenly saw two more puffs of smoke from the receding satellite. They were hatches exploding. And, good God, emerging from them, suited, two astronauts, little straddled blobs of light, two bobbing balloons glittering as they turned in infinite blackness. The goddamn thing had been manned!

"I should have guessed," Clarke said, choking, horrified.

They had powerpacks, we could see that. Hearts in our mouths, we cheered their brilliant attempt to escape their doomed coffin by suiting up and hoping the individual power packs on their backs would overcome the accelerating force which was driving them to a cold death on the lonely reaches of the universe. We saw the buggy turn too and watched it race back towards them, by now its cockpit voices a garble as Alex read a stream of guide numbers and Grainger adjusted them.

Clarke, noting the technical panel glossing the side of the image, exclaimed, "They're going near the limit!" It was orange all right, very close to red. Every second, though, because of the contending forces of each object's solar orbits, the three pieces — satellite, buggy, and Earthbaby were growing further apart.

The little figures, though, vapour trails clear behind them as they held on to each other, seemed to be closing the gathering entropy of the system, raising our hopes. Then they stopped.

"They're out of fuel," Clarke said, horrified.

It was up to the buggy now, the system of forces making the figures dwindle again.

We could hear Alex screaming, "Go! Go! Go!"

We knew Grainger would be pounding every button in there to accelerate, relying on Alex to feed him what he needed.

"Unfolding solar," she yelled.

The great wings spread gorgeously. My instinct was to recoil at her move, then I remembered there was no drag in space.

"We're gaining!" Alex screamed.

And so they were, their acceleration faster than the slowed-up bodies of the astronauts whose abandoned craft was now beyond visual range.

"Jesus! Mach two. Can they turn this around?" said Clarke, watching the tech panel.

"There's contingency built in," Adam said.

We heard Grainger, then, asking Alex tersely, "Red line?"

We all knew what he meant. The craft was reaching that horizon of speed and distance that would make it impossible, soon, for it to return to the space station. There it was, right on our screen, now hitting the red exactly. Grainger's instincts had known it.

"Go! Go!" Alex shouted back.

A few seconds later, again Grainger was asking, "Red line? Red line yet?"

"You can do it!" we heard Alex say. "You can do it!"

"Fuck! Are we over, or what?"

"Contingency! We can do it!"

"We're over?"

"Yes, but…"

"Fuck!"

Then there's a yelp and silence because, as we see on the screen, Grainger has wrenched the buggy around with full power-follow, and Clarke, who knows about such things, grimaces with the knowledge of how their bodies and brains are scrambling in the forces, not to speak of the craft itself, which, in the slightest trace of atmosphere, would have simply split into pieces.

But Grainger does know his stuff, blanked out as he and Alex must now be. The buggy, out there on the edge of the screen, continues outward a little, stops, gets larger. It takes a good thirty seconds or so for them to come round again, Alex obviously the first to recover because we hear her weeping and crying out despairingly as she sees the little doomed figures give what appears to be a last wave, as, clung to each other like sky-divers who will fall forever, they dwindle to sparks, flare once as they turn and go out, beyond perception.

Clarke told me he didn't know what he would have done. I suspect, though, he would have gone to the extreme limit. I'm trying to be fair. Alex is shattered and will not speak to Grainger at all. To his credit, Adam is not taking advantage of this. He has a grudging old-style respect for Grainger — you know, the old 'a-man's-gotta-do-what-a man's-gotta-do' bit. What more can I say? Except this. No-one will know whether we could have saved them.

What we are all united on, though, is this. NASA has manipulated us. Surely studying the satellite's telemetry with their sophisticated instruments would have told them this satellite had a crew. After all, Alex had been puzzled by its earlier course corrections. If not, then their intelligence network in the Eurosoviet must have had some information. No-one really believes they didn't know this. As to whether we were in danger, I suppose there's a difference of opinion, although I know where I stand.

I told Alex about the locked bulkhead. "On the way back, did you see anything under our dark side?" I asked her.

"No. I was too shaken up to think about illuminating it. Besides, if there's any weapons down there, they wouldn't have them stuck in full view."

"I'm pretty suspicious they're there," I said, "tucked inside. What if the satellite had been waiting for the right orbital angle to quickly observe us on the underside to see if we were loaded, or at least get close enough for its radiation sensors?"

"Right," Alex said, getting very agitated. "And when NASA realized they were moving around on us, they wanted the satellite out of the way before they detected anything and could report it. I murdered those people, Lilly. I will never forget it."

I watched her eminently-controlled face grow childlike, not with the look of innocence, but that other look children have — the one when they hate utterly.

"They'll pay for this."

I wish I could believe her. ❧

"How did you sleep last night? Your quarters satisfactory?" Lesley asks him, sipping the pink liquid.

Only in the bright light can he see the crowsfeet around her eyes. He realizes he's still wearing his glasses and takes them off, moving his head into the shade. She too moves out of the sun.

"Yes. Not bad. I still have to watch my back, you know. I could do with a firmer mattress."

"I have a very good camping mat in my tent, actually. You can try it some time."

"Maybe I will."

Tremaine is acutely aware of her, as if, through the banter between them, they are talking about something else, about how they are sharing with each other and every other live growing thing in the universe this one intense late afternoon in the ongoing mystery of being. If it weren't for the greatest of luck, I would never have known this, he thinks.

"It's really nice being older in many ways, don't you agree?"

"I was just thinking the same thing. Since the crash I've certainly begun to feel more alive than ever before."

"The world always does offer up an infinity of possibilities when you least expect it."

He thinks of Perlita again, but rallies to the moment at hand. "Yes. There's a lot to appreciate in the world."

He grins at her, making it obvious to whom he's referring.

"I think you might find you're going to enjoy yourself here," Lesley says, leaning back over the edge of a table, her hips thrust forward.

He notices how her arm thrust back onto the table, supporting her weight, is still firmly muscled, the elbow-joint over-straightened, bending slightly inward, one of the physical characteristics that distinguishes men from women. It delights him to look at it, the paler inside skin stretched out like that. He'd love to put his mouth on it.

He gestures to take in the sweep of the plateau with its forest borders.

"Don't you find," Tremaine asks Lesley, "that there's an enormous relief when you confront actual unvarnished reality after you've spent all day dealing with simulations? I mean, you're practically the inventor of virtual realities. How do you feel about them?"

"Good question," she laughs. "In actual fact, the virtual reality movement goes back fifty years or so. As I understand it, it was an extrapolation of the magic realism movement in art grafted onto theme park design and movie set-making, that sort of thing."

"Jock used to have a collection of plastic sushi meals arranged on plates from the nineteen eighties. They used to display them in the windows of the old restaurants. I tried to pick one up and eat it."

"And then there was the cult of the silk flowers. Anyway, I believe the art-gab of the time went on about how if you achieved virtual reality, then somehow actual reality itself would change. I had no intention of starting the kind of virtual reality fad we have now. I got the idea of using simulacra for a very specific reason: preserving the experience of ancient sites without wrecking them, or having to build complete replicas to satisfy the tourists. It's like McLuhan says — the new technology arises to solve a problem of limited scope and then runs away with you, defining its own environment. I had no idea we'd see the world turned into an ersatz copy of itself."

"We've come to a pretty pass, I must say. The old world of image-making was something you could stand back from ultimately. There was always the consciousness it was artificial."

"We might be fooled by fake sights, sounds and smells, but we've still got our sense of touch to define what's real."

As she says this, she slides a finger over his chest.

He catches her descending hand in his and holds it lightly. It rests there, connecting them. "And even that, I hear, is being worked on," he says. "Once they actually get to that point with magnetic counter-attraction or whatever, what does that mean?"

"If we can't tell the real from the simulated, then I guess the simulated becomes as real as the real."

"But don't you think there's some other essence, some magic feeling about things that are actually real? I mean, I don't think people can be deceived except momentarily or by their own suspension of disbelief. Do you?"

"It would be nice to think that."

"You don't believe it?"

"What else have we got but our fragile senses to perceive anything? Simulated environments simply underline that old subjective philosophy notion that nothing exists or is real until we are there to perceive it. I agree, the ramifications are horrible."

"Yes, why take the trouble to keep what's real if you can make it up cheaper? In fact, it goes beyond that, it means we think we can do reality better. Fucking human arrogance again. I can see the point of what you've set out to do with recreating your ancient sites, but why else would anyone want to make a virtual reality? What's wrong with the one we've got?"

"Did you ever stop to think that this is what God did when she created the so-called real world? That the whole universe is merely a hologrammatic projection from her one vast mind, a masturbatory attempt to stave off her own ultimate reality, which is simply an infinite loneliness?"

There's something in Lesley's eyes when she says this, a deep well of need that makes him want to hug her tightly to him, to share their fragile existence, to assure her that what she says is not so. Tremaine breathes deeply in. "Whew! That's pretty frightening. Given everything, how do we ever get to confirm our reality, our existence?"

She looks at him, connecting deeply.

"In extreme danger. Or in great sex. Or when we actually die."

"The first two I don't mind. But that last one...."

She looks at him as if she is going to say something significant and secret, but then decides against it. "Perhaps it's not as final as you think. There's more to be said on that subject. "

Faint in the distance, they hear four bleats of a horn. People appear from tents and dig sites, checking the arrival on their communicards with outlying watch-posts.

"Who is it?" Lesley asks Donald Grey who strides up holding a cluster of plastic bags filled with small artifacts from the dig.

"Looks like Edgely."

She fills Tremaine's glass with a small ladle, holding it with her hand over his to steady it. Then does the same for Donald. The look that passes between them is easy and familiar. She gets around, Tremaine thinks, happy for her.

"You know, folks, I think we've found evidence of the Maritime Archaic today. This will create quite a stir."

"Great stuff!" Tremaine says, enjoying the lighting up of Grey's paleolithic face.

"Wonderful!" Leslie exclaims.

With a wide grin, Donald strides off with the lesbian tent retinue close behind him, eager to get to the lab.

"Do you know what he's talking about?" Lesley asks, amused.

"Not really. But I'm sure you do."

Then he sees the jeep. Perlita is in it too.

"There must be something happening for Edgely to come back so soon," Tremaine says.

"I sense we're going to have to do some more work together."

"I'm game," he says, gallantly, laughing to himself.

Oh my faithless heart.

*   *   *

"With communications stifled, ain't nothing much left but pillow talk. The Eurosoviets are palming one of their negotiators onto us with the blow-by-blow in a few days."

"So we still don't know what happened exactly?" Tremaine says.

He's still stunned at Edgely's news of the destroyed satellite.

"Your crew ashed the two Eurosovietniks somehow. That sure don't cop a plea with me."

"There has to be some explanation. Lilly and Alex couldn't possibly have been a party to this."

"Someone flashed some pretty jivey programming to duck-blind that satellite, and nothing came up from the ground to do it."

"It could have been Grainger, even Adam for that matter. Lilly and Alex are utter loyals. There's no way they'd sell out to Foreman's boys at NASA."

"True when you were alive, the charismatic Andy Tremaine. But to them you're shrimp food now."

"Add on the pressures from NASA command and the other crew members…." Lesley cuts in. "Lilly has motive to stay in our camp, what with Jock being killed, being intimate with you (sorry, yes we know that) and being of mature years with little to lose in terms of career. But Alex is young. She's ambitious, a survivor. After all, she IS one of those vestigials from the Japanese techno-lapse, isn't she?"

"What has that to do with it?" Tremaine snaps, amazed at how sharply he's responding to her, a little shock running through him at the incipient racism in her remark.

The others don't seem troubled by it, however, especially Edgely. He switches disconcertingly into his formal speech mode. "She means that people from that kind of disrupted childhood and institutional upbringing are statistically prone to a sharp disjunction between their inner and their social selves."

"They make great spies, to be blunt," Lesley finishes. "They lead secret lives."

"But Alex has always been superb, physically, emotionally, socially. Utterly reliable, a complete team player, unfazed under stress...."

"Everything's possible," Lesley says enigmatically, her eyes flashing warmth and sympathy for him.

"We're not talking personally, here, Andy boy. This is just statistical.... We need to be sure. And since it looks like she did the figuring for the satellite job...."

"What are you getting at?"

Edgely mops his brow, agitated. "If the world at large becomes convinced there's no way of cutting off Foreman's nuclear balls in the near future, the whole resistance movement will collapse."

"Right after we got the news, Perlita and me started to do some figuring on this. Assuming they're going to send a quiver-full of nukes up to Earthbaby, what next? We have two choices. One is to somehow destroy the station...."

"Fuck...." Tremaine exclaims.

"...Two is to get the crew that's already up there to either mount a resistance or disable the damn things. Anyhow, prevent them from making the weaponry effective."

"The gun may be loaded," says Perlita, "but until you pull the trigger...."

"If there's any resistance from my crew, Foreman will just replace them with another one."

They are all looking at Tremaine as he gazes into their faces one by one. It has happened. To him. Innocent bystander who has merely been doing his job all these years, to suddenly find himself at the centre of an incredibly crucial world event. Because, yes, he does know how to disable Earthbaby — by destroying the laser umbilicus. But that would also doom the crew to a lingering no-return cosmic journey.

"At least their resistance would buy us time," Perlita says.

"Put it this way, brother: we have to establish a conduit between us and Lilly, leaving Alex out until we're sure of her. That way she might get some preventive tactics going while we fight the good fight down here without threat from the big eye in the sky. Any ideas?"

"Trouble is, Bill, their communications link is completely secure. Earthbaby can't pick up any random signals. They're completely locked in to what NASA chooses to send them up the laser. God knows what they believe about anything right now. It all goes through James."

"And that's the other player in this," Lesley adds. "From what you told Perlita, there's an outside chance James is reachable."

So they've all gone through the data, carefully analyzed it. Strange the intonation Lesley gives to the word 'James.' Obviously they've had some scheme in mind for whatever contingencies might arise. And this is one of them. He protests, as much, he realizes, to play devil's advocate as anything. After all, their impression of James is second-hand at best, and his own old paranoia reasserts itself.

"Oh come on, folks. That's stretching it, isn't it? Just because the guy exhibited some quite normal feelings...."

"How else can we connect with Lilly?"

"Jesus! One second you get me paranoid about Alex, and the next you're all eager to recruit a fade-out like James!"

Edgley looks over at Lesley. "Shall we tell this Lazarus here about his erstwhile bosom buddy?"

She nods.

"He was probably in love with you," Perlita says seriously.

Now there's a double-take for you, Tremaine thinks. Despite the situation he can see the three of them are allowing themselves a chuckle at...good grief!...a blush flooding up into his cheeks.

"So he's gay. It's been decades since that mattered any more, certainly not enough to blackmail anybody, even if he is in the Lifeists. They all hate women anyhow. Where did you get this snippet of gossip, anyway?"

Edgely nods over at Lesley. "Lesley knows."

"How?"

Lesley stretches herself, rolling back her shoulders, getting out the tension.

"I've known him since he was a child. We have a special relationship. I'm his English Aunty."

"You're related?"

"Through marriage. My fourth husband was his uncle, the sculptor brother of James's father, General Cardoman. You know, the Japanese techno-lapse riots hero."

"He's Cardoman's son! I never knew that. In the family tradition, eh? So how well did you know him?"

"James was hardly ever at his own home. He always hung around us and stayed for holidays. He's always led a schizophrenic life, poor boy."

"Does he know you're deeply involved with the Tribals movement and the Society?"

"Of course not."

"That's why Lesley can't approach him — at least not at first — too risky," Edgely adds.

"So you want me to?"

"God no, Andy man. Perlita here will do it." He gives her a hug. "She's our communications expert, right babe?"

"How?"

"At first over the computer," Perlita answers him. "The way I did it with you."

"So you were the one." Yes. Making sense. Perlita has that capacity to feel things out, gradual, instinctive, able to subtly push, retreat, assess, weigh the ambiguities.

"Some kind of very enigmatic message, at first," Lesley says.

"But we need your clearance first, old boy," jokes Edgely, covering some nervousness.

"On what?"

Perlita smiles at him. "The message will say something like, 'Tremaine lives.'"

Now he gets it. A phrase like that could simply be the slogan of a wacky underground resistance cell grouped around his memory, determined to carry on his good works — that sort of thing. At any time up until a crucial point the phrase would have that enigmatic ambiguity to it, until James and he actually got to meet face to face once again. Plenty of time to pull out without letting the cat out of the bag that he actually is, physically, still alive.

"I see what you mean. You think being resurrected from the dead could be very risky for me — quite comical when you think about it! So you want my approval."

"We'd be as careful as we can."

"It's either something like this, or somehow destroying Earthbaby, and maybe everybody on it, I guess. Since I owe you my life.... It's a small price to pay...."

"Even if we could get James to deliver the message to Lilly that you're still alive, and nothing else, that could still make a difference."

"Yes. That woman knows her stuff. If anyone can do something...."

"It's agreed then?" Bill sighs, relieved.

They each take turns shaking hands with him, then hugging him.

Outside, there's a whispering tropic dark. Lesley puts her hand firmly in his.

"It's about this mattress of mine. Coming? You're wanted. Dead or alive."

"Is all this real?"

"As much as any one can tell," she laughs back at him.

Like some eager puppy, he follows her to the dark outline of her waiting tent. So what if this *is* a pre-arranged award? So what?

RUN ARCHIVE TAPE
THE CREW ASSEMBLED IN THE COMMUNICATIONS CENTRE, GRAINGER AND ALEX AS FAR FROM EACH OTHER AS POSSIBLE.
COMMUNICATION SCREEN LIGHTS UP. ZOOM ON SCREEN SEGMENT. JAMES.

I don't even have to run an analysis to see that James is a man in deep conflict, although his cover of official brusqueness and formality would be quite effective to the normal observer. As a public relations expert his basic tool kit consists of false images — virtual realities which smother the real ones. But he looks as if the blatancy of the lies he's forced into mouthing offends even his trade's professional 'integrity' (a paradox if ever there was one!)

His function was to introduce President Foreman and the President of Agriminco. Bring on the clowns, I thought. And there they were, delivering their little platitudes about Alex and Grainger's "…invaluable service to the Western Commonwealth by thwarting the attempt of enemy forces to cripple and destabilize peaceful scientific research into the possibilities of deep space habitation…." and so on. Obviously, the speeches were for later public consumption on the general networks.

Looking at the tape, I can see that all of us without exception visibly wince when Agriminco's President (referred to by James, diplomatically, as 'Board Chairman') delivers his last line: "We gave them the tools…" (judo chop), "…and they did the job." This was followed by Foreman threatening that any further Eurosoviet "aggressive acts" would receive similar treatment, ending with his election slogan: "Whatever needs to be done, it will be done."

Obviously, Alex and Grainger were expected to make some sort of reply, having been so commended by such highly-esteemed personages. Now I notice on the tape that for the first time since the dreadful incident they look at each other. At least they are sharing a common response of distaste. I can see the slightly inquisitive look on

Grainger's face, as if asking Alex, "Do you want to say anything?" Alex's head gives a small dismissive nod and Grainger opens his mouth to say something but decides not to. (To his credit, I think.)

Surprisingly, his eyes flash a signal of "get me out of this, please…" to Clarke. Generous hearted as always, Clarke steps into the breach adroitly with: "My two crew members involved are unfortunately still recovering physically and emotionally from the incident, but wish me to convey their thanks to those of their colleagues at NASA who have been so supportive of the Earthbaby project so far."

Once the charade was over, James came on again to deliver what proved to be an unsettling message. Because of the "attack" (which the incident had now grown to become) NASA and the consortium were going to be re-evaluating the original research plan for Earthbaby in the light of Earthbaby's need for continuing protection.

Adam expressed everyone's secret thoughts later at suppertime: "Goddam it. We're no fools. Does this mean they're going to curtail our programme and replace us with a Lifeist army crew?"

No-one took it up.

"Let's just go on as normal," Clarke pleaded.

'Dissonance Reduction' they still call it: the human ability to somehow cope with totally conflicting emotional situations. We've all been going through it on Earthbaby, starting right from the first day when each one of us, filled with expectations of what we were supposed to do and how we would do it, suddenly found ourselves skewing ninety degrees off course. With every new turn of events, the actual reality of our situation has become more clearly at odds with what we initially envisioned. Even given the most benign habitat and supportive authority structure, there are already more than enough shocks to the human nervous system as it tries to adjust to an outer space frontier settlement. It's amazing our little band has maintained any semblance of sanity and cohesion at all.

Naturally, my chief concern has been trying to keep Alex and Grainger's feud from getting out of hand. It's unfortunate that their deeply held traumatic feelings arising from the satellite incident seem to be getting transferred onto each other, creating what I fear might become an irreversible breach. If the respect and affection they shared before the expedition could have been carried on through the incident, they could have supported each other, reassured each other, shared their feelings. But the way it is between them now doesn't help either of them to handle the terrible shock of their recent experience.

Strangely enough — considering what I thought was the somewhat narcissistic, superficial personality of Grainger — I would say that Alex has the advantage in all this. At least for now she can see herself as fairly blameless, merely a dupe of the Lifeists and a victim of male arrogance. Besides this apparent level of righteousness on her side, she has a healthy anger response to being deceived by NASA. In consequence she is coping quite well with the abhorrent idea that she helped murder two innocent people.

Grainger, on the other hand, at first acted very stoically, 'taking it on the chin like a man' and expressing his very real justification that both his and Alex's lives were in his hands. Searching through the archive tape I found a segment where, in discussing the incident with Adam in Adam's greenhouse, he comments bitterly:

"It's all very well, once you're sitting safe and sound at home, to second guess the situation. Just wait till Alex has to sit in the hot seat, then she'll find out what real life is all about."

His other justification, naturally, was that the satellite was out to destroy us. It was the old military, "better them than we" justification for killing a fellow human being. Despite all this, he could not seem to whip up for himself enough righteousness to protect his self-image from some very real damage. Part of this at least is due to Alex. The esteemed one he thought he was protecting from danger, is the one who is being the most dismissive and scornful of him. His trauma, therefore, is compounded by a severe narcissistic blow.

Beyond that, though, lies something else. Searching the archive, looking through the tape of the sunbuggy launching area to study the demeanour of the pair when they returned, I fast forwarded it too far, running into the next evening. Skittering back through the yards of empty tape, I suddenly saw a change-code light flash from the recorder, indicating a presence in the area. Locating it, I was surprised to see it was Grainger, revisiting the buggy, entering, then just sitting there, staring. This he does for some minutes, then leaves, going down one of the nearby corridors beyond range. Searching the archive tape codes to follow him, I realized there is a whole area there, near where I saw the locked bulkhead, that is unmonitored. Did he encounter the same door I did? Has it set him wondering? Interesting.

Also interesting is the fact that Grainger's composure begins to slip noticeably after this incident of his sitting alone in the buggy. His body language on the latest tapes — especially when alone — and his very pre-occupied demeanour suggest he is likely falling into a depression. The mother in me, I suspect, can't help responding to this new and vulnerable person, his usual defenses and bravado painfully stripped away.

Far from exacerbating the leadership contest with Clarke, it is to this father-figure that Grainger has so far offered up his wounded psyche, albeit in that complicated male code of joshing and oblique emotional sharing that I have always found so infuriating.

I shall be treading a very delicate counselling course here because I don't want Alex to lose the emotional liferaft which is enabling her to manage the horror of the situation and her very real, though innocent, part in it. On the other hand, at some time or another, she is going to have to come to terms with the fact that far from being a simple coward, Grainger was acting with great responsibility and quite possibly saved her life.

As for myself, I'm not sure that being replaced by a Foreman crew would be entirely unwelcome. For ever and ever, it seems, we humans have believed the way to solve our problems was by leaving behind the rubble of our previous existence and moving to the new green valleys of the promised land. Ever since the ice-age set us moving we've done nothing but trash wherever we wondered. That's maybe our big mistake. Instead of ever searching for new Edens, we should simply remake the one we have.

The holographic picture windows on this station, the plasticky veneers, this wretched simulacra of earth makes me want to puke. Thank God I at least managed to sabotage having the usual musak soundscape incorporated into this wretched environment.

I think of Jock and Tremaine, and I think of the two Eurosoviets. How many days would their packs continue life support? Would they still be conscious, looking into each other's faces? That's real, at least.

I must get out of this cabin and visit the observatory. I need to look out into the true dark of space, into absolute emptiness reaching forever. ⌒⌣

There's a lot to be said for experience. I can't believe it, Tremaine thinks; how the pale slip of her body can have wound itself so intensely around my nerve-paths that I can still feel her active on my skin. Surely the first human speech must have been babblings of pleasure between the sexes. This morning the whole camp will know every lurid detail, probably better than they, themselves, who lie together made amnesiac with ecstasy.

Tremaine looks down at Lesley still asleep as the beginning throb of tropic dawn filters orange through canvas walls. How confident she is, the way she takes her pleasure at the moment he discharges wildly into her, hooking her legs and arms around him tight to keep him in. And then one, two, three strong long strokes of her pelvis, breath held, her whole body rigid for one moment, two moments seething, before her total outburst, her come-scream arabic, triumphant.

His heart aches as he notices her small and pendulous breasts, her scarred, child-loosened abdomen, the wattling at her throat as her head lies on the pillow. He runs his hand gently over the slight ageing curve of her spine below her neck. How delicate are the prominent bones of her shoulders, and the veined long hands that gave him so much pleasure. Yet how bravely alive she is, how goddam beautiful her lovely active haunches are.

Is three days a kind of watershed? After the third night with each other does that mean everyone assumes there's an ongoing intimacy? Good. It can't get any better than this. Nevertheless, better be careful old man, you could be in for a hard fall.

Not since his twenties has he allowed himself such immediate intimacy and flat-out emotional involvement — twice, now, in very short order. Still. These are unusual and charismatic people he's getting involved with. Think of the hundred or so young, bright bed-mates he's had the good fortune to wake up with over his long active life; very few of them could compare with Perlita. And of them all, Lesley, on the cusp of seventy years old, must be the most skilful, sensitive lover he's ever encountered.

Even their work with each other over the last three days has taken on a sensuous quality, a kind of love fest as they recreate the NASA complex in ever more realistic detail, all the while touching, their eyes messaging constantly, voices soaring with wit and affection. He has grown to be fascinated with the way her mouth purses as she concentrates on her imaging, lips pouting out, hollowing her cheeks, like someone practicing speaking French.

This rush of closeness and compatibility is pretty dumbfounding. There's still the one part, though, he hasn't given her: the laser-beam security complex. Hold back, his instincts tell him; keep it as a last trump card, to be used only when Lilly and Alex are safely gone from Earthbaby. Does Lesley sense he still has something to reveal?

He doesn't want to believe that everything going on between them stems from an ulterior motive on her part. But maybe he should play it safe. Safer than he has so far, anyway. He's been infatuated before, after all. He should parallel this withholding of a piece of critical information from her, with keeping a part of himself emotionally in reserve as well. Suppose his earlier paranoia is right: that, benign and pleasant as it all is, Lesley is part of the manipulative set-up to get him firmly on side — as at least part of Perlita's motive seemed to be. Look at the bump in his heart he had to contend with when she revealed her connection to Edgely!

Thanks to Lesley and his own fickleness he's over that. Besides, nothing is simple. People are complex. James, even, look at how that might work out. And Perlita did feel for him, that's obvious. So, whatever Lesley's initial motives, it's not very egotistical of him to think she too is developing romantic ideas corresponding with his own. But if this thing with her goes on much longer....

That brings him round to the present. Three days since Perlita was going to begin her wooing of James. He slides off the mat and eases over to the tent flap, pushing it aside to gaze through the nylon flyscreen. To the East burns dawn's red edge: but on the West horizon stars still shine. He fixes on Mars, looks past it at the angle he knows would show Earthbaby floating there if he had glasses strong enough. How are Lilly and Alex managing? To be able to contact them, that would be something.

Leslie turns onto her back and he studies her as she wakes, floating slowly back into herself from wherever her soul has been, her gaze deep and loving, vulnerable, until her eyes flare with their usual animation.

His shrink could have a heyday over his entanglement with

Lesley. Undeniably, there's something deeply thrilling to him about Lesley's charismatic maturity. But who cares? He's crazy about the warm crinkling of the lines around her eyes when she smiles, the gauntness in her cheeks, her close-cropped boyish hair.

"You've got a damn good mattress, there, Lesley."

"You're welcome to use it any time."

"Aren't we due to hear from Perlita today?"

"Thinking about her, are you?" she jokes, coming alive with a great cat-stretch then rolling over, tackling his legs with her arms, trying to bring him down.

Without his thinking it bursts out, "I hope YOU aren't otherwise attached."

She jerks him off-balance and he flops down beside her. She sidles onto his lap and kisses him, nuzzling his cheeks with her long straight English nose.

"Right now I'm in between things; so I guess you're lucky for once."

"Yes. I think I am lucky," he says seriously.

*   *   *

This time Perlita comes in by rent-a-plane, a tiny amphibian with a quiet electro-methane engine. They are all having breakfast, listening to Grey's speculation that the Irish not only made it to Newfoundland and the Gulf of St.Lawrence in the fifth century as Robert McGhee established in 1990, but came as far south as the Antilles. How else could this iron gouge (a rusted lump of barely discernible shape) be found in a Late Archaic gravesite unless it came in by some convoluted trade pattern like the Rama chert flint-stones from Goose Bay in Northern Labrador?

Tremaine is about to leave the shade of the shelter to greet Perlita as she extricates herself from the little rent-a-plane, when Lesley stops him. An ominous hum heralds the appearance of a Lifeist helicopter, buzzing the field. It circles and banks, taking a look, then drops out of sight over the forested crater rim.

Perlita's worried about the copter a little.

"Don't worry," Grey tells her. "Just checking out the amphibian. They do it all the time. A few times they've come down to check the place out."

"More to get free beer and ogle the women than anything," Lesley says.

"We just show them around the dig and get the women to flirt with them a bit. After a couple of beers they leave. They're just young locals."

Perlita tells them Edgely is hiding out in her house for the moment, expecting to meet with a Eurosoviet negotiator. In case the Foreman boys had wind of who was coming and was doing some extra surveillance, he thought it best if she got her friend from the tourist hotel to bus her down to the Hispaniola airport, where she got the rent-a-plane under Andrew's assumed name (Herman Pantalone), so there'd be no apparent connection between the camp and her house.

"Right. I almost forgot. I'm her uncle from New Haven."

And yes, after the initial contacts, she actually did get to see James. She took a risk, because he could have just had her swept away by Lifeguards, drugged and tortured if necessary. So, just in case, she made sure she had a quick-ease suicide drug she bought in a pharmacy; and then she arranged their meeting in one of the Tribal Society's Gyro bars in the tourist area of old San Juan.

She dressed up like a prostitute, trying to make herself look like a transvestite so anyone shadowing James would assume she was just a casual pickup. That must have been difficult, Tremaine is thinking, but by now they're in the communications shed and Lesley insulates the three of them into the copper room.

Perlita is triumphant and excited, exuding that sensuality she had after getting the bus through for the election. Even though Lesley is there, her manner stirs him.

"So what's the next step, after your brilliant work, Perlita?" Lesley asks.

Only the English can get away with expressing themselves in those kinds of words and in that kind of tone, Tremaine thinks. From anyone else it would sound trite and insincere.

Perlita looks at Tremaine. "James wants confirmation you're actually alive."

"What kind?"

"I'm afraid he won't accept anything but actual meeting."

"You see, Lesley," he says, "the boy knows from hanging around you that you can do anything with virtual reality."

"On whose ground? That's the problem. Andrew mustn't be put

in danger."

Lesley's very firm saying this, and it pleases Tremaine that she does it with such a tigerish protective tone. That proves something, doesn't it?

"That's to be decided. Of course, I didn't let on this was anything to do with our Society. As far as he knows, I'm just a member of a small cell of Oxfamites. I left it obscure."

"So how did you convince him there was a good chance you were telling the truth about me being alive?"

"I reconstructed the conversation you had with him about the Agriminco president getting into Jock's chair, and what happened when he tried to warn you, then ran off looking sick."

"So, wasn't that enough to convince him? That you knew that?"

"Maybe at first, but when you think about it, there were lots of people around and it's just possible it could be a reconstruction."

"How did he react?"

"He was elated. At first, that is, right after what I said. But then he checked himself and got very angry, very suspicious. He had an anxiety attack while we were sitting there, you know, by that pink fibreglass sound sculpture in the Gyro courtyard? He said, 'For Christ's sake, you Lifeguards are making a hell of a scenario out of nothing here. Okay. So I liked the guy. Wouldn't you be upset if one of the people you knew and worked with had a terrible accident like that?' From what he said, I gathered James feels he's already being watched, but that might be just part and parcel of Foreman's operations once you achieve a certain level in the hierarchy."

"That would make sense," Lesley says. "Yes. He's suddenly been launched into a high enough position to be considered a threat by Foreman's paranoid power hierarchy. Before, he just had to go through the motions and rake in the goodies, like most of his cynical generation. I'm worried, though. The kid was pretty inscrutable in some ways. And enormously bright. What if he's playing double agent here? He had plenty of time to prepare for the meeting with you. His whole reaction could simply have been a ploy to find out how much you knew, then get your trust by intimating he's in some kind of trouble himself over the incident with Tremaine.. I mean, what if you do arrange a meeting with Andrew, then Poof! They grab him, stuff him with info-drugs, and we all fall down."

Perlita seems taken aback by this. Tremaine looks from one to the other. "I could go equipped with quick-ease, like Perlita did."

It astonishes him how calmly he says it. He wonders whether he really would do that.

"You might not get to use it," Lesley says, distress in her eyes. "I think that at least I should see James first."

"That might make sense," Perlita agrees. "We'll have to check this out with Edgely."

"Wouldn't that still be a problem, Lesley?" Tremaine asks. "I mean, even though he won't know till you meet him that it's anything but a visit from Aunty, that's pretty big stuff when you reveal you're a tribal working with the Society. In fact, better risk just me than the entire movement, don't you think?"

Perlita watches the truth of that turn Lesley pale.

"I'm sorry. I think it's too risky for Andrew. For God's sake, I know James. I know he won't turn *me* in."

By now she has reached over and is holding Tremaine's hand.

"Once people get brainwashed by these Lifeist reactionaries, you don't know what they might do," Tremaine says. "I'm damned if I'm going to sit here and let you put yourself on the line like that on account of me."

Perlita looks at them both, and smiles.

"I might have to get back to him and see if we can work out something else. In the meantime, I guess we'd better wait for Edgely to…let's say…get some objectivity on this and put it into perspective — don't you think?"

"All right," Lesley says, tightening her grip on Tremaine's hand, eyes suddenly gone moist, but being brave and terribly British.

"All right," he echoes her.

Crazy about her now, absolutely crazy.

SOCIAL DYNAMICS RESEARCH PROJECT; EARTHBABY
(JOURNAL OF LILLITH SHAWNADITHIT)

O utraged! That's succinct enough to describe how I feel. The beginning of it comes several days ago now, precisely where I left off this journal last time.

I traversed the dimly-lit plastic corridors, noticing, by the way, the slight 'bump' where the passageway angles 'up' to the observatory entrance. The artificial gravity field here on the station is constant for every part, no matter what its 'slope,' but, conditioned as we are on earth to putting out more effort when we see the ground tilt up, or put our feet onto a stair ready to climb, we automatically make the same adjustment here on the station, with comical results.

Stumbling over the threshold, I was a little startled to see the set of asteroid scanning screens were still lit up. Looking up, I discovered Grainger reclining in the observation cradle at the viewing end of the telescope. Absorbed as he was, he didn't know I was there. I thought of leaving quietly, but remained because my attention was caught by a computer enhanced image on the scanning screen which made my stomach lurch.

It was two dots, two five-pointed little stars close together: the doomed astronauts.

Jesus! I thought. What a thing to do to yourself. It must have been quite a feat for Grainger to find them and track them like this. Of course, once locked on, the tracking system would hold them for as long as they stayed in perceivable space-time, re-enhancing their image on an information feedback loop until an obtruding light-source or gravitational warp of a larger body close enough would rub out the last trace of its existence and the loop would be truncated.

I was standing, dumbfounded, when Grainger spoke. "I caught them by accident when I came in here the night after it happened. The scanner has a programme for highlighting asteroid material it may encounter that's giving off infra-red. I thought — holy shit! — it's found something with organic compounds — you know, some prim-itive lichen somehow photosynthesizing on one of the dirty-ice aster-oids or something. Then when it brought it up, I realized what it was."

"Why didn't you just cancel it out and let it go."

"I wanted to, but I couldn't. They were still alive, you see."

I thought: I can't bear this, to be standing here with this gruesome image ever so imperceptibly fading into oblivion. "They must be gone by now, Grainger. I'm not sure this is a healthy thing for you to be doing."

"I don't give a shit about what's healthy. I just give a shit about what's right."

"What do you mean?"

"It's a deathwatch. I owed them a deathwatch at least."

So he probably saw them die, not knowing the precise moment of course. And now he needs to see them buried. On board a ship, there's a finality, when the bodies go over the side, but here....

"It wasn't your fault Grainger. You have no guilt to bear over all this."

"Alex doesn't think so."

"She may be the perfect bionic woman, the perfect communications guru and the perfect social relations expert, but she is not the perfect person."

"But she's also right. I spent hours and hours backtracking the computer scan on the astronauts right to the point where we pushed them into orbit. Then I ran a tandem model on our chase in the buggy. If I'd kept going, we might just have been able to pick them up by using up all the contingency factor in the red."

I couldn't think of what to say.

He climbed down then, and walked morosely away from me over to the wide quartz port that was all that separated us from instant death. It struck me, thinking about it, that in the vacuum of space, all of our tissues would instantly explode, the gasses in our bloodstream and cell units rushing out, tearing the membranes, the very molecules of those membranes themselves ripping into their separate atoms until, in the immense zero cold we would simply puff into little condensing gas clouds. That would happen to those astronauts eventually, once their pressure suits decayed enough in direct sunlight, fibre-fatigue set in, and the fabro-titanium skins ripped apart. So Alex had been right. A lucky guess. And here was poor Grainger, taking it on the chin, obsessing, berating himself....

Since I was feeling angry anyway, I decided to put it to good use, as I sometimes did with Jock. The theorists may go on about the father figure and all that, but the first and real authority a man feels is his mother. And that holds true even if you're not Jewish. I went over to him and rather forcefully turned him around. "Now you listen to me. You model male prodigies are always going on about your vaunted rationality. Well if this isn't the most irrational, whining, little boy, acting-out, breast-beating, attention-getting charade.... If any one's to blame for all this it's that asshole Foreman and his boys. They're the real murderers, those bastards...."

I had hit the right button. I could almost hear his mental gear change.

"And it's suckers like me who help them do it. When I signed on for this project, I thought it was going to be really something. New frontiers of knowledge and all that crap."

"Well. It still can be, can't it?"

"It's fucked, Lilly. The whole thing's fucked."

I didn't answer.

"What's the point of it anyway? I mean, going out there and blasting a few asteroids into each other, sticking the dirt into trashbins and bringing it back to earth, for what? So a miserable lot of third world wage slaves can churn out more junk for us to litter the solar system with? Shit! There's not much difference between me and my dear old Dad wasting his life driving a dump-truck in an open-pit nickel mine."

"Whatever happens, you'll get your chance to do what you dreamed. Of all of us here, you'll be the last one they'll replace. I mean, what if you discover an entirely new sort of mineral? Or even, like you first thought, you encounter a new life-form?"

"Come on, Lilly. You know it looks more and more as if we're just a cosmic accident, that as far as life in the universe goes we're it; and when the human race snuffs, who'll be around to give a shit?"

"I can't speak for our descendants, but I can for me. I know you really acted responsibly, Grainger. One of these days Alex will get over her trauma and come around."

I don't know whether I believed it, but it was what he needed, and he did brighten a little.

"Thanks Lilly. I really appreciate your being around."

"Come and talk any time, Grainger. That's part of what I'm here for."

This was followed by one of those pleasant awkwardnesses. The kind when two people suddenly connect in some shared feeling of mutual support.

Grainger felt constrained to stumble around it.

"Well at least you're able to do your job, Lilly. What's it like always being more aware than anyone else about what's really going on in any situation?"

I laughed. If only he knew. "Well, you never really completely let go, I have to admit. I'll be blunt with you. I found a piece of archive tape, quite by accident, with you sitting in the space buggy, then heading off up the corridor into the technical division. Are you sure there's not something else you want to tell me. Some other secret worry?"

"Christ! You know everything."

"I just wondered. I found a sealed bulkhead there myself the other day when we were loading."

"So did I. In fact, I was about to do a little investigating just to satisfy myself. Let's lay this question to rest once and for all."

Opening a hatch in the counter under the scan screens, he pulled out a little gadget and handed it to me. "Radiation counter. I swiped it out of the tool kit today."

So we went along, past the buggy launch zone and got lost once in the dim light, until I recognized the hyperbaric chamber facility, which I'd learned about in case we had to use it to repressurize anyone whose outside suit failed. That helped locate us; then there was that bulkhead: locked, sealed.

We took out the counter and held it against the door.

Nothing. Only the standard cosmic rate making the needle quiver a little.

"So what do you think?" I said.

"I don't believe it."

"Me either."

"The fucking facility is insulated, naturally. Probably lead-lined to hell."

"In that case, we'll never know."

"Oh yes, we will."

Grainger hustled ahead to the space buggy dock. My heart was thumping. I felt like a teenager. Here's the thing that's attractive about men like Grainger. They really do carry you in their wake. And that can be really exhilarating.

"You sure you can do this without a trajectory programme?"

"Sure. There's lots of goodies built in on board for this in-close stuff. We'll just crab our way along the underside."

Once the buggy was clear of the dock, I felt myself go into weight-lessness. My heart, as much as my stomach, sensed the loss of gravity and went into a slight vaso-vagal panic. Then it decided it was really just back floating in the womb and settled down again.

Although the canopy tint was extremely dark (much like arc-welding glasses, I've been told) the sun belted brightly through once we'd cleared the shade of the dock lintels. Once we slipped under to the shadow zone where we thought the bomb bay might be, we were able to detint the roof and use the buggy's illuminators to light our way. Coming to a slight bump in the smooth contour of the under-surface, Grainger, suspicious, delicately rolled the buggy so our side bumpers engaged and we could inspect the graphoplaque skin through the side port.

"Look at that. They've done recent work here."

Sure enough, the bump was a newly-installed hatch. You could tell by the shine of it, in contrast to the mat finish of the older materi-al, abraded with microscopic craters from dust impact.

Easing right over it, Grainger got me to hold the counter.

Even when you know, deep down, that betrayal is not only pos-sible but likely, it's still a shock to have it confirmed for you in stark detail. Once again that seething rage which threatens to overwhelm me completely one of these days boiled through me. I thought of Jock, of Tremaine, of all of the innocents who are regularly put to the wall by those power-addicted psychopaths we throw up to rule us.

How did they brainwash us into thinking they were at all neces-sary? Where did this breed come from? When did that bad seed emerge to rape its way into the human gene pool while its first victims stood amazed and bewildered? And now, here is the godhead of that ancient perversity, its ultimate iconography.

So we floated there, in celestial darkness, inches away from the humming menace, the radiation counter belting out roentgens a cou-ple of notches over the safety limit. I felt sick imagining the horror contained in this deadly cradle.

"Let's get out of here before we fry," Grainger said, and took us up into sun, both of us grim and hard breathing.

"As soon as they can, they'll be sending a crew of Lifeguards up," I said.

Grainger nodded. "Quite likely. This whole thing's just been a charade."

"Oh, they might keep a few of us on, you, Adam, useful types."

"Whoever's willing to stay, I guess."

He meant it to be enigmatic. His look, though, told me I had an ally. If only something could be done to give us a chance up here....

Well. At least we know something for certain we didn't before. Score one for sanity. As for understanding Grainger, this night has been a revelation. Amazing how people can turn out to pleasantly surprise you sometimes.... ❧

ovedrunk like two infatuated teenagers, Andrew and Lesley are breathing in the frangipani scent of the upland night air, hugged together, their legs interlocked on a wooden bench in the moonlit camp. Sweet-voiced Beatta, large and awkward with beautiful gaze and pre-Raphaelite waist-length hair, sings and plays guitar while the rest of the lesbian tent listens and lolls about her. "So they seem to be a true collective in everything," Tremaine says.

"That's right. They're all in love with each other. I think that's really sweet."

"They seem to really like you."

"Well. I stayed with them for a while when I first came here. I was recently widowed, a bit chewed up. They were a great comfort to me."

"So no one got jealous about you?"

"If any of them go to bed with each other for more than three nights in a row, they think that's being exclusive, and the others get snarky about it."

Three nights. Tremaine chuckles to himself. It must be a universal concept. "So how do you feel about being exclusive with me?"

"I could ask you the same question," she teases. "I saw the way you looked at Perlita in the copper room today."

"Where is she, by the way?"

"In the communications shed with Grey. Edgely's getting in touch tonight."

"This damn communications censorship makes all that stuff riskier. How are you getting around that?"

Lesley nibbles at his ear. "We have our ways… Hey, here's Grey coming now."

With Perlita close behind him, Grey hurries over. "We got a signal from Bill."

"What's happening?"

"He wants you to meet him at Perlita's house."

Perlita says, "He's with the Eurosoviet negotiator. Everything looks good. So that helicopter yesterday meant nothing."

Tremaine goes to disentangle himself, but Lesley tightens her legs around his and won't let him go. He gives her a hug then shifts her around so she's on his lap.

"Am I going alone or what?" he asks Perlita.

"I'm going back with you, just so I can get dropped off at the airport. Bill thinks there's a little more work to be done on James."

Lesley gets up off his lap and strokes his hair. "I'd think of going with you, but it's only a two-seater. And besides I've got a lot to do here with our NASA simulation project."

"I wish we could do this in the morning," he says, not meaning it but conveying his reluctance to leave her.

"We'll take care of her," Grey says.

"No big goodbyes," Lesley says, kissing him lightly at first then clutching him tight and murmuring, "Take care, please, take care."

"Love you," he says simply; then gathers his gear and walks out of the lamplight with Perlita towards the plane.

"You be pilot," she says. "I only got my light-plane license last year and I don't like night flying."

Tremaine is glad of it, to be back in the air again after all this time. Even though it was only his daily commute to NASA, leaving the dull earth every day always relaxed him. To take a copter up again after what happened to him might be a bit of a freak out: but these cute little lightweights are a joy to handle. He slips in the navigation fiche, getting Perlita to electro-point their destination while the little craft scoots along the runway, lifting in a moment, the quiet methane engine purring neatly.

He circles once to gain height over the mountain rim and sees Lesley standing with Grey in the light-pool from the lamps, waving up at them. The lesbian tent are in a group standing off to the side. His last glimpse of her is to see her walk over there, to be taken up into the midst of them.

He can hardly believe it has been one week since Perlita brought him here.

Over the mountain rim the little plane bumps through the turbulence. Dotted with lights in the silver moonlight, the island spreads out before them.

"Okay, Andy. We're right on course."

*   *   *

Twenty years ago, the new airport was constructed to knit together the two separate countries of the Island into one protectorate. Tremaine can't help being astonished at the obviousness of the old border which the airport straddles. To his left the landscape is virtually barren, the land eroded down to its rusty gnarled bones; to his right, lush and verdant, lowland rice paddies are rimmed with terraced vineyards, rising to forests. The old French possessions are always left the worst, he thinks, no matter where in the world you find them. Perhaps because the French clung onto their colonies longer than anyone else, and so they were the last to get their independence; and then only at the cost of enormous social devastation.

There's not much traffic in the skies. A big jet passes thousands of feet over them, lights blinking, and a copter comes humming out of a dark valley to their right. As it crests the ridge and comes into full moonlight, he sees it's the same kind of yellow Sikorski as the one that buzzed the camp. Should he mention it to Perlita? She's dreamily asleep in her seat, slumped sideways in her seat straps.

As he begins to skim down to make his runway approach the copter cuts across and tucks in behind him. He checks the navigation fiche and the air-control matrix beside it. Already the automatic descent sequence has him green-lit to land on lane three of the light plane strip. Soon they'll be throwing up the laser hologram to signal him down.

So what's the copter doing on his tail like this? Now they're bathing him in their landing lights. So what. They're coming in too, probably. The bright light flashes over Perlita's face and she comes to, abruptly. "A copter behind us, same as the one over the camp. Probably just a coincidence they're coming in the same time."

Perlita glances back at it. "They're moving across now."

Tremaine clicks on to the hologram signposts, his own lights now revealing the tarmac. He notices the copter drop behind one of the service buildings as he brings the amphibian to the ground, barely a bump, proud of himself. He's just taxiing around when he hears the copter again. It hasn't landed; it's hovering just over the service bays where it can see them.

"I don't like this, Perlita. How long before your plane leaves?"

She looks at the copter hovering. "It could be anything. They're always messing around with those things. They could be waiting for a medical emergency patient off a plane, for all we know."

He pulls to a halt in the parking lot, lining it up with about ten others and switches off. "Probably just paranoia, but I think we shouldn't take chances."

Perlita undoes her straps and crouches down. "The sky busses leave every half hour. Do you think they saw there were two of us?"

"I'm pretty sure they couldn't, not from that angle and with the light the way it was. Besides you were pretty slumped down asleep."

"Okay. If they're tailing us, they'll probably send a Lifeguard out on foot to see who gets out and where they go. You've got all the right I.D. and the rental registration for this thing if they question you."

"So what's your idea?"

"What if you get out of the plane and lock it up as if you're alone and go in to the terminal for a drink and a burger? I'll wait to see the coast is clear then scoot around the parked planes here and go in the side door there. I'll head for the washroom until the last minute, buy the ticket and get on the airbus."

"Okay. I'll wait until I see your plane's left, then take off again if it looks safe."

He squeezes her hand and does as she says. As he walks into the terminal the copter lifts up and takes off again, disappearing over the airport buildings and the runway hotels. What a relief. He checks his inside pocket to make sure his I.D. is there and goes in, going through the motions as Perlita has suggested.

In a few minutes he sees her, lining up with the small crowd for the air bus. She turns and looks at him, but gives no sign except to round her thumb and forefinger into an O.K sign. He winks quickly and turns away, idling with his drink by the window until he's sure she's safely away, the bus booming up into the atmosphere.

Before going back to the plane, he cases the parking lot. No one there. He unlocks the plane, gets in and taxies to the launch beam. He punches the take-off request and it flashes green. In a moment he's up and away, breathing easier. He takes the electro-point and dots it onto the navigation fiche at a point just offshore of Perlita's house. He can run it up the launch ramp near the village as Perlita suggested and walk up the cliff-side to the house itself. A Eurosoviet negotiator eh? What has Edgely got in mind this time?

Humming along, he allows his mind to fill with images of Lesley. The way she taps her nose with the end of her finger, like a child surprised to find it there. The way she tugs her heels into her groin in the lotus position when she sits down. The way she's always pulling her shoulders back to counteract the slight widow's hump her spine is developing. And the beautiful blurring of her eyes as she reaches behind her to undo her brassiere and present herself to him when they start to make love.

The moonlit night is poignant and breathtaking as he flies through it heading for the coast; at seven thousand feet wrinkled volcanic mountain ridges loom crocodile green below him. The feel of Lesley is in his heart now, suspended there, like the amber afternoon at Perlita's. And he, like the insect in that pendant, he too is suspended in the night, going on, going on, forevering...forevering....

And then it is shattered. Out of the dark cleft of a valley the yellow Sikorski rises. In low-cast moonlight its silhouette moves like a killer bee across the range below him. He holds his breath. A couple of ridges over to starboard there are lights. The resort area. Okay. He's just got time to do a bit of shadow flying. If he can lose them they'll think he's put down on one of the airstrips that are down there. Quickly he veers down, down, dropping over a ridge into a valley, keeping to the shadow side, then turning all his lights off.

It's scary going down the dark side like this, but he feels a fresh through-wind coming up the valley from the coast. That's the advantage of these lightweights, as sensitive as gliders. Like a stream of water the moving air compresses and bounces around the juts and headlands dimly seen to his left. He rides it with a touch of the right aileron like a canoe through rapids.

In a few minutes he sees the copter's lights flick over him, crossing the valley into the lighted side. The Sikorski sifts along it and passes him, unnoticed, the louder noise of their own motor drowning out his.

Judging adroitly, he allows himself to just skim the upper cliff edge where moonlight glows eerily along the valley crest. As soon as the copter takes a turn out of sight he slips up into bright light, crosses the ridge quickly to port and slips sideways into the valley next to it, again hugging its dark side. Once more he sees the copter, still to the right of him, climbing.

They've lost him, all right. They're getting up to take a general look around, puzzled no doubt. Yes. There they go veering further to starboard, away from him over towards the tourist airstrips.

He makes another valley skip to port, holds there for a while then comes up again. All clear. The navigation fiche has gone crazy so he has to reset it, finds his course again, and in a few minutes sees the sparkle of the sea.

There you go, he says to himself as he lands, the brief cascade of water from the pontoons for a moment reminding him of his crash. He taxies up the boat launch and parks by a quieter stretch of the road where old abandoned boats are rotting by the shore. He folds the wings and tucks it between two of them making it less obvious for any copter to spot.

There's still some life in the old fox yet, he thinks as he climbs the twisting road upwards. As he reaches the end of the drive, he hears some-one step out behind him and whirls around. Gun in hand, ready, it's Bill.

"Sorry to scare you, old chap. But you were a bit late."

"Fuck, Bill, my nerves are already shot. A copter was tailing me. But I lost him."

"You sure of that?"

"Definitely. They'll be checking the airstrips in that tourist area South-East of here by now."

"Better safe than sorry, but don't get too discombobulated brother. There's dozens of these rent-a-planes all over the country, a hell of a lot of them muling dope. Could just be they're increasing surveillance of everything that moves."

"Maybe, Bill. I hope you're right."

They're approaching the house now and Tremaine tells Edgely the whole story, starting with the copter buzzing the camp as Perlita landed.

Edgely gets thoughtful. "The way Foreman's tightening up, just about everybody's working as a Lifeguard these days. Still, we better get more careful with the camp, it's good we're going to do our business over in the Virgins for a while."

"All I remember of that is Neil's garage."

They're in the familiar house now, surrounded with warm wood and rattan chairs. Tremaine runs his fingers over the valleys and ridges of the crocodile skin on the wall.

"Our launch is coming in before dawn to take the negotiator off. We're going with it to Neil's. So if they *have* been dogging you, they'll lose your spoor."

Tremaine's just thinking how that's going to keep him away from Lesley, when Bill goes to the bedroom and yells out: "Come on out

Rivka! It's safe my little Lubichka."

The Eurosoviet negotiator. Northern Russian, Tremaine thinks as Bill introduces her. Rivka Plotkin. She has a drink in her hand which she finishes and puts down to embrace him heartily, double-kissing him on both cheeks. Her body pressed against him is large and firm. Her skin has a damp night sweat from the tropic heat. She's a woman in her early forties, with high Slavic cheekbones dominating her mobile fun-loving face, skin tinged with that Siberian gold, cheeks radiating that glow which emanates from a vigorous disposition egged on by a constant infusion of alcohol and nicotine, both of which he can smell on her breath. Exotic, but what a shame wildly chaotic changes in Eastern Europe and Central Asia over the last fifty years have perpetuated cultures enslaved by self-abusive habits largely extinct elsewhere.

But her gutsy decadence doesn't put him off in the least. She's of that flagrantly heterosexual feminist wave which was the first to finally cut through the sexual confusion caused by the lingering tradition of man as the initiator. Coming from where she does, she also has the air of one who takes her practical pleasures wherever she finds them, knowing they could become scarce or disappear any moment. And although her clothes are more formal than the various breast-revealing and body-decorating fads of Western fashion, her gauzy blouse conceals nothing.

"Plotkin," Tremaine says. "Are you related to the lyricist who wrote that post-war musical, *Moscow Nights*?"

She hums a few bars of the old Russian classic, 'Pod Moscovnie Vechera,' swaying her wide hips voluptuously.

"He is my Great Grandfather, Grigor Plotkin. He visited Toronto once in 1975, with Canadian-Russian friendship group. He was hiding in house of young writer for some while, but does not manage to defect. Otherwise I would not be here with you, now! He is pulled back to USSR by love of my Great Grandmother who at that time is Chief Milkmaid of Minsk area co-operatives."

Rivka gives him a gap-toothed grin, then goes to pour herself another vodka, from a bottle she has brought with her, she explains. When he at first demurs, thinking her supply limited, she cajoles him into having a small shot of it.

She hands him the glass, swivelling her large hip into him. Mae West, he thinks.

"Nasdarovja!" he says, chinking glasses.

With her tousled straw hair and streaked eye-shadow, Rivka has a just-fucked look to her. The odds of Bill having in any way resisted her seem pretty picayune. After downing another vodka, he notices her English slipping more and more into Russian idioms and rhythms.

"You Trans-Americans don't know how to combine pleasure with business. Believe me, Andrewchik, you have much to learn from us."

Bill roars with laughter, patting her ample thigh.

"I'd say you're a damn good teacher, Rivka."

She grabs his head in a hammer lock and pulls his nose into her breasts, playfully, giving a throaty growl like a tiger about to eat him. Then suddenly she has released him and has grown serious. Tremaine cannot believe the quick change flickering over her face.

"Yes, there is great sadness everywhere; and that is why we must laugh when we can, and love each other."

She slumps into a chair and stares disconsolately out the window where a few fishing boat lights make a network of red, white and green, and an old-style lighthouse, kept up for tourists, blinks like a pulsar out on the point.

"You see, my Lubichkys, those great steppes of Russia are swept by wind. What is the wind? My friends it is a force unseen yet every-where felt, the breathing soul of the soil of our motherland. And so we Russians believe very much in the reality of ideas, also unseen, and these ideas, like hurricanos, sweep right through us, unchecked, unstoppable. In nineteen-nineties, we need Democracy. We take instead this hurricane of Capitalism.

"It comes like wolf among us, hungry foul-footed monster. This capitalism monster is trampling on culture, is destroying community, is deliberately de-stabilizing everything so can re-develop again. With us, international conglomerates could have feeding frenzy much big-ger than even old Third World had been for them."

Bill, open-mouthed listening to her, automatically pours anoth-er vodka into her held-out glass.

"In West, ancient power of democratic tradition is check on ris-ing capitalists — not enough, but something. In Russia, nothing to check but old communist regime. We not realize Capitalism is work-ing for you only if person has capital to begin with."

As punctuation, Rivka downs the vodka Bill has poured her in one gulp. Tremaine, astounded, remains speechless as she ends. In an attempt at coherence, Bill explains.

"You should know, Andy, that Rivka here is also Director of the Political Science Department of the Minsk Regional University."

"Believe me, that is a serious decline in fortunes from the position of Chief Milkmaid held by my ancestor seventy years ago," Rivka chuckles.

"We Russians tend to be digressive," she apologizes. "Now we must negotiate how we shall stop these Lifeist lunatics from plunging world into chaos. In time I was speaking of, my grandmother's exactly, we lost great chance to be our own governors, choosing instead to accept false consciousness of Western media, which is drug to us. Victims of fashion trends and virtual realities, we become mindless desirers of commodities and alien values — like all hinterland peoples — bewildered and dismayed. Mutual Aid is replaced by Self-Interest. Many old people are starving. No more is possibility of communal action which overthrew old communist state. Divide and conquer is your saying."

Her cheeks flush red with remembered anger. She goes on. "You Americans, you call it, New World Order. And is how we became serfs again! Only this time with more powerful and sophisticated absentee landlords: IMF and all their multi-national cronies, hand in hand with home-grown criminal buccaneers."

"The old apparatchiki authoritarians, they are neat and obedient children toilet-trained too early, conformists, normalizers. It is natural to them. They welcomed this new regimentation, computerized now so no-one could hide from them. We were hypnotized by mind-numbing advertising and media. No more troubles, no more thinking."

"Until the Japanese-American car wars de-stabilized the system again," Edgely finished for her.

"Yes. Then more new ideas from European Union are sweeping like wind across the steppes. Workplace Democracy, Mutual Ownership, City State Freedom, The Real World Movement, Ecstatic Religion. And so we now are in equal Eurosoviet Union. Still many problems, but is not bad for everybody. And I ask myself, is all this, so painfully created, threatened by reversion to old days?"

Tremaine sums up her lecture. "Turn and turn again, Rivka, Now we see Foreman's second coming of the New World Order. Only this time it's with a de-technologized Japan reverting to shogunism, and only one international corporation, rather than a bunch of them fighting over who gets to run things."

"Point I am making," Rivka continues, "is what is happening in perverse part of world you live in is archaic: Eurosoviet people are just now waking up to reality of it. Our part of this world is mosaic of separate city states, almost utterly non-violent — only in sports we compete. And is no real army. Destruction of our Eurosoviet satellite and astronaut murder has done much to unite Eurosoviets. But ordinary people think, huh! This crazy Foreman exists only in your mad part of globe. Clearly, he want to expand Trans-American empire; but our Federation finds idea of forceful opposition inconceivable. Deep down, our people are thinking Foreman will just 'wither away.'"

"That's the problem with not taking these clowns seriously right at the start," Tremaine puts in. "I remember Jock thinking the whole Lifeist movement completely comical. It was only when they managed to complete the buy-out of the privatized army that people started to wake up."

"I think it's about time you told Andy the news about the satellite, Rivka," Edgely urges her. "You can see you have an ally."

"Something new?" Tremaine asks.

"You know was pushed by space-buggy. Two people murdered. One is old schoolmate. But is not all. Detectors tell presence on Earthbaby of nuclear weapons."

"They slipped them by you, Andy."

A withering ache runs through his heart. "Yes. But not by Jock. He must have found out, confronted them — he was like that — and they got him before he could tell us. That explains the spin crisis on the shuttle-launch — from a cargo overload. The assholes loaded it in secret and made a shoddy job of fuel compensation. Those bastards! I should have double-checked, I had no idea they'd risk a thing like that."

"It's not your fault, Andy. Obviously Foreman and Powers didn't want the world to know until at least after their coup."

"But now the world shall," Rivka says. "And before it's too late."

"Will they believe it?" Tremaine asks.

She smiles at him. "They will. If you tell them."

"Rivka also happens to be a political news producer for Eurosoviet Network News. A multi-talented woman we have here."

"You're with ENN?"

"Andy, lubichka, I think is time we bring you back to alive. Bill will interview you. His face is famous in our part of world as in yours. Once we Eurosoviets are convinced Powers and Foreman can threaten any part of world with neutron bombs and laser scorchers, support will grow for underground movements in Trans-America."

"I'm willing. But what does this get us?"

"There is para-military force, financed by Eurosoviet federation. A hang-over really. They do special jobs in case city state violence threatens others. Not people to my liking."

"Once we've gone public with the nuclear threat on ENN, Rivka feels the Eurosoviets will get us swat teams able to invade and sabotage NASA's shuttle launch site. If we can stall Foreman from getting his missile crew up to Earthbaby for a few months, it's possible we can turf him out once the Eurosoviets get really activated."

"It all hinges on destroying the backup shuttle," Tremaine concludes.

"Right. That's why we need James as our inside man, so the Eurosoviet swat team can get in there."

"Is Perlita trying to get him to come for a face-to-face meeting with me?"

"Yes. Once we're at Neil's, Rivka will tape us. She'll broadcast it through the ENN communications satellite for their evening news. In the meantime, Perlita will have forewarned James to watch it as further proof you're alive. Then she'll send him on, through the society network, to meet us at Neil's."

"So does Neil's have a communication centre like the one at the dig?"

"Yes. You'll see it. The antique car on the roof conceals the broadcast aerial, and the rest of the works is inside an old van."

"And Bill has given to me NASA virtual reality tape you make with Lesley," Rivka says. "That will be needed, also entry codes to the complex, if possible, for surprise, yes?"

"If we can get James," Tremaine replies, "then we should be able to figure out some way to sabotage the normal entry security system."

"We'll get him," Edgely assures them both. "Perlita's good at her job."

Rivka stands up. "Okay. It is done." She kisses them on both cheeks again.

"When's the boat coming?"

"Another hour and a half," Edgely says.

She takes one of their hands in each of hers.

"Perhaps we would all like a little rest, yes?"

She staggers a little leaning on Edgely, hitting the edge of the table. The vodka bottle tips over and starts to roll. Tremaine catches it before it falls to the floor.

Edgely gently leads her into the bedroom where she falls instantly asleep.

"Man, she is quite something," he comments, yawning himself, and flopping onto the sofa.

Tremaine sits down by the night-bound window, listening to the sounds of the far-off surf, imagining Neil's boat slapping the wave-crests, skimming towards him. So much to do. But he wants only to think of Lesley, that's the size of it, to be alone and private where he can secretly cradle the thrilling ache of her love in his heart.

SOCIAL DYNAMICS RESEARCH PROJECT
(JOURNAL OF LILLITH SHAWNADITHIT)

Since the cameras had been disabled in Central Control, we thought it would be safe to tell the others there, but Grainger whispered that our voices might be picked up by the ones in the neighbouring corridors. Consequently we jammed into Clarke's cabin, double-checking that the privacy mode was on before saying anything.

Clarke, Adam and Alex were pretty astounded at our news. Everyone felt that this was something we shouldn't have had to bargain for.

Clarke, ever the peacemaker and negotiator, tried to put the best light on it. "I don't see that it makes that much difference to how we conduct ourselves up here. For one thing it might be that these items..."

Items! we all exclaimed — disparaging the euphemistic military language, and causing Clarke some embarrassment

"...Okay, then, weapons...aren't necessarily put on board for military purposes...."

"What!" we all exclaimed in unison.

"Now hang on a minute, it's just possible they were loaded under Agriminco's auspices, for the asteroid mining project Grainger's involved with," Clarke protested.

All eyes on Grainger, shaking his head in disbelief and grinning.

"Now don't try to throw this thing on me," he joked.

"Or me," said Adam. "I'll grant you though, speaking also as an employee of Agriminco (and how many people in the world these days aren't?) I wouldn't put it past those managerial assholes to have jumped the gun on this. I mean, do we know what kind of bombs these are? Maybe they're just part of the old arsenal from the twentieth century that they bought cheap to knock the asteroids around with."

"So what are you saying, Clarke?" Alex cut in. "As senior officer, commander of this project, what do you think our policy should be on this?"

"Just keep going on as if they weren't there," Clarke answered her. "Even if they *are* there as a military threat. That doesn't mean they'll be using them right away...."

"Yeah. Only if they feel they have to do some terrorizing...." Grainger scoffed.

I couldn't help noticing that his whole demeanour had brightened up since our discovery.

"The essence of the problem," I said, "is this. Many of us suspect this whole Earthbaby project has been a charade, a stop-gap measure until, let's face it, Foreman's military coup succeeded. (And I think, having no information to the contrary, we can now assume it has succeeded.) Given that we had a clear understanding as researchers what our duties were, now we have this *new* situation, what kind of response by us would seem to be most apt?"

"Exactly," added Alex. "Do we let them get away with perverting the original intention of Earthbaby or not?"

"Regrettably, I don't think we have any alternative but to follow whatever orders NASA might give us," Clarke says quietly.

"Even if," I say, "they decide to replace us?"

I notice him then, looking rather pale and shaky as he keeps looking down, apparently concentrating on wiping his glasses. Where they have come off his nose there are two pale white spots, a slight dampness glistening between them. He's having an anxiety attack, I think to myself. Either that or he's feeling ill for some reason. Poor bastard, I thought. What a thing to happen at the end of your career. Officially, he's the guy directly answerable to NASA and the Lifeists, and he's being presented with a hypothetical mutiny.

"I think we do have an alternative," Alex continues firmly. "I think we can legitimately protest this illicit cargo and ask that it be removed."

"See how far that gets you," Grainger says cynically.

Alex casts him a withering look. "At least it's serving notice that we do not think this cargo is appropriate."

I'm still looking at Clarke, wondering if he's okay. "If we could get into the bay, we could dump them out into space. Without their triggers, they can't explode can they?"

Grainger picks up the idea. "Say Clarke, this is a great idea Lilly has. You don't have a code card for that area do you?"

"Personally, I wouldn't want to get near those damn things," Adam says.

Now everyone is looking at Clarke. With great difficulty, he replies with a kind of strangled, "No. I wish I...."

Then suddenly he stands up, looking pale.

"Excuse me, but..."

I go over to him and steady him as he staggers a little. The others scramble up to give him room and I ease him down on the bed.

Grainger opens the cabin door and ushers Adam and Alex out.

"Let's clear out, guys, give him room. Lilly will handle it."

Good man, I think, already checking Clarke over for my immediate concern — heart attack — wondering whether I'd need an emergency stripper dose or not. No. It appeared more like some kind of anxiety attack complicated with asthma or hyperventilation.

My own cabin is two doors away from Clarke's. I whip in here and scrabble through the drugstore: the old tried and true. I sit Clarke up and get him to belt down some tranqs, waving to Grainger to close the door on us for privacy. Clarke grabs on to me as if I were a life raft in the ocean, and I rock him gently, feeling him relaxing until he can speak and I lie him down.

"I'll be okay soon," he gasps. "I've had this before."

"Very often?" I ask.

"No. Nothing to worry about."

Then he told me the story of the first time it happened to him. It was as he crossed the empty football field of the military academy where he spent four crucial years of his life, every moment regulated like clockwork. He found himself clinging, in the midsummer mist of the early morning, to a soaring goal-post, looking up to the very top of it. There in the grey shifting light its tip scratched the grey slate sky. "It was the first time I thought of the world turning. No, not thought of it, felt it. I was frighteningly conscious of it, Lilly. Three thousand miles an hour. I had to hang onto that pole as if I was on a merry-go-round."

I told him that sounds like Mountain Fever, that's what my grandfather would have called it. You get up on the top above the snow-line there and suddenly nothing in the world seems solid. It's as if you were in the crow's nest on a huge high ship and the whole mountain starts to pitch underneath you. Too close to God, he used to say, can sometimes drive men stark crazy. And isn't that the situation we're in on Earthbaby?

Clarke seemed surprised to know that other people are subject to these things. He went on to say that these events, few in number, and never noted in his medical file because he never reported them, didn't seem to particularly relate with major traumas in his life, though he'd figured out they might be peculiar delayed reactions. The first, for instance, came a good year after his father's death in Vietnam, a loss which, through pension arrangements, actually meant his passage was paid through university and officer training school.

"Didn't your wife die of cancer quite recently, Clarke?" I asked him.

"Almost two years ago."

"So probably this is for her."

I saw him bite his lip, and he turned his head away onto the pillow. "It's okay, Clarke. I'm not going to record any of this in your file."

Funny how I thought to say that. He was embarrassingly grateful. All I was doing was responding, I realized, as if he were Jock. These men who have legendary coolness and skill under stress often have little quirks like this in their makeup. Their subconscious just grabs onto them one fine morning, catching them unawares, and throws them out of the ring

Like Jock one morning, trying to hide from me the fact he woke up completely unable to move his legs. He couldn't believe the problem was purely hysterical. He also couldn't believe that once his conscious mind knew what the problem was that he wasn't instantly cured. "Move," he kept shouting to his legs, pounding on them like a dead radio.

It took two weeks of tranquilizers while lying on the beach in the Caymans to fix that one. And then there was his chronic back-ache. That was another instance of it, when the crew had to carry him around strapped on a braceboard.

I reported to the crew that Clarke's attack was nothing serious, just some temporary dizziness due to stomach trouble. Clarke was asking that the meeting be delayed 'til the morning to give everyone time to think about the situation. Adam and Alex were happy with that. They had a date to run a growth projection model on the computer to calculate the carbon-dioxide/oxygen requirements for (as Alex put it) "the plants and animals on the station." When they went off together to Adam's solarium I suddenly had an image of them walking hand in hand like Adam and Eve into a reconstructed Eden.

Okay, I'm aware I'm blabbing on a bit here.

Oh Christ! The truth is I'm going around a little incident I'm still a bit uncertain about. After all, I have my quirks too. I've done things I didn't consciously intend, driven by the old subconscious needs as much as any one. Hell! This intimacy with Clarke must have unhinged me somewhat. Maybe writing will make sense of it.

Dream on!

In the privacy of my cabin as I was putting the drugs back in order, Grainger came in behind me. I was suddenly keenly conscious of him.

"I've got a yen to look at the bomb bay again Lilly. Maybe there IS some way we can break into it. Want to come?"

"Yes," I said, "though I think you were right, when you said before this whole thing's fucked. There's nothing we can do."

Just for the hell of it, I took some gaffer tape and a coffee-cup lid to cover the observation camera by the buggy dock. Grainger, naturally, had to hoist me up and hold me so I could reach the lens.

When he let me down, I knew I was a goner. He suggested we sit in the buggy for a while, but we didn't get that far. We kissed against the wall under the blind camera and I felt my suppressed libido come surging back. Dazed as I was, it was I who had the most marvelous inspiration.

"The hyperbaric chamber," I gasped.

Grainger thought this was hilarious. There was no observation camera in there for one thing, and for another, it's one of the few places on the station without artificial gravity. I felt so free inside the small cylinder, bumping gently against the sides, connecting, then parting as we undressed each other, our clothes floating airily about us like God's and his angels' on Michelangelo's Sistine chapel ceiling.

Appetite. Raw appetite, that's all it was, as I arched myself backwards as if floating in the sea, Grainger's large hands under my buttocks, drawing me towards him, lifting my pelvis up to his mouth, draining out of me a huge welcome flood of relief…. I'd had this before, in a menage a trois with Jock and Andy a few times, a pure lust release, a physical withering.

Later, I sobbed my heart out, remembering Jock's wonderful unjealous loving. I also knew I had crossed some kind of threshold by "sleeping with the enemy" so to speak. I know Grainger is not exactly my patient, but I mourned the loss of my own self-respect by breaching my long-held professional principle not to get involved with clients — or potential ones any way. Obviously our intimacy was going to have an effect on the crew's group dynamics. Not very professional of me. But right then, and for some time afterwards, I didn't give a shit about all that, or the world below with all of its turmoils. Truly, I was in heaven. ✀

E dgely manages to rouse Perlita's jeep rental friend at the tourist hotel to fly the lightweight back to the airport. They watch it take off, then the three of them descend quietly down to the dock just in time for the cruiser to pick them up. Tremaine recognizes the young men who plucked him from the sea. "This one's the admiral of our navy," Edgely jokes, digging an elbow into the ribs of the wheelman.

Tremaine can see by the light of the cabin below that Edgely looks exhausted. So does Rivka.

"Why don't we all get some sleep?" he suggests.

Alone, in the same cabin and the same bunk as before, Tremaine fixes the sound of Lesley's voice in his mind, the murmur of it threading through the hum of the motors, turning into a real dream that lasts him until morning when he wakes, feeling calm and illuminated, the morning sun through the blinds striping the cabin walls.

Already the Virgin Island docks are alive and bustling, as they hustle into a little van with smoked glass windows and jounce over the cobbles to Neil's garage.

"Yes sir," Neil greets him. "You sure do look a lot better than the last time I see you."

Tremaine remembers being helped to pee in the bottle, the welcome coke in his dry mouth, the even more welcome oblivion offered by the pills in Neil's palm.

"I've got a lot to thank you for," he says, shaking hands.

Rivka sprawls on the beat-up sofa, enjoying herself immensely.

"What atmosphere," she says, panning with her little handheld around the litter of old motor bikes and car parts. She wants to get started as soon as possible so she has time to do a little editing. Also, as she puts it, once she's got it on tape, she doesn't have to worry about either of them dying suddenly or getting shot in the streets.

Neil patches another camera into the switching panel to catch reaction shots. Then, directing Rivka's coder onto the ENN satellite, Neil arranges the time slot for reception, so they can splice it into their night-time newscast.

How different this is, from the last time, Tremaine thinks, seeing himself on the monitor looking surprisingly healthy.

"Okay," Edgely says. "Let's do it, brother. Let's get this revolution started."

T remaine is alive! Some suspicious part of me still doesn't believe it, and I go over every possible scenario associated with why James would tell me, and me alone.

It's two days later. Lucky Grainger wasn't in my cabin, when I saw the little light on the console start blinking on the private link with NASA reserved for 'personnel evaluation' as it's euphemistically called. The idea of that channel, of course, was so that NASA and I could privately communicate if one of the crew started to go off the deep end.

I thought at first that NASA might have been closely monitoring the observation cameras and were going to discuss some crew behaviour they were disturbed about. Clarke? Or perhaps, now the lifeists were in control, they were going to give us new policies on sexual behaviour. Had they seen Alex and Adam fucking in the space garden? Me and Grainger bopping into the hyperbaric chamber?

"Lilly," James said. And I read the urgent note in his voice right away. "Are you alone?"

"Yes. James?"

"No-one's monitoring this. Don't record it. I'm going to read the headline of the Eurosoviet Fax News. *NASA Head survives Foreman assassination attempt: Earthbaby Armed for world domination.*"

"Good God, James. Please don't play games with me like this."

"It's true, Lilly. I've got to get off this channel in case someone happens to monitor it. Things are going crazy down here. The Eurosoviets are meeting to collaborate on counter take-over policy."

"We know about the bombs," I said stupidly.

"If I don't get in touch again, do what you can. Goodbye, Lilly."

My heart thumped to hear the fear and loneliness in James' voice.

"Everything will be all right, James. I'm with you."

I don't know if he heard me because of the two or three second delay in the transmission. The channel light was already off when I looked down at it again. I sat for a while to make sure it wasn't a hallucination. God. This changed everything. It wasn't hopeless after all. I rushed out to get Grainger, then instinctively bit my tongue when I saw him. What I knew could cost James' life.

Then I began to think, surely the Foreman and Agriminco boys would have thought to put an undercover operator on board, wouldn't they? Of the three men, who could I really trust? Each one of them, in his own quiet way, could be a dissembler. Grainger, for instance, so boyish and charming. He was doing very well with Alex until pure circumstances truncated their relationship. And now he's turned his attentions to me. Is that suspicious? And quiet nervous little Adam, so young, so innocent. What a good cover; not to mention his involvement with Alex. Then there was Clarke. Well, my mind founders. Instinctively I would trust him above the others!

Then I think to myself how I am supposed to be an expert in judging this sort of thing, reading the emotional dynamics of others. At the same time, I remember the caution given me by old Professor Davies during my training: the easiest person to con is the con-artist himself. How true.

Grainger, though, must have felt my inner elation, probably thinking it was to do with our zestful coming together. His embrace was ardent and thrilling and it was all I could do to break away, my whole being feeling like it had dropped to my groin.

"Listen Grainger," I said. "Maybe we'd better cool it for tonight. I really don't want the other crew members to know just yet. I think it could be very disruptive."

I was perversely amused by the surprised look in his eyes. I doubt whether there were any women in his life before who hadn't keeled right over hungering for a second or third night of love after the first one.

"Who gives a shit, Lilly? We won't be up here much longer anyway."

Then I did a peculiar thing. That's lust for you. I looked him square in the eye.

"Are you working as undercover agent for Foreman or Agriminco?"

"Of course not. Why the hell would you say that?"

"Because if you are, and you're seducing me for that end, I'm telling you this. If I find out, I'll kill you."

He looked at me and knew I meant it.

"Does this mean," he said grinning, "that you and I can make love tonight?"

Jesus. I can barely keep writing now. The smell of him lingers on these very sheets. He did me differently this time, from behind, somehow reaching my G-spot. I'd never come quite like that before. All right. Enough of that.

But I must say, even as I drifted in and out of ecstasy in the aftermath of our loving, I still resisted telling him about James. When, for propriety's sake, he left for his own cabin early this morning, I stayed awake, speculating on how Tremaine had survived, and what the state of things on Earth might be. I felt I had to tell someone.

Alex. I knocked on her door. Sleepily she opened it and we sat on the bed.

"Something's happened, Alex. I was going to keep it to myself. But I can't stand it and you're the only one I can trust."

"What?" she asked, her mouth slack, her eyes blurry.

Just then I saw on the floor a hastily squished tube of contraceptive cream. Damn. I suddenly felt I couldn't trust her not to tell Adam about James.

"It's all right," I said, quickly changing my intentions. "I guess I just wanted to tell you that Grainger and I...."

"Just don't go overboard, Lilly. I think the guy's a self-involved creep. Sorry. I shouldn't have said that."

"You did though. I think you're seriously misjudging him. But what can I say?"

Alex looks at her watch. "I'm going to sleep in, Lilly. Say I'm sick, will you?"

"Sure," I said, and pulled the covers over her like a child.

So here I am back in my own cabin typing away. And why didn't they think to make these beds wider? That way they could have made two less cabins! There's another design fault for you!!! ◠

T hree days since the world learned he was still alive and Rivka returned home. Outside, in the real world, rain has started to pour from a hurricane blowing in the night a hundred miles away. Its roiling electric energy is scrambling the microwaves giving Neil trouble trying to bring in Eurosoviet satellite signals from ENN news. It's smuggled-out footage of various uprisings throughout the Americas. But, of course, (who knows?) maybe it isn't. Anything can be manufactured these days. In the same way, anyone watching the broadcast of his own resurrection might have had legitimate doubts about it's actuality. The ENN images flicker and jump over the screen, the picture scrolling no matter how Neil tries to adjust it. We're still somewhat subject to nature, Tremaine thinks.

"Look at that," Bill exclaims, as much to himself as to anyone. "It's a humbling experience to see what's going on out there."

Edgely's grown quieter, less ebullient these last few days. It must be pretty dumbfounding for him now all the different groups among the Tribals are generating all this motive force against the Foreman-Powers authorities. He dabs his brow with a powder pad, a reflex habit acquired from years in front of the camera which he'll probably keep to his dying day.

"Sit down and take it easy, Andy boy. Lesley's gonna be here, soon. So's your old buddy James. Lookit this shit goin' down in Chicago. And hey! Here's Rivka."

From the Minsk bureau, Rivka gives an encouraging political analysis, mentioning the scandal over Tremaine's attempted murder and adding a personal note about her meeting with the two of them, ending on a wish to see them both again for a celebratory interview in the near future, "…as satisfying and fulfilling as the last."

Her smile and arched eyebrow are not lost on Bill, but he keeps his mouth shut since Perlita comes through the door and sits beside him. She's been sleeping in after arriving last night, mission accomplished with James. He's due later on tonight.

At every encouraging news-byte, Perlita clutches Bill's hand enthusiastically. She has no doubts about the truth of it all. A believer. Tremaine wishes he still had that kind of innocence.

How much can James, can Rivka and the swat team — can anything really be relied on? The only thing Tremaine is really certain of right now is this almost painful expectancy in his chest, waiting for Lesley's arrival. Waiting always gets to him.

Neil gives up on the monitor and wanders off into his back room to find a half-smoked split. Tremaine smells it whenever he gets up to look out the rear window onto the backyard palm-trees. Their clattering fronds browning, but not yet dead, these hardy survivors might yet propagate themselves in some future untainted world. Tremaine thinks of their amazing ova spilling into the sea in some hurricane like this one, tossing like liferafts till they come to rest on some empty shore like miniature Noah's arks. And isn't that how they came to colonize all the islands of the South Pacific? Earthbaby: space coconut, floating through the universe.

"Come on," he mutters, hoping Lesley isn't caught in the rain.

Then the van with Lesley is suddenly there. On his feet immediately, Tremaine is just as quickly held back by Neil and Edgely. Of course. If she's being watched and he were to rush out there....

"Oh sorry," he says.

Neil pulls the main switch creating instant darkness and silence. Tremaine can hardly wait for the exchange of signal-codes. Then the little van, lights off, drives in, bringing with it a clean whiff of rain-washed cobbles.

"Just made it," Lesley says cheerily as the first flash of lightning brightens the backdrop of the descending garage door and Tremaine's exuberant greeting is drowned by thunder.

Laughing, they clutch each other, snatching kisses in the vibrating dark until Neil flicks on the lights again.

"Okay, you two lovebirds!" Perlita teases them, grinning.

"One down and one to go," Bill comments.

"How is he getting here?" Lesley asks.

"Not directly. He was going to check in at the Frangipani on the other side of the island and Sonny was going to bring him in."

Half an hour later, Neil, checking the outside scene through the video-scope, raises a laugh. "Oh you should see this now. That boy Sonny is one hell of a whimsical I tell you. He bring him in by scooter. They near drowned."

Once James is in, they all greet each other in a strange kind of silence, muttering greetings out of awkwardness and choked emotion,

Tremaine finding himself hugging the younger man in a confirmation of the living reality of each other.

James seems haggard, on the edge of a breakdown. They sit him down with rum-laced coffee while Lesley dries his hair with a rough green towel.

"Any troubles getting here?" Bill asks Sonny.

"No sweat."

"There was a copter quartering the beach right after I got there," James interjects.

"Storm blow him away," Sonny finishes, his intelligent East Indian face remaining untroubled. "We get surveillers all the time now."

"Was it a yellow Sikorski?" Tremaine can't help asking, anxiety rising in his throat.

James looks up abruptly.

"Andy shook one off the other day, so he's a bit paranoid about them," Bill says.

"It was a Sikorski," James answers.

"No sweat," Sonny says calmly. "Lots of those up there these days. Part of the drug corps."

James stops shivering, cradling the warm cup in his hands. "So you're really here. I can't believe it. I'm glad you made it Andy."

"So am I," Tremaine grins.

James sits with Lesley standing behind him now, lightly resting her hands on his shoulders, like any favourite aunty. And James has his hands affectionately over hers drawing in her amazing warmth, what Tremaine has come to feel is her astounding life-force. She'll exhibit that, no matter what, until the very moment she dies. Then it will all go away from her, all at once.

"It's made all the difference, Andrew, since Perlita told me you survived. Amazing. I hope we can get these bastards."

Tremaine, affected in spite of himself, is acutely conscious of Edgely sizing James up. It's all or nothing now, isn't it? If Foreman can get his henches onto Earthbaby, he can lay a lattice work of neutron bombs throughout the Eurosoviet and terrorize the world for ever. And this shivering complex little neurotic holds the key to stopping that.

Without being asked, Neil and Sonny go off to Neil's "lock-up" as he calls it, where there's a scuffed old Billiard table, a bed and a fridge. Better they don't know any details, just in case.

James takes his hands off Lesley's and pats the arms of his chair. "So. What can I do for you gentlemen?"

Bill pulls his chair over, close and intimate. "Be our Trojan horse, James. We want you to be our hero…"

The effect on James is startling, his face rapt and illuminated in an instant.

Jesus, Tremaine thinks. To catch him just like that. What an acute perception that old bastard has…

James came on the communications monitor again today in Central Control. It was another of NASA's dreadful Big-Brother style announcements. A shuttle launch would be forthcoming in the next few days, bringing what they called a "supplementary crew" for protection and security, which would also "enlarge the colonial capacity of Earthbaby and render it more effective as part of Pan American manifest destiny."

Clarke, grabbing the moment, voiced our astonishment. "At this stage in Earthbaby development, doubling the crew size will surely create a terrific strain on our habitat's bio-chemical resources. May we be made aware of what steps are being taken to accommodate them?"

We saw James turn to confer with an unseen advisor. Then he replied stolidly, "We'll be giving you all that information once the launch is underway."

I saw Clarke bristle at this, and almost cheered as he calmly reminded James that, as Commander of the Earthbaby enterprise, he would not in any way be willing to put our habitat in danger by allowing it to become overloaded. Again there was some conferring. NASA was giving thought to the problem, James stated. In fact, there was a committee presently re-assessing Earthbaby's colonial development in the light of changes in the overall global situation. Unfortunately, the shuttle-launch window of opportunity would brook no delay.

"Cut the bureaucrap, eh guys? " Grainger cut in. "What we want to know, is whether or not any of us is going to be replaced up here and returned to Earth."

This was a question James said he was not at liberty to answer, and forthwith NASA terminated the communication.

Once the laser video channel was shut down, I thought of coming clean to the crew about James' private communication with me, but I held off, cautiously, until I could assess the others' reactions to the announcement, sensing each one was churning over the various possibilities. Taking into account our recent discovery of the weapons on board, it was obvious that at least two or three of us were slated for replacement.

Replacement. That was the word, and I used it immediately to try and establish that quite likely *all* of us would be returned. This way I thought I could avoid any division amongst us. Of course, from James' previous communication with me, I was quite certain the new crew would have completely militaristic purposes and I hastened to present this idea. "Otherwise," I said, "If these were legitimate scientific or technical support personnel, they would have let us know who was coming up and what their function would be."

I then slid in: "Besides, what do we know about earth events at this point? Anything could be going on down there."

Grainger took the bait and ran with it for me.

"Lilly's right. We were never shown the aftermath of the election. And all those assholes managed to do was cause us to murder two Eurosoviet astronauts — I bet that didn't go down too well in that part of the world."

I saw Adam give Grainger a sharp appraising look at this last remark — a look I am still trying to analyze from my memory of it. But it was Alex's face that registered the most emotion. Grainger's mention of the astronauts was like a healing touch to the animosity constantly between them. Although her face set itself back into its rather formal pose immediately, I could tell from that instant she was beginning to transfer the blame of her traumatic experience away from Grainger. She was shifting it over to Foreman where it really belonged, just as, through my sessions with him, Grainger had begun to do so.

Continuing to look at Grainger, who locked onto her gaze, she supported what he'd just said. "That's right. With the way they've been censoring our communications, they've created a reality for us which probably doesn't cohere with what's going on at all."

"Wait a minute, though," Adam chided, directing his remarks to Grainger. "That doesn't mean we all have to go off half-cocked and create an equally inconsistent reality ourselves. A paranoid reality at that."

Clarke, who'd sat quiet up to now, tried to calm things down.

"What's true is, we have a lack of information. That's our real problem. I think we should concentrate on getting as much as we can, however we can, before we make any assumptions about anything."

"Which may be leaving it all too late," I said. Then almost bit my tongue, hoping nobody was reminded, as I suddenly was, of the way

Clarke had delayed in the spin crisis on the way here with almost fatal results.

"You seem very certain of yourself, Lilly," Adam said.

"Foreman's crowd has done nothing but lie to us," I shot back.

"We have no hard evidence for that," Adam said.

"What about those bombs in the bay, then?" Alex said — startled, I think, by the tack her lover was taking.

"There could still be a legitimate explanation," he answered lamely.

As the discussion continued, I remained puzzled by Adam's continuing opposition. Maybe, in an attempt to discredit Grainger, he'd simply got off on the wrong foot and was stuck with it. Or was it some deeper instinct for self-preservation that meant throwing in with the winning side, even at the cost of losing Alex's respect? How I wish, now, we hadn't agreed to dysfunction the cameras in Central Control. How I would love to have a critical second look at his reactions.

A discussion started about the legal basis of our contracts with NASA. Grainger and Alex made the point that none of us could be replaced without citing due cause, mental or physical.

"Look Adam," Alex said. "You want to talk about realities? Well, whatever the reality of the situation now, our contracts with NASA were the reality we came up with. As you say, why go creating other realities? On the basis of that one alone we have the legal right to stay here."

"All that contract gives us is the right to sue in court after the fact'" Adam said. "Isn't that right, Clarke?"

"Don't ask me'" Clarke replied. "As far as I'm concerned, when the time comes we'll see where we go from there."

God, I thought, how predictable people are.

Adam may have been balling Alex a few hours before, but he was no match for the gathering alliance between her and Grainger which now had him floundering. It was an alliance, furthermore, which I began to suspect had deeper roots than the question under discussion. Was I getting paranoid? Jealous?

Then I began to be enthralled by the subtext of the whole debate, even though I had a big stake in its outcome. All my training and experience in human dynamics seemed to coalesce at this point and I sat, rather amazed, watching a pas-de-deux spin itself out between Alex and Grainger. I noticed every little flicker of eye-to-eye contact, every body-language movement. For instance, when Alex spoke to

Adam, she leaned forward and grasped her hands around her neatly side-by-side legs. But when she addressed Grainger she released her grasp and leaned back slightly, her knees coming apart. Grainger, of course, continued to flash the odd smile towards me, but it seemed tokenistic compared to the intense way he leaned forward to catch Alex's every word. I had an absolute awareness that I was watching these two, without their even being aware of it, falling desperately in love with each other again, completing the courtship ritual they had previously begun. The end result, I thought bitterly, was going to be both Adam and I doomed to be cast off like broken-stringed kites.

Shortly afterwards the debate broke up. Adam insisted he had some cloning work to complete in his greenhouse — as we'd all come to call it. Clarke perhaps anticipating his removal, wanted to catch up on his log-books and record-keeping, so at least everything would be left neat and tidy and his duty would be done. As they both rose to leave, Clarke decisively and Adam reluctantly, looking to Alex for some sign, the remaining three of us sat awkwardly, eyeing each other.

I was sure Alex and Grainger would find some excuse to be alone with each other and would hie themselves off to bed forthwith. But no such thing happened. Effusive and charming, Grainger immediately came over to me, took my hand raising me from my seat and, winking at me, mentioned that he and I had some chores to attend to in the observatory.

The result was that Alex stumbled after Adam, muttering some excuse about having promised to give him a hand earlier. In the corridor, Grainger hugged me passionately to him. Rather dazedly, I let him take me to my cabin. Once there, he tore into me voraciously. Greedily I accepted him.

A happy ending, but it shook me to think I had been so certain of my supposedly expert powers of observation, when all that I thought was happening was simply a fabrication created by my own jealousy.

Because of our violent passion, the aftermath was particularly sweet: we drifted off in each other's arms. So that's how Grainger came to be still there when the alarm buzz came from my console. I slid out of sleep and out of Grainger's unconscious embrace, pressing the connecting button. It was James again.

"I've seen Tremaine. Don't worry about the shuttle. It's all being taken care of."

His voice was whispery, eerie, filled with a manic elation. A sickening feeling hit me in the stomach. *What if this guy is going crazy!*

"Are you sure? We're all pretty worried about that up here."

"You'll see. Goodbye."

Before I could say anything, he was gone. I disconnected, my heart thumping, trying desperately to fix that tone in his voice, make some decision about it. What the hell could I believe any more? What else might I be so wrong about? And that's the crux of my report this time as you will realize from what follows. I twisted about and there was Grainger, sitting bolt upright.

"Did you hear it?" I asked, hoping he hadn't. No luck.

"The whole thing."

I needed a confirmation of my reality right then. I had to trust him.

"Remember what I said the other day about killing you if I found out you were spying for NASA?"

"Now I know why," he said. "What's the rest of the story?"

So I told him about James' previous message: how he'd read the Eurosoviet Fax Times headline to me.

"But God knows who to believe."

"Look at it this way," he said. "If James says the shuttle launch is taken care of, then we can just relax until whatever's going on down there is over with."

"What if the launch does take place?"

"I don't know."

"I can't believe it's not going to touch us, somehow."

"The only thing I want to have touch me is you."

I wish he hadn't said that. They were Jock's same words a month or so before he was murdered, coming back from all the hassles at NASA. Normally, when I think about Jock, I feel a clear driving anger. But tonight the rage had a different quality. It was still there, but it didn't energize me. Was this because of emotional exhaustion? Or was it because of Grainger beginning to colonize my sexuality this last little while?

Anyway, I went a little numb after that, but I didn't totally withdraw. I reached out to Grainger as he reached out to me, as we clung to each other, two tiny specks like those doomed astronauts, two short throbs of life drifting through the great dark infinity in a fragile egg-case.

This is all so incredibly tiring. ᙅ

Waiting. Always the worst of it. The last few days, pretending to be a tourist on the island, Tremaine has found himself consuming an unhealthy amount of chemical-tasting pina coladas in an attempt to keep down the tension. Yesterday afternoon he had wandered alone into an ancient church, its roof and much of its whitewashed stones stained green with moss.

Inside it was cool and his eyes took minutes adjusting to the darkness. A small stained glass window, grimed over, let in a thin dash of light over an untended altar. The end wall was a mural depicting a dying Christ on the cross attended by his mother and Mary Magdalene — the figures all black skinned. Oh yes, these people would have understood suffering like that; not as something abstract, but something familiar and every-day. How cruel everything turns out to be, how fucking cruel and useless. Leaving the restful darkness, he pushed through the creaking doors, steeling himself. The sun was a brutal kick, a whiplash.

It's been a tense day with the arrival in port of a hundred or so keelhauler gang members on jet skis. Such gangs of hooligans are taking advantage of the disrupted situation now Foreman's Social Service Corps are being kept busy by brushfires of resistance everywhere. All day, Neil has kept the garage locked up tight, everyone inside taking a turn at armed watch in case the keelhaulers decide to go on a rampage. There was a frightening hour when the keelhaulers burned a few boats in the harbour.

This finally brought them attention. They left, pursued by two yellow Sikorskis, scattering across darkening waters in fading twilight. Their trails glowed a deep purple as the sunset sea turned pink. Watching, Tremaine could see three or four of them capsize and disappear, hit by lucky shots from the copters which were so far away, by then, that he could barely hear them.

Fortunately the launch was left intact.

Now Tremaine watches the digital clock move towards midnight. That's when the personnel shift takes place at NASA, and when the new random latch codes for security are changed. For one micro-second, the computer cancels the other proceedings and then publishes the new latch mode. During that moment, that split second, the complex is unguarded, insecure if you like. Tremaine remembers hearing the shift sometimes at night when he was working late. It was like mice scurrying, a barely perceptible ripple of electronic laughter as each gate and door electronically set itself, one parameter slightly behind the other like long lines of dominoes falling.

"Yes," James had said, fingering the capsule containing the programme stick Lesley had given him, "I'll load this virus as soon as I can."

"You're sure you've got it right. How to load it I mean?" Lesley had asked.

"Don't worry Aunty. Here, let's go over it again."

It was brilliant of Lesley to come up with it. The viral effect, as she'd said, would be only temporary. Instead of one micro-second, the changeover would delay for one minute. Happening as it does, night after night, no one will even notice. In that minute, the swat team will break into the launch area and ash the shuttle. And all trace of the virus would disappear right afterwards.

"I thought I'd have to do something really outlandish and brave," James said.

Bill patted him on the shoulder, "Believe me, you're already doing it. We're counting on you."

And now the time of reckoning. This evening the swat team would have gathered, probably landed by submarine. A couple of missiles into the back-up shuttle silo. A quick in and out. Then most of their troubles would be over.

Perlita sits biting her nails. She would have loved to be in on the raid, somehow. Tremaine remembers the proud way she had unloaded the gun after the bus skirmish during the election. An inappropiate rush of desire for her courses through him, remembering that incredible coupling with her.

"Do you think they'll be able to get in and out in one minute?" she says, more to herself than anyone in particular.

"Sure Honey," Bill assures her. "These guys are real experts. And from Andy's and Lesley's simulation they know right where to go."

"This clock is dead right, isn't it?" Lesley asks.

"Right on," replies Neil from the shadows.

Three minutes to midnight. It strikes Tremaine as very unreal that the five of them are sitting like this, staring at a digital clock.

Two minutes.

Lesley reaches for his hand. He squeezes it.

One minute.

Midnight.

Nobody moves or says anything.

Somehow Tremaine can't imagine the shuttle blowing up in the next thirty seconds. There's no noise. No picture to respond to. The clock flicks again. It must be over by now.

"When will we know?" Tremaine can't help asking.

"We have an open radio channel to Minsk," Neil remarks from the shadows.

"Give me a toke will you?" Perlita begs.

He hands it to her. She drags and passes it around.

Tremaine tries to pull it in, but it's been too many years since he last smoked and he coughs violently.

Lesley is just nervously laughing at that, clapping him on the back, when Rivka's voice comes over the speaker.

"My friends. I hope you can hear me. We've just got word from the team. My friends, I'm sorry to tell you. We have failed. The security blocks remained intact, they could not get near."

"What happened? Do you know if…?"

"It's no use, Lesley," Bill says. "We're receiving only."

The radio drifts in again: "I'll be back to you later when we debrief the team. No casualties, but the complex was definitely in a state of readiness."

"Oh shit!" Lesley wails. "This means it wasn't just a programme failure. It means they knew. It means that James.…"

She rocks forward in her chair, devastated. Tremaine tries to comfort her as the first sobs rack her body, but she won't respond.

"Couldn't they have at least tried to put a fucking missile into it anyway?" Perlita says. "Shit! Why wasn't I there?"

Bill gets up, walks over to the wall and pounds it with his fist.

Tremaine's mind has leaped ahead. If they know about James, then they must be close to zeroing in on all of us.

Obviously Neil has had the same thought.

He yells. "Let's get out of here!"

Adam looked pretty bleak today. I think he and Alex are over their honeymoon period now he has dared to disagree with her. I'm being a bit snippy here about Alex, but there is a level to her that is very self-contained ultimately, and I can imagine that relationships involving amorous intimacy will plumb that hard nut of self-interest in her sooner or later, and brunt up against it.

A shame she's had such a hard beginning, being a refugee from the Japanese de-technologization era. But everybody has to contend with something in one's life or background; so maybe it's a part of her personality that would be there anyway.

Adam had invited me previously to visit his hydroponic bios-phere, so I went along with him when he asked if I could talk to him. We entered the huge bright area through a maze of code-labeled cloning sheds and came out at the border of what appeared to be a large field. Actually its colour was not uniform. It was a nutrient bed supporting different varieties of protein algae, some of which I could clearly see grew more vigorously than others. And I mean vigorously.

"Look at this variety," said Adam, planting a stick into an ebullient froth of bright green foam. "Watch closely."

I did so, and was astounded to realize that I could actually see the mass growing under my eyes, rather like the way you can see the hands of a huge old clock like Big Ben moving around the dial if you concentrate.

"Lots to eat once it's processed," I said. "Though I prefer real food, I must say."

"Depends on your definition of real," Adam laughed. "But I know what you mean. This is why I'm growing the garden."

And there it was. The phrase 'hanging gardens of Babylon' came into my mind. Great gushes of leafy vines fell down from the wired up dome of the ceiling, creating a welcome pattern of light and shade over bushes and trees of every tropic variety: stubby date palms, papaya with neatly chevronned grey trunks, Smyrna figs, glossy leafed bananas, oranges, endless varieties, all still immature, but amazingly grown in the last few weeks and ready to bear in a few weeks more.

I stood there astounded.

"All the product of cloning, growth hormones, hydroponics and twelve-fold solar energy," Adam said — not proudly, I noticed, but with a bored, cynical tone.

"Art and nature so allied," I said, quoting Shakespeare. For by then I'd noticed the sustaining network of dripping pipes holding it all together in its artificial Eden.

Suddenly it made me shudder to be standing there. I had a flashback of Jock in the hospital after the crash, wired and tubed, made bionic by the emergency ward's life support system. How pathetic all those heroic efforts seemed, how intrusive and arrogant. I had a deep sick feeling about the whole space station at that moment. How wasteful and purposeless all this was. I shook myself, suddenly wracked by an existential shudder that ran right through me.

"Are you okay, Lilly?"

"Yes. Yes," I said, welcoming the human touch of his arm around me. "Must be the change in humidity or something."

"Quite likely. Also there's islands of extreme temperature deviation because of the shading pattern. I've had some trouble with that. Come over this way a little."

"To tell you the truth," I said. "I think what you're trying to do here is tremendously impressive, but I find I'm getting sick of manmade environments, no matter how brilliantly conceived."

I was astounded when Adam grasped my hands fervently. "Me too, Lilly. That's part of what I wanted to talk about. I guess it struck me when we were arguing yesterday. I guess what I really meant to say was that I didn't give a shit any more about fighting to stay up here, keeping it all going. There's no real sense to it. All I want to do is find some small corner of the real world down there where I can help things bloom naturally."

I thought, yes, Adam comes from a long line of kibbutzim who spent their lives making the deserts bloom.

"Well, this is a very high-stress environment we've got ourselves into. You might well be having a temporary loss of initiative."

"No. It's more than that, Lilly. Lately I feel disgusted at the idea of asserting myself in any way except the way nature intended."

"You mean, you want to give up all this?" I said, sweeping my hand around.

"When I was a student working in the lab, I was always filled with a sense of wonder discovering how nature had so cleverly worked things out. But every so often, particularly when we were doing experiments on gene exchange and chromosome shifting, I would get a peculiar mix of feelings: a kind of excitement, the kind you get when you do something fearful or forbidden, followed by a wave of disgust and loathing. I remember that feeling often lasting for a month or so. I couldn't generate enthusiasm for what I was doing. Don't ask me how I managed to stay in the running for my scholarships. That made me feel sick too. The competition between us all."

"I know what you mean," I said, remembering a couple of students who'd fucked their way to Ph.D.'s. "It's a pretty disgusting system."

"I had quite a philosophical crisis near the end and began to have terrific arguments with my girlfriend. She was doing research on manipulating insect genes. You might have heard of her: Carmina Zielinski."

"Wasn't she the one who managed to eliminate the cane toad plague?"

"Right. She created an artificial parasite specific to their spawn."

"Did that prove to be benign, by the way? I heard it began attacking other amphibians."

"Well. There's a lot of debate about that. I suppose she was very clever in the way she got to me. She began to present me with the idea that nature itself was artificial, if you like, that it was just as perverse as anything humanly created. She was just developing into one of those Marxian futurists who came into prominence in environmental studies departments shortly afterwards."

"Jesus! Those guys. We used to call them Frankensteins."

"Right. The ones who celebrated the Great Die-Off as a necessary calamity. So there'd be a clean slate to artificially recreate a new, rational world ecology."

"Those who talk most about rationalizing things are always the most insane."

"Anyway, she had a friend who was studying the gene form of the proactive hormone which causes the male praying mantis to ejaculate. The males and females were in cages, moving so slow, robot-like. You'd almost think they were artificial."

At this point, Adam actually shuddered at the memory of it. I held onto his hand because I could see he was developing that aura which emanates from people about to undergo a psychic catharsis.

"You mean," I said, "this was all they did all day: watch these things copulate?"

"Yes. And you know what happens. The thing is, it's so mindless and sickening to see these smaller males allow themselves to be caught like a moth in the thorny arms of the females. Then they shift their abdomens while she waits, motionless, holding onto them, until they've penetrated her. At which point, of course, she slowly bites off their head, thereby triggering the release of the hormone which in turn causes ejaculation to take place."

"So what was the point of all this?"

"She forced me to watch, then made me admit she was right about the irrationality of random natural history. Of course she used a lot of Gould's chaos and calamity theory — or should I say misused it — to build up my confidence that what we were all doing was morally justified. Now it was our turn to rebuild an artificial biological world in our own image and for our own purposes in tune with our human moral aesthetics. In fact, because I was so sickened by what I had seen, we talked long into the night about how I could create an ecology where plants could thrive entirely without the interaction of insects."

"Which you've produced here. I mean, no bugs to bite, no bees to sting...."

"And no butterflies... or insectivorous birds, for that matter," he finished.

"So she managed to keep you on track."

"Yes. A few months later, though, we split up."

"How so?"

"I may as well tell you. I couldn't have sex with her after that."

"Because she had manipulated you, you mean?"

"All that, I guess. But also the very visceral shock I'd had watching the mantises. Truth is, Lilly, until I got on board here, I never even tried having sex again."

Somehow I kept a straight face. After all it's fairly common for obsessive research types on an over-achieving treadmill to become asexual. It's the twenty-first century's form of monastic and convent life.

"So this has been good for you, then," I said. "Getting it on with Alex I mean."

Adam looked a little chagrined. "It sure was, at first; but to tell you the truth Lilly, the last few times Alex has seemed very distant when we were making love. I'm just not able to satisfy her, I guess."

Poor kid, I said to myself. I just bet Carmen Zielinski's basic personality was similar to Alex's. That hard nut of self-involvement just under the social surface. Brilliant, nice, warm, but ultimately unreachable people: clones, let's face it, of the media ideals propagated over the last five decades.

"I don't know what I can say to help you, here, Adam. I mean, some relationships are a take, and some aren't."

"If it hadn't been for the satellite incident, I'm pretty sure she'd have got it on with Grainger. I was lucky."

"He's too old for her, Adam. It was just flirtation. You have no worries there."

I laughed, wondering if he got my drift.

"I just thought, since you know her so well, Lilly, there might be something…"

"Yes," I said. "I do know her well."

And then I thought, hell, if Alex can be good for Adam, then why not the other way around? They're both young. Like him she's a high-achieving young professional with no time to develop much experience in the relationship business.

"Don't get discouraged, Adam. All this is happening in a very artificial environment. To be blunt, the boredom factor would be a big one as far as Alex is concerned. I think you should try a less earnest approach. A little more fun and laughter. You know, get her out here and pull her into the bushes. And there's always the hyperbaric chamber. We're going to be a long time up here together, after all."

"We are?" said Adam. "I thought you said we were going to be replaced."

My big mouth. Now what could I say?

"Well, I just think there's a good chance this shuttle launch won't take place."

"But yesterday you were convinced it would. Is there something I'm missing out on here? Did Clarke get some word about it?"

"Clarke?" I said.

"I thought you and he were kind of close."

Boy, these young people can be pretty dumb sometimes. "What do you mean by that?"

"Oh, I'm sorry, Lilly. I just got the impression that you two being unattached, and the right age for each other...."

The right age. That one hit home. In his eyes, he wouldn't see Grainger coming on to me. Too young. Hell, I thought. I should just seduce this young puppy and show him a thing or two. That would cure him of his stereotypical notions.

I grabbed the lens of one of the observation cameras and twisted it up to the ceiling. "If you need a little advice on your technique, don't be afraid to ask," I joked, flaunting myself a little.

This flustered and confused him enough to distract him from the shuttle business. "Thanks, Lilly. You're a peach."

I left him to tend his plants, his eyes roaming through the garden for a good seduction spot. What a manipulator I am becoming! ∽

At the wharf, Neil screeches to a stop. Tremaine, at the very back of the van, leaps out first, Bill right behind him. Thank God for quick tropic sunsets. Lesley jumps into his arms and he lowers her, grabbing her hand, running. They vault on deck, Neil and Bill already casting off mooring ropes.

"Can you hear them?" Perlita says. "The Sikorskis."

Damn them. They're back, lights blazing.

"Get inside!" Bill yells.

Without questioning, Tremaine follows Lesley down the companionway.

They all huddle in the cabin, the copter noise getting louder and louder. Tremaine winces as the growl engulfs them, crescendos, then, thank God, recedes.

Neil looks out of the port. "They're hovering over town."

Then a blast rattles the open hatch, blowing down something heavy topside.

"They ashed the garage!" Neil yells. "Fucking pricks!"

Pink and brown rolls of flame light the night-sky where missiles struck home. Another gas pump explodes. Over the flames' roar they can still hear copters growling, see their search-beams tethering them to the scene.

"Will they come back here?" Perlita whispers.

Sitting ducks if they do.

Tremaine grabs Lesley. "If they start coming, make a run for it."

"It's all right," Edgely says. "Look. They're going."

Sure enough. Away.

But Perlita's face lights up in anguish.

"Dear God. Please don't let them hit the Frangipani next!"

Magically, Neil has a phone in his hand, already punching it.

He puts it to his ear. Connects.

"Sonny! Get out! Copters going ash you! Go!"

He puts down the phone. In town the flames from the garage are throwing up beautiful firefly sparks.

"They gettin' out," Neil says, numbed.

"What about us?" Bill asks.

"Yeah. Everybody agree?"

"Better than sitting here," Lesley says.

"Let's go," Tremaine agrees, his ears listening for other sounds.

They're just pulling away when the Frangipani goes up, like distant thunder. Rounding the point flat out, planing high over calm waters, they see its smoke rising.

"Rough. Rough." Bill mutters bitterly. "Fucking rough."

A minute later there's a great thud against the boat's hull. Falling off its plane, it smacks to a stop, rolling.

"What's happened?" Lesley asks in lurching sudden silence.

Neil's leaning over the side of the flying bridge with a spotlight.

"Goddamn scooter!" he yells.

Its handlebars are jammed between skeg and prop. Bill helps him free it with the gaff-hook.

"How's the boat?"

"Thanks be to God it's one of these newfangled soft-bodies, not some deadhead. Let's get the fucker on board. It might come in handy,"

They pull it up quickly, dripping. A bullet-hole is drilled through the dashboard.

Just then the driver's body, face down, comes heaving into the bow-light spill. Tremaine's surprised to see it's already been worried by sharks. As they watch, another one torpedoes in, its head swishing side to side. How come it's the predators who survive? As Neil gets under way again, Tremaine watches the mangled body dwindle in the wake, remembering the spot, close by here, where his own death was luckily thwarted.

"What do we do now?" Tremaine asks Lesley.

"Get back to camp. James didn't know about that or about Perlita's."

So Leslie must think James....

"Then what?"

"Then you'll tell us the rest of what we have to know to destroy Earthbaby."

In the spotlight her eyes are clear and cold.

This morning the news was sudden and shocking, opening up all kinds of possibilities which I am having a hard time reconciling. And yet the day had started happily enough with my spending a few hours in the lab running routine tests on the crew's body fluids. I was humming to myself, idly fantasizing how I could educate Adam in sexual technique, contemplating what I might fancy for lunch — that sort of thing — when I heard a commotion down the corridor.

I got to Central to see Alex and Grainger standing together, talking to Clarke who stood with his hand resting on the main console like a captain on the bridge.

As if I should know, Grainger asked me where Adam was. I felt a little bump of guilt over my harmless fantasy for a second. Then I realized they thought I might have been with him as I was yesterday.

"I guess he's in his garden," I said, noticing a slight reaction from Alex.

"They've launched the shuttle without telling us about it," Clarke said.

"How do you know?"

Alex seemed proud of herself. "Grainger and I caught the launch from the observatory."

So. Alex was back to helping him was she?

Grainger flung himself into a nearby couch.

"Those bastards! Trying to catch us off-guard. Lucky you noticed it, Alex."

"What does this mean," I asked, looking significantly over at Grainger — referring of course to James' message that the launch wouldn't take place.

"That you have to take everything with a grain of salt, I guess."

The others looked a little nonplussed at our exchange, so I quickly diverted attention.

"I'll get Adam," I said.

I tore back to the garden, finding Adam in the cloning sheds.

"Stunning news," I said, panting. "Grainger and Alex just told us they saw that the shuttle's been launched." He twisted the tap on a main feeder tube and I watched the yellow liquid spurt along its transparent length.

"They were in the observatory?" I could see his mind churning over that one.

"Yes. Working with each other again, apparently."

"So you were wrong, Lilly."

I knew he meant about more than just the shuttle launch.

"Everyone can make mistakes," I replied.

"That's for sure," he said bitterly. "You know, now that it's happened, actually happened, I'm beginning to feel really pissed off about this whole thing."

"Well let's get back to Central and see what's up."

Adam gave only a curt nod to Alex and Grainger when we returned. Now we were all together, Clarke, indignant, taking on the mantle of leadership rightfully his, inquired from NASA why we hadn't been informed of the shuttle launch. I was impressed by the quelled note of outrage in his voice. This was the kind of role Clarke was born to and it showed. I thought of the I Ching ideogram, 'Great Power Held In Check.'

The communications control officer on duty seemed rather flustered and had to gather his resources, mumbling a few vaguenesses about his own lack of authority in the matter, promising to pass the query on, and so forth. Clarke demanded James contact us at once and sat there steaming while the duty officer consulted with his superiors.

One of Foreman's media officers, whom I recognized because of his long face and yellowish eyes which reminded me of a doberman, took over. Obviously surprised by Grainger and Alex's observational acuity, he tried the jovial, mano-a-mano approach. Say, you guys are right on the bit. No way we can put anything over on you, eh? Then he went into a version of: we-were-only-trying-to-save-you-from-undue-worry. As soon as NASA were certain the launch was a success they had been intending to give us a full report, he assured us, at least as far as the slingshot trajectory portion was concerned. After all, that was the launch-phase we had trouble with and it might disturb us to be anxious about it.

This didn't appease Clarke very much, especially since he'd been reminded of the spin crisis on the way up and his own lack of decisiveness in the emergency. He demanded further clarification, which

James had promised us, about the shuttle's crew. Who were they and what was their purpose? Were any of us Earthbaby colonists going to be replaced?

With Doberman's vague and obfuscating answers, Clarke grew more heated and demanded to speak directly to James. Doberman blinked a few times then avowed how a man had to have a holiday some time, and the recent strain on James was such he'd decided to take a vacation.

"So who's in charge down there?" Clarke asked icily. "Are you?"

Doberman lifted his head like a dog sniffing the wind and moved it a few times from side to side, his eyes never directly registering on the screen. You've got us again, old boy, was his drift. James' departure had been unexpected and things were a little up in the air at the moment as to the critical path of the organizational authority lines, ahem and so forth.

"In that case," said Clarke, "I refuse to carry out any NASA directives until you characters have made up your so-called minds."

"Good for you, Clarke," I cheered. I couldn't look over at Grainger and my mouth was dry. What had really rattled me was this business about James. It wasn't that he was crazy, or had misinformed me about the shuttle as maybe Grainger would like me to think: deep in my heart I knew the worst had happened. We would never hear from James again.

I didn't voice this directly. But I could tell Clarke was worried about it, too.

"Damn politics down there," he said. "You never know from one day to the next who's in and who's out."

And what was I to do with the horrible suspicion that Grainger was responsible, that he was a Foreman plant who'd successfully deceived me?

"So there we are," Alex growled.

Adam, his chest heaving in what I recognized as contained fury over everything falling down around him, practically exploded.

"Fucking hell. I've had about enough of it up here. Those damn military assholes (please understand I don't include you in this Clarke) can have the whole goddam thing, as far as I'm concerned."

"Don't you care about your work going to pieces?" Alex chided.

Adam bristled. Obviously Alex had echoed a past theme of Carmina Zielinski.

"I'm bored with the whole idea of it," he said diffidently. "I want a life in the real world with real human beings."

This last was said with such challenge to both her and Grainger that Alex was taken aback. Good for you, Adam, I thought. I could see she was doing a little reassessment, and if Grainger hadn't been there, I'm sure she would have responded positively to this new, rather more exciting version of Adam. Damn it, though, the little bitch continued to hang around Grainger all through the last few hours of the day-phase with one excuse or another, off in the observatory checking the shuttle progress and all that.

So there Adam and I were, marginalized by these two as I'd horribly dreamed it a few days ago. Finally I went off with Clarke to check him over in the dispensary because he mentioned his legs felt weak.

He was getting edemic, poor bastard, so I told him to lie feet up and swallow a couple of diuretics.

It gave me the chance to have him to myself and I decided to do a little reality testing before I committed myself to a plan building up in my mind.

"Tell me, Clarke," I asked. "Do you know more about what's going on than the rest of us — being a Foreman appointee after all — or are you just as much in the dark?"

He looked at me rather curiously.

"I don't know, Lilly. You seem to have a stronger feel for what might be happening down there."

Again I had to resist the urge to tell him about the messages from James, my certainty he had been dispensed with, and my suspicions about Grainger being a Foreman plant. All I knew was, I had to be extremely careful. One thing I could do, though, was test his resolve one way or the other.

"Social dynamics is my business, Clarke, just as guaging certain strategies is yours. My instinct is that things are pretty volatile down there. Look at this business with James for instance. One thing is certain among power-groups everywhere, things change. It strikes me we just might make a mistake by rolling over and playing dead right now, especially since these weapons are on board."

"You think we should resist being replaced; is that it, Lilly?"

"At least somehow playing for time. I mean, Clarke, this is an unjustified take-over of your field of command, whatever way you look at it."

I think I worded it just right, especially at the end there, for he looked at me forcefully, the same flame of righteous anger he had talking to Doberman flaring up again.

"You're damn right, Lilly. I've been thinking much the same myself."

"Everyone is right behind you, Clarke."

"What about Adam?"

"Don't worry. What Adam needs is a sense of noble purpose to what he's doing. Seeing the rest of us fighting for the right will stir him up."

"And are you sure about Grainger? I sense you two have been… developing a special relationship."

What an irony he should bring it up at that moment. If I told him my suspicions about Grainger it might well keep him from resolving to resist. I stammered a little, trying to decide. Clarke, though, took my confusion for embarrassment over having an affair.

"Lucky young bugger. Well, I take it there's no problem with him, or with Alex."

"No," I lied, thinking, I'll handle Grainger one way or the other. "You've got a full house Clarke."

"All very well," Clarke said. "But how do we do it?"

"Easy. We have a malfunction with the magna-grabs. They've given trouble before, remember, during the construction phase."

"Lilly. I have to warn you. These guys don't play around. This could have very serious consequences if it goes wrong."

"If you're worried about consequences of failure to the rest of us, Clarke, you can always take the heat yourself. You can claim we were merely following your orders."

I knew that would get to him, but he persisted with his objections.

"Still, Lilly. You should never lead troops into a battle you know you can't win."

I decided to come clean, then. I could feel the crucial moment had arrived.

"I know how you feel, Clarke. But I think there's a good chance we *can* win."

I then told him about the messages from James, that Tremaine was quite likely still alive, putting a very positive light on it all, of course, not even expressing my own doubts about whether or not it was all real, and especially leaving out my suspicion of Grainger.

Clarke was stunned at first. Then outraged. Then positively elated with the prospect of contributing to Foreman's downfall.

"We should have a meeting on this right away."

"In the morning," I said, "Would be much better. You and I won't get much sleep thinking about it, but we should let the others get their rest. And I think people are more likely to act in concert the closer the threat comes."

"Maybe we should leave it until right before the shuttle's due to dock."

"Even better," I agreed.

Again I was thinking to myself just in case Grainger's a plant we don't want to tip our hand too soon.

Clarke left after that, his edema considerably lessened. On his way out I gave him a big hug and a kiss. He received it awkwardly but eagerly.

"You're quite a magical person, Lilly."

I could have cried seeing his brave lonely figure making its way down the corridor to his cabin. His wife must have been lucky.

So far, so good. And now I'm sitting here, in my own lonely cabin, finishing this, thinking banal thoughts like, 'you win some, you lose some,' my heart wracked with thoughts of Grainger and Alex probably fucking their brains out. Large as this complex is, you know, I've never had the feeling it was ever *still*. Always I'm conscious of how we're coasting through the universe, all of us, everything. I think if I ever get back to earth I will never lose this feeling — that even back on so-called solid ground I'll feel adrift, uneasy.

So what will I ever do if Grainger...?

Shit. That's him! At the door...

SAVING C:\Earthbaby\Journals of L.S.\ Socdyn. doc ∽

They lie on separate bunks, numbed and exhausted. Above him, in gaps of his troubled sleep, Tremaine hears Lesley sob. He wakes enough to put his hand up to comfort her, but her previous coldness has invaded him too, and when he does not encounter any part of her he makes no more effort.

He wakes again an hour or two later and lies in the dark, vaguely angry. Given the world's general craziness, didn't he, Tremaine, as the last civilian head of NASA, have every right to try protecting the spacestation's crew; or, for that matter, his and Jock's phenomenal work: Earthbaby itself? It's not his and Jock's fault the world degenerated into stupid political wrangling since they first conceived the project, for God's sake. What difference would it have made if he'd told Lesley about the laser-beam umbilicus support system to Earthbaby anyway? It was obviously James who screwed up, or worse, James who acted as mole to infiltrate them.

And there's the real source of Lesley's coldness and sorrow. Damn it, though. What a perceptive bitch she is, cottoning on to him like that. How did she guess he's been holding back on her?

In the morning he tries to jolly her along, but although she's polite, as are Bill and Perlita, (both distinctly hung over) Tremaine is conscious of a gathering alienation from them. After breakfast, he relieves Neil on the bridge, watching the digital flux stay in phase on the course setting Neil has prescribed, keeping his eye on the depth sounder for patrol subs and his eyes on the sky for those damn yellow Sikorskis.

The day is not bright and tropic clear; rather, the sky is packing up with accumulations of cumulo-nimbus, and the air has a supersaturated feel to it that prickles his skin. The sea is running a chop counter to the swell; so the boat bottoms with a jar occasionally as it slides off one surge and awkwardly into the other. He resets the trim tabs and pushes the throttle up a notch, but the result is like a car on a corduroy road. He cuts it down again and lowers the planing angle.

Then Perlita calls up to him.

He backs down the companionway, expectant and nervous, Neil passing him to take over the bridge again. At least let's clear the air, get back to that openness between them all before the disaster of yesterday.

When he turns around, there's a figure in the cabin who looks like a gone-to-seed clone of a steroider: shaved head, muscle-shirt, yellow and green rambunctious tattoos to the end of his fingertips. So where did *he* come from? he's thinking, when the voice gives it away. It's Edgely, courtesy Perlita.

"It's your turn now, man. Now we know they're on the watch for us we better get super cautious."

No jokes. No banter. Tremaine watches as Bill heads back to his cabin, Lesley following him.

Perlita has his fake identity fiche. Her uncle by marriage from New Haven. The tiny photo, he sees now, is quite vague, a vestigial remnant from the old identity cards when the visual was the important thing rather than the DNA imprint.

"We just have to do something to play down your media image. We don't have to go as radical as Bill because you haven't been on TV much, so you're not instantly recognizable like he is. They wouldn't have seen the Eurosoviet telecast either. You've got these thick eyebrows, still your original haircolour. We can pluck them and dye them white like your hair. And as for that, we can give it a lifeist booby style. And see this sunjacket with the fishing logo? That changes the image. Remember, if they monitor the boat, you're on holiday doing a little tuna fishing with your companion Lesley. Neil's the captain, Bill's the crew, and me, I'm the cook, right? Complain how you were conned by the travel agent into thinking there were still fish in the sea."

Having given him those instructions, Perlita works away at him for five minutes in a moody silence. "All right," he says. "I know something's up. Is everybody somehow blaming me for all this disaster?"

"No. Not exactly."

"What do you mean?"

"Lesley thinks you've been holding stuff back about the NASA complex."

"What made her think that?"

"When she analyzed the general structure of the virtual reality tapes you made with her. There was an anomaly in a portion of the main building."

"Why didn't she come to me with this?"

"Apparently she kept going around and around it, hoping you'd come through with something. When you didn't, she persuaded Bill it wasn't anything crucial; so he went along with her rather than put pressure on you."

"So why blame me now?"

"Not blaming, Andrew. That's not the right word. I guess they figure they might have tried something different if they'd known the whole story."

"The whole story about what?"

"About whatever it is you haven't told them yet."

"And what if there isn't anything? What if I don't even know about whatever there might be that's showing up as this anomaly? Maybe it's some security guards' recreation room — a video-game parlour, let's say. Or some goddamn obscure workshop that tests astronaut toothpaste that I never knew existed."

"Well. They do have unconfirmed information about some system. Once we get back to camp you can go over it with her."

In the meantime....he's just saying to himself....in the meantime....

Neil yells down the hatch. "Monitors! Monitors!"

"Get up on deck!" Perlita yells.

Fuck it! Whatever the situation, Tremaine thinks, now I've got to play my part, so we can all at least survive from moment to moment. Most of the world lives like this. And that's the trouble isn't it? How can you be wise and principled if life consists entirely of lurching from one crisis to another?

He plunks himself into the fishing chair as the Sikorski dips down to wave height and zooms in on them. Jaded young assholes. They're flying that thing almost carelessly, bored with it, hours and hours of flinging it recklessly across dull blue seas.

It hovers menacingly overhead, its boombox blasting a heavy bass sound-massage tape through its loudhailers, at the same time deliberately pounding him and Neil with a gale of prop-wash. He looks up like an innocent tourist, a mixed expression of fear and annoyance. The crew is jerking to the boom-box rhythm. He sees one of them reach up and take off a virtual reality mask. Now they're going to go into some real action: harassing a tourist boat. They stay fixed over the deck and he thinks for a moment they're going to veer off elsewhere, but it's only to slap their floats down on the water and draw alongside.

Mercifully, the sound system turns off as they come on the loud-hailer.

"Heave to, there. Prepare for inspection."

Neil pulls back the throttle and slides the clutch into neutral — without turning off the engine, Tremaine notices. Inside the bubble, the pilot and his crew are decked out in the latest techno-gear. Their helmeted heads on top of their thin, unexercised limbs, shiny with lurex, make them look like insects. The wedding of man and machine, Tremaine thinks. Machines becoming more like men, men becoming more like machines, and in this new age they meet in the middle: bionic, symbiotic, over-amplified, addicted to numbness and useless replication. They would be laughable except for what gives them power: the weapons they brandish with casual arrogance.

In a moment they've grappled on with a magnetite gangplank and are on the deck. Their chief, wearing prostheticant boots with fake hinges at the knees to simulate artificial legs, sports a display of chevronned hologram logos of various stages in his climb up the social service corps ladder. His helmet is a different colour and bears the Lifeist cross. He points his light-weight Uzzi at Neil, gesturing with it to make him get out of the control seat on the flybridge and step down. As Neil climbs down, his underlings, one woman among them, head below. They stand at the hatch, weapons pointing down, shouting a warning. Then the woman goes down covered by the other two who then go down behind her.

Tremaine, still sitting in the fishing chair, clutching onto a useless rod, finds himself the focus of the chief's attention next. Still speaking through the sign language of his gun, which he obviously loves to show off, he indicates he wants their papers, then waves Tremaine and Neil to stand by the rail together as he goes over them. They do so, somewhat confused by the next set of signals as the Uzzi is waved in the air.

"Turn around you assholes," says the chief, speaking through the enhancement microphone of his headgear — as if they should have known instantly what he meant. They do so. Tremaine looks down into the water. What an irony if he should wind up shot and drowned in there after all. His spine tingles with the knowledge his life is subject to the careless whim of a brain-dead fascoid. He hears a bit of a commotion behind him — Bill, being escorted up onto deck.

"This is a fully documented operation here," he is saying. "Ain't no need for you to throw your weight around."

One of the men snaps, "Get over by the rail with the others, Fatso, and shut up."

Tremaine has a great urge to turn around but resists it.

"Who does the old blonde bag belong to?" he hears the chief asking.

"The old guy by the rail," the woman answers.

At her words, even enhanced as they are, Tremaine freezes. He knows that voice. Then Lesley is standing next to him, her face impassive, neutral, just bearing with it as he is, and next to her, Bill, trying for the same demeanour.

"Find anything else down there?"

One of the men answers, a leer in his voice.

"Yeah, Chief. An island bitch. Jack's still down there with her."

The woman guarding them giggles. Probably coming down from ecstasy.

Bill can't take it. He's about to wheel around but Lesley restrains him.

"Stay cool, Bill," she whispers. "They're just trying to provoke you."

"Maybe I'll go down and help him out," they hear the chief say.

Then the woman again: "Isn't that one of those sea-bikes we were chasing yesterday? In the stern cuddy over there?"

The jet-ski wave-skimmer. And Tremaine knows that voice, knows it. If only he could get a look at her face under the helmet.... No. Don't turn around or whoever it is might recognize....

Neil looks worried.

"Fuck!" Bill mutters.

They leave the woman on guard while the others investigate.

"Keep those eyes looking out to sea or you wind up fishbait," she tells them.

An image of her is almost forming, annoying. And what the hell's happening below with Perlita?

The chief comes back. "Okay, we got a little problem here I see." The words float out eerily from his enhancer. "Everyone turn around."

Reluctantly, Tremaine follows the others, keeping his head down, pretending to shade his eyes by putting his hand in front of his face.

"You! Black fatso." The chief points the Uzzi at Bill. "Get over here."

Bill goes forward, his massive old body still carrying authority.

"Get him down," the chief orders.

Grinning, his underling does so with one swift kick at the back of Bill's legs so he crashes backwards. Angry, Bill goes to get up, but the chief sticks his Uzzi in his face. Meanwhile, the woman's attention is distracted. Tremaine steals a glance over at Neil, at Lesley. Neil shakes off his question with a look that says, ride it out, ride it out, just as the woman turns her attention back to them, gun up, wary.

"You want to know about the sea-bike" Neil says. "We bump into it so I bring it on board. Ain't nothin' to do with him."

"Oh yeah? Way Chief figgers it, this here black fatso was riding it," the underling answers him. "Or maybe it was him, Chief. Maybe this one."

All attention on Neil, now.

"For Christ's sake, it was like he said," Lesley says, playing the angry tourist. "And when I get back to New Haven there's gonna be hell to pay for this."

"Hey listen," Neil cuts in quickly. "We know you guys got a job to do, right? So take the bike. Take the bike and whatever else, and our tourist friends here can go home happy."

Shit. Now the attention's on them. On him. They expect him to say something.

He looks up. The woman's gaze hits his directly. He sees the flash of recognition. It passes between them. Janet. The one who avoided talking to him in the cafeteria that last day. His heart pounds. She stares at him. By what little threads do we live or die? The word of the Eurosoviet broadcast, confirming he is still alive, must have zipped through the NASA complex even through all the censorship. She reacts by pointing her gun aggressively straight at him. Somehow she's got herself transferred out to this sordid detail. How far gone is she on drugs and despair? He tries to make his eyes plead to her. The longer he can hold her gaze....

Then she turns from him abruptly and addresses the chief. "You know what chief? I think I recognize this guy."

"Yeah?" he asks.

Lesley looks at him, Neil too. Bill is helpless on the ground. Rushing them while they have the Uzzis is pointless.

Janet turns to him again. "Ain't you one of the organizers of that social service rally I went to last month in Connecticut?"

His relief is so profound, he almost forgets to answer her.

"That's right. It's true what the Captain here's saying. We heard shots in the night and then we came across this thing. Bumped into it."

He smiles at Janet, winging his gratitude over to her. Surviving. All there is.

"Okay, okay." The chief sounds bored now. "Let's get that thing out of here."

The underling brings up the bike and takes it across to the copter. Then the chief calls for Jack on his helmet intercom. No reply.

"Fucker must have taken off his helmet."

He digs into a pocket and brings up a code reader.

"While we're waiting for Jack, may as well try this thing out."

Tremaine recognizes it. A DNA scan device.

The chief runs it over Neil's bare arm, then checks his ID card to see if it matches. He goes to Bill, still prostrate on the ground as his underling returns from stowing the bike in the copter. Janet reaches for the scanner.

"I'll check the rest if you guys get Jack. That prick."

"Give him time to finish with her," the chief laughs, and takes Bill's arm, pushing up the sleeve.

Tremaine sees Perlita's head quickly appear out of the hatch. There's a shrill buzz from the scanner. Yes. They'd have put Bill's DNA on file, his own too, have them both coded as wanted men. That's why Janet....

The chief rears back in surprise, reaching for his Uzzi. The underling, Janet, all stare at Bill, struggling to get himself up, to try and grab onto.... Tremaine, charging forward, with Neil and Lesley, sees the chief's Uzzi coming up, hears a *pop!*

But it's the chief who lurches away, drops. The underling turns. Too late. *Pop!* And down he goes. Just in time, Tremaine clings on to Janet, saves her, as Perlita marching forward from the hatch, is aiming again.

Tremaine sees Perlita's face is scratched and tear-stained. Bill leaps up.

"Baby, Baby!"

Perlita doesn't respond. She drops the gun and stands at the deckrail holding on. She spits into the sea, spits again.

"Give me some water. I bit his tongue off."

Lesley runs for it, in the locker by the fishing chair. Perlita takes the bottle, but before she can drink it she pukes over the side. Lesley takes over, holding her, getting her to rinse her mouth out while she sobs and screams between the retching.

Neil has taken the gun from Janet.

Lesley, her own blouse soiled, takes it off and wipes Perlita's face with it. She sags to the deck, gasping, looking up at Janet.

"Who is she?"

"I know her," Tremaine says. "She tried to help me before you came up."

"I wish I'd ashed those assholes like you did," Janet says to Perlita. "Every one of these crews has one woman on board. They change us around when they get bored. If you don't co-operate, you get lost at sea."

Now her helmet's off, Tremaine sees Janet clearly. Her holocaust haircut has given way to a frontal-lobe bald-patch, a prosthetic derivation from brain surgery. Her eyes are afraid and bewildered.

Tremaine looks down at the bodies. He's filled with adrenalin, a small tick of angina going down his left arm, but he's not woozy at all.

"Let's get them while they're warm," he says to Neil.

The chief and his underling are easy. There. One small moment of horror and they're gone into the sea. Lesley tells Perlita she's going downstairs to get fresh clothes for her. Perlita won't let her go. "There's blood all over down there."

And so there is. Going down with Neil, Tremaine knows this will get to him later, but some kind of sustaining anger, mixed with the adrenalin carries him on. Neil momentarily falters, seeing the dead white thigh skin where the man had rolled down his uniform. In order to rape Perlita, the fascist bastard.

"Oh Fuck me, man," Neil says. "Are you sure he's dead?"

He leans against the cabin door, one foot skidding in the red slime, clutching the doorpost. Thank God for shoes, Tremaine thinks, his anger still driving him.

"I don't give a shit, Neil. He's going over and that's it."

But he is dead, and they struggle with the awkward carcass weight, both bloodied from the unclean kill, finally making it up to the deck through the hatchway then running with it to tip it over the side.

Then they look at each other in their horror, noticing Perlita similarly bloodied, and Leslie, and now Bill, too, from hugging her.

"The pump," Neil says.

Furiously Bill helps him mount it. Janet, not as bloody as the others, helps him handle the hose. They start the engines for power, the pump's inlet hose flung into the salt-curing sea. The outlet hose begins to gush its cleansing baptismal flood all over them.

Like children, Tremaine thinks. Like children on a summer day.

I'm going to write this exactly as it happened so I can reread it and maybe make some sense out of it. Usually I write at night, after the events, so to speak, when all is relatively calm and over with. Today, though — this morning — I need to finish last night's report — hastily saved when Grainger appeared unexpectedly at my cabin door.

Now, did he come fresh from dallying with Alex? There was no evidence of it, except a clean fresh-washed smell about him. Suspicious? Not really, because he has that rather nice habit of making sure he is clean and shaved before our little liaisons.

As if nothing much had happened, he came in and embraced me as I stood up, uncertain how to respond.

"What's wrong?" he said fatuously as I withdrew from his embrace.

"What's wrong?" I repeated. Then again, "What's wrong?" trying to think.

I stumbled out a few phrases that I thought might sound plausible enough.

"For one thing you've been clung tight to that young computing machine all damn day; so I haven't had a chance to talk to you about the shuttle or anything."

"I wasn't clinging to her; she was clinging to me. I saw the opportunity to engage her in a mutual project that would show off her skills to advantage. And they did. We caught the damn shuttle launch didn't we? I thought you'd be pleased our quarrel was getting patched up. Isn't that part of your job up here, to maintain a cohesive social unit?"

There was a lot of truth in what he was saying, the clever bastard.

"You don't have to go so far as to have her fall in love with you again and break things off with Adam, for God's sake."

"I don't think you're reading this right, Lilly. As far as I know, those two are fucking away right now."

"How do you know?"

"I saw Adam go into her cabin just as I was moseying discreetly along to you. It was a rather wink-wink, nudge-nudge moment, to be honest."

He must have guessed my perplexity. Was he telling the truth or was this a masterful piece of pseudo-reality he was foisting onto me? Jealousy can play tricks, old girl, I thought. Look at how Iago was able to completely distort Othello's perceptual ecology.

All right. I hadn't tripped him up on that one, but suddenly I had another disturbing idea: "How come you two decided to look out for the shuttle launching?"

I thought I had him there.

"Oh, we weren't exactly looking for it, not at first. Alex just suggested it as a means of monitoring the NASA complex."

"Why would she want to do that?"

"I guess because I'd told her about James coming on with that crazy message for you about not worrying about the launch and all that."

"You told her?" I practically screamed. "You told Alex?"

Grainger reared back as if shot.

"You didn't tell me not to tell anyone."

True. I didn't. I let that pass. My mind was spinning now.

"When did you tell her?"

"Two days ago. The very next morning after we heard James come on the personnel channel...."

Oh my God. So Alex knew also.

"Did you tell her the rest of it?"

"You mean, Tremaine being alive and the Eurosoviet broadcast stuff? No. I thought it politic not to."

"But you didn't think it politic not to tell her about last night's message?"

"Oh Jesus, Lilly. I'm not perfect."

So Alex knew. But she didn't tell Adam. If she had, he would have been bound to mention it to me in our conversation. Just a second. Maybe she did tell him. When he brought it up, was he playing innocent to get confirmation, or more detail? Whether she told him or not, it still means there were at least two people beside me who knew.

Not likely, but Alex could just as well have betrayed James, couldn't she? I really couldn't have entertained that thought until a little while ago, but now I found I could. What did anyone really know about her? Moreover, come to think of it, there was very little objection raised by the Foreman and Agriminco gang when Tremaine proposed her for the crew....

Stop thinking like this, I said to myself. You are going to go crazy. So crazy you'll start suspecting that Grainger himself, consummate deceiver, *deliberately* told Alex — and then let me know he'd told her — just so my suspicions would be divided rather than landing solely on him. All right. What about it?

I took a deep breath and plunged right in.

"You realize that James' disappearance signals a falling from grace, don't you? Not to say, a horrible annihilation. Whatever he was planning to do, someone found out and told on him."

"Whoa there, Lilly! Not necessarily so. Suppose it's just as NASA says. The strain got too much for him. Maybe he went over the edge with drugs or whatever and they put him in the detox tank. They're all pretty wacko down there as it is, so how do you know he's been ashed or whatever?"

"However," I persisted. "Someone ratting on him is a possibility, right?"

"I'll concede that. Okay. A possibility. But we haven't the faintest idea what's going on there really, except from what James told you. I mean, they could have been shadowing him for months if he was working for the underground, and just took him off at the crucial moment."

"I wasn't thinking of anyone ratting on him down there."

I let that sit and sink, looking at Grainger carefully to gage his reaction. I was relieved to see it took a moment before the significance of what I had said registered.

"Oh come on," he said. "Alex could never...."

I kept thinking: these guys are trained. These guys are fantastic actors....

"I didn't say Alex," I said coldly.

He put his head in his hands and rubbed his eyes, realizing (or pretending to) where that put him. Then he looked up at me.

I'd never seen him look so old. What I'd said (if he wasn't acting) had completely devastated him.

"Fuck!" He got up wearily. "So when are you going to kill me?" he said in a bitter, choking voice.

My own voice was on the edge of hysteria.

"I can't help it. I have to think of everything."

"You poor bitch. You can't trust anyone, can you?"

"No!" I cried, tears starting out of my eyes.

How he could push the buttons in me.

"No!" I said again. For he was right. Ever since Jock....

Then he had me in his arms, comforting me. I yielded to it. So what. So what if I was going to be betrayed. What else was there to do but trust at least one person in this stinking universe?

Carefully he stripped me, gently laid me down, entered me slowly, lovingly, his hands tangled in my wet hair, his mouth drying the tears on my cheeks. He couldn't have just been with Alex, I kept telling myself. Yes he could. He couldn't be a plant for Foreman. Yes he could. And Alex couldn't possibly be... Yes. She could.

Then I came, truly came. ᥦ

L ike a phoenix, Tremaine thinks. Like a phoenix. Something truly powerful is pumping through him now as he wheels the big yellow Sikorski up into the sky out of the sea. His ascent is at first a little awkward, causing Perlita and Bill to stumble into the bulkhead. He sees them look at each other, then strap themselves into seats as Lesley has wisely done.

Below him, Neil stands with Janet sharing a big split on the boat-deck, giving a wave, the whole scene rapidly miniaturizing. Anything could happen between them or nothing. Neil's first job will be returning to check on Sonny. Then what will the pair of them do with their places reduced to ashes? From this height, there's nothing to show where bodies have foundered, nothing except a few dark shadows which could be coral outcrops, cloud shadows, sharks, old wrecks, anything. How lucky he is not to have been devoured, but to have survived intact, loved, and soaring safe away.

He starts at the crackle of the communicator: "Monitor 47, report due 1900."

He's afraid one of the communication switches might be left open, so he turns them all off, clearing the panel.

"Can you guys sort this out while I fly this thing?"

Bill proves to be the expert. He finds the right reply channel but leaves it closed, checking his watch.

"Couple of minutes yet. We should say something, just to satisfy the receiving computer for a while."

"The medium is the message," Lesley laughs.

Perlita still looks sick, but she tries to keep her end up.

"So what we do with dis t'ing now? We steal it or what?"

"That depends whether they have it locked permanently into a location grid or not," Tremaine answers her.

Bill is going over the control panel again.

"It may be built in," says Lesley, looking herself.

Leveling off, Tremaine aims at Hispaniola, appreciating the forward thrusters.

"Here's the little fucker," Bill says, crouched down by Tremaine's left side.

"Great!" Lesley says. "Can we turn it off?"

She takes a look at it, finds the crucial relay.

Bill says, "Give me our co-ordinates."

Opening the reporting channel, he reads their position in.

"Just letting you know, Control, fishing launch checked out okay; but right now we're surveilling a large tug pulling a couple of barges. End report."

"Wait thirty seconds, then turn off the location sender."

Lesley counts, then trips it.

"It'll be hours from now before they figure out we've somehow disappeared. Then they'll come nosing around here trying to find some tug and its barges, figuring they had something to do with it."

"The camp, then?" Tremaine inquires.

"Right on."

In his mirror, he sees Bill sit again, pulling Perlita against him. She's crying, her sobs quiet, heart-wrenching.

Lesley, bless her, reaches her hand into his.

"How are things with you, my co-pilot?" he says softly.

*   *   *

It's nighttime now and Tremaine's mentally exhausted, though he feels he could stay awake forever. They have to keep low to bump radar, but until the moon comes up utter black prevents him from seeing waves below. Unable to use his own radio/laser sensors, he's been going on instruments, as in the old days, judging how much margin to leave for low-lying coral islets. The fact they haven't crashed yet might simply mean he's too high up, and therefore radar discernible. Thank God these military Sikorskis have anti-radar stealth profiles.

So he pushes it down, foot by foot, suddenly seeing a coral head practically scrape his belly. Jeez. What a relief. Too low to lock onto auto-altitude, he manages to hold the needle right on scale until he's a couple of miles from the big island.

At that point he slows down, practically hovering, asking everyone to keep an eye out for shoreline, for lights, anything to give him bearings.

"There!" Lesley points. "Wait for the beam to come round again."

Sure enough, a far lighthouse, flashing behind headlands, illuminates the sky just enough for a massive cliff to show against the dark. He gets Lesley to put in a navigation fiche and does a quick radio/laser burst to get a reading, knowing monitors wouldn't catch it, low and sheltered as they are from where the radar must be on shore.

"Okay," he says, getting the bearing, "a little ravine work and there we'll be."

"I wish I could fly this thing for you," Lesley says, kneading his stiff neck.

"Just don't stop what you're doing. That'll get us there."

And it does, though he can barely talk when he steps out.

Grey and the crew are terrified until they hear Bill's voice and realize what has happened. They hustle to cover the Sikorski temporarily until it can be concealed tomorrow. Tremaine has parked it close enough to the communications shed so they can string tarpaulins from there. Lesley greets each of the Lesbian tent one by one while he waits, dazed from the flight, uncertain.

Then she takes him by the arm and leads him to her tent, to the place where they began together. He lies flat on his back, eyes closed, relishing solid earth beneath him, allowing Lesley to pull his clothes off, lifting himself slightly to help her. Despite his numbed mind, his body responds to her touches.

"You've done well, little boy," she teases him, fully intending to ride him before they sleep.

"You've done well, and tomorrow" — a gasp as she straddles him — "you'll do even better."

That depends, he thinks. With a shudder he remembers how the dead man's blood had made a smudge of red on her hair.

*   *   *

In the morning Grey tells them Rivka has communicated through the computer coder that Foreman's boys have launched the shuttle. So the whole campaign has been a complete wipeout.

Perlita, blunt, straightforward, still dreadfully rattled from yesterday, comes out with it. What all of them have been thinking: "What if James was a plant? This is all my fault, not cottoning onto him."

Tremaine notices Lesley turn white at that. "What bloody nonsense. There's no basis for that at all."

And yet she had said yesterday it was safe to go to the camp or Perlita's because James didn't know about them.

Tremaine remembers the yellow Sikorski following him and Perlita in the lightweight to the airport, and how he shook them, coming back here, to camp.

"They were tracking him," he says, looking at her. "And us. I'm sure of it. So when he got back, they had him, and he didn't get a chance to put in the fiche."

Tremaine puts his arm around Lesley. Poor bitch. Either way it must be hard for her. On one side imagining the torture and probable murder once they'd got it all out of him. Drugs, hopefully. But you never know with those bastards. On the other hand, the alternative reading — James callously sacrificing her along with the rest of them. Who would ever know?

Bill answers to Perlita first: "Don't worry, honey. You did good. I think it's like Andy here says. I hate to say it, Lesley. But I think that boy is gone."

Lesley twists out of Tremaine's arm.

"It's done now, anyway."

She walks off into the scrub, pulling her hat down, hands stuck in her pockets. He lets her go. Would any of them ever know the truth of what really happened? *I mean, for God's sake, it could be Lesley, all the time in cahoots with James as far as that goes....* God, how the snake of suspicion slithers through every paranoid thought.

He looks after her, trudging along close to the trees. Blood, nerves, skin, bone, all to be dispensed with in ten years or so — twenty, what difference in the long scheme of things? All her bundle of molecules, when it decays, will be traceable back to elements eventually. Dust to dust. Ashes to ashes. Nothing lost there. But what of that complex of knowledge and feeling? Where does it all go? Back to nothing also?

Nothing. Is that, then, what it is all made of?

N ow we've done it. It's not my watch, but I hardly think I'll sleep. God, this is thrilling. This sense of power is somehow linked with a fantastic sense of self — a self so aroused, my normal self feels pushed whimpering into a corner.

And yet our situation is, as Clarke predicted, fraught with danger. As I write this, I'm sure the crew of the shuttle is planning their next boarding strategy. Unless they manage a code exchange, however, they won't get NASA's help without us knowing, because we can monitor everything.

I managed to persuade Clarke not to tell the crew about our intention to resist the shuttle docking until the last moment. I wanted there to be no time for a spy to send NASA a warning. If there *is* a mole in our own crew, I wanted whoever it was to be caught off guard, even to the point of being uncloaked under the sudden stress.

While we waited for the shuttle's arrival I went on a bit of a binge. The rest of the crew seemed similarly disposed, so I thought it best to give out a ration of joy-juice. I must say it created a jovial ambiance and cemented a kind of camaraderie, though I wondered about poor Clarke being so obviously left out. I began by doing nothing but drink and fuck Grainger; and the hell with whether or not he was working for the other side, something I convinced myself I was less and less concerned about. At the same time, I noticed myself constructing safety nets against that denied possibility.

One of those nets, I now recognize, was my wild flirting with Adam, sitting on a string hammock he'd rigged up. (Obviously, his new seduction spot.) With poor James probably murdered — Grainger continued to argue about this, but weakly, since NASA continued to evade answering any of our direct questions about the shuttle crew — there was no point in keeping secrets any longer, even if there was a Foreman plant on board. I took the opportunity to tell Adam (and later on, Alex,) about the messages I'd received from James concerning Tremaine's miraculous survival and the Eurosoviet broadcast with Edgely. What a relief to unburden myself to the whole tribe!

Adam became quite passionate about "those murdering hypocrites." Of course it could have been a cover, I'll never be sure. By the end of our conversation, however, his heavy breathing, his choked voice, and his hands lingering in mine as we parted, made it clear I could seduce him if I really wanted to.

By the same token, I must admit I batted my eyes a bit while a little high with Clarke one evening, empathizing with his celibacy. In fact, I went so far as to give him a little hip action while he was hugging me, something he does now whenever we meet or part to discuss strategy in his cabin. Yes, if I wanted to, I could have a wild time up here and damn the consequences.

But of course there are consequences; and today, with only a few hours left, Clarke and I broached to the others the idea of resisting the docking. Clarke was magnificent in bearing and demeanour, his voice ringing with calm authority. I felt quite a throb of desire for him. He didn't mince words as to the consequences, but promised to take all responsibility on himself as we'd discussed.

Grainger was the first to support him, with an offhand, "You don't have to take the can back for me, Clarke."

"What have we got to lose?" put in Adam, looking towards *me* for approval!

Alex frowned. "If these guys are as ruthless as they seem to be, we could lose everything." She sat rather rigidly, with crossed legs, one foot jigging nervously.

"Are you with us, then?" I asked.

She flushed. "Of course. I just didn't want Adam to see this as some wrap-around movie."

"I know full well what we're getting into. I just happen to think this is the wise and proper thing to do."

Alex reached out and touched him. "I just wanted to be sure, Adam. You're such a romantic."

This rather pleased him.

I had been expecting to judge from each one's reactions whether any of them could be a Foreman plant. Not a hint. In fact, as the conversation went on, every last one of them expressed a gleeful kind of eagerness. I exchanged a triumphant glance with Clarke over seeing my professional instincts so clearly justified.

I must say, though, I held my breath when the shuttle, heaving into view, synched beautifully with our independent solar orbit and drifted there, glittering.

"Requesting permission to dock," came the Captain's self-satis-fied voice in the traditional phraseology.

I could almost see the big bird itself rear back in surprise when Clarke, his voice as calm and even as you please, replied simply, "Permission denied."

"Ah, did I hear you right?"

"Repeat: permission denied."

"I have orders to dock, Earthbaby."

"Orders invalid: permission denied."

Flustered as he was, the captain forgot to switch transmission.

"Fucking hell, guys, they won't let us dock. Get NASA for God's sake. Christ, I was looking forward to a good gravity shit."

We all had the relish of hearing his confusion and frustration as he attempted to get orders from NASA who seemed equally astound-ed.

NASA's first response was to call on us through Central and demand an explanation from Clarke. Operating on the "less is more" principle, Clarke merely stated that in his judgement the safety and welfare of the Earthbaby crew would not be served by allowing the docking. He then terminated communications.

By now, although the shuttle Captain had switched off his feed, Alex had clicked into the communications beam of the laser umbili-cous. Unless they could contrive a code, something they had not been prepared for since our resistance was so unexpected, we could moni-tor everything that passed between NASA and the shuttle crew. This was something NASA and the shuttle suddenly realized. Their discus-sion terminated with NASA ordering the captain to gain access to Earthbaby by whatever means possible, "Including the use of extreme force."

This last was an obvious attempt to scare the shit out of us, and to a degree it worked. Up till then, our nervousness, coupled with the vision of a pompous authority being startled into helplessness, had caused us to chuckle and even laugh outright. This announcement was enough to quell that.

"What can they do?" Adam asked.

"Who knows?" Clarke replied. "But whatever it is, they're time limited."

"They're slipping into the dark side," Alex reported.

This meant it would be virtually impossible to monitor them visually as we had been doing. Because of radiation interference and shadowing, our instruments would only be able to pick them up as a large presence.

"I could take out the buggy and keep an eye on them," Grainger suggested.

"Good idea," Clarke said.

I hastened to demur, babbling on about how Grainger could be shot from the sky. Losing a crew member aside, what would we ever do without the buggy if we were stranded for a few months and needed to do outside repairs? Things of that sort.

In truth, I'd caught my breath, shaken with paranoia. What a brilliant scheme for Grainger to defect to the other side and assist their operation! There were all sorts of possibilities, including his picking up a couple of them unseen from the shuttle, armed, and bringing them back on board through the buggy-launch area.

Fortunately, Alex and Adam agreed with me, feeling at this stage that it was an unnecessary risk and that Grainger's bravery might be better employed at a more crucial time. I was shaken by the thought I'd have to watch Grainger's every move, double-guess him. Unless, of course, I was wrong.

By now Adam and Alex had the shuttle imaged, Alex attempting to braid in an enhancer programme. It looked pretty good, but, as Grainger explained, "You won't be able to see the little green men pop out of it in their snowsuits."

My suspicions of him took another reverse turn when he then proceeded to explain in highly-charged technical jargon to Alex how they might apply some of the observatory's asteroid mineral sensing devices to the hook-up. If he's on their side, I thought, then why is he trying to assist us so assiduously?

I was left moping about it while they went off to figure it out. Adam, Clarke and I stared uselessly at the imaging. Adam finally broke the silence.

"Well. We've done it now."

"Right," I said.

Adam hugged me tight, surprising me by whirling me around a half turn.

"I feel like I'm at the Boston Tea Party."

Clarke laughed. "Very apt, Adam."

Just then the screen clarified so much we could see the shuttle clearly.

"Look at those guys!" Clarke said. "Bloody geniuses."

Alex and Grainger returned grinning. I swallowed my enthusiasm. How much I would have loved not to feel that terrible confusion about Grainger. All right, what he'd done made us all feel a lot safer than before. Now he couldn't possibly make clandestine trips to the shuttle. But it wasn't enough to completely allay my suspicions.

Lucky, though, that they did their job so well. Half an hour later we did, indeed, see the little green men pop out of their craft in their snowsuits.

"They'll try testing all the hatchways," Clarke stated. "Maybe blasting one open in a safe-lock zone."

Adam looked from one to another of us. "What'll we do?"

"Wait till they are actually in contact with our outer skin," Clarke said. "Then we'll show them something."

Softly the menacing little figures deployed themselves about the Earthbaby complex. In fact, we could see one on the dome over Central where we were. Probably he couldn't see us because the light was behind him, illuminating the graphoplaque skin. He reminded me of waking in a tent in the desert and looking up to see the sharp clear black silhouette of a scorpion crawling over the fabric.

"Shield mode!" Clarke ordered.

Suddenly there was panic. The little figure realized what was happening as the shield swept across the dome's surface, threatening to bump him into space. Worse yet, it might trap him inside the couple of metre's space between it and the dome, there to languish until oxygen ran out and he was left like a smudge of a fly killed on the wall.

How we whooped and shouted as we saw them on the imager all heading back to the shuttle. First blood, I thought. Our first encounter with the enemy and we had won. Now we were together as never before.

I looked up to see Grainger's eyes alight with excitement — and alight with desire. For me. ∽

G rey, working the communications shed in the early morning, brought bad news. Tremaine was sitting with Perlita and Bill outside in the new dawn air. Perlita, swigging down a glass of biting orange juice at Bill's urging, seemed to be making a reasonable recovery. The news swiped that all away: her house had been destroyed. She was utterly crushed. Still twitching from the remembered horror of the day before last, she began rocking and moaning in distress, constantly spitting into her handkerchief, wiping her mouth while her eyes glistened with tears and anger.

Tremaine and Grey don't want to intrude on her grief, leaving Bill to console her and urge her to go inside with him.

Why the hell would they demolish Perlita's house? How did they know about it? Why didn't they wait until she was there; or all of them were there? Perhaps they don't care any more, especially since the Foreman boys have got the shuttle up there, about to dock with Earthbaby. Given the low calibre of their personnel, and the stress of the times, their kind of totalitarian centre cannot hold for long without breaking down into inefficiencies here and there. And do they know anything about the camp here too? If they do, it's not through James, who knew nothing about it. Are they just waiting a little to trash the whole thing and everyone in it in one big fireball?

Tremaine can't help wondering to himself whether the ancient crocodile skin on her wall had somehow survived. What is for certain is that the amber afternoon he'd had with her in that beautiful place would never be again.

Grey's take on it is somewhat more optimistic. Perlita has long been known as a local figure in citizenship politics. The whole affair might have more to do with Foreman's social service core punishing those involved in local election resistance than with her international role as a member of the society.

That makes sense too.

A quickly rising red sun hard-edges dark green forests surrounding the tussocky plateau. It reminds Tremaine to deal with hiding the copter.

Grey finds an ideal hole for it: the excavated pit of the archaic habitation site. Palisaded for protection on its open side, the tiny village had backed against a pumice knoll. Tremaine eases the copter down close to the rock-face. Its massive floats compress subsoil blackened by ancient hearths. Tremaine imagines that fugitive band comforting each other around their sanctuary fire, making brave plans for an uncertain future in the face of some newly-evolved political dictatorship bent on their destruction. Nothing much has changed.

Grey directs the workgang covering the ugly machine. Tremaine wants to be able to get it out of there in a hurry if necessary. The crew stakes camouflaged tarpaulins around it. From the top of the knoll, Beatta throws on cut palm thatch. Three thousand years from now, will future archaeologists dig the thing up and wonder how and why it got there?

Bill meets them halfway back to the shed.

"How's Perlita?"

"Lesley's taking care of her."

He still has on the remains of Perlita's make-over on the launch. But the effect is tragic and defeated.

"Some good news, anyway."

"Why? What's up?"

"The Eurosoviets are sending that video vamp Rivka again. Sounds like they're getting aroused, sending swat teams in all over Trans America to tie in with local resistance movements."

"Good. Lots of diversions. Amazing how quick a loose confederation like that can mobilize when the need arises."

"She's bringing a team into here, with some image-generator laser projection equipment we might find handy. Truth is, though, it looks pretty hopeless if Earthbaby isn't disabled."

Tremaine looks back at the habitation site. Amazing, really, how easy it is to be fooled by appearances with crude camouflage like that, let alone those simulated environments like Lesley's.

"Listen Bill, I've been thinking. Earthbaby may not be so invulnerable as it looks. I might have something to say about that when we get back to the shed."

"Lesley had an instinct you might. Good."

Grey's group starts gathering around them.

"Let me know if you need us. In the meantime, we're going to test trench what we think might be a neolithic decarnation site."

Lesley meets them at the shed door.

"Perlita wants to sit in with us. I think it might be good for her to focus on something else. After all, we're all trying to hang in here."

"What's a decarnation site, Lesley," Bill wants to know.

"A special enclosure where they leave bodies to rot and get eaten by vultures and animals. When there's no flesh left, they take the skeletons and bury them."

"Charming."

The shiny copper walls of the communications shed reflect the four of them from every direction. Perlita is making a brave attempt to hold together, but the shine of tears stays in her eyes and periodic shudders ripple subtly through her limbs.

Under cover of her stiff-upper-lip British veneer of forced cheerfulness, Lesley too is depressed and moody now the adrenalin shots of the past few days have brought their inevitable hangover. Tremaine remembers his first time in here with her. Full circle.

Bill, bless him, is trying to stay collected for Perlita's sake; but is himself harried and bristly, mopping his pate ever more nervously. He starts off, ritualistically really, trying to set a kind of solid tone for Perlita's sake as much as anything, reviewing the current situation. Their last chance was to keep the shuttle from reaching Earthbaby. Well, by this morning it will be there — presumably with arms and men. All that can save the situation now is to destroy Earthbaby itself.

Which is where, Tremaine knows, he comes in.

"Couldn't the Eurosoviets send up another satellite like their last one? Only armed this time?" Lesley asks.

Bill rubs the bridge of his nose and sniffs. Getting an allergy attack again.

"Now the Lifeist army boys have been shuttled up to Earthbaby, it's a cinch for them to ash a satellite with a missile before it gets anywhere near them. Unless we can think of something else, we're stuck ladies and gentlemen."

That echo from his broadcast days.

They all look at him. Tremaine watches Lesley's image skid across the blurry monotone of the copper walls as she gets up from her chair and stands in front of him. His heart kicks with sadness at the way she looks this morning, her age showing, trying to keep herself together. She puts a hand out and touches him. He feels guilty about his random thought last night that she might be the traitor.

She turns her head to take in Edgely and Perlita, then reaches back for his hand. He returns her light I-love-you squeeze. She's looking at him in some kind of knowing way, her mouth nervous and twitchy.

"If it's something kept strictly between the four of us, wouldn't that be okay?"

Yes. He does love her. Wants to stay alive with her, wherever, however.

Tremaine draws a deep breath, hears himself talking. Part of himself can't believe it.

"There could be a way. But it would have to be soon, in the next couple of months or so, before Earthbaby goes functionally independent."

Bill is alert again, vitalized, camera-ready.

"What do you mean by functionally independent? Isn't it already?"

"Not at all. Not until the various life-support modes are fully functioning and in phase: oxygen production from the space garden for instance, completed solar-cell charging of Earthbaby storage batteries and so on. Along with that goes a complete solar orbit cycle to test the efficacy of all the station's automatic attitude adjustments to enable heating-cooling, radiation release.... Well. A myriad of things, which in fact the on-board computer systems have to take time to actually learn phase by phase — from the mother computer so to speak — while braiding in the actual contingencies Earthbaby encounters as it orbits.... Anyway, until then, Earthbaby's functions are controlled through a laser umbilicus."

Lesley's eyes open with awareness.

"Which means in the meantime that Earthbaby's existence depends on ground control?"

"Almost completely at first, gradually phasing out over several months. By now, enough control will have been transferred so it wouldn't whizz off into space without it, but it would be pretty uninhabitable and disabled until reconnected."

"Is this control system the piece Lesley felt was missing from the hologram reconstruction?"

"Yes. I should have told you about it before. But it was early days then and, primarily, I didn't want to risk my crew — especially Alex and Lillith. Also, I may as well be completely honest, I didn't want to see something Jock and I had worked on for fifteen years get demolished almost before it had begun."

A healing flicker of hope darts into Perlita's eyes. There's a deep silence, Lesley tightening her grip encouragingly.

Edgely turns towards him smoothly, choreographically, mirror walls reiterating his movement. Beat, beat, like something done in theatre.

Then: "Now you won't have to worry about your crew. They'll be on their way back already, now the replacements have got there."

Of course, now the way is clear, Tremaine realizes. How strange to find himself here. In this surreal burnished environment, could he really be about to say the words on the threshold of his tongue?

"I don't care about Earthbaby now. In fact, I've come to think the whole thing is a huge folly."

"Yes," he says straight into Lesley's loving face, real and vivid before him, "a huge folly."

"Better late than never," Perlita says.

Through all her brave agony she manages a smile.

SOCIAL DYNAMICS RESEARCH PROJECT
JOURNAL OF LILLITH SHAWNADITHIT

My watch.

I don't mean my time-piece, though I notice it figures much more largely in this process than in normal times. I'm talking about guard duty in the old sense. My image of it has always been standing somewhere on the camp perimeter ears pricked, eyes uselessly straining into darkness. How different this duty is, though: literally "watching" an unmoving screen image, hour after hour. Thank God I have this ongoing journal to create in this curious little old laptop.

There is of course no real "night" up here except that of the artificial illumination program which keeps our bio-rhythms in sync. The station itself always has a "light" and a "dark" side which itself changes on a gradual basis as Earthbaby spins around its own axis to equalize temperature differences. More than that, its vertical attitude is adjusted as well so that one or other surface does not have a perpetual "winter" or "summer." Here in Central, because of the dome, a portion of every "day" and of every "night" is illuminated "naturally" (through all the filters, of course). And right now as I write, (on the night watch!) the dome is steadily brightening — an odd feeling because I've never seen this before although intellectually I've known it must happen while we are all asleep.

All this musing about comparative "time"! Sitting here, through these hours, I've suddenly had the feeling that I am, in fact, living *inside* a kind of huge celestial "watch," like a mouse in a clock.

Anyhow this is the kind of mind rambling one does in a situation like this while waiting to see if those little green men are going to suddenly emerge from the shuttle to threaten us again. Another five minutes and it will be Alex's turn. Clarke has left me with the task of organizing these watches. If we have to spell each other off like this for a meaningful amount of time, I think it might be an idea to create two "shifts," (not a good prospect for group dynamics, however you slice it). That way, however, it might be possible to keep two people at it all the time — one to check the other — not just to make sure they stay awake but just in case one of the pair is a plant. Yes. That's still remotely in my mind.

Ah. Here's Alex now. Typical: she's a few minutes ahead....

Storing this 'til later....

Back again. In my room now, but not immediately after. In fact, checking my watch, it's been over two hours!

What a hullabaloo! And thank God Alex was on the scene when it happened. There we were, just chatting, nothing untoward happening, the shuttle image glowing on the screen, when suddenly every damn alarm bell and buzzer in the place starts up. In two seconds, I couldn't even think. In a matter of moments the other three, ripped out of their blissful sleep, joined me and Alex in Central, everyone having to yell to be heard — What's happened? What the fuck's going on? I kept my eyes glued to the screen, interpreting their questions to mean — Have we been invaded? Is the skin breached, or what?

"Nothing!" I screamed, pointing at the screen to make myself clear.

"Nothing!"

Alex leapt to the control panel. Grainger joined her. I couldn't hear what they were saying to each other: the din went on and on. Then Adam joined them. Clarke and I sat numbed while they went at it, bringing up formats and scrabbling at keyboards. How they could even think I don't know; but lucky they could — for that limited time anyway — because if they hadn't been able to stop it we'd have all gone mad.

Of course that had been NASA's intention. Fortunately, Alex was able to override the signal coming through the laser umbilicous which had been programmed like a virus to throw the alarm systems into chaos. Gradually, starting with those in Central —smart girl — she managed to turn them off. Palpable relief as we heard those in the far distance dopple down one by one.

Clarke was immediately back in control.

"Anything happening on the shuttle, Lilly?"

My eyes had been glued there.

"No. Nothing."

"I think we can expect more of this sort of thing. Will they know we've been able to override and stop it, Alex?"

"I don't think so, Clarke."

"Then quite likely they'll leave us to suffer for a while, turn their program off, then communicate with us to give in or they'll turn it on again. If that happens, pretend we're still getting tortured by it. That way they won't turn their attention to something else for a while."

"What else?" Adam asked, a bit shaky.

"We computer people should look at the independence schedules," Grainger suggested. "Wouldn't surprise me if they go after every system we haven't control over."

Adam looked scared. I guess we all did. My own heart thumped. I mean, with all the resources they have down there, it's a bit terrifying to think of what scheme they might cook up next. On the other hand, everyone realized the shuttle's window was getting narrower every day we held them off.

If only we can survive for the next week or so until they leave. Without a back-up shuttle ready, it'll take them weeks, months, before they can try again. And as Grainger said, remember the story about that early Russian astronaut who got stranded in space for nearly a year when the Soviet Union collapsed?

In a few months, who knows what might have happened to the situation down there? ～

This morning Tremaine found Rivka sitting cross-legged under the flamboyant tree, squeezing the last juice from a ripe grapefruit into her mouth and humming happily. At a party last night, right after her arrival, she cut quite a swathe through the workcrew. How the hell does she do it, traipsing around the world making programmes, teaching in her university, negotiating with the other city states — and doing it all so passionately and fully?

She grins at him and then points with the dripping fruit peel: "My boys! My lovely boys! They are here! Of course, there are girls too. They always look good in pictures with rifle straps between their tits."

He can see Grey's van drawing up to the communications shed, loaded up with the last of the Eurosoviet swat team, ferried over to the island by Neil and Sonny. Eager young things, conscious of their macho image, they jump out and look around, stretching and shaking themselves. According to Rivka, now that the other side of the Atlantic has realized the danger they may be in from the Powers-Foreman alliance, there will be scores more of these little guerrilla groups landing over the next few weeks.

"When are you leaving, Rivka?"

"Right after I do some video interviews. But there is someone who came in with our team your Lesley will be glad to see."

She throws the grapefruit peel into the bushes and gets up, smoothing her rumpled jeans down over her thighs, tipping her head up at him coquettishly.

Tremaine looks back at the group, still clumped together, as Bill goes over to greet them.

"Who do you mean?"

"Look. There he is."

As he squints in the rising sun, Bill waves at them to come over. Now Tremaine can see the slight figure detached from the others. "I'd better get Lesley."

*   *   *

"Sorry," Bill says. "I had information James had made it out to the Eurosoviets a few days ago, before Rivka arrived. I wanted nothing more than to tell you, Lesley. But I couldn't really say anything until we'd all had a chance to check him out. The Euros especially."

He runs over that part quickly, as if it is just routine, but Tremaine knows what he means.

Leslie, so happy, almost unable to unlock her arms from around James, didn't really catch the subtlety or care about it. How wonderful to see her renewed like this. And he, Tremaine, too, instinctively hilarious, yet that nagging paranoia which forces him to translate every gesture, every glance James makes, probing for certainty as he asks him questions about his departure from NASA.

How did he know Foreman's boys were on to him? He figured something was up when, the moment he got back from his supposed long-weekend vacation, they asked him whether he knew where Lesley, his aunt, was now residing. Did he still have contact with her? He figured Foreman's intelligence had come close to knowing she was with the Society in some capacity. And then, weirdly enough, one of the security officials had called him in for an interview and asked him if he'd ever heard of some organization called the Regulators. He'd never heard of them except as some vague rumour coming from the alien cults. What was that all about?

Tremaine, watching him closely, almost misses a quick flicker over Lesley's face as James mentions it. He must ask her about that. Is there something she knows about regulators that he doesn't?

"They've got some paranoia about this regulator thing," she says. "There's a special corps here to try and root them out, whoever they are."

The day before James was meant to load the virus for the swat-team raid he managed to make a quick connection with Lilly, telling her not to worry about the shuttle being launched. He wished now he hadn't done that. It would have given her false hope. But he was getting ahead of himself. First, when he returned, he realized they had moved up the shuttle launch schedule. Also there seemed to be a tremendous amount of secrecy about it, who the crew were and all that. They kept him entirely out of the loop. The complex seemed to be swarming with vastly increased security forces.

Then, the devastating thing, the day of the raid when he loaded the virus through his network computer, the way Lesley had told him, it obviously didn't take, giving back a pile of erratic error messages, nothing like he'd expected. Taking a risk, he'd asked one of the top security guys he was friendly with what all the extra security was about.

The big rumour was that Powers and Foreman had broken with each other, but of course it was all being kept quiet for the moment. Apparently something really big connected with the break between the two was connected with the imminent launch of the back-up shuttle. So that was why the whole place had been gone over, including a complete change and updating in security measures.

A little later, the offices in his zone were visited by a computer team. The local network was out of order. James figured it was because of his attempt to load the virus. Lesley nodded. That was entirely possible. They were obviously going to run an analysis and James was scared what they might find since they seemed, like everyone else, super security conscious.

He'd tried to somehow warn us all about the situation, but outside communications were temporarily suspended until after the launch. The raid was scheduled at midnight, so James decided to clear out to the Eurosoviets right away, before NASA security made a connection between the raid and his messing with the security codes. He'd boarded the airbus to Miami and then the direct to London where he got in touch with ENN. But before he left that evening he'd gone back into his office, copied a whole range of the new security codes and the laser beam co-ordinates and put them on a fiche. That way he could persuade the Euros about his authenticity.

(At this point in his tale, Tremaine reminds himself that unless the Lifeists are really dumb, they will have changed all the codes if someone who might know some of them had defected. Especially someone they had been suspicious of. And as for the laser-beam co-ordinates…well, they can also be worked out independently, with a lot of trouble mind you. Still, what else could James have brought out with him?)

That was a hell of a risk making a last trip into his office, wasn't it? Was it really necessary? And how did he manage to make contact with Rivka to get to the Eurosoviets? Tremaine is all the time studying that nervous smile for in-authenticity, that glint in James' eyes for a sudden shading as James gives his perfectly plausible answers.

God, Tremaine realizes, James has become almost anorexic, a

held-together bundle of nervous energy, thin-boned, ethereal, like a bird. What if he's gone through a bout of AIDS? Never thought of that. An experience like that could have been what converted him in the first place, if he's genuine — that glimpse into a possible black death. A seven-out-of-ten cure rate is still not the best of odds.

The encouraging part of the news James brings, however, is that internecine warfare has clearly broken out between Foreman and Powers. Inevitable in the long run, but a surprise to have it happen so soon. Rivka is going to mention it in her report. His election as President has given Foreman the impetus he needed to go it alone. Powers, however, must have suspected something because Foreman's boys have run into a lot of resistance. Foreman's ego perhaps made him move too quickly.

The whole affair, though, makes it even clearer why Foreman would have armed Earthbaby, since he can now hold the key card in any dispute with Agriminco. If only the Eurosoviets and the resistance movements can take advantage of the situation before Foreman consolidates himself, there might be a chance. When would the Lifeist crews now inhabiting Earthbaby be able to get their weaponry ready for a launch state? Getting the computers to work on that might give a good idea whether it's days or weeks. A lot depends on where Earthbaby is located in its orbit relative to the earth. Unless the trajectories are feasible, any threat to use the neutron warheads is an empty one.

Destroying the laser. That's the key. Then Foreman's crew on Earthbaby will be doomed to ride through the universe with their useless weapons forever. That threat cleared away, maybe the rest of the world will have a chance to sort out the Trans-America mess — especially if the two factions destroy each other.

Another civil war to go in the American history books: only this time on an even bigger scale. Not a happy prospect.

After lunch, Bill gets busy going over the diversionary plans with the newly-arrived swat-team. Perlita recognizes she's too shaky with post-trauma stress to be involved with anything for a while.

"I've got to get over this. I've got to get back to normal."

"You will," Leslie tells her. "Don't be hard on yourself. None of us is normal right now. You got the worst of it, and it'll take longer."

"Oh fuck. I'm okay for an hour. Maybe even two. Then it just rears up and grabs hold of me. Shakes me like a dog."

Leslie tells her, "You saved all of us you know, Perlita. You're a world treasure."

James reaches out his hand. "And you were the one who brought me home, don't forget that."

Rivka recognizes the symptoms and is very loving towards her. A little while before she leaves, she asks Perlita whether she wants to go with her, have a holiday and recover. Bill thinks it's a great idea, but Perlita will have nothing of it, not wanting to leave him.

"Look," Bill assures her, "what we have to do here will be over in a week or so. I'll come join you then. In the meantime we can keep in touch."

Perlita, clasping tight to him begins sobbing, realizing she is useless, perhaps even a drag on the operation though nobody would say so.

"Okay. I always wanted to see St. Petersburg."

At sunset, Perlita and Rivka make their departure in Grey's van.

"See you in the movies!" Rivka yells, a couple of the work crew running alongside the window kissing her goodbye.

With the laser-generating equipment Rivka has brought in, the simulation of the NASA complex is now projectable. This means they can produce what Lesley calls an "emulation," a virtual reality walk through. The first swat-team had used it in training for their unsuccessful raid.

"I wonder," she murmurs, "whether we can use it on the actual raid. You know, the way I used it to create false environments on historic sites."

"Let's think about that," he says. "Maybe something will occur to us when we fire it all up tomorrow."

They walk with the exhausted James who is to bed down in the communications shed. Tremaine remembers being there his first night in the camp, Perlita gone away from him. Poor old Bill looks a little abandoned too now she is gone. But it's also a relief for him not to have to worry about her every moment. Tired as he looks, Tremaine knows Bill will be waiting up to hear from Rivka that Perlita's arrived safe and sound.

Tremaine puts his arm around Leslie, his new-found love, and they stroll outside.

"I'm over the hard part of all this, especially with James alive and well," she tells him. "Now I can concentrate on loving you for a while."

He hugs her. "Until the next crisis. At least we're together in all this."

With his hand on her hip — the way they walked through the camp together before the first time he made love with her — he's once again thrilled with how unique she is.

They've come to the end of the scrub, standing under the dark portico of a giant cottonwood at the edge of the forest. Turning, arms linked and close, they gaze at the last hint of sunset behind the camp. Some of the crew are singing quietly to a guitar round a fire over by the dig where the copter is hidden. As full dark descends, the Milky Way haloes the universe directly above them and they move against each other, old body memories making it natural and unconsidered. The cushioning of her belly and breasts breaks something open in him.

"Slowly," she says, hands on the back of his neck, pulling his mouth onto hers. "Slowly so I can relish every damn beautiful…"

That very moment, a soft explosion destroys the fuel and equipment shed.

A shock wave eases past like heavy surf. They cry out, falling. Another rush of air, oven-hot and deafening washes over them.

They are still alive. Under thick trees. On their backs looking up. Debris, alight, insanely beautiful, like flocks of burning birds. A yellow Sikorski churns right through the warm and wounded air above them, moving in.

Tremaine gets himself up and squats, thinking: "This is it. This thought in my mind is the thing that we must do to stay alive here."

Then, focused, no other thought, with Leslie running with him — did they speak? she seems to know his thought as clear as he does — Tremaine skirts the edges of the smoking turmoil and all the suddenly lit-up spaces, keeping to the forest edge until they are above the little cliff behind the dig — the lightly covered copter just below. Recklessly they jump and land beside it, flinging the largest fronds aside. "Get in!"

Work, damn you! The blades churn into life, flinging off the last camouflage. He counts a desperate pounding twenty seconds utter minimum of warm-up and pulls the harness down. They rise, rise up above the smoking camp, hearts pounding as another copter passes right across them almost in collision but ignoring them.

"They think we're one of them," she yells. "We look the same."

At this he turns the searchlights on like all the rest. There are three or four of them he figures, sent in to mop up, but leery of the smoke and night and near collisions like his own. Cruising low, he senses that the other copters' lights are all above him, staying safely out of it. If that's the case....

He goes back down again into the smoke, remembering to turn on the air filters; then he slips sideways towards the billowing heart of the destruction until the luminous orange of the fires below reach up to them and the craft vaults away like some instinctive animal in the violent surge of the updraft. A sudden clarity as they break out of the lower level of the smoke column close to ground where a dangerous inrush of clear air drawn in to feed the fire threatens to carry them into it. But he holds off by driving into the teeth of it.

Above, the smoke palls out, concealing them. If he can stay down low across the small plateau, keep his copter tree high and follow the forest on down the mountain slope, that plume of smoke will hide them till they reach the deep night shadows of the valley chains. Below, the ground is clearly visible in his lights, tussock grass, bushes, erratic stones, the jeep trail...

...the jeep! No. It's Grey's expedition van, jammed with the swat-team crew. They hear the copter and react — an immediate spray of gunshots pinging off his armoured undersides. A stray bullet might damage the stabilizer vanes. Flash memory of his spinning plunge into the sea — his heart makes a violent bump in his chest, causing his fingers to tingle, a few angina tics down his left arm. Tremaine swings quickly away.

"I'll land ahead of them and get out so they can see me."

"No! Some of them hardly know you."

True. Besides the van is almost safe into the forest. Almost. Bad luck because his copter being here has drawn another one over to see what's going on. They too must have seen the van.

He twists right round putting himself between the other pilot and the van, then accelerating straight towards him on a ramming course. It veers off and climbs away, but remains dancing around him. Tremaine can imagine how they are trying to identify him — this idiot playing chicken like that — or attempting to make contact on the radio, getting more suspicious by the moment.

"The van's clear," Lesley yells.

Sure enough. On its way now under the forest canopy. Impossible for the other copters to track it, even with the best of lights.

"Let's get out of here!"

But then there's another copter, dancing on the other side of him, lights aimed straight onto them so that Lesley is eerily illuminated, her face in the sharp shadows a death's head. Is he going to end it all in a crashing copter after all? His plan to skedaddel down the hill over the forest under the cover of the smoke and into the dark valleys is no good now. He guns straight back into the smoke and confusion, catching the others by surprise.

They're on to him, though. A dash of small arms fire rattles off the copter's belly again. He has to keep over them or the next few rounds will come through the perspex windows or blow off the tail. Oh shit! Another one! This time straight on top of him coming out of the smoke. He's saved by a fresh billow of smoke pluming up from the fire. Something else catching fire. He can't see, but down, down he thinks. Get the damn thing down and we'll make a run for it. The jeep. That might still be there.

He's in and out of the main plume, subject again to the crazy winds of the roaring fuel fire. He can tell when the others are above him by their blasts of light. His own lights at last reveal the ground and he drops onto it, a touch too fast and canting too far to one side because of the side-draft. They land with a clunk, and he holds his breath as they almost tip over. Lesley is already opening the hatch, as he undoes himself from the harness. Then they are out of there, running, coughing.

They stumble instinctively away from the centre of the noxious fumes, until gasping, wretching, they breath easier and Lesley bangs into a rope. It's a line still holding one of the crew's collapsed tents. A wonder it hasn't yet caught fire. If the jeep's anywhere at all, it must be by the communications shed. Unless James and some others got away in it.

They trot that way, trying to see through streaming eyes, panting. Yes. The jeep is there. Tremaine reaches it, turns to look for her… Too late.

All around her, now around him — armed men — in the reddened light looking as if they have sprung from the ground — sprung up from dragon's teeth the fire has sown there….

SOCIAL DYNAMICS RESEARCH PROJECT: EARTHBABY
(JOURNAL OF LILLITH SHAWNADITHIT)

Emotionally exhausted. The others sprawl in various attitudes on whatever dry patch of grainy vermiculite they find between immaculate orchard trees. I monopolize this bower where I sat the other day with Adam while I type this out — removed from them. I think: this is the first time Adam's garden has been actually inhabited. We are its animals. Our walk-about space suits, like discarded skins, hang carefully from hydroponic supply lines. We monitor our movements and our breathing, hoping to conserve oxygen now we're reduced to what little these plants recycle while the station remains locked in the twilight of shield mode.

I should, of course, be trying to record all this objectively, but I find my consciousness fixing on the outrageous pistil of a banana tree flower, the glorious energy of a fountaining palm tree. What a consolation we living things derive from other living things — despite the fact their existence is genetically engineered and rigidly cloned.

This analytical writing part of me, producing these inadequate words, seems trivial when I think of the ultimate mystery of existence itself. If only there were singing birds, feathers iridescing as their throats turn to the sun. (And will I ever see such achingly beautiful life-forms again?) I hear this removed, professional part of me saying, *a keening of consciousness such as you are experiencing, my dear girl, often attends a state of life and death emergency.* Doubtless.

Now we've traveled much further along the critical path begun by our decision to resist the shuttle's docking, we find ourselves stripped down to essentials: technical ones (since we've become exiled into the only inhabitable part of Earthbaby), and emotional ones (at the point where the hard part begins and the true stuff shows). I know there will be a great psychological boost once the shuttle's dark shadow, like a clinging vampire, lifts off our throat and hastens towards the native soil of Earth. Why it hasn't already left is surprising. Perhaps they think we might break at the last minute.

Only another thirty minutes before their window closes, that's what Grainger and Alex have estimated. At this hour, in our programmed night-time, we should all be safely snug in bed in our cabins; but in this never-completely-darkened biosphere we are all awake.

I check my watch again. Half an hour, half an hour. What more can they do to us? If nothing, then we will survive, recover, even without the laser umbilicus to feed us. But we are on the edge. If it hadn't been for Alex and Grainger anticipating, and working through the days and nights.... And Adam, of course, with his Garden, our sanctuary: dear Clarke a focus of confidence and leadership. And Myself?

Keep writing. Tell how, when the bastards thought we had to have been driven mad by the constant alarms, they contacted us. Aha, but we had won that one already and were confident — practically sneering at their ineptitude and bombastic frustration.

Imagine our consternation when, sitting down to supper, we noticed the artificial gravity field begin slowly weakening as the dynamos ran down. We managed to hold down our panic until a lifted glass of milk spilled upwards and threatened to drown Alex as her indrawn breath sucked its loosened molecules into her nose and throat. So this was their next trick. Since they were deprived of a gravity shit, I guess they figured we should be too.

It was far less scary, however, than you would think. Once everyone's vaso-vagal system had adjusted to it, we found it quite amusing to be able to float about touching things up in the dome area which we had never touched before. When Grainger cupped his hand behind my neck and scooped me into a face-to-face embrace with him, I couldn't help remembering that fantastic time we had months ago in the gravity-free hyperbaric chamber. I was looking forward to bedtime, in fact, although the problems of a gravity-free existence in the body of the station were going to be complex to handle if this became our permanent living situation.

Already a variety of objects were littering the airspace. I hated to think what might be going on in our individual cabins and the clinic, so I went to investigate. There wasn't much I could do. Each one was a dreadful mess, even Clarke's which had been the neatest originally. The damage was especially worse in terms of left-open bottles of creams and liquids, not to mention items of clothing and bedding, razors, toothbrushes....We would have to spend some time in a ruthless clean-up and securing operation.

So much for that. I returned to find Clarke and Adam flying about sucking up stray droplets from the atmosphere with dustbusters. Grainger and Alex, trying to hold themselves steady by pressing their knees to the underside of monitoring consoles, were trying to manipulate floating keyboards moored, luckily, by their expansion cords to the fixed-down computers. One of the monitors had gone adrift and I could see Alex swipe at it to bring it back to her. The two unsecured chairs at that console had gone astray and had been ushered into the upper reaches of the centre to keep them out of the way.

Well, again they did it, those two. Apparently they found a way to access an emergency back-up system which the NASA boys were unable to completely disable. All well and good, but the mess, including those two chairs, started raining down on us since the system re-established itself quite rapidly and things which were temporarily stuck up high suddenly broke loose with the increase of gravity. Still, what a cheer went up from us! What a boost to our sense of invulnerability!

It was only a vague headache and dullness an hour later which made me groggily realize something else was amiss. I might not have got to the point of actually figuring it out completely if the CO_2 alarms hadn't started to beep. Scary was not the word for it. Clarke managed to keep us fairly cool, ordering us back into the spilled litter of our cabins to don our oxygen-supplied walk-about space suits. From the clinic I grabbed several other oxygen cylinders and we put our heads together to garner other air supplies: from the space buggy, from the supply cylinders for the hyperbaric chamber: everything we could think of.

It was Adam who gave us the best news. He'd rerouted the oxygen monitoring units so air produced by the garden was no longer being recirculated throughout the entire station. Instead of mixing with the oxygen production system (which NASA had cut off), it was now being retained in the garden area at a higher concentration. By sealing off the garden area, we could assure ourselves of a relatively self-generating oxygen supply. This depended, though, on getting out of the shield mode which we could do once the shuttle had gone and the plant's photosynthesis rate could speed up again. In the meantime, we left Alex and Grainger, suited up in the airless centre, to try getting the auxiliary oxygen supply back on again. The rest of us lugged all the air cylinders we had collected into the garden.

This time, no luck. Foreman's boys had us. Grainger and Alex came back looking grim as they divested themselves of their suits.

"Lack of oxygen is not necessarily our main problem," Adam reminded us. In the long term, it's the incapacity of the garden to absorb enough CO_2 that could do us in — unless plant synthesis is increased by getting out of shield mode. Then the garden could do the job normally done by the CO_2 scrubbers in the air replenishment system."

Clarke checked his watch.

"We'll get out of that mode as soon as that damn shuttle takes off."

So here we are. Waiting for them to leave. Watching the minutes draining away. All secretly contemplating the primitive future we might have on the station from here on, totally relying on the viability of these growing green things, desperately dependent on their not dying of some weird, as-yet-unknown disease. Fertilizing them ultimately, with our own feces as nutrients. Not a very pretty picture. On the other hand it does seem strangely simple and concentrated.

I watch my timepiece. So, too, do the others. Leave, damn you. Leave so that at least we can get out of this blasted shield mode into the full light of day, so to speak, in which these plants will thrive and save us. Christ. They're cutting it close. Do they believe by now we are dead? Doubtful. They know the CO_2 alarms would have sounded and we would have taken some kind of emergency measures — if only getting into our space-suits. This part, though, taking sanctuary in Adam's garden, they may not have figured out.

You would think they would have tried to contact us again with a last attempt to blackmail us into letting them in. Pretty callous of them to return to Earth knowing we would soon run out of oxygen and die of suffocation. I guess that would make it easier for the next crew to come equipped and ready to blast their way in and throw our dead bodies into the forever darkness of space. Bastards!

Seconds to go now. Everyone is up on their feet, wondering.

"They're not going," Grainger says.

Head in hands, we wait five minutes, just in case.

No. They don't go.

"They can stay in that thing for weeks, until the next window," Clarke says.

All eyes on Adam now.

"I give these plants — and us — about two days if we stay in shield mode."

We all look at each other.

Now what? ❧

If he's going to die, Tremaine thinks, better he should have taken his chances with Lesley in the helicopter. Being blasted out of the air would have been quick and active, the way Jock went — poor bastard — not even knowing. God how he misses him.

How fucking ridiculous he should go like this — executed by some brainless louts in total obscurity. And not even able to say anything brave and noble to anyone who matters...Lesley especially...his heart and mind threaten to collapse when he thinks of what they might be putting her through. And then his wonderful daughter. Perhaps when this has all passed she will come to this place and find out what happened, from whoever survives. Perlita for instance. What luck she went off with Rivka. And Bill? Did he get away with Grey and the others in the van? Then there was James. That was a hard one to figure out. Surely a lot of people must have been killed in last night's conflagration.

There's been a lot of activity in the camp — bright lights run by growling generators, heavy truck motors, copters landing and taking off. Over the hours his brain has been registering it all, trying to make some narrative sense of what was happening.... And waiting.

And all night too he has tried to keep the image of Lesley's face as they pulled her away from him, the last squeeze of her hand, her command to him: don't despair. But he is despairing.

Dawn light filtering through the shuttered windows means he can see better. That's less frightening. Despite everything, he must have drifted off for a while. Blessed unconsciousness. He should try to get back to it, gather whatever strength he can. Voices in the adjoining copper room must have woken him. Manacled as he is to this iron bedstead, he cannot turn enough to look directly in there. He can only see the cathode flicker of TV monitors through the half-open door. He listens.

"Fucking disloyalists. You wait and see, Mich, once I put the report in on them, the boss ain't likely to use those assholes again."

Disloyalists? Who are they talking about?

"Whaddya thinka that shit they give us, eh chief? All that crap about some flare hitting the fuel shed by accident, so they can't put down in the smoke? Oh sure!"

"Yeah. Nice way to give the whole camp warning so they can clear out and the bastards don't have to fight them. Very convenient."

"Right. Too fuckin' chicken to get grounded. Then they woulda have to take on that fucking Euro swat team."

"I'm gonna say in our report our agriminco boys coulda done better in a couple armoured APC's. Then that fucking swat team wouldn't a got away."

"You're right there, Chief. That's Lifeguard training for you, eh. No fucking initiative, all herd mentality."

"Just plain yellow, more like it. Why d'yer think those copter divisions come over from Foreman's side to Agriminco's in the first place? Because they know the wind's blowing our way, that's all. Never trust none of these disloyalists, I say."

So that's what's happening, Tremaine thinks. Foreman's helicopter divisions have defected to Powers — thus, *disloyalists*. A big move. Useful to quell uprisings. And the raid wasn't meant to be such a fiery debacle. Was it just the swat team they were after? Or was it Bill and the rest, including himself?

"So. It's just about time. You wanna go in and get the guy ready?"

"Why don't we both go. You never know with these kind of guys. They can go crazy and land a couple. It'll be easier with two."

"Yeah. I'll be glad when this is over with. This place gives me the creeps."

Tremaine's body goes into extreme alarm. A fear-sweat breaks out over his chest and abdomen as he tries to jerk upright. He strains to lift his head, sees the two men coming in, coming striding quickly towards his bunk as he lies helpless. Backlit by the window, their faces are in darkness. One holds a devastator. Are they going to kill him?

Not yet. One stands with the weapon while the other undoes his manacles. Thank God. No quick shot in the head as he lies there. At least he will be able to walk upright. Yes. They are lifting him off the bed. Holding tight to each arm. Nauseous and dizzy he doesn't resist. Let them think they have nothing to worry about....an old man....offering no resistance....going along with them.

Meanwhile he is breathing, gathering oxygen into himself. He will wait. He will be compliant, until the moment it's clear there's nothing else to be done. And then... At least he will take one or both of them if he gets half a chance. He will go out yelling in their faces....

Into the copper room with its eerie ghost reflections. He looks over to that section of the copper wall where Lesley's image had been mirrored every day as she worked with him at her keyboard. He had come to fancy the copper had been etched with her likeness. Appropriate to have it end here then, where it more or less started.

Now he can see the two men guarding him are not in any kind of military uniform. Something familiar about them though. Both with that old corporate look sporting mafia-style ties. Ah. Now he knows. These are Powers' boys. Agriminco security. Maybe from Powers' personal elite corps.

One good thing. They haven't treated him particularly roughly. If he remembers the psychology of such things, they usually beat you around quite a bit if they mean to kill you. Kind of working themselves up to it. You never know.

Now they've dropped him into a chair and are putting on those damn manacles again. This is the worst part: being so defenseless. They can do anything they want to you. A wave of dizziness overwhelms him so he has to lean forward. His heart is yammering badly again and a pain tic is beginning to stroll down his left arm, numbing his fingers. Not a good sign.

The thing about pain and fear, Jock once said to him — that was when he was being carried around strapped to a board — is that it throws you inside yourself. That's the real horror of it, because it's the same as going crazy. You lose touch with the outside world, with reality, with other people. The more you can think yourself outside of yourself, and the more you can project yourself inside other people, the better you can handle it. Okay, Jock. I'll try it. You —, you're gone, Jock. You know what it's all about. Now it's my turn. Every one gets a turn.

He draws a deep breath and tries to think of Lesley. If only he could get that old familiar surge of anger coming from his guts that would save him from this state of terrified helplessness.

One of the men sets up a tripod. Then mounts a camera on it. So, they're going to video him? Why the hell would they do that?

"Hey!" he yells, getting the cameraman's attention. "What the hell is going on here, eh?"

Saying something makes him feel better. Somehow he managed to get that authoritarian tone into it he would occasionally summon up as head of NASA. The guy looks up and is about to answer when the one behind Tremaine warns, "Don't fraternize, Mich. He'll find out soon enough."

Tremaine twists himself, dragging the chair around enough so he can see the other one. Hugely built, this one definitely looks familiar.

"I'm sure I know you," he says.

Then it hits him. This is one of Powers' henches, one of those who hoisted the old guy and his care-chair into Jock's place at the Earthbaby launch.

"You're a Powers' man. You were with him at NASA during the shuttle launch."

The two men look at each other. Mich raises his eyebrows and grins as if to say: so what's the big deal if he knows who we work for?

"Listen. Just let me know one thing, What's happened to Leslie? You know, the woman who was with me?"

Mich looks up from adjusting the camera. He'd be willing to say, but his boss isn't.

"All in good time. Better you keep quiet, understand?"

Something in his tone, though, gives Tremaine hope.

Now he notices they have set up a large hologram screen. Mich is bending over the camera again. This time Tremaine suddenly sees himself on a monitor. He thinks of Bill, the interview with him at the launch site, getting passed the society's number. A lot has happened since then.

Then the large hologram screen scintillates with the image of another suit-and-tie Powers' hench.

"You guys about ready there?"

"All set."

"Okay. We want an I.D. first. Get him to say something."

"Tell him who you are," demands the big hench behind him.

"I'm Andrew Tremaine. Still, Goddammit, Chief Director of NASA corporation. And I want to go on record as saying I am being detained completely illegally."

"Voice print positive. It's him all right."

"Yeah. We figured we had the right guy too."

The on-screen hench turns his back to them, looking behind him into the void of the hologram screen space.

"Do you wish to speak to him now, sir?"

For a moment the screen goes blank, then there's Powers himself — President of Agriminco — ultimate, and now *only* corporate conglomerate in the American Protectorates of Trans-America. It's a flattering half-view of him, legs kept out of it, sitting in his care-chair.

Tremaine's inner terror loosens a few notches. If Powers intends to talk to him directly, chances of a whimsical low-level torture and execution drop considerably. He knows a lot about men like Powers. They attend to you only when they want something.

"Mr. Tremaine. The genuine article. So your appearances on ENN and Worldnet were not merely an electronic replication as General Foreman believed. I told him he was wrong."

The voice is firm and clear. Too firm and clear and not quite how Tremaine remembers it. His suspicions are aroused. What if this image isn't Powers? What if this is an electronic replication, like Foreman clearly thought he was himself?

"Oh, I'm still alive all right. No thanks to you and Foreman."

"I understand, Mr. Tremaine, you were almost shot down by my helicopter squad. You lead a charmed life."

Maybe the extra tone in Powers' voice is just normal enhancement public figures always use on the media to give their voices more resonance and depth. So now it's definite that Powers has indeed inherited what was once Foreman's helicopter squad.

"You and General Foreman have hardly contributed to my survival. For that I have others to thank."

"I take it you are referring to that unfortunate accident of several months ago. It's a far-reaching assumption to claim it was sabotage, don't you think? I must say I was shocked to see your treasonous slanders of the leaders of your nation on Worldnet, and appalled at how misguidedly you let yourself be used as a pawn for Society propaganda."

Amazing. Powers — if that really is Powers — actually believes what he is saying.

Over many years spent among the extremely rich and powerful, Tremaine has learned to recognize that for such people the construction of a virtual reality constantly maintained by sycophants and like-minded colleagues is a self-deluding necessity. Orwell's double-think isn't something the rulers impose on the masses. It's something they impose on themselves. Powers needs to criminalize and demonize him, to put him on the defensive. No use arguing.

One thing is certain. At this particular moment he is completely at Powers' mercy, unless some elaborate game is being played with him and this isn't Powers at all. Whatever the case, he himself must retain the illusion of strength. He adopts a business-like tone.

"I have compelling evidence — even from General Foreman's own aides — that both Jock and myself were meant to be murdered to clear the way for the militarization of NASA and the use of Earthbaby as a doomsday weapon."

"If there was a plot against you, I had nothing to do with it. I always feel violence is the last resort of bad management."

"My sources also tell me that since his election you and the General have fallen out with each other."

That's taken the old bastard off-guard. Tremaine searches for a trace of emotion on the wizened face of this ancient autocrat. In his youth he had been dashing, bold, multi-talented — a fine musician and athlete — if the profiles coming out of his own media monopoly can be believed. Then the dreadful polo accident in Argentina, only a few years before development of nerve re-growth techniques which would have saved him. Now he is reduced to this hard old ego, given to the single pleasure of being right.

While Tremaine has been studying him, Powers has gone into one of his characteristic rants. This has to be the real McCoy, no-one can fake it like this.

"Historically, the problem with management has always been the over-diffusion of decision making. Take the triumvirate of Caesar, Pompey and Crassus. Caesar, of course, realized the advantage of unitary management..."

Powers judo-chops the arm of his care-chair for emphasis as Tremaine saw him do at the launch. That must need re-upholstering frequently.

"....after the treachery that brought him down, Rome was never as powerful again."

What a ludicrous performance. Tremaine is overcome at last by a deep and abiding anger over how a great part of the world has come to kowtow to such as these. His greatest desire is to live to see their downfall.

"Treachery, Mr. Powers? I take it you are referring to General Foreman?"

That has struck home. Before Powers can say anything more, Tremaine adds, "With his control of Earthbaby — which I now know was illegally armed — Foreman holds the trump card in any negotiations. Unfortunately, our team was unable to prevent the back-up shuttle launch and the replacement of our original crew."

Powers remains silent, staring fixedly. So he's been thrown off his script, has he? One for the good guys, he thinks inanely, almost bursting out laughing as the thought rattles around in his over-excited brain.

"Yes. Quite a campaign you've waged, Mr. Tremaine. Quite an entrepreneurial spirit. Especially given the rag-tag resources at your disposal. I'd like to remind you, however, that I class your actions as treacherous also. Nevertheless, I may be prepared to forgive and forget under certain conditions."

Ah, here it comes. Tremaine is momentarily ashamed at the flood of relief. But how much does he know? Does he know about their planned attack on NASA? And what about Lesley? Have they got anything from her?

He forces himself to remain silent rather than to ask any revealing questions. Keep the body still. Pretend great composure. Not that it makes any difference. He does it for himself.

Powers taps the arms of his chair, thinking.

"I say to myself, Mr. Tremaine here, is a man who knows more about the deep-space orbiter and about the functioning of NASA than anyone alive. How can I use him in the best interests of the American protectorates and the world at large? What common interest might I find with him of mutual benefit to all so that his rehabilitation may lead to a peaceful retirement in his declining years?"

Playing with him. Enjoying himself. Tremaine lifts his chin high, pulls his shoulders back, makes his voice as strong as he can. He knows he's still in shock, but now he can feel again that welcome adrenaline flow as the full depth of his panic subsides and nausea in his stomach abates.

"If you are talking about the destruction of Earthbaby, Mr. Powers. There may still be a way. But before I agree to any mutual collaboration, I must insist my collaborator, who was illegally detained at the same time as myself, be released immediately and brought to me unharmed."

Powers allows himself a little smile.

"You will be informed shortly of the terms and conditions of your probation, Mr. Tremaine. In the meantime, make sure you know who is standing behind you."

Another tiny smile flickers on the old man's face and the screen goes blank.

Standing behind him?

Mich has the shackles' keys in his hand, ready to free him.

"Mr. Powers likes his little jokes," he says, then twists his chair around.

Two other men are standing in the doorway.

Between them, smiling at him, is Lesley.

Adam's two-days estimate was too short. We've survived twice that. Despite being in shield mode, the plants proved hardier than he expected, processing a greater amount of the accumulating CO_2 into useable oxygen — which, in turn, we consumed at a slower rate than anyone predicted. But a few hours ago, with the CO_2 levels rising because of the plants' slowed-down photosynthesis, we had to get back into our suits and breathe from cylinders.

Given the stress we're under, we've become intensely aware how vulnerable we are in this hi-tech virtual oasis. Normally, we Spacelings don't let ourselves think too much about the systems keeping us alive; or we would become paralyzed with anxiety attacks like the one Clark had a while ago. In emergency situations, though, the research tells us that high adaptives, which most space crews tend to be, will temporarily de-intensify their ego-survival instincts in favour of an intense intellectual engagement with material situational problems. On one level, having never experienced such a crisis until now, I find a curious intellectual satisfaction in having the theoretical data confirmed.

As the hours passed over the last three days, though, I found another adaptive syndrome beginning to operate in myself which has a curiously poignant ambivalence. Occasionally, I found my *primitive* instincts over-riding my *intellect* — urging me, against all logic, to feel secure and at ease. Is there some hard wiring in our gene pool which gives us this built-in response to warmth, lush vegetation, organic smells, even though — as in our case — we know the whole bag is patently artificial? I suppose this is at the same level as imprinting ducklings to think Labrador dogs are their mothers. What a dream it would be to laze like weary nomads in an authentic paradise of this kind that once actually existed. Imagine that first true Eden.

But it's all gone, hasn't it? That's the poignant part — just like coral reefs and caribou herds... Oh God, how miserable to think we will all probably die here — in Adam's ersatz attempt to recover a semblance of it.

Once it was clear the shuttle intended waiting for the next window to leave, a debate started about what to do next. I haven't the strength of will to analyze the dynamics of this discussion fully. In fact, reading through the first couple of paragraphs of this journal, I can't believe I've just written such semi-formal academic tripe.

To be honest, I don't give a shit any more. What I would really like to do is become a Viking berserker and murder every one of Foreman's men in revenge for killing Jock. Then spend the rest of my days fucking the hell out of Grainger — and/or Clark, Adam, whoever, for that matter. (Are you coolly assessing my state of mind, oh future clinical reader? Or will I reach some deeper part of your consciousness with this tangled narrative?)

All right. Let's take hold of ourselves here.

Nothing in the debate we had surprised me. Adam, understanding that it was *his* project and *his* expertise that was crucial to us, began to assume more of a leadership role. Interesting to see how circumstances have re-motivated him since we talked. He was strongly in favour of having one or more of us suiting up and going back into Central Control to take off the shield mode so the plants — his special loyalty of course — could step up their photosynthesis. Clarke was inclined to go along with him, feeling we could take our chances with repelling boarders so to speak — the direct military approach (naturally). God, how horrible it is to be able to predict people's tendencies like this. Alex, (ever-cautious and tending to be counter-suggestive though never openly confrontational) threw in her line: "They have weapons, but we don't."

"Actually," Clarke informed us, "we do. One anyway. As expedition commander I was issued a small arms AP."

We all swallowed on that one, but didn't require an explanation once we thought about it. What if someone had got space-fever and gone totally crazy? "AP means Anti-Personnel," Grainger informed Adam, who, startled, raised his eyebrows in what I found a comical expression. What an awkward specimen he is.

"I've kept it locked in my cabin, of course. Up to now, that is."

Clarke reached into his jacket and produced it.

"Well, well," Grainger chuckled wryly. "I can't say I'm completely surprised. I might as well tell you I was also issued one by Agriminco."

He produced it.

I thought, Oh spare me! Two alpha males producing their potency totems. In other circumstances it would have been funny, especially when Grainger commented: "It's a little more high-tech than yours, Clarke. The latest Destructo-Cone: takes out everything in an area about ten by ten."

Clarke looked around at each of us. "Is there anyone else?"

Adam burst out, "Who the hell would *need* one?"

We looked then at Alex. She made a slight grimace and shrugged. Not her? I looked at her sharply. Hmm. She was the least transparent of the whole crew. There was something about her I couldn't fathom. But my suspicious instincts had always proven to be unfounded by the way she actually behaved. Then they all looked at *me*.

"Hey! Are you kidding?"

Clarke grinned. "You *are* the Social Dynamics officer, Lilly. And let's face it, you have everything you need to know about all of us. More than we might know about ourselves, in fact."

He said that affectionately, referring of course to the intimacy that had been between us when he crashed out. In fact, I felt very loving toward him — especially in these poignant circumstances. It must have showed in my look because his gaze lit up for a fleeting moment with a sweet, sad look of gratitude.

"People in my trade are supposed to rely entirely on their manipulative charisma. And the drug cabinet, of course."

Then Alex threw in her bombshell.

"Okay. So we have two weapons, wielded by two competent — but if you excuse my saying so — not exactly ruthless swat-team-calibre professionals. Clearly, the moment we begin to use these weapons in any way, we become justifiable homicides for Foreman's shuttle crew who outnumber us and outgun us. So I don't see us winning that one and getting out alive. There's only one chance to survive as I see it. And that's by simply surrendering."

She had voiced what all of us had been thinking since the shuttle hadn't left and we knew our air would eventually run out.

Clarke coughed nervously. "Well, that's certainly something to think about."

Grainger sat, still hefting his destructo-cone.

"Okay. Let's think about it, then. Personally, I'm sure Alex is right in one respect. We are outnumbered and outgunned, and in any face-to-face square-off we'd probably lose. But that's not the way it's likely to work. We do have the choice of battlefield, and know our own terrain. If we do have to engage them it will be in a form of guerrilla warfare. So, as to your point we are doomed to lose in a shoot-out, I think we'd have a better chance than you think."

"I'm not exactly assured by your male posturing here, Grainger," Alex scoffed.

"Call it what you like. My argument still stands and I think Clarke, as a military man, will back me up on this."

Clarke did indeed nod in reluctant agreement.

"And what romantic notion, Alex, makes you think these guys are going to accept our surrender? Don't forget they've shut down our air supply with the sole aim of killing us off. Oh, they might want to keep you and Lilly around for a while, of course."

That last part shocked her, shocked me, because I knew it would be true, whether or not they decided to ash the lot of us.

Alex clenched her hands and caught her breath.

"You're making unfounded assumptions, Grainger. They may not have thought of our going into Adam's garden, but they'd assume we'd get into our suits and breathe whatever supplies we've got. They're just escalating the distress so we'll give in and let them board — as they have all along."

Pointlessly, I uttered, "If only we could hold out another week."

Adam looked over to our cache of remaining air cylinders.

"Impossible unless we go out of shield mode."

I knew from Grainger's face that his adrenaline was kicking in. He was all fired up to use that destructo-cone.

"Come on, Grainger," Alex challenged him. "Would you really be prepared to use that thing?"

Cunning little devil. Grainger flushed. "Well, if I really have to…"

But the damage had been done. Adam was coming round to her side.

"Maybe Alex is right. I know we made a pact to resist. But at that time our lives were not clearly at stake as they are now."

"You're damn right circumstances have changed," Grainger argued. "Not just up here, but down there too. Who knows what's really been going on? These bastards don't give a shit about us now. We're just a few extra kilos of troublesome protein mass to them. If they don't ash us with a couple of these, they'll just set us adrift out there…."

Yes. Out there…with those Eurosoviet astronauts. I think I saw

Alex flinch a little at the memory.

That Grainger was probably right in his assessment of the Foreman boys' ruthlessness struck me forcibly. I thought of how they had callously disposed of Jock, then probably Tremaine and James. The others would not have the personal knowledge and the anger drive I had, of course. When Alex asked Grainger whether he would really use his weapon, I knew what my answer would be and it rather shocked me, but also made me feel clean and clear.

I guess it was natural for the others — to some extent or another — to go into denial over the fact that someone could quite arbitrarily and whimsically eliminate them as sensate beings. Or that one of us would be capable of doing so. It did seem ludicrous. But I was convinced we had nothing to lose, so I bent myself, with all my skill and subtle influence, to bring them round to Grainger's point of view. I knew I was getting there when Alex kept saying, "I don't see the logic in this. Nothing makes sense. I just want to get through this somehow." I still can't fathom her.

Adam fell back on his only certainty. "Fuck! All I know is the plants will die and so will we if we don't get out of this shield mode the moment the CO_2 level gets into the red zone."

Finally, after another hour or so, I took a chance.

Clarke had said practically nothing compared to the rest of us. I looked around at them all.

"Look, we all have our particular jobs and specialties as part of this crew. It strikes me this is Clarke's call. Can we all agree we'll go along with what Clarke decides one way or the other?"

Each of them thought about it and nodded in turn. I made them all put hands together, pledging. Then I sat back.

I could tell it was agonizing for him, but Clarke did magnificently.

"First, if we do surrender, we don't have to do it right away. That simply cuts our chances. I'm going on the old adage, 'if in doubt, do nothing.' That's because circumstances might change again. Perhaps to our advantage. Our strategy should be to stretch out our resources to the limit — Adam, we'll go with your expertise here — then we'll unshield and play it by ear…resisting any boarding attempts and playing for time. Unless that shuttle is really oversupplied — and it might be — they'll have to take the next window out. All agreed?"

Adam was fully swung over. Alex, pale, nodded. Bad thoughts on my part, I know, but I couldn't help thinking: I hope she doesn't let us down....

All that was four days ago. And except for being in our suits, using up air, nothing has changed. A black blotch, the shuttle still clings to us. We are down to the last few full cylinders. But what's really crucial is the plants' declining ability to photosynthesize which Adam has been checking almost minute by minute. Should they begin to die off, then there's no chance for us, no matter what the circumstances.

I see him now, looking at his instruments, fretting. Then he looks up. I can tell before he speaks that this is it.

"It's right on the edge. Another half an hour, whatever, and they'll all start dying back."

No sense discussing it. We save our breath. Grainger is the one to go. Clarke removes Grainger's partly used air cylinder and insists he replace it with one of the last full ones.

I'm stopping this for a moment. Need to touch him. Look in his eyes... remind him to take his weapon....

...By now, he'll be in Central Control.

Typing this at this moment, I must admit I do so in a strange air of unreality. During the discussion — four days ago now — we were not yet in our suits. We were able to see and touch each other if we wanted. In fact, Grainger and I made hasty love in the shield-mode twilight last night while the others slept. I remember that last excruciating orgasm, and the guilt afterwards that we had used up more than our portion of the remaining oxygen.

Now we are all separate from each other behind our visors. And when we speak to each other there's no directionality to the sound. It just comes into our ears. In fact we don't even bother to look at each other when we speak, just sit still and mutter back and forth as little as possible. Typing is not as awkward as I thought, since we're not pressurized and I don't have to wear gloves. The cylinders we have on our backs, though, — plus a that last few propped in a cache where we can all see them — is the sum total of the breathable air that remains.

We wait. What if Foreman's men somehow managed to get into Central...and Grainger's run into them...?

But now.... Aah! Grainger's activated the unshielding. It begins, like a slow dawn cutting into our twilight.

How welcome the sight of it! Oh God, let there be light, and light for us all at the end of it .... ∾

T he thought crosses Tremaine's mind he could ram the copter's throttle wide open and belt into the black hills surrounding the Agriminco complex. Not now, of course, with four of the swat team riding behind him and Lesley. But how about when the swat team jumps out to begin the exercise? He shakes the idea out of his head. There's no sense in it. Working with this Agriminco goon squad means a better chance to disable Earthbaby than trying to go it alone.

"It's a brilliant idea of yours to lock onto NASA's Earthbaby communication beam," Lesley comments.

"That's how I got away the first time."

So they will use that same narrow corridor, insulated from detection, he flew up into when he escaped that day from NASA. Too bad they didn't have James' co-ordinates, but several computer runs administered by Lesley with sophisticated Agriminco equipment have charted the beam's complex cycle. At this time of year, they have to make the raid in late afternoon, so they can home in to it where — almost flat to the horizon — the beam tangents off into space and, in turn, is then bounced off a synchronous sidereal reflector set up on Gaspra asteroid.

Lesley activates her emulator: "Here it comes."

Then there it is, vivid and real below him, NASA's familiar heli-pad looming larger as he descends towards it.

"Great, Lesley. Okay. We're in security-check range now. See that pixel board? That's the automatic identifier which tells them whether we're friend or foe."

"Right, I remember." She takes aim with her image generator.

Bop! The blank board turns green and flashes up their copter's serial number.

"Good. That gets us through the front door," he tells her. "Make sure you keep the identifier flashing for half a minute after we land, or they might get suspicious."

Tremaine tries setting down; but, meeting no resistance, the copter's floats drop right through the heli-pad's roof. A weird sensation that, just ghosting through things.

"Want me to set this thing down, now? I mean on the real

ground?"

Lesley hits her buttons again. There: everything simply disappears. The real bare scrub of the Agriminco compound waits ten feet under his floats. He lands. Over to his right, he can see the armoured vehicles of the outside team who will create the diversion when the copter goes in. They're lining up waiting to file into the transporter which will drop them on a Powers-held safe runway on the West coast of Puerto Rico.

Lesley fires up again. In a moment, he finds himself parked on NASA's helipad. This could get dis-orienting.

"All right," she commands. "Let's get out."

The swat team storms onto the virtual helipad, practicing landing, running and covering each other. Tremaine grins, thinking how, if he hadn't landed, they could easily have leapt out into nothingness if they'd been told to.

"Now. Here we are at the elevators.... Got that?"

The swat team boys nod. It's Tremaine's instinct to register them as separate personalities, but they've given no names. All wear such a mask of professionalism, they seem androids. Indeed, their protective kevlar suits and traditional balaclava hoods ward off any human interaction.

"So," Tremaine continues, "assuming we've made it into one of the elevators and have descended.... next, here's the coaxial corridor."

He signals Lesley to project the next scenario.

Christ. He could believe this is real except he's conscious of uneven scrub beneath his feet rather than the seamless rubberized NASA floor so familiar to him. Lesley has given him the virtual- reality walk-through unit and he points with it, leading them into the laser-generated maze of passages. He approaches a door. Hesitates.

Over his intercom he tells her, "Wait a minute. It doesn't look right, somehow."

"Think about it," she says.

"Yes. I've got it now. There's a short stair about here, going off to the right into a generator room. It's just I've never used it, so I forgot."

"All right. We can fix that. Give me a moment."

Lesley programs the changes into the scenario.

"Magic!" he yells.

At every turn he checks Lesley's emulation, projected from the computer simulation they'd worked on at the camp, reconstructing it here and there, the swat team familiarizing themselves with its layout. Tremaine leads them past the Gaspra asteroid feed into the central nacelle. Used to it now, his whole body has re-oriented itself into being in the complex. His whole mental apparatus has begun treating it as reality. He half expects to see familiar faces of security guards, or to open doors of rooms to find an old colleague hunched there over his screen or checking gauges. Then he takes them down the last turn, up to the very door of the laser-generator room.

"This is where I'm stymied, because what you need is a code and a key."

"You can blast it open," one of the swat team boys says. "Just use one of these blasters. We'll give you a couple when we leave tomorrow."

Casually. Just like that.

*   *   *

The Agriminco security boys latch the apartment door behind them. While Lesley goes out onto the small balcony, Tremaine flings himself into a lounge chair in the living room. It's one of those damn auto-ergonomic items shifting around to pummel him into some ideal posture. Fucking thing! He can never figure out how to work the program properly. He gets up and sits on an old-style couch where he can see Lesley, flak jacket flung by her feet, standing on tip toes, straining to peer over the buildings of the Agriminco complex and the perimeter fence.

"What's up?"

She points into the ramshackle denuded hills. Beyond the second ridge he can just discern a rising wisp of smoke.

"Over there. Where is that?"

"The Freemont Lifeguard Base maybe? I'm not sure."

"Does that mean Powers is winning one?" she says, scanning the horizon.

"It could also be Agriminco's Claresville algae reconstitution plant in that direction. Hard to tell."

A thin brown stick, she turns to look at him, declining sun belting through her pale wisps of dangling hair and sweat-damp blouse. Her face in shadow, a blank. Any moment she could burst into flame.

"I'm telling you Lesley, I can't believe how amazing your emulations of the NASA complex were. At one point, walking through that projection, I thought I could just open one of the doors and see some familiar faces behind it."

"Well, don't forget it all comes out of your amazing memory for detail."

"Tomorrow you'll be seeing the real thing. But, you know, I'd prefer you stayed in the copter, rather than come down to the laser security nacelle with me."

He joins her, looking down where the assault team in the trampled compound are still running routines through Lesley's emulation. Let's hope for their sake and mine I remembered it right. Because of their extreme viewing angle and the setting sun, the virtual NASA complex is mirage-like, a shimmering series of transparent overlays. Where the hologram projections achieve a momentary solidity, Tremaine is surprised to see people temporarily disappear behind virtual roofs and walls, then re-appear again as the edges of the emulation drift into photon decay.

"I never knew you could hide behind a hologram just like behind a real tree."

She comes with him out of the appalling sunshine into the room's shade. He hugs her close. Like everything else she is fragile, she is temporary.

He smells her, taking her up into his nose: the ordinary sweat of the day, the subtler aroma of her skin. She opens her blouse for him as he slides his mouth over her breasts, drops to his knees and inhales her belly, pulling her hips so his face is buried in the musk of her absoluteness. Her hands in his hair, her hands undoing herself as he tastes her essence. Onto the couch. She shudders and falls, opening to him. When they come astoundingly together, his body feels shaken to pieces. His panting lungs are filled with her. He utters her name again and again. Real. She is Real.

When Tremaine opens his eyes, he thinks his sight has gone. No. It's only the sun dropping suddenly behind those hard black hills. Lesley's sleeping head is cradled in the crook of his elbow. Oh God he is so alive again. He is so determined.

He thinks over the arrangement for him and Lesley to get their release after the raid. Why take two old crocks along with the swat team in the first place? With what we've shown them, they can do the job themselves. I guess old Powers wants some guarantee. And their freedom depends on success. Very simple really: to take off and fly to wherever they want in the attack helicopter they will use to get into NASA.

What else could they have done? They didn't really have much room to bargain. But it was a better deal, risky as it might be, than trusting Powers to carry out his promise to escort them into some safe haven. After all, once he and Lesley have truncated the laser beam, their usefulness to Powers is over. But where to fly away to afterwards? That's the problem. If only they could contact the society —or Rivka, Perlita and the Euros (assuming the van has made it away, and Edgely and the others still exist).

If only they had a communicator. After the raid, they will have to pick one up somewhere. Using the one in the copter would make the call traceable back to the society, even if it was encrypted, since the Lifeguards would know where the transmission was coming from and move in. Tremaine remembers his first contact with Edgely, climbing in the copter up the laser beam angle. Full circle, yes indeed. But Lesley might still remember Rivka's code, and a few others with encryptable numbers and channels. He'll ask Lesley about it when she wakes up.

He eases his arm out from under her so he can turn onto a more comfortable side. God, life is tiring sometimes. No wonder old people just suddenly decide to pack it in one day, stop moving, stop eating, stop caring…. He spoons against Lesley's body. Taking comfort….

Tremaine's return to consciousness is reluctant. He spirals up a dense whirlwind, emerging into consciousness, at last, to a choral wail of sirens. Lesley is sitting upright on her knees looking through the sliding doors onto the balcony.

"What's happening?"

She's almost laughing, pushing back her hair from her eyes. "A missile just blew up on the far side of the complex. It must have come from the hills."

"Well. At least this time we managed to finish what we started before getting fired on."

She laughs: "Let's get some clothes on and see what the hell's happening."

All the action is around tall aircraft service buildings rimming the airfield. The missile landed on their far side, shielding their block from any blast damage. A row of hangar windows begins glowing pink —

fire spreading behind them.

"That'll keep 'em busy for a while."

He sounds casual, but he's beginning to worry. Last evening's smoke in the hills. Now this. In this kind of chaos anything can happen. What if this complex is destroyed and themselves with it? Or tomorrow they don't even make it to NASA? Or once there they can't escape? No one will give a shit what happens to them.

A loud onset of engines peppers the night sky with copters. Magna lights ablaze, they circle, sort into battle order, then scud purposely towards the hills. A loud cobra hiss signals a defense missile launch from the compound behind them. Too quick for the eye to follow, it overtakes the copters, just in time collides dramatically with its incoming quarry, sends the copter formation reeling away from the blast.

They hear the curious windchime tinkle of falling shrapnel.

"They were ready for that second missile," he says.

"The first must have been a surprise then," Lesley adds.

"Yes. Otherwise they would have been on red alert. Underestimating the enemy. This means things are more up in the air than anyone expected."

"Do you think the Euro swat teams are mixing in to it as well?"

"That would be nice. Let's hope by now they're scattered all over the place, keeping both side's resources occupied."

"It's worrisome, though, isn't it? It means we have to play everything by ear."

Boom! Boom! Two loud cracks assault their eardrums. Supersonic attack jets pass over, their exploding rocket bombs echoing around the complex. Now the sky goes crazy, everything being flung up there. They stand dumbfounded.

Lesley is on the ball.

"Away from the windows," she says, grabs his arm and hustles him into the bathroom, closing the door.

He sits sideways on the toilet, she sits on the bathtub edge facing him so they can hug in the crashing darkness. Mortar-fire — from the sound of it still concentrated on the airfield. Lucky the transporter has left.

Then there is a quietus except for insistent alarms and vehicle sirens. They wait a minute then emerge into the living room. The balcony doors are gone, shards all over the apartment. Tremaine pushes at the apartment's entrance door. Still locked, still intact.

"How far down is it, Lesley? I don't like being trapped like this."

"Five floors. Not thinking of the old bedsheet trick are we?"

They strip the beds and Tremaine knots the lengths together. He crunches over the broken glass on the carpet to drop them over the balcony. By now the main sirens have quit. Deep in the hills, the copters appear to be doing their job; at least there's a lot of action out there. There's still an ambient noise from the fires — yes, mainly over by the airfield itself — they can hear shouts and beeping back-up signals from fire engines. Smoke drifts their way and they cough getting caught in a drift of it. Their ladder isn't long enough, by far.

Lesley hunts in the cupboards. Damn. No extras. They tie on pillow cases and towels. With the size of the knots they don't add much to length. In the old days they could have used curtains. Once tied to a rail stanchion, the assemblage dangles a little past three floors. Too short to drop down from. It won't do to have one or both of them lying down there crippled and winded.

"I have an idea," Lesley says.

She runs the sheet rope around a stanchion, ties the two ends together, throws the loop down. It reaches to the second balcony below. Now Tremaine gets it. They can shinny easily down to the lower balcony, undo one of the knots and pull the ladder down after them. A couple more times and they will be able to reach the ground.

Because of the smoke they go to the far edge of the balcony kept clear by a stiff breeze coming down from the cooling hill ranges. Knots of curious bystanders empty out of nearby buildings, but none of them are looking their way.

Tremaine drops over first. Easier than he had thought. He swings himself inside the rail and drops to the balcony floor. The balcony door is blown in like theirs. The apartment looks empty. Lesley has started down and he helps her over the rail.

He's beginning to untie one of the knots when Lesley shouts to him from inside the apartment. No need to use the sheets. The front door is unlocked.

Quickly they hustle down echoing concrete steps outside. There's a small group standing by the front entrance, nicotine addicts, taking the chance to toke up without getting slapped with a summons. They all try to hide their butts until one of them says, "They ain't security."

A young girl sucking on a Xylotol cigarette yells, "What the hell's happening? Any idea?"

"No more than you do," Lesley replies.

They move away towards the perimeter road. It could be the security fence is breached. This could be their chance. Smoke drifts over them and they cough badly. They will have to go a long route round, more into the breeze coming down from the cooling hill ranges. This means they run into little knots of confused bystanders who don't have a clear emergency or defense role, low-level service people, clerks and warehouse workers. They all have that under-class "look" for both sexes and all colours, something resistant and connective, a defiant tribalism against the oppressing establishment. Like the smokers group.

Nearer to the turmoil the perimeter road is barricaded, but it's easy to wend their way through subsidiary roads and buildings, the wind stronger by now, thankfully clearing the air. Then they are at the scene.

"Just a minute, Lesley. Let's think this thing through. If we get a good chance, are we getting out of here?"

"Why not? They don't really need us, you know that."

"I thought about this earlier. What if they fuck up?"

"Why should they? Is there anything more they need to know? Once they get past the nacelle and blast into the Laser-generating room, that's it."

She's right. They do know their stuff.

"Okay. Then let's think about our chances. Are we better off scrapping around in those hills out there, or in a copter?"

"Good point, but we're assuming the raid goes as planned and none of us are killed or wounded, and that they actually do allow us to get out of there in the copter after we drop the swat team."

Right again, of course. The nagging thought he has comes not from logic but from desire to be the one to actually destroy the thing he has largely created. And also, much as he has no feeling for them, the moment he destroys the beam, he reminds himself, he will be condemning a group of human beings to slow death.

"All right. If the perimeter is breached and we can get out, let's do it."

Done. They come upon the scene.

Damper machines launch fire-quell packets rapidly into the blaze. They tint the smoke a grotesque green. Port wine red and tawny orange lights bobble from a host of vehicles, lighting up workers' faces. Yes, there are some dead. Two are being loaded by four stretcher bearers into the back of a Medcorps van.

Without warning, Tremaine and Lesley find themselves lit up in the high beams of a security hover car. It also illuminates the Medcorps guys easing the stretchers back out from under the corpses. On instinct Tremaine takes Lesley's elbow and strides purposefully towards the van and the four stretcher bearers. He knows by its lights the security car is hovering behind them. Two of the men secure the van's doors, as they approach. One of the others addresses them, raising his voice over the din.

"You the medics?"

"Looks like we're too late," Tremaine yells back.

Relief. The hover car has heard the exchange and moves on.

"How many more in there?" Lesley asks.

"Quite a few. Guess they'll all be dead though."

"Pretty brave of you guys doing this job."

"It ain't easy, that's for sure."

"Let's get this over with," his Buddy calls out.

The four trudge back into the ruins.

Lesley clutches Tremaine's wrist and drags him to the front of the van. No one in sight. She opens the unlocked driver's door. Keys in the ignition.

"Get in."

She starts it up and drives carefully away, angling to where the fence should be.

Tremaine squints through the cab back window into the van's interior.

"You are really nuts, Lesley. Do you realize there are four dead bodies back there?"

"They won't mind."

"That's what I love about you."

He turns his attention to where they are driving. Obviously along the edge of the airfield. He can see some traffic markers. She speeds along, then encounters bumpier ground, and right after that, just in time, she sees a deep ditch.

Lesley turns sharp left and avoids it, running alongside. It goes on as far as they can see. On its other side, Tremaine glimpses the perimeter fence.

"Follow along," he says.

Right then the van tips and plunges forward sending them into the windscreen. A goddamned shell hole. Luckily they are just on the edge of it. By gunning it in all-wheel drive, Lesley manages to lurch it out. One of the lights is broken.

"There!" Tremaine points.

The fence is down. Lesley negotiates potholes and upthrown mounds of earth. This is where a hover-truck would do better. Reminded of that, Tremaine keeps an eye out for the security car.

"Cut the lights Lesley. Can you still see?"

The moon isn't up yet, but the ongoing fire lights her way.

The van's big tires roll over the tangle of wire. Tremaine prays some of it doesn't wind round an axle. Then they are past it, gunning into the shadow of the nearer hills over the stone-littered plain.

When they reach the first gully, Tremaine begs her to stop a moment. His back has been wrenched and he needs to try stretching it without being thrown around.

Left leg crossed over his right knee, he leans forward feeling the spasm start to give way as he stretches.

In the relative silence, there's suddenly the chime of a communicator. They both startle.

"Where is it?" she says.

In the glove compartment. Tremaine opens it, picks up the tiny noise-maker and is about to turn it off, then thinks better of it: "Yes?"

"Hey! Where the hell's the van?" It's the guy they spoke to.

"Sorry. Emergency call back at medic central. Thought we'd take these bodies in and get there fast. Don't worry. Take it easy for a while. We'll be right back."

"Okay, Doc."

Tremaine closes it down then asks Lesley if she knows any of the society's numbers. She does. Lesley takes it. She wants to ensure it is capable of mutual encryption. It is. Since Foreman's election, all microwave links have been severely curtailed, but this is a privileged unit. The first number doesn't work.

"I'll try one in Toronto. There's a society cell on The Island there."

This one seems to get through. Tremaine watches her concentrating face as she punches in a series of numbers, listens again, inserts another series then disconnects.

"What's happening? No good?"

She takes a breath to reply, but the phone rings first.

She answers, gives out a series of meaningless code words he doesn't understand, listens a moment.

"Yes. Yes," is all she says.

Tremaine, impatient, takes the phone from her. It has gone dead.

"You didn't get a chance to say anything? What about a safe contact location?"

Already Lesley is backing up the van.

"We're getting out of here."

A ray of light illuminates the van's interior as he looks behind them to see where she's going. The bodies are all in a bizarre tangle.

Next thing Lesley is speeding back the way they came....

"What the hell's happening? Where are we going?"

"They say the shuttle's still up there. They think the crew resisted it docking. But that won't make any difference to Powers. He'll want Earthbaby disabled anyway."

"My God. We can't let them cut the beam. That's Lilly and Alex for you. They must have realized what Foreman was up to and persuaded the others into it."

"So we have to go on the raid tomorrow, and see what we can do."

Naturally. But what? My God this puts a different light on things.

"What the hell can we do? How can we stop it now? "

"Don't worry. We have all night to figure it out."

He clings to the dash for support and they are soon at the security fence gap, much easier to see now it is back-lit. But instead of going through the mortar-shelled range, they stop and abandon the van. This is much better for his tense back.

They take first to the ditch, hasten along, reach the perimeter road, find their way back through the ranges of buildings. They go up to the deserted apartment's balcony. The sheet rope is still there. First we break out: then we break in. He clambers up first, then helps Lesley over the rail, dragging the sheets in behind her.

They don't bother making the beds. Just collapse, grimy and exhausted.

"So," she says. "Here we are again. Now, where were we exactly when we were so rudely interrupted?"

Then they both burst into gales of laughter.

Well, chronicle reader — if ever there is one besides myself — always expect the unexpected. I say this because I'm going through a bit of a shock to my sense of being human, to being a Worldling. And I need to write this now as much to maintain my own sense of reality as anything else — a sense of reality which has been roughly shaken.

Grainger returned and we all squatted down together like nomads meeting in the desert, tense but buoyed by being again in the strong tropic light of unshielded mode.

"The monitor cameras are still functioning, " Grainger told us. "This means one of us could be out there watching for where they might try breaching the skin, the same as we did before."

"Hell" I said. "That's a real break. We could sweep them off by shielding againóat least temporarily."

Somehow, with Earthbaby's skin now unprotected, we'd expected an immediate invasion. But this hadn't happened. Once bitten, twice shy. They'll probably try something else. And the sudden unshielding might have been a shock to the shuttle crew if they'd thought we were all dead, or at least totally incapacitated because of the laserbeam systems being cut off.

Clarke wondered how the air quality was improving. Adam took another reading.

"CO_2 is already down. I bet we can start normal breathing in a few hours."

I watched the sky panels' reactive rhythms as they responded to radiation intensity in subtle waves of darkening and lightening blues.

We all realized that sending someone out now, while we still had to breathe from the cylinders, wouldn't make any difference to our total consumption. The question was, were we going to have any cylinder air left after a few more hours to keep someone out there for much longer after that?

We drew up a watch schedule, persuading Grainger to rest up for the first eight hours, so he'd be alert if defensive action became necessary. Alex volunteered very forcefully to go out for the first four hours.

She wanted to see whether she could put some of the computer mess together and see what might be working I would go after that, then Clarke. Adam would stay to tend the garden.

So Alex, seeming to move lightly even in her suit, stepped into the air lock to do her watch duty in Central.

I blew Grainger a kiss when the others weren't looking. He grinned, still pumped, lifting his thumb. I allowed myself a rush of irrational hope. Something could have gone wrong with one of the shuttle's systems. Nothing was infallible. Maybe we would win this one after all.

Then I threw myself down on the vermiculite growing mix under the densest shade I could find, lying on my belly, head down with my arm shading my eyes. When I woke up it would be my turn if nothing had happened. It would be scary to be out there alone. Again that light touch of paranoia about Alex. Why was she so insistent at volunteering to go out first? Oh shit. I was too tired to care. I actually fell asleep, listening to the comforting murmur of the others' voices....

I awoke with a great sense of joy under the bright blue sky of the greenhouse dome. I felt light on the earth, as if I had been floating and had just gently landed. I had been dreaming of Jock loving me and I could still feel his touch on my body. He was still there beside me. Life green and golden. I had woken at last.

"What a terrible nightmare I had, Jock. I..." But the words of course never came out of my mouth. I climbed the last two steps into glaring full consciousness, into a bitter and unwelcome reality.

I sat up, gasping. How horrible it is to have something ripped away from you like that. I took no comfort from the dream. None. How could my stupid head have contrived such a vicious delusion? I pulled myself together. What time was it? When was my watch duty? Another hour.

I looked around. Where was everybody? There was Clarke asleep. Grainger too. Good. If anything happened, they would have to take the brunt of it. And Adam? Surely he hadn't gone out there with Alex? Fucking on watch duty? Ho, ho! A bit difficult with the suits on. I got up softly and began threading my way through the perfect, identical trees. May as well check on her, after all. Even if just to quell my irrational suspicions.

Alex was, in fact, so engrossed when I got to Central, she didn't notice me. But not with Adam. He wasn't there. The observation cameras were working as Grainger had said, and I gave them a quick scan. All clear. Then I saw that Alex had managed to put the mess of computer gear together that the gravity change had disturbed. What a productive little devil. Suited as she was, she didn't hear me. I quickly switched my voice mode to single communication so the others wouldn't be shocked awake with my voice in their ears.

About to say hello, I came up behind her in time to see she had on-screen what appeared to be a geometric abstract painting. Then I realized it was actually a close-up of one of those late twentieth century town sites down on earth; you know, basically a grid with a few curling crescents, the house blocks all neatly arranged. In the corner was a bunch of computer lingo symbols and the operating label "search for congruent modules: array construction number....completed."

As I looked, the screen zoomed out miniaturizing the town site and bringing in others. I recognized part of the California coast around San Diego, the desert... Then there was a scurry of activity and the screen clarified into a whole complex series of town sites, now the size of dots, interconnected by lines of varying widths.

"What's that?"

Alex startled...? Or caught out?

"Lilly!"

She turned to face me, blocking the screen

But not soon enough. The screen resolved itself and I saw, "Operative Planet 3 (followed by code numbers) your download completed."

Alex realized I was reading over her shoulder. She turned around and blanked it. But it was too late and she knew it.

"What the hell is going on Alex?"

She had a tense determined look on her face which scared me. We were alone. But the suits were tough, and I was bigger. Unless she had a weapon. And she did. She drew it and pointed it at me.

"I f you haven't already, switch your audio to single mode Lilly. I want to talk to you alone."

My heart was pounding. I found myself really angry. So. Double-agenting was she, the little bitch.

I sat down very slowly. "I'm in single mode, Alex. Go ahead. I'm listening."

All my life, I've said to myself: why didn't I listen to my paranoid instincts? Now here was another instance. Pissed off as I was, it took me a moment to comprehend that the sound in my ears was Alex crying. I could see her face screwed up in her visor.

I sat very still and composed waiting for her to get control of herself. I sat there thinking my way through what my sweet old professor Davies used to call a "reality check." I imagined the look on his face as I went through my "situational parameters": I am orbiting Mars in a crippled space station threatened with imminent invasion. I am in a space suit breathing compressed air which will last about another thirty minutes. Across from me is a young woman (probably crazy) who is sobbing while pointing a devastator at my head.

I did start thinking rationally again, though. What had precipitated this situation was my seeing the confirmation message on Alex's computer. But without the laser beam, how can Alex be communicating with anyone? And even if she's doing it with old-style speed-of-light radio micro-wave, that would take at least ten minutes to Earth and back. But the response had been immediate.

Then Alex spoke: "We're on our own now, Lilly. They can't help us any more — for all sorts of reasons. That's why I had to send them my last piece of work. Of course they'll be disappointed to have Earthbaby out of the loop. But they'll develop some other link in a few years I suppose."

You have to be very soothing in these circumstances.

"Take your time explaining, Alex. I'm in single communication mode with you. It's just you and me. But you know, I'd be able to concentrate more on what you're saying if you just didn't point that thing at me, O.K?"

"Oh my God! I'm so sorry to scare you Lilly. This isn't for you, of course, it's for them."

Not only did she turn it away, she put it back into the spacesuit's copious pocket where it had been hidden.

"Who do you mean by *them*, Alex."

"Oh. Of course, the shuttle crew. Not the regulators."

"The regulators are the people you were referring to before?"

"Yes. I was going to tell you all this Lilly. Once we'd got ourselves stabilized up here. You see, I've been helping out in the solar grand circuit branch. There's quite a lot of us. In fact I rather suspected you might be one yourself — but I guess they really need only the high-level computer-patterning people like me at this stage."

In my ears, her disembodied voice. I was trying to hang on to what Prof. Davies called the charismatic thread — that subtle psychic connection between patient and therapist. But our helmets and visors prevented all but the most elemental eye contact or facial gesture reading. And add to that the traumatic circumstances we were in …. Well, I was drifting away, disorienting, a panic attack constricting my throat — and here was Alex jabbering away about regulators turning the solar system into some kind of super computer!

Come on: get focused! I commanded myself. — otherwise it's all just a black hole and entropy.

Years of experience produced just the right tone: " I wonder if you could help me get a little broader perspective on this Alex. I just want to make sure I'm understanding you properly."

"Haven't you noticed when you're in a plane how the townsites you go over look exactly like circuit boards in a computer, Lilly?"

"Now you mention it."

"So think of all that in-built circuitry — the electric power lines, the communication cables, the different conducting densities of the buildings, the roadways and so on, and how those complexes in turn are interconnected with the major power grids, major switching stations."

"Yes, but we're the ones who build them, randomly. Not these regulator people."

"Exactly. But our tendency to construct communities like that is pre-programmed, don't you see? Apart from whatever else we might do as humans, those are our material manifestations. I mean, look at termite hills, for instance. They're marvels of engineering constructed entirely by using the principles of the arch. Now, do you suppose there's some master termite who controls the rest of the colony's building activities? No. But when the colony acts as a mass, somehow these arches get created; though each individual termite is only conscious of mortaring on his own little burden of dirt. Or think of the way the different corals grow on the reefs. How do those millions of tiny individual cells, creating their own little individual calcium houses somehow combine to form each coral species' distinctive pattern?

"It's meta-consciousness, Lilly. Our individual brains, which we think of as completely separate and independent, are just like electrons in computer chips. True, you can't predict what an individual electron or proton might or might not do at any given moment, but apply quantum theory to it all and you get an ongoing statistical certainty."

"Jungian archetypes and racial memory. It's just you're applying those theories to computer and communications theory, Alex."

"Yes. Jung and others like Reich and McLuhan had an understanding of meta-consciousness. But it's only been in the last twenty years or so that the regulators have made themselves manifest. They actually exist as meta-conscious beings, Lilly. To them, we are a kind of wildlife area which they are managing."

I tried to keep the doubt out of my voice.

"So what, if anything, do we produce for them?"

"I think it's consciousness. I think they harvest it throughout the universe."

"Good God! How do they do that?"

"Well, they skim a layer of it off as we sleep, probably. But the major harvest is when we die. That's when they are able to drain all of it and begin recycling it through the universe. I don't understand everything, of course: just the notion of my body as site in strategic interventions and that I am just one of the selecteds."

Oh God, the words these alien abduction types come up with. A hang-over from that ludicrous post-modernist babble at the end of the twentieth century. I resisted an overwhelming urge to giggle at the sheer absurdity of it all — not just what she was saying, but the whole situation in which I found myself. I hung on to what little control I had left.

"And I take it you've had an ongoing communication with these regulators for years now. Through what means?"

"Well, it manifests itself through the computers I use of course. But the regulators' transmission device is of another order. They're able to make use of binary proton theory. You know, that experiment where there seems to be communication between separated proton pairs that is simultaneous and without an apparent cause and effect sequence? In fact, it was through their intervention I was able to wrest some of the Earthbaby control sequences away from the laser beam to make us more independent. Not quite enough, though."

"So what have they done to help you, specifically?"

"They protected and preserved me through the de-technologization massacres. They gave me hyper-awareness, and also, on a few occasions, material intervention."

"Can't they do that for us now?" That will test you, I thought.

"It's not possible right now."

"Did they say why?"

Even through her visor, I could see Alex looked disconsolate — betrayed even.

She started weeping again.

"I guess they felt they couldn't do much more. The last time they intervened materially was with the spin crisis on the way out here. It requires a tremendous concentration of resources to counteract material reality. That's why miracles are rare events."

Well. I could buy that. And so it went on for almost an hour.

M y immediate therapeutic instinct when she began to tumble out the general outlines of her fantastic tale was to pretend belief, and to pretend complicity — a standard practice of our hypocritical trade — so she would think I was bonded with her in her delusional ecology. But having done that for half an hour or so, I felt a great longing to believe as she did. How wonderful that would be. What if even some of what she was saying was true? I mean I am not dealing with your average half-baked rave bimbo here, but one of the world's most intelligent, highly-trained professional women.

My mind began to race along, independently of my skepticism. What if, indeed, we were not alone in the universe? Furthermore, was there actually some kind of understandable purpose for our evolution — even if it was to be little electrical impulses rushing through giant-size computer chips, or grazing herds being nightly milked of our consciousness? Such absurdity gave the idea more credibility.

At the end of it, we were comforting each other, encouraging each other that the invasion wouldn't take place, clumsily touching hands, unable to hug properly with the suits on.

I did want one thing from her though, and despite my confusion I'm glad I managed it.

"I'd feel a lot better on this watch if I had some protection, Alex. Would you give me your devastator?"

It was a gamble. I thought she might stiffen up and refuse. But she didn't. Once it was in my hands I felt a great sense of relief; but the way of her giving it so freely also added to my confusion.

She trusts me.

"Get some sleep," I said. "We'll talk about all this later."

Sitting here writing this up in the solitude of my watch duty, I simply don't know where I stand, or what to do. Tell the others about it right now? They have so much to deal with as it is, and besides, this one is strictly my department. Alex's story is so complex, I can't think of it as resulting from a temporary breakdown. I worry a little about why she chose not to reveal she had a devastator. But she could have seen her possession of it as part of her secret life. And to explain how she got it — which I didn't ask her about — might well involve her having to explain her long-term relationship to the so-called "regulators."

I recognize how tempting it is to throw yourself into a belief system like this one. Right after they murdered Jock, I was on the verge of joining a Tibetan Buddhist group, overwhelmed with my temple-mates' utter faith in magic and reincarnation. I've always been attracted to the Fideists and the Mysterians. Because after all, what do we really know about just being here?

If only we could remember clearly how it is that we wake from the mists of the unconscious as children and suddenly comprehend the essential "facts of life." Maybe this would give us a clue to the great mystery of being and our real relationship to it. What if we were "born" into a universe where the laws governing our existence were all entirely different, but just as apparently coherent as the ones we now have? Let's say where time — if there was such a thing — ran in the opposite direction — or where there was no death, only a series of transformations into something else.

It doesn't really help a hell of a lot that I know far more than Newton, or even Einstein or the quantum theory boys of the late twentieth century. We've all been stuck in this basic paradigm of being and non-being, consciousness and unconsciousness, since the (alleged) beginning of our universe. Why should there even be a universe in the first place, for instance?

So now this is my problem. Is her story real, or is it just a very long-term complex behavioural delusion on her part I'm being sucked into?

The computer messages I saw, for instance. Surely some one or some thing must have sent them? Well, not necessarily. Those messages could have originated through a series of avatars she may have created as self-evolvers years ago. Right! That would explain the simultaneous computer response. The messages aren't coming from out there. They're generated within the computer itself!

And a lot of what she says is characteristic of cyber-zombifica-tion: and we all know how many affinity groups that addictive syn-drome mentally destroyed twenty-five years ago. But how could a cyber-zombie have survived and been promoted the way she has?

I know that children who survived the Japanese de-technologiza-tion revolution frequently claimed they did so by being touched by angels. Part of her story could be considered a variation on that notion, too. Okay. So she could have braided together a neurosis using angel-cult theory as well. Put that together with her deep base knowl-edge of computer language arrays, and no wonder the whole thing has such coherency — how the pieces all fit.

We have, of course, known for three decades there has been, and probably still is, other life around in the universe, although it has shown itself to be pretty basic compared to us. If what she says is true, then the world is in for quite a culture shock!

And so I sit here, scanning the cameras, mouth dry with anxiety, trying to assess not only Alex and her story, but my own psychologi-cal state.

Oh my God! I just noticed it. The weapons hold ….

An outside hatch is open!

They're co ⌒

They lie in dawn light hoping the raid will be called off because of last night's debacles. No such luck. So here's two security guys at the door rousing them up.

"Rough night, eh?" the perky young one says, looking at the glass all over and trying to be cheerful.

The older guy with him looks glassy-eyed and pale. He hands Tremaine a breakfast bag. Tremaine is starving.

"Rave bars? That's all?"

"Things ain't exactly normal around here today, Buddy"

Tremaine lets it go.

"So our copter survived, eh?"

Lesley comes in from the balcony.

"Yes. She's down there ready to fly."

They gag down the reconstituted algae and soya bars, swill the over-sweet taste out with black coffee Lesley has managed to make, and go down to the compound.

Lesley makes sure of the equipment. Good. It's all there.

The swat team cluster in the copter behind him, tense and abrupt in their movements.

"Got the blaster buttons?" Tremaine asks.

"Be careful with these things. Remember, push them onto the surface, make sure they adhere, then a full half-twist to the right."

"No problem." He tucks them into his flight suit.

Lesley lightly taps his wrist and smiles encouragingly. Concentrate on the moment, he reminds himself, each moment as it comes, crucial or not.

"Okay, folks. Let's check the heading and away we go."

Normally he'd enjoy flying this machine. It's a powerful one with a fast cruising speed. He holds the speed back a little. He has to jibe with the ground force's attack time after all, or their plans might not succeed.

He notices Lesley working rapidly with the emulator generator, testing the angle of the projection every so often with a neutral beam that he can see sweeping across the landscape below them. The swat team boys don't seem suspicious. They know how crucial it is to mask the heli-pad pixel board with the positive ID overlay. They probably think that's all she's doing. Wait 'til they find out.

She also has the van driver's communicator hidden in her flight-suit. Turned off, of course.

The navigation dashboard display gives him the exact co-ordinate and the e.t.a. for intersecting the laser beam corridor. It only takes a few minutes, then a little dinkering around and they are locked on. For over an hour they belt straight along it, not a word said as they traverse a dead azure sea.

With the rise in sea-level the land masses are much smaller than when he was a youngster flying over these waters for the first time. Tremaine can tell by the deeper coloration where drowned recent shores used to be. And low-flying as they are, he can even spot under-water villages with their roads and houses still intact.

A few more minutes. He glances over at Lesley. Her look tells him she's ready.

They are losing altitude rapidly as the beam's corridor angles in more closely to the NASA complex. This is an advantage because the horizon begins to blur with heat currents and vague confusions of low-lying coral and cloud forms.

Tremaine gingers up the team with: "The coast is right ahead." And the moment they pass over it he says, " Getting close now boys. At this angle NASA will come up suddenly."

"If you keep your eyes open," Lesley adds, "we might spot the ground team down there somewhere."

Good for her, a wonderful diversion. He takes a quick glance in the mirror. The four of them are all looking out and down into the scraggly jungle, rather than straight ahead. Perfect! Lesley's eyes are fixed on his face, waiting for the word.

"Go!" he whispers.

Her fingers fly — and suddenly there it all is in front of them. So real it startles him: the perimeter fence, the ugly sloping blank main wall of NASA headquarters, looming up at them. What a good job she's done reconfiguring it all while they were in the air....

"We're there!" he yells as the swat team jumps into action. "Get the doors unlatched. We need a quick exit."

He holds his breath. Knowing it is an illusion, he can discern movement warping at the hologram's edges. But he needn't have worried. The boys actually cheer when the landing pad comes into view and Lesley overlays the identifier pixel board with her fake green go-sign.

This is where he has to be careful. He inches it down by feathering the blades instead of slowing the revs. There.

"No challenge! Looks good! Go for it!"

The boys on the port side leap almost together and disappear through the virtual landing pad with a wild yell. On the starboard side they are a little slower and the second one doesn't fully let go as he sees his buddy fall into nothingness. He twists himself and is about to make it back in when Tremaine jerks the harness down and kicks the craft over to one side, shaking him off. He too drops with a yell.

He won't die, Tremaine thinks, since they are only about fifteen feet above scrub bush. In fact, Tremaine roars away quickly, hearing shots fired wildly as they rise. Below he can see Lesley's images peeling off the terrain and a brief glimpse of the swat team crew tangled in the scrub attempting to fire at them a last time.

"Great stuff!" he tells Lesley as she shuts the emulator down.

Now, straight ahead of them appears the real NASA complex. His stomach lurches looking at it, remembering the thousands of times he has made his way in to it, usually with Jock by his side, eager, excited, animated with the sense that anything is possible. All those years, and what has it come to? Well. Now the swat team is dumped, thanks to Lesley's genius, it's time to get out of here, establish contact with the society and retire to somewhere sane and friendly like Finland.

Just then, the ground invasion force, exactly on time, begins their attack by lobbing mortar shells into the compound. With any luck NASA radar security will be distracted enough not to notice their own approach.

He keeps low, aiming to go around to the far side, leaving the bombardment behind. He can make a quick skim over the city, in fact over his old house. That will do for a final closure. Elation floods over him. So far everything is going their way. Lesley has the communicator to her ear. Evidently she has got through again and they will know where to go to make contact.

There's a lot of noise as sirens wail and answering pom-poms from NASA rain destruction into the invasion force fire zone. This won't last long. NASA doesn't realize it's not a full-scale attack, just a diversion. Another five minutes and the Powers' forces will pull back out again. Lesley talks on the communicator. Then she closes it down with an odd look on her face.

"Did you get a contact location worked out? What's happening?"

"We've got to go in there. Got to get to the beam."

"What? Is everyone going nuts? We did our job, for Christ's sake. First they want us to leave the beam alone, and then they want us to wipe it out again?"

"No. But they need an intervention. The beam's still functioning, but all life-support systems are closed down. The crew needs them turned back on to keep the shuttle crew locked out."

"Are you sure? Who's giving you all this? Do you know who you're talking to? This could just be a scam! It's crazy! It'll be suicide for us to go right in there."

He's close to the NASA shuttle bays now. They loom like mantises, arms of gantry cranes waiting for prey. That's what living in space is doing to us, he thinks, forcing us to grow protective exoskeletons, morphing us from endoskeletonic creatures into insects.

Shells are flying thick and fast, but none have hit the towers yet. Slipping sideways, he pulls into a narrow ravine he remembers and drops down hovering between a bank of trees and the climb of a volcanic rockface. He has to think this through.

Lesley is adamant.

"It's no scam. They need this intervention. They said it was crucial."

Here he had thought they were all through it, safe and sound.

"Oh my God. I'm not sure I have it in me, Lesley. I'm an old guy, you know. I can't take a lot more of this."

"I know, my Darling. But I'm even older than you. Look at me and tell me honestly what you want to do."

He takes a deep breath.

"What do you want to do?"

Lesley hangs her head, speaks quietly.

"Go back and turn the systems on, I guess. What else can we do?"

Just then the phone rings. Lesley answers it.

"Just a moment, please."

She hands it to Tremaine, laughing.

"It's your friend the van driver, doctor."

"*What the fuck gives? We waited for hours with those corpses and no van.*"

"Sorry. We got hit. Look, I'm in the middle of an operation

here."

He hands it back to her. She turns it off.

Utter madness to go in there, but he imagines Lilly and Alex gradually stifling in that damn metal box so far from home.

"All right. Let's do it for real this time. Get the identifier overlay for the pixel board cranked up and let's see what happens."

He seems not to be thinking beyond the moment, and that's a good sign. Up. Up. Out of the ravine, and once more....

SOCIAL DYNAMICS RESEARCH PROJECT: EARTHBABY
JOURNAL OF LILLITH SHAWNADITHIT

T ime only for a quick note in this brief interlude while we wait
to see whether the shuttle crew will actually invade us by using
the weapons-hold hatch they managed to open.

Clarke, more familiar than anyone else with military systems,
assumes the weapons hold area is a quickly conceived, last-minute
add-on and was not pressurized, since weapons storage has no need to
be. The access door leading into the hold from inside Earthbaby is the
one we couldn't get into and about which we hadn't been briefed. It
comes off the corridor near the hyberbaric chamber. Behind that
sealed door must be a pressure lock, or there would be a major
blowout of the access corridor if the hold door were ever opened.
Clarke's assumption is that the weapons-hold pressure lock would be
designed to be operated from our — that is station — side, not the
hold side. In order to get in to the station, then, the invading team will
have to blow the air lock, presumably remotely so they would not be
endangered in the ensuing pressure outrush. His theory was confirmed when we saw the crew going in and out, transferring from the
shuttle pieces of equipment, wire spools and so on, which suggested
explosive devices.

As a safety feature, automatic emergency bulkheads exist
throughout the station which slide rapidly shut in response to excessive pressure decreases. This means we don't have to worry about
being blasted out of the station or exploding into a mass of molecules
in the zero pressure of space as long as we are some distance away
when a rupture occurs. The puzzle is, then, how would the invading
shuttle crew be any further ahead if they blasted open the air-lock into
the access corridor when the only result would be to have the whole
area sealed off by the emergency bulkheads.

"I know you can blast anything open with enough juice,"
Grainger said; "but those emergency pressure bulkheads are pretty
heavy duty. Certainly a devastator wouldn't do much."

" And they'd be crazy to blast any of those," Clarke added. "The
results could be catastrophic."

He was right. Almost every item not bolted down would vomit

238   *Earthbaby*

out of the station including all the trees and growth medium of the garden. A nice mess.

So what is their strategy if blasting their way in just gets them up against an emergency bulkhead?

For the answer Grainger and Alex brought up the station blueprints on the computer. A quick search through the maintenance back-up system revealed that a pressure breach in that area would be sealed by an emergency door just the other side of the space buggy launch area, in the no-gravity zone that included the hyperbaric chamber. I searched Grainger's face, remembering the great times we had there, but he gave no response. His mind was on other things, locked into working with Alex in that cyberspace world they both inhabited so easily and which I didn't.

Further investigation by Grainger and Alex made it clear what the shuttle crew were up to. Plans showed there was a manual service airlock through a hatch close to the chamber which led to another subsidiary airlock, then through to a manually removable panel in the exit corridor from the detox chamber. The logic of this arrangement was twofold: not only was it part of the emergency repair system designed to give access to isolated damaged areas, but it also gave a shortcut for outside workers suffering pressure loss to be shunted very rapidly from outside through a zero-gravity chute straight into the hyberbaric chamber.

Adam, remembering the big fuss over his forgetting to put his watch through the sterilization chute, was appalled they clearly planned to use this route in the opposite direction — so to speak— because it meant they would be boarding Earthbaby without detoxification, introducing God knows how many viruses and bacteria into the system.

"Normally," Alex said, scrolling through systems and databases at a great rate — a meaningless blur of data pages to the rest of us except Grainger — "there should be back-up contamination sensors operating in the exit corridor leading from the detox chamber, which would also close emergency bulkheads. Unfortunately, we don't have independence on that system. It's linked to the air/oxygen system they've terminated from the laser link."

Grainger stared grimly at the screens.

"So, that seems to be their invasion scenario."

He'd been hyped before when he and Clarke had been talking

about resisting the boarding party. But now the reality was upon us, it was a different matter. This was no war game. The last thing we might all see, ten minutes from now, is a red flash and we would be "neutralized personnel" in the "opposition reduction scenario" in the shuttle-crew invasion reports.

Alex summarized it for us in her old efficient calm voice: "We'll hear the hatch blow. There'll be a slight pressure drop. About five minutes later they will come into the detox corridor."

I couldn't believe this was the same Alex I had spent an hour with just a short time before. "How many of them will there be?" I asked in general.

Clarke calculated quickly: "There could be as many as eight, even ten."

Alex must have read my mind, because she turned to me and said, "Are you prepared to kill them all, Lilly?"

The others looked bewildered, especially Grainger. I made a quick decision. To tell them she had been communicating with some alien agency and babbling on about "regulators" while pointing a devastator at my head would be completely unproductive at this moment. Whatever was Alex's state, at least she was on our side. And, goddammit. Could I really pull the trigger if it came to it? Maybe Alex could kill a lot better than me. Who knows what she might have had to do to survive the Japanese de-technologization chaos.

To everyone's astonishment I took out the devastator.

"So you *did* have one," Adam exclaimed.

I handed it over to Alex.

"It's hers."

"What the hell is going on?" Grainger demanded of me.

"There's no time to explain."

Clarke assumed command then.

"I'll be the one to wait for them in the corridor and take them as they come out of the hatch. Then you behind me, Grainger, at the exit into Central. Then you, Alex, Lilly and Adam. You should go into the garden and seal yourself in as much as possible. Alex to be the last stand."

I could see Grainger was overwhelmed by this. It was clear Clarke's strategy was the most workable. But for Clarke to throw himself into the most vulnerable — even suicidal position, with such calmness and firmness went straight to his heart as it did to all of us.

"Sorry to countermand you commander. But I'll be at your right elbow."

"And it doesn't make sense for me to be with Lilly and Adam in the garden. Since it'll be too crowded in the corridor for three of us, I'll stay here in Central as backup."

Clarke was going to protest, especially to Alex, but the look on her face was enough.

"I'm staying in central here with Alex," I put in.

"Me too," Adam said. "I may turn out to be not completely useless."

In the meantime, here we all were, crowded into Central, breathing our precious air. Adam must have read my mind. He checked his watch.

"By now the air in the garden will be breathable."

I, for one, desperately wanted to get out of this suit and feel my body free at least one more time before being gunned down. There was nothing we could do until they blew the air lock open and the emergency bulkheads slid home. So we might as well breathe real air in the meantime. Alex felt one of us should stay in Central, in case we didn't hear or feel the expected explosion. She volunteered forcefully saying she could also fiddle with the computers to see if there was some way she could reactivate the air/oxygen sequences that had been cut off from our control. I hesitated to leave her there alone, but it was clearly wasteful of me to stay with her, aside from my desire to get out of the suit.

Before I could say anything, her voice was in my ears again. She must have switched to single mode because I was the only one to react.

"You did really well Lilly. I won't let you down. Don't say anything to the others just yet. I'm going to see if I can get the regulators to make an intervention."

Hell, I thought. Chances are very high we'll all be dead in ten minutes. Let's face it, when you come up to a full-blooded realization of what that means, you understand why it is even skeptics start to pray out loud. What's there to lose? So I allowed myself then, and I am allowing myself now, to think and pray that *maybe what she says is all true.* "All right," I said. "Good luck, Alex. I hope you succeed."

Grainger was beside me going into the garden through the air lock. What a great relief to get out of the suits and unload the weight of the cylinders. It was wonderful to have everyone hug each other, to feel their real living bodies. Crazy, I know. But my senses were keened up. How different from each other the three men smelled. I thought of Alex still out there running her crazy obsession which I now wanted to be real. As soon as I could I got Grainger aside and told him all that had happened.

"She seems so damn consistent and plausible, Grainger. Could there possibly be anything in it?"

"Rumours about this regulator stuff have been circulating around the tech boys lately. It's like all these things, Lilly. When push comes to shove, there's nothing there. Otherwise we *would* have an intervention to get us out of this, instead of vague excuses why it's impossible at this time. Ho ho."

"I want it to be true. I'm scared as shit," I told him.

He hugged me tight.

"Look, as far as we know, the whole invasion might not even happen. What Alex and I did was describe what *could* be their plan. They may not even realize the opportunity is there. They may be doing something entirely different. Getting the weapons unloaded and put back into the shuttle hold to take them back to earth at the next window, for instance."

My whole being lightened up at his words. I wanted so much to believe him. "Do you really think so?"

He looked at me very keenly, searching my face. He loves me, I thought. He loves me. Oh what a rotten irony.

"Actually, Lilly. I don't think so. I think we are really up against it."

"I love you," I said.

He clung to me hard and whispered, "And me too, And me too."

But he didn't say "I love you" right out. Then he went off to talk strategy with Clarke. Okay. I understand. This man thing. Didn't want to say anything too sentimental. Scared but still has to behave like Horatio holding the bridge. I began to feel what all those old epics were made out of.

So here, in my isolated patch of shadow, away from the others, I sit, heart pounding, waiting…and yes, praying for Alex, anybody, to pull it off…. ❧

Wary of flak and missiles, he winces as they zoom over NASA's perimeter into the shuttle-launch area, flat out across its maze of guide rails, shunt engines, fuel bunkers and the rest of it, charging right between twin towers of shuttle silos, hurtling towards red-tinged smoke billowing from clamorous bombardments laid down by Powers' ground team.

Miraculously unchallenged, they swoop towards his familiar helipad. Lesley overlays the arrivals identifier board, keeping it flashing green, and Tremaine lands where he's come in so many times before. He grabs the devastator from the console and they sprint out bent over as shrapnel pings around them.

Two security guys huddle, sheltering in the elevator foyer. Tremaine waves at them. They've been totally taken in by the pixel board.

"Jesus!" Tremaine yells over the ongoing racket, "I thought they were going to blast us out of the sky. You guys okay? Any one hurt?"

Luckily, these two are new, otherwise they might have known him.

"No sir. But we weren't expecting anyone to be landing."

"Me either. Thought we'd better get in here while we had the chance."

A whistle and crash nearby sends another cloud of smoke and debris their way. That ground force was supposed to avoid this helipad. Idiots. Still it's worked to their advantage. The security guys have scuttled to shelter in their lunchroom.

Tremaine pulls Lesley over to the elevators. Too bad he doesn't still have his executive key. But the door opens almost immediately. They go down and emerge into the coaxial corridor. It's deserted and quiet with everyone no doubt scared shitless and gone into hiding.. Down here outside explosions become muffled vibrations.

They're into the nacelle, running now. That damn door into the beam security area is heftier than he remembers. But it still wasn't designed to do more than keep out unauthorized personnel. Not exactly a bank vault. He finds a blaster, presses it carefully over where he thinks the lock bolt will operate and it sticks there.

"Ready? Okay!"

He twists it a half-turn clockwise and runs with her back down the corridor. She pulls him around the corner where the service corridor intersects, and in a few seconds they hear it explode. They wait for smoke to clear, then peer out. All clear.

But the damn thing hasn't opened. He puts another blaster on and again they shelter. This time, the detonation has peeled back enough metal so they can see where the lock has shattered away from the latching pin. He kicks the pin and it opens.

The round room is lined with monitoring consoles. A solid titanium pillar containing the beam elements is in the centre.

"Now what," he says. "I know how to turn the whole thing on and the whole thing off. But I can't figure out all the rest of this mess."

"Leave it to me," Lesley says.

She hunts around the room, reading dials and gauges. Then she cottons on to the system and begins re-establishing programmes one after another. Following her around, Tremaine begins to make a little sense of what she is doing.

"Here's the big one," she comments. "Air recycling, conditioning, virus and bacteria scans, pressure balancing and all the related sub-systems....There! It's reactivated!"

"How are we going to make sure they don't turn it off again once the raid's over and they come in to inspect this thing?"

"It might take them some time to realize it."

"Not with that lock blasted to hell on the entrance door."

"Actually, I can see there's a security programme here they've had to breach in order to turn these systems off prematurely. I just might be able…"

He watches her face, impressed and in love with her.

"That would be good. Then we can get out of here and in touch with the society again."

She doesn't answer. Then she says, "Aaah….!" And he knows she has done it.

"It'll take them a while to figure that one out."

Now it's done, he's feeling uneasy. This raid won't last more than a few minutes. And how long can they expect their luck to hold?

"Come on. Let's go."

He trots, holding the devastator in front of him with both hands, his heart leaping at every turn. At last, the elevator. He hits the button and the doors slide open. Oh shit! The two security guys.

But they needn't have worried. Tremaine twigs they are getting out of the danger zone and are embarrassed to be caught out.

"Any damage up there? How's the copter? We were just going to check."

"Everything's still intact, sir, far as we can tell."

"Good. Why don't you stay down here: keep out of harm's way for a while."

"Yes sir. I think it's quieting down a bit."

As they exit, Tremaine sidles in to take their place, hiding the devastator behind him in his right hand. He wipes sweat off his forehead as doors close and they begin to ascend. Up. Up. His pulse is beating in his head. One moment, two moments, Lesley's grip tight to his free hand. At last the doors open onto the heli-pad.

An inrush of acrid humid air. The raid seems more hand-to-hand now. He can hear the rattle and whizz of small arms fire under howls of tank shells and roaring engines. He restrains her.

"Wait! Don't rush out there."

He moves out slowly, trying to perceive the copter through a drift of smoke. It's still there.

He hands her the devastator.

"Take this. I need both hands to get it started."

Sprinting. One moment, two moments, still alive. He grabs at the door, Lesley right behind him. He swings it open…. Then he stops dead.

Someone's in the pilot's seat, devastator pointing right at him.

Lesley screams, "James!"

Tremaine jumps, evading a direct hit. But an electric shock rips through him, stopping his heart in mid-beat, causing his body to twitch and fall. Blackness for a second. Then he comes to, gasping deeply, feels bobbling in his chest and then his heart thumps back into frantic action.

"James!" Lesley is screaming again, devastator raised.

For one moment, held-out arm stick thin, James points his weapon towards Lesley, registers who she is, begins to swing it back to Tremaine still on his back, helpless. Tremaine just has time to notice James' face, incredibly haggard in floodlight, eyes insanely aglitter….

Then Lesley fires… and James keels over onto the back of the co-pilot seat.

Tremaine isn't thinking now. He scrambles to his feet, adrenaline pumping, hauling himself into the copter. Still weak and shaken, he tries to pull out James' body, has to be satisfied with lifting his legs and toppling him over the seat into the back. Lesley jumps back there with James, while Tremaine pushes the ignition button, hearing the vanes start to turn, praying, praying....

It starts. Warm up fast, please warm up. One moment more, one crucial moment.

Eyes locked onto the dials, Tremaine tries not to think of the exploding air around them, or someone blasting them off the landing platform in the next micro-second. In a moment of quiet he hears Leslie's voice behind him. James is still alive. He starts sobbing in Lesley's arms.

Tremaine pulls down the harness. Up. Up. A spatterdash of shrapnel stars the windshield. The copter starts yawing, but he keeps the harness down driving it upward and forward into free clear air.

Now he gets it. James is one of the incurables. And this the last stage of AIDS dementia. Probably for months the bastards have been subjecting him to psychotropic drugs under the cover of medication changes and mood stabilizers. Poor little fucker. He's been driven between real and hallucinatory worlds having no idea what's really happening to him. And who has been using him? Powers, Foreman, or both or neither...? Well that explains a lot, and also doesn't explain it.

In the meantime he concentrates, trying to still the trembling in his arms and legs. A burst of small-arms fire rattles off the copter's belly. Then a pall of smoke smothers them. He's flying badly, lurching side to side like a ship rolling in heavy seas. The smoke clears and his heart bumps again to see how close he is to crashing into hydro lines. He goes under, lifts again. Where is he? Pins and needles chase up and down his hands and arms. The sun. Put it behind. Get out of there.

He can tell by Lesley's breaking voice that James will soon be coming to the end of it. She is trying to sound firm and reassuring. He recognizes the forested ridge ahead of him, gives himself lots of clearance because he still can't fly with anything like his old finesse. At least there's some quiet now, and light behind him makes it easier to see.

James' voice has turned into a little boy's: "Am I going now? Am I going?"

"Yes, darling. But where you're going there will be more. Don't worry. There is more."

"Is there really more?"

"Yes. You know you can trust me. This isn't all there is. Believe me this isn't all there is."

"I want some more."

In the silence Tremaine thinks ludicrously of Oliver Twist. More Boy! More!

Over the ridge he slips to the side, recovers, follows a narrow ravine downwards. A stream leads through it to the sea, he knows. He's flying better as his trembling subsides. Boy, wait 'til the bruises come up from this little episode. Lift up, heading is due East…leave the whole mess behind. But where the hell ARE they going?

He keeps his voice gentle.

"Lesley?"

"He's gone."

In a moment she climbs into the seat next to him.

"I'm sorry Lesley. But he was suffering…not knowing what he was doing…and his next shot…."

"It's okay. I had to do it. It's going to be okay."

"You saved me…. I was completely helpless."

"Are you all right, Andrew. Are you okay?"

"Yes. Still shaky. But I'm okay. But what about you?"

"I don't know yet. He's gone though. And I killed him."

"I'm so sorry…."

Now he has time to look at her quickly. She's holding her arms around her stomach, leaning forward, fighting nausea. He too feels dizzy every time he shifts his eyes away from the windshield. He stops looking at her.

"What's ahead of us?" she asks him.

"Nothing. Just the sea."

"That's good. They'll be able to take him easier."

What does she mean by that? The Gods?

"I always suspected James was the one. But only in the back of my mind. I never thought it would come round to me to be the one…."

"He was finished anyway, poor beggar. Much better he should go quickly with you to hold him, Leslie. Besides, what else could you do? You were forced to do it."

He wants to touch her, but he's busy with the controls. Already the twilight wind-change is blustering, distorting the copter's attitude.

Lesley is turned looking back at James' body, now.

"Now I understand. It's as if it was all arranged, isn't it? Some weird notion of poetic justice. I never killed anything in my life, you know that?

In her voice is a warning of hysteria he has never heard there before.

"You didn't kill him, Leslie. You helped him die. It was a suicide act. It was for the best. You're not to blame." Rattling off every phrase he can think of to calm her down.

She turns forward, puts her head down against the instrument panel.

"This is hard. This is so hard to bear."

Then she straightens herself, shakes her head with determination and picks up the communicator

Good, Tremaine thinks, she's going into action. We'll soon know where we're supposed to be going....

She fiddles with the communicator. Tries it. Tries again.

"Nothing. Goddam them! ...nothing!"

Suddenly, the communicator rings. She answers.

"Oh shit!" she says. "It's that damn van driver again."

Then, without pausing, without a word, she throws it out the side flap. He catches a glimpse of it tumbling down into the thorn bushes and cottonwoods speeding below them.

Stopping himself from exclaiming, he looks at her face strangely illuminated in the declining light. For some reason, he remembers Perlita and that amber moment on the deck of her old house. This is another one of them.

"Are you going to be okay, Leslie? Is everything all right?"

Lesley speaks to him in a soft, spellbound voice.

"Don't worry," she says. "We accomplished a great intervention. Everything will be all right now. Everything will be perfectly all right."

Intervention? The very words she speaks seem suspended in time. Behind them, a warped red sun teeters on the brink as they speed across beach, then reef, then sleeping cobalt sea.

Now what the hell do I do?

"Neil's still operative," he tells her, conscious he may be intruding on a sacred silence. "I'll just head for the Virgins and set down on a beach somewhere. Okay?"

She doesn't answer, just nods assent without looking at him. One look at her face and he knows she's gone. Her lips are moving. Maybe it's shell- shock, he thinks, using the old word for it. In the dying light he sees the diamond glint of a tear caress her cheek. Working quietly, carefully, he sets the navigation display, and puts the craft on course.

Strangely, now, over the silver-plated ocean, everything seems exactly as it should be — just as Lesley said. James is dead, at peace behind him. Lesley is by his side grieving and enchanted. He lets out a long and tight-held breath, trusting every moment to complete itself, flying to that place where sky meets curving sea.

This may be one of the last times I write in this journal. First, I must try to calm myself, find a proper perspective. To be still alive. Isn't that the main and glorious thing? Patience. That's the thing to wish for. All of us, Foreman's crew included, are going to be stuck here together for the immediate future, at least until the next window months away. Anything can happen.

Now Earthbaby's systems are re-established, it seems oddly comforting to be able to re-inhabit my own locked and bolted cabin, to have some hours at least of solitude, of contemplative privacy. Yet at the same time, I am struck with a bitter sense of loss. How I regret informing Grainger of Alex's fantasy about the regulators. If I hadn't, everything might have turned out differently.

In the meantime, my duty is to record here exactly the events, astounding as they may seem, which I know will become a focus of attention for legions of future historians. Whenever she found some babbling childish narrative of mine confusing, my grandmother (the one who taught me to write by hand) would chastise me with, "Begin at the beginning, Lilly, and go on from there."

As Alex had predicted, the invasion began explosively, the bump resounding through the station, enough to alert us garden dwellers. Quickly we donned suits and breathing tanks, ready to go when Alex arrived to warn us. We hustled into Central where I noticed Alex had by now completely re-established the computer console. Every screen was flickering with cascades of data being processed by a variety of search and execute programmes.

During our rest period, Clarke and Grainger had had time to reassess their defense plans. The removable panel in the exit corridor from detox was large enough for two of Foreman's assault team to jump out simultaneously. Clarke knew their training would mean they'd be through in a split second, weapons already emitting on a held-pulse mode, probably of one point five seconds duration. (This setting would still enable their firearm's reserve capacity to emit one high-intensity micro-flash immediately afterwards.)

Even if Clarke's and Grainger's reflexes were fast enough to down the first two, chances of getting a second pair, let alone third, would be minimal. Not only that, but in such a narrow corridor, Clarke and Grainger could be hit with bounce pulses, stunning if not fatal, fired through the opened lock previous to anyone actually emerging from it.

The revised strategy, then, was to let Foreman's goon squad enter the corridor unimpeded. Finding no resistance, they might well relax enough to amble down the corridor, becoming more convinced at every step and at every unmanned intersection that we crew were either all dead or incapacitated. Arriving at Central, they would tend to group at the corridor exit before cautiously entering the large open area, which would appear empty to them.

As soon as they were clear of the corridor, however, they would suddenly find themselves subject to a three-point ambush: Clarke to the left positioned behind the food provisioning machines, Grainger to the right around the corner of the cabins-access corridor, and Alex straight ahead, hidden until the appropriate moment behind the computer console.

I think all of us (Grainger particularly — were comforted by the idea that this ambush, if well conducted, could lead to at least some — if not all—of the assault crew surrendering, rather than butchering the whole squad two by two.

And so we took up our positions. I chose to shelter with Alex behind the console, Adam with Clarke behind the food machines. If they were shot, Adam and I would try to take over their weapons and carry on.

I was glad of this arrangement because I wanted to keep an eye on Alex who was still scrolling through her data bases with a hand-held remote, gazing up at them from her position on the floor. Suddenly she made one of those moves computer people do — a quick sharpening of attention followed by a rapid flurry on the keyboard. She had put down her weapon to do this, and I thought to myself *what if she has gone into reality denial and is entering the cyber-zombification stage?*

Slowly I reached out and took her weapon off the floor. She glanced briefly at me then back at her screen again, muttering, "Damn! I thought something was happening there!"

She didn't seem to care I now had her weapon. I looked it over to make sure I knew how to operate it. It wouldn't be long now.

But we weren't prepared for what happened next. A great blast of laser plasma, magenta coloured, beautiful but deadly, roared out of the corridor and vibrated around the room.

Clarke's distorted voice — "Laser grenade!" — crackled in my helmet phones. "These boys aren't taking any chances."

And you bet they weren't. Thirty seconds later another one flashed over us, higher intensity because less diffused by its shorter journey into Central. I couldn't see for several moments — could only hear Clarke's voice again.

"If they pitch another one at the end of the corridor, we're dead. Let's get out of here."

I stood up immediately, weapon in hand. Alex also stood. But she wasn't going anywhere. Her face was illuminated, her fingers flying.

"They did it! They did it! They intervened!"

I went to grab her, but as I did so I was conscious of something happening in Central. A bunch of lights went on and with them a series of alarms. And then I could hear and feel a kind of drum tattoo throb throughout the station — emergency bulkheads thumping closed in rapid sequence!

We all stood stock still. Alex, fingers still moving, screamed out an Arabic ululation of triumph.

"There, you bastards!" she ended, hitting a final enter key. "Look! Look! You can see them being sucked back into detox!"

And indeed we could. On the observation camera, a tangled mass of space-suited bodies were flying through the air, impelled by the force of the emergency suction system which didn't give a damn about anything but vacuuming every unchecked molecule out of the station. We saw them all bunch up and bang around the detox lock then crash against the chamber's outer wall which is where they would normally enter the station in the first place.

Alex programmed a close-up of Detox, which had instantly sealed itself to contain contamination, and was beginning its business.

Because of Earthbaby's continuing attempt to stabilize its newly-restored systems, air pressure and oxygen levels were obviously not fully operative in the detox chamber. It looked like two of them had lost their air-tanks, ripped off in the melee. Worse off, though, were the other two who had lost their helmets. Faces distorted, they gasped with bulging eyes. It was pretty horrible. These were the two who died soon after. There was nothing we could have done about it.

As the chaos of bodies sorted itself out it was clear others might have suffered broken limbs in what must have been a terrifying couple of seconds, rather like being sucked out of a hole in a jet plane. My thought then was I would have a lot of repair work to do and would need the others to assist if any assault crew were to survive their experience. (Yet, thirty seconds earlier, I was prepared to slaughter every last one of them.)

Well, that was the sudden and amazing end of it — or so we thought. I turned my attention away from the observation camera and caught something on one of Alex's monitors. A moving shape. Was it a woman? I realized it was the NASA communication channel which had also been turned back on. In the hubbub, I heard a voice-fragment from the console say, "Let's get out of here..." Then the figure moved on and there was nothing but vague outlines of flickering monitors.

"The regulators!" Alex crowed. "They intervened! They intervened!"

My first thought was, "My God! It's all true!"

A great rush of happiness flowed through me. I started to say something to Alex about the NASA communication channel being on, but my voice was drowned out by Grainger's wild Indian war whoop and the next thing I knew Alex pressed another button and the console screens went blank.

Grainger grabbed Alex and the two of them started dancing crazily in their suits. Of course, at the time, I thought Grainger was the only one besides myself who knew what she was talking about. I was sure Adam and Clarke thought the whole thing was some computer miracle Alex had achieved, or some miss-timed screw-up in their invasion plan caused by the NASA ground-crew re-establishing the control systems a few minutes too early. I thought Grainger would break off from Alex and come over to me, but instead Adam joined in with them, leaving Clarke and I standing in our suits smiling at each other, our bare right hands still holding our weapons, our left hands clasped.

It was only later that I realized Adam was already one of Alex's initiates. And now I fear, Grainger is becoming one too. I know, I know. I went through this jealousy thing about him and Alex before, didn't I? And it all proved to be unfounded. But this time I'm sure the young witch has him. Let's be realistic. Alex is the hero, isn't she? Without her, fantasy or no fantasy, we would all be dead, beat up, raped, God knows…. And what a better consort than Adam Grainger will likely make for our new queen, should she decide to take him on. I still have that image of them taking off together in the space buggy like two teenagers in Daddy's car.

Okay. Calm down, Lilly. Get back to where you were. I must also remind myself we've all been so stressed for so long, and then so stimulated and elated with what happened, so continuously pumped with adrenaline, there's no doubt we're all a little whacko in our judgement right now, and we're all destined for a big depressive drop which could last for some time. I don't know what to believe any more.

Patience. Patience old girl. Get back to telling the dear reader about the last big surprise in store for us all.

The detoxification took at least an hour. By that time, the air/oxygen systems had re-established; so it meant we could operate without suits. We commanded Foreman's squad to divest themselves of everything according to protocol, otherwise we threatened to open the outside airlock and rid ourselves of them instantly. That got their co-operation.

There seemed to be two older and two younger guys still intact. One of the older pair, with a broken leg, couldn't stand; and the others had to help him painfully take off his suit. The other two who had lost helmets were unmoving by then. We decided to leave them in there and shoot them into space after the four others had passed through. These four were pretty shaken and bruised; so they were pretty compliant any way. We hustled into the detox exit room so we could collect weapons and gear they'd put into the detox chutes. That's when we had the big surprise.

"Look at this flight suit," Clarke said.

Grainger ran his fingers over the stars on the collar.

"It's a Lifeist Army General's outfit!"

We all scrutinized the observation camera to figure out to whom it belonged. It soon became clear enough even though we realized he'd been contriving to keep his back turned to the camera. He didn't seem badly damaged. That's because, I sneered to myself, he would be hanging back a long way from the others, so his trajectory into Detox had been shorter and less violent. His suit, being of top quality, had also protected him from concussions, his helmet staying on.

His bulky pathetic old body stood out from the other three who were all younger and in better shape. Later I learned the two who died were younger privates who had a more standard issue suit. Now you fucker, I thought, how does it feel to be stripped of everything, powerless — *entirely at my mercy.* Oh how wonderfully does the world turn sometimes. I caught my breath at the chance to wreak terrible vengeance on him. How dare he defile Earthbaby, Jock's last creation, with his vile presence! Horrible things flashed through my mind I can't bring myself to write down. Lucky I wasn't able to get to him, or my jaws would have blood on them. Then I completely lost it.

The others were as amazed as I to find they had captured Foreman — President of the American Protectorates. But my violent reaction bewildered them. Here was Lilly, always in control, the social dynamics officer for Christ's sake, gone completely berserk. As dear Clarke held me, calming me down, I heard Grainger, before I could stop him, inform the others about me and Jock. Well, Grainger, you stupid big mouth, thanks to your patronizing explanation of my female hysterical fit, now every one knows my deepest secrets. I should have known I couldn't trust you.

Writing about it has brought it back again. I'm sitting here pulse racing, thinking to myself, My God. He's in my power. I can snuff him out just like that, just as he did to Jock. And yet I couldn't help noticing how pathetic he looked as he emerged naked with the others, behind two relatively uninjured hunks carrying the injured man. What an inferior bedraggled old physical specimen compared to those well-hung goons of his. After the four others had passed through, Clarke took it upon himself to operate the exit airlock to launch the two dead ones into space, saying a dignified prayer as he did so. My respect for that man grows daily.

All of them, including Foreman, I soon realized, were beginning to suffer from some degree of nitrogenosis because of extreme pressure fluctuations their suits hadn't entirely protected them from. Normally, that wouldn't have been a big problem, but with all the bruising and especially the broken leg, complications could easily settle in. I had no compunction about ordering the three youngsters into the hyperbaric chamber. Somehow I could excuse them, especially being under orders from the top man directly. But I was nauseous with anger, breathing very rapidly when I came to Foreman. I wanted to torture the damn murdering bastard slowly to death.

"You'll have to deal with Foreman," I told Grainger and Adam. "I can't even look at him."

Normally, the gravity is left off in the chamber, because recovery is usually faster in emergency in a weightless state and comfort is much higher. But in their case we re-applied the gravity field so they wouldn't have to be strapped down in order not to fly around at night and bang into each other. Once they were all in there, lying on recovery couches, I was able to control myself enough to fiddle a bit with the chamber controls until they were comfortable and the blood gas tests looked as if they were normalizing.

Their overt injuries were not life-threatening. Besides the middle-aged one with a broken leg — who later turned out to be Foreman's personal assistant — the nicely built one had a sprained wrist, the third a broken ankle. Foreman had a dislocated shoulder. I suspected interior bleeding in all of them which might show up later, since their faces were extremely pale.

I wished Foreman had been in a much worse state than he was. Even now, I am thinking now how I might torture him in the hyperbaric chamber later on. Raising and lowering the air pressures would ensure he would die an excruciating death from joint pains, interior bleeding, ruptured vessels, deafness from blown eardrums, blindness, the whole works. And by adjusting the pressures I could prolong his suffering for days and days of screaming agony.... Sorry, I'm having trouble controlling these violent fantasies of mine. There's a fine line between such things being therapeutic and becoming obsessional.

We were told the shuttle pilot and co-pilot had remained on board. They were just shuttle pilot staff, no special corps like those with Foreman. In fact Clarke recognized their names: Risto and Tupac. Clarke spoke to them over the docking intercom, bringing them up to date with events. They expressed relief that Clarke and the rest of us hadn't been injured or killed. No threat from them. They would just be waiting to get the hell back home at the next opportunity. But everyone felt it wiser to have them stay there. Things could get crowded. And security could get to be a problem with more of them on Earthbaby than we are. Grainger and Clarke worked a few minutes with them to apply the magna-grabs so the craft would be locked onto Earthbaby and they wouldn't have to keep all the systems running. In fact, they said they were quite comfortable because they got a partial gravity effect from the station, and there was lots of room to go round.

Thinking of all this now, it seems we are going to be quite busy.

We decided to draw up plans tomorrow after a good sleep. So there it is. And I suppose I should try to stop this seething in my brain. My memory keeps reiterating that first shock of recognizing Foreman. And the other thing I can't stop thinking about is Alex and Grainger.

How do I know he went to his own cabin? What if, right now, he is in hers?

How cleverly Alex took advantage of the emotional crisis of the invasion to begin making him her acolyte. He wouldn't listen when I went through all the logical reasonable explanations for the systems coming back on. And when I told him about seeing the NASA communications link, the shadowy woman's figure, the voice, he looked quite skeptical, as if I were deliberately lying to confuse the issue.

"Let's leave it, Lilly. We're both outrageously tired, and my watch is due in a few hours. I'm going to bed."

Now I think of that voice… Let me try to bring it back… It was difficult to hear above all the hubbub in Central… Tremaine's?… No! Maybe I'm just projecting… Could it have been Tremaine's?

My God. If only I could convince Grainger of that. That's the way. Try to open communications up with the outside world, with the society and the Eurosoviets. Then we'll get all this straight. Tomorrow. I'll think about it all tomorrow.

But oh what pain it is to think of Alex initiating him right now, probably, into the ecstatic mysteries of her cult, bonding him physically and psychically to her. Must get that image out of my mind….

If Grainger is starting to believe in all this, will I lose him if I don't believe in it too? Oh God. Am I going crazy or what? There's no logic in this. None…

Shut up stupid. Stop writing this crap and go to bed. ❧

"**G**o around behind the first headland. We can look for Neil's boat in the harbour."

These are the first words Leslie has spoken in hours. He can't read her face. No moon, not even a hint of dawn. It's difficult to see anything except red/green channel-markers leading to onshore lights.

They drop out of dark sky a few kilometres along the coast from the harbour. Impossible to judge how narrow the beach is between palm-fringe and shingle's edge. First try, he splashes down in two feet of water. Then he hops it up on shore, as close to trees he can.

When everything is shut down, he can hear a new wind clattering palm fronds. Once dawn comes it will freshen further. In the meantime the sound of the surf is a quiet murmur. He sits exhausted, so tired he is unable to concern himself with what to do next. One thing for sure, he doesn't want to sit in this eerie quiet with James' dead body right behind him.

"I'm getting out, Leslie," he tells her, pocketing the devastator..

Mutely she comes with him.

"What shall we do about James?" he asks her. "It's too stony to bury him."

"It's easier for the spirit to go free left in the open air, like the Zoroastrians do."

"You mean just leave him on the beach?"

He remembers Grey talking about the de-carnation site. In this hard rock part of the world it makes a lot of sense to become part of the food chain.

Leslie reaches for the rear door and opens it. He scrambles in with her and they pull James out. He weighs practically nothing, almost bird-like, almost pure spirit already. By Tremaine's foot a black land crab scuttles into its burrow. It won't take them long to discover him.

He takes the heavier end, holding James by the wrists, avoiding looking down onto the head lolling backwards with open white eyes. They carry the body close to the litter-strewn tide-line, easing it down onto a sand bed thrown up between two coral rock-heads. They both stand over him for some moments, Leslie murmuring a brief goodbye.

He goes down to the water's edge and rinses his hands, rubbing damp sand between his fingers, rinsing off death's touch. She follows him, crouched over, heedless of surges inundating her ankles. His feet too are wet. When he stands, he can barely see those small waves sucking at the shingle. This is a protected bay. From further out come drum beats of heavier swells thumping on the reef. Welcome in his nostrils is the iodine tang of seaweed. Once back at the copter they can't discern where James lies. Already he's begun to be part of it.

Leslie goes back in for a moment to retrieve the computer heart of the laser-generating device. He helps her down with it.

"This is going to be a bugger to carry."

"I need it to communicate."

"I think I see a path here."

It leads to the top of the headland. There's the hint of a horizon now. Lace surf seethes across reefs. Below them is the wind-chiming harbour, a forest of boat masts anchor lights swaying. As he sets the computer down on weather-worn rock, fleeting shadows of lizards scatter. A thorn bush has scratched his carrying hand. He licks the blood along its length and holds it in the wind to dry.

A rush of jubilation for a moment clears away his tiredness. Dawn, and we find the intrepid couple are still alive folks! Towards the end he was worried the fuel would run out. There was something wonderful in the way she threw the phone through the window. Now, what the hell is she doing with that thing?

He sits on a ledge beside her as she animates the screen. Its colours paint her face in changing hues, its various boot-up beeps and buzzes, so familiar, suddenly seem weird and out-of-place. Little fucking aliens taking over: there are millions and millions of them now. How simple on this island it once was to hoist your sail and ride the wind, dip your home-made fish-hook into living seas, then return triumphant for a family feast. No more.

Moment by moment as the atmosphere brightens, the circle of his vision grows wider. He catches his breath as the first pink streak distinguishes sea from sky. Then sunrise primal red, volcanic orange silhouettes a black confusion of clouds and islands. Leslie's little glowing box seems insignificant, though she, herself, priestess-like burnished in the fiery morning light keeps tending it. The world keeps rolling through the universe, tipping them now into the full face of the sun.

Two black dots ascend sky high, start circling, then purposely drop down with wide-spread wings. There go the undertakers.

Sunrise quickly over, the ordinary day immediately begins, long-shadowed still but every object in it round and real.

"Did you get anywhere?"

"They'll notify Neil we're here. They'll find us. Meanwhile I'm starving. Let's see what's open down in the harbour."

"That's a relief. Anything about Lilly and Alex on Earthbaby?"

He sees a flicker of hesitation on her face. "Guess we'll find out more about that later."

"No one can rest easy until we're certain that place is totally neutralized. I hope we did the right thing."

"Of course we did the right thing."

"But until we find out…. That's the trouble. Not having direct communication with them except through the laser."

As he says this, her first flicker of hesitation and a flashback of her telling him in the copter they needed to re-establish the beam, come together in his awareness. My God. How did anyone outside NASA know the situation on Earthbaby? And every communication about what they had to do came through her. Who was on the other end of the line? And this whole incident with James….

She's looking at him very directly. Fortunately he's backlit, but he wonders how much of this is showing on his face. As she continues reading, his mind is beginning to skew. If only he can connect with Bill. Bill he can trust.

"What's happened with Bill, Grey and the others?"

"Bill and most of the crew have joined Perlita and Rivka in Europe."

So he won't be able to see him and check all this out.

"There's more news. I'll read some of it out to you if you like. 'Rumour Powers dead or incapacitated, Agriminco executives using look-alikes.'"

"Powers may have died in the meantime. But I'm sure I spoke to the genuine article."

"Next: 'Foreman's organization unravelling, many defections, local crime lords taking over. Long-term chaos expected as infrastructures collapse throughout American protectorates. Euros collaborating with Society cells to negotiate cease-fires and local stability.' That's it."

Leslie finishes and closes down.

"In the meantime let's eat in a harbour café because I'm starving and we'll both probably collapse with post-traumatic shock in a few hours, but I want you to know I love you."

He picks up the computer and starts to follow her down. Then he stops.

"I love you too, Leslie. And I'm on my last legs. But I have to speak to you. Otherwise I can't go on."

She gazes at him steadily. "All right. I think I know what you want to ask. But please don't panic. Please trust me for a while. I can't handle it just for the moment."

Asking to take her on faith. Can he do that? In the blunt searching light she looks old, slightly stooped, too tired, like himself, to bear everything. But the look she gives him is wise, loving. My God. What haven't they been through together! More life with each other. That's all he wants.

"Okay. Let's go then."

She reaches her hand out to steady him coming down the steep rocky path. "There's also really big news, but I'll talk to you about that later."

"Oh great. How come I'm always the last to know about things?"

"It's in my nature, as a woman, to keep you under close supervision at all times. Didn't you know that?"

SOCIAL DYNAMICS RESEARCH PROJECT:EARTHBABY
JOURNAL OF LILLITH SHAWNADITHIT

When Earthbaby was being planned, I was the one who suggested the crew number should be five. Despite its small size, five offers a wide range of social possibilities through multiple variations of alliances. Thus it has traditionally been the small-group size of choice in social dynamics theory.. Most triumvirates don't last long because there's only one possible combination other than unanimity — two against one — and only two different pair bonds can be made. Four most frequently leads to stalemate. Five is most successful because it offers so many combinations: one to four, two to three, two versus two with one neutral, two to one with two neutral and so on. Pair bonds may evolve in ten different ways. The number's inherent possibilities show up in poker and cribbage "hands" of five cards, in five-year plans, and the "Theban Five" who founded the most civilized city of Ancient Greece. (Not to mention our five senses!) The worst social situation, happening only rarely as far as social dynamics goes, is when the group regularly divides four against one. (Particularly if you are the "one"!)

This is the situation I almost found myself in as the week progressed. There is a new high priestess on Earthbaby. Her chosen consort is Grainger, victor of the leadership contest between himself and Clarke (the old king) which I predicted from the first day. Chief disciple is Adam, who, I am positive, continues to "minister" to Alex on a regular basis, sufficiently enough, doubtless, for her to hold him in thrall through what we shrinks call "intermittent reinforcement."

This threatens to put Clarke and myself outside the temple precincts. If I hadn't taken instinctual steps several hours ago, Clarke might also have been a novitiate in their congregation as well, and I would have become totally isolated, peripherally identified with the Foreman Goons whom I tend and feed with only the most minimal help. I say minimal because Alex and Grainger, inseparable now, spend their precious time at the elite activity of working on Earthbaby's systems-independence schedules. Adam, of course, has to play the god Pan in his domain. At supper time I heard him yammering on to Grainger about the possibility of cloning future inhabitants of Earthbaby — in Alex's likeness, no doubt.

Naturally, I reveal none of these thoughts, pretending I am unaware of the new dynamics. A complex game this. Alex, in fact, continues to praise me in public and display intense affection for me, as if she still regarded me as an intimate and a believer. I go along with it, of course. Let her think she's deceiving me.

The slippage was not immediate. In the morning after the invasion, Grainger greeted me as if everything was perfectly normal. He put his arm around me while we were all drinking coffee, and asked me pleasantly if I was feeling rested. But the veneer was thin and I could see through it like plastic wrapping. Both he and Alex looked quite exhausted. Naturally.

I asked whether there had been any communications from NASA. No. And none between the shuttle pilot and NASA either, because we were now able to monitor that channel as before. NASA had closed it down. How convenient for Alex, I thought, remembering her quick move to blank the console. If NASA had been overtaken by friendly forces who were responsible for the "intervention" she could keep that information from us.

"That doesn't mean we can't send. We should issue a statement and a request to open up the link," I said.

"Alex thinks we should discuss all the issues first, so we are all agreed as to what to say. I think she's absolutely right."

Clarke called the meeting to order, but his chairmanship of it seemed immediately tokenistic. The other three had obviously been discussing strategy. With some degree of awkwardness, Grainger started up with how recent circumstances made it imperative we should be looking at a whole new mission and strategy for Earthbaby. Now Earthbaby had been so magically saved it would be a tragedy to lose it again. There were many issues we all had to think about. Primary among these was assuring complete independence until such time as it seemed safe to reconnect with world forces sympathetic to us. The fact we had Foreman himself as a captive on board had to be discussed and dealt with also. Maybe we could use him as a bargaining chip. Sending him back to earth with the shuttle crew seemed ridiculous.

At this point Adam raised a somewhat alarming long-range problem. One of the more banal functions of the usual shuttle visits was to replenish the water supply. These journeys were now out of sequence since Foreman had used the back-up shuttle and there was nothing in its payload. In short, there were too many inhabitants on board. Any increase in plant and human consumption as well as solar-electric conversion into oxygen and hydrogen for air quality and fuel needs, meant an inevitable shortage in Earthbaby's closed system. Although the problem was not immediate, it could become crucial in a few days, especially as plant-life increased in volume.

So far, no-one had mentioned the regulators, but I could feel it was soon going to come up. I interjected that all of these issues really depended on reliable information. At least we should try to communicate with NASA right away, so a deal could be worked out if necessary. Possibly, NASA had been taken over by friendly forces. I was hoping this was the case, of course, so Grainger and the others could entertain the idea there was a less mystical explanation for the "intervention." We could also get a better idea of the situation down on the planet, as well as who was alive or dead, by having a controlled debriefing of the captured crew one by one before we launched into any new strategy.

Then Alex piped up at last to tell us that we did indeed have communication, and that was with the regulators. Already that morning they had informed her the re-establishment of the systems might be only temporary; thus it was imperative for her Adam and Grainger to work on the independence schedules day and night as they already had been doing.

"Exactly how do they communicate with you, Alex?" I asked innocently.

"Currently, they manifest themselves only through existing computer networks, Lilly. These they can penetrate from the epi-phenomenal universe they inhabit without serious disruption. They don't want to disturb the world's existing microwave envelope."

"So these come to you as a kind of old-style e-mail message then?"

"Yes. That's a reasonable analogy. But they won't message trivia, only consequentials."

"What does that mean, exactly?"

"Items and issues that are important, that might have consequences."

One of these items, she went on to explain, was that Foreman had instituted special cadre corps for rooting out regulator members. Consequently a large number had been brutally exterminated. This act was something which should not go unpunished. She seemed very agitated and angry about this.

At first I thought it sounded farcical for Foreman to bother harassing an arcane cult, but chatting later with Gerhardt, the hunky young weapons guidance officer, confirmed her information. Did she really pick this information up from the regulators? Or did she get it from one of the shuttle crew? How I wish I knew enough about computers to determine whether the "information" she gets is really from "outside"(by this instantaneous split-photon-pair technique she told me about) or generated by a complex programme from "inside" as I suspected from the beginning.

I now realize this regulator stuff is quite a wide-spread cult, especially among techies — as Grainger remarked when I first told him about Alex's beliefs. With Foreman ruthlessly suppressing it, the movement gained credibility in my mind. So it wasn't entirely an individual fantasy. That made it even more complex, rather like the society except with religious overtones. At least I agreed with Alex about somehow punishing Foreman for his war crimes— if you can call them that. I still can't bear going anywhere near that murderous fucker. I still have that fantasy of killing him in the aerobic chamber.

Alex's remarks opened up the whole regulator business of course. Wholeheartedly supported by Grainger and Adam, she launched into an uplifting spiel, about how we were among the first disciples of the Dawning New Age that prophecies had predicted for thousands of years — about hope and meaning and all those long yearnings humankind has had since first consciousness. Oh yes, I found myself being drawn in at times, but there was something that terrified me about her intensity, about how easily I could turn into being the same way— an unthinking fanatic.

Seeing where the land lay, then, I made no objections, I bided my time, playing the friendly open-minded skeptic. I waited until it was over, and her disciples had finished their congratulations.

"I would like to believe all this," I said. "But I, for one, need more proof."

It was Grainger who came to her defense. And that rather broke my heart. Having someone torn from you sexually is one thing. Having them so suddenly ripped out of your consciousness as the intimate sharer of your world view and your inner thoughts is somehow more devastating. We had shared so much, trusting each other's acceptance and confidence.

"But what more could you want Lilly?" he asked. "It's not as if Alex made this all up after the fact. She told you all about it before the raid even took place. You knew she was hoping for an intervention. You told me so. (Oh how much I wish I hadn't!) You also told me you wished it was all true. And now it's all happened as Alex had wanted. Why aren't you happy like the rest of us?"

Clarke, bless him, came to my support.

"I'm with Lilly on this until I know more, Grainger. I mean we're being asked to throw away the belief system we've had all of our lives up to now. I agree, these events seem miraculous; but as you once said yourself, this regulator stuff is pretty well confined to super-techies like you three. I mean I haven't the faintest idea what Alex was talking about with the regulator communication technique. Personally, I don't see how it should affect us one way or the other. Some people are believers and some aren't. If this is a legitimate organization who have helped us out, then maybe they'll continue to do so."

At that the meeting might have broken up, but I was determined to institute some communication with NASA. Twisted and warped that information may prove to be, but were we henceforward to rely only on Alex and her regulator channel? I grew more suspicious when Alex tried to obfuscate and delay. She turned my own debriefing idea against me, saying we should wait until we had the results of that exercise, and more news from the Regulators —which (naturally) would not be forthcoming for a while — before attempting open communication.

I wasn't going to let her get away with it.

"What possible harm could come from telling NASA we have General Foreman and the shuttle crew in custody and are awaiting communication regarding further negotiations?"

Well, I won that one. But it was a phyrrhic victory.

The message was sent, and within minutes we received a reply. I was quite deflated when the image of the one I call Doberman appeared. He was brief and quite threatening, insisting we immediately return Foreman and the crew in the shuttle at the next window or future consequences would be dire indeed.

So my idea of persuading Grainger and the others that friendly forces had overrun NASA and created the "intervention" was a lost cause.

Well, not much was resolved. My debriefing suggestion was approved, but I was left to do it myself along with all the medical labour. Clarke, bless him, pitched in. Alex and Grainger went off to spend their precious time at the elite activity of working on Earthbaby's systems-independence schedules. It was a long hard day.

That's why I was so surprised that night when Grainger appeared at my cabin door. He was really exhausted.

I made my voice sound very casual. "How's it going?"

"She's a hard driver. I'm really wiped."

He flopped down beside me in the old familiar way, and I almost went on automatic pilot, reaching out to caress him as if nothing had happened.

"These young ones can wear you out," I said nastily.

He caught my tone.

"Here you are, Lilly, witness to what might be the most important moments in human history, and all you can do is express some immature jealousy. Alex can't help it if the regulators decided to make her one of the elect. It just happens they want people with her skills because of the solar computer project right now."

"So you do believe all this stuff, don't you?"

"Well, as I said at the meeting, it seems there's overwhelming evidence for it."

I knew he was a computer expert, of course, so it made me reconsider things for a moment. Alex might be able to fool me, but could she fool Grainger? Then I remembered how he had probably spent the night with her.

"Is it the song you believe in, or is it the singer?"

"What do you mean by that, Lilly."

"Have you checked all this stuff through, Grainger? I mean, don't let yourself get blinded by one night of passion, for Christ's sake."

"What the hell are you talking about, Lilly?"

"I'm asking whether you can distinguish between virtual reality and actual reality?"

"I have to be completely honest with you, Lilly. It's probably been decades since what you are talking about was considered possible. Actually, the question is no longer relevant in today's world. 'Reality' is what presents itself at any given moment in time to our consciousness. I'm old enough to have some grasp of what the old world meant by the philosophical construction they called 'reality'; so I can at least talk to you about it in terms we both vaguely understand. But people Alex's age don't have those distinctions any more. They're useless notions."

"But I need an answer. Don't you see. I'm in total confusion about all this."

If he had comforted me, if he had reached out to me, if he had even denied being with Alex or said something about giving it time to sink in, that it didn't really matter one way or the other…everything might have been different between us. But he chose not to. In retrospect I believe he didn't want to. I believe he was subconsciously wanting to create a distinction between us, something to give him an excuse to rearrange his emotional alliances.

"Well. I can't give you the answer you want, Lilly. As far as I can tell the regulator stuff is as "real" as anything else in this universe. Mathematics, for instance. You know that question: 'Is mathematics a discovery, or is it an invention?' Alex tells me mathematics is in fact one of the early manifestations of the regulator's meta-consciousness. So you see, lots of things now make sense that didn't before. If you don't want to believe in it, that's your affair. But don't try to warp my own sense of what I believe is Alex's profound sincerity."

Anger rose in my throat. "What about my sincerity?" I asked. "Does that still mean anything to you? Or has Alex changed your conception of that too?"

A mistake. He winced, mumbled something about being driven away after coming to make peace with me, and the next thing I knew I was alone and devastated.

Thus things went from bad to worse. So, we had come through the fire, all of us. But not unscathed. Why couldn't I accept his having a relationship with Alex, after all? Yes. That's what I should have told him. I stumbled out of bed and went to his door. It wasn't locked, so I quietly opened it. No Grainger. And the bed was neat and tidy. Down the corridor I went to Alex's cabin. Locked. I stood there in the twilight of the corridor, imagining them tangled together on her triumphant bed, my stomach churning in a mixture of anger and sexual longing. I leaned against the door, my ear to the molded outer lining. But I couldn't hear anything. With the soundproofing I didn't expect to.

So that is how I drove him into her arms. ✒

At first Tremaine and Leslie were wary of making themselves too conspicuous, choosing to sit just inside a small bar with a good outlook onto the harbour. Early as it was the rubinesque black bar-owner conjured up a couple of goat-meat rotis for them, and brewed some Jamaican Blue Mountain coffee. Her main man was breaking coconuts with a machete out on the front steps.

They'd been there half an hour or so when Tremaine noticed a small army patrol picking their way along the waterfront, carefully inspecting the mix of local and tourist craft moored there. The man with the machete paused for a moment, drinking coconut milk from a half shell, and looked down at them.

"Who are they?" Tremaine asked.

He laughed. "Rat patrol. One week now they keeping this island pretty clean, you bet."

"Where they from?"

"Eurosoviets."

"Yeah? So what's been happening?"

"Making it tough on the Foreman's bastards, man."

He waved the machete in the air, significantly.

"Guess they get some help," Leslie grinned at him.

He winked and chuckled, then pointed the machete down to the harbour.

"There's your boat. She come for you right now."

Sure enough.

Tremaine took the copter's ignition fiche and handed it to him.

"Can you give them that, and say it's the other side of the headland?"

"They already on their way. A small place like this, everybody always know everyt'ing."

They shook hands and scrambled down the cobble street, in time to catch the mooring rope flung by Sonny. His handsome East Indian face flashed a warm grin. Neil saluted them from the bridge. So it was easy. Their insides relaxed at long last. A hop over the shining rail, hugs, greetings.

"Where are we going?"

Not Hispaniola this time. Too hot for them in the Caribbean any more. Got to get out of Powers' country. To Nassau by tomorrow morning, then plane to New York. Don't worry, Neil told them, we've got people there in the Bahamas, and also on the ground at the other end in New Jersey. That's a heartland Foreman enclave.

Tremaine could see how Leslie was going into herself again over the James trauma. She went below to be by herself where she could wash up and visit the head. Tremaine took Neil aside and told him all about it. Sonny radioed the Eurosoviet shore patrol to confirm the location of the copter. Maybe they could make use of it if they could keep it from the Powers crowd. In the last couple of hours the tide had come in. Quite likely James would be gone by now.

Tremaine commiserated with Sonny over the Frangipani. No-one was hurt, thank God, and the ground being so wet from the downpour the flames didn't spread. He seemed to treat it all with remarkable equanimity. After these troubles were over he'd rebuild it again.

Down to the familiar cabin where his back was healed that time. Already under way, the boat was lifting as it began to plane. Leslie came out of the washroom, red-eyed and stricken. He hugged her.

"I brought Neil up to date on everything. Don't worry. We're safe now." Without ceremony, they both collapsed onto the bunk-beds and fell asleep.

And now it's a day and another night later. Full moon, and Tremaine awakes to see it broadcast its silver network on the waves. Always that mysterious tidal union with the sea.

Through the port window in the lunar glow he can see an arc of the boat wake forever unrolling. Within it, a kaleidoscope of phosphorus luminesces continuously. Ah God. These still moments are wonderful. The clock says time is passing, but does it really? Maybe not inside yourself. Maybe you don't even age at times like this. You exist without effort, without expenditure — like those suddenly-appearing porpoises now surfing the bow wave.

Silhouettes in formation, taking every advantage, they ride on some shear-point of multiple forces until a side-swell disrupts them. Then they shudder a moment, leap up, recover their balance…supple and perfectly motionless again in the ocean's commotion. If he were one of the world's one billion Hindus, he would believe without question one of these dolphins was James, already gone into his next transformation.

He stares enthralled 'til the first flick of dawn and they are gone, just like that.

Calm waters. Jesus this all seems so easy. But he won't quite relax till he gets there. On the side table a photo of Janet. My God, he must ask Neil what happened with her. Obviously something. Then where is she?

Eighteen hours of sleep makes you hungry. All that hard work resolving inner conflicts. Very soon they should be there. Now Leslie is awake, pulling her knees up to her chest for her break-of-day back-stretch.

"What's up?" she asks.

"Watching porpoises."

"They can read minds, did you know that?"

"Makes sense. Makes a lot of sense."

While Sonny's at the wheel, they sit down with Neil. He asks him about Janet.

"She's gone back to NASA. They took her no problem. Claimed she defected from the Helicorp when it went over to Powers' side."

"Is she all right, though?"

He means of course her shattered and drugged-out self.

Neil taps his shirt pocket where he keeps his roll-ups.

"Janet? Now she does this stuff only — one, maybe two splits each day. She got purpose now, Man."

Clearly a hint of pride in his voice. Neil, always coming to the rescue. His life-role. And thank God for that. Tremaine still remembers the sight of him on the bridge of this very boat, come to pluck him out of the sea.

"Working for the Society? Good on you, Neil."

"She's in NASA external communications, troop movements and all that. Relays stuff to me."

Tremaine looks at Leslie. Is this how she got the information about the Laser? And about Earthbaby's resistance to the shuttle docking? No sign of it on her face. She coddles a bright yellow coffee mug in both hands, close to her lips. Next to Neil she's so tiny, a wisp of a thing. She sees he is looking at her, takes it for a love-look so she smiles, squints her eyes with affection.

"So. Getting a station put back together, Neil?"

"Little by little. Right here on the boat. Could use some of that stuff in the copter. So listen, this is what Janet says is the big NASA rumour. Crazy, but you never know. Ain't nobody seen Foreman in a long time. Word is, Man, he went up with the shuttle to Earthbaby!"

Tremaine comes fully awake. What if it's true! Foreman has always been strictly a power-desk man. Once the missiles and bombs started flying, his tendency would be to run for cover. What better place. And to be able to preside directly over his big threat in the sky. Oh Yes. Psychologically it all goes together — beaming his big ugly mug down from the heavens into several billion TV sets and image wall units, spouting his pieties with his finger on the button like all those video-game villains and heroes he must have grown up with.

Leslie is struck with the idea too.

"If only we could communicate with Earthbaby directly. Let them know what's happening here, and find out what's going on up there."

"Trouble is, as you well know Leslie, the only communication you can get with Earthbaby is through the laser."

"Or…" she says, "someone who has access to it."

Neil shakes his head.

"Not Janet. She's radio external only. Got no clearance to that other part."

"What about the shuttle?" Tremaine asks. "I know it's usually through the beam; but doesn't it have a co-terminous piggy-back system in case of beam truncation?"

"Secret frequency and it will be encrypted, for sure," Leslie comments.

"Hey!" Neil says. "Janet could get that."

"Shuttle's next window is three days away. After that it's months. She'll have to hurry."

"But what help would it be?" Leslie asks them.

"We could open the channel. That way we could hear everything that's going on between the pilot and NASA. At least that'll give us some clues as to whether they boarded or had to give up."

The boat throttles back and its bow drops to horizontal coming off plane. Neil rises, pours a mug of coffee for Sonny from the pot.

"She'll do it. That is one good Gal, you know."

SOCIAL DYNAMICS RESEARCH PROJECT: EARTHBABY
JOURNAL OF LILLITH SHAWNADITHIT

I see by the date it will soon be a week since "Intervention Day" as Alex insists on calling it. Only this new "morning" do I feel capable of continuing this journal. Hopefully, I'm beginning to achieve some measure of rationality and purpose.

(At this point I am attaching a fragment I wrote in some moments of lucidity the day before yesterday. Some things may be resolving themselves — as always in unexpected ways! Here it is.)

What an emotional mess I'm in. Oh sure, I'm still sane enough to write out the technical words for it — post-traumatic stress following the invasion, confused belief system about Alex and the regulators, anguish from the narcissistic blow of losing Grainger, seething anger over the vile presence of Foreman, callous murderer of dear Jock. (*Lifeists* they call themselves. What a disgusting perversion of language!)

It's this last that's most disorienting because most unexpected, dredging up all this buried grief, making me yearn for some kind of ritual closure and release. And if only he weren't here to muddy our triumph over his invasion force. In my brief rational periods, like this one, I recognize Foreman's presence here — and his future disposition — is really the main issue our crew has to deal with. Even in my own head, the realization we have abducted the world's most powerful person is psychologically daunting, as it must be to everybody, but especially, I suspect, to Clarke. Unlike the rest of us, who represent other interests, Clarke was directly appointed by Foreman and his lackeys. Foreman is not only The President, but also his commanding officer.

I now realize my insistence on communicating with NASA was a double blow. Not only did it seem to support Alex's claim our success was due to a Regulator intervention, it also brought home to us how the "Powers"-that-be view our actions.

In our minds we were merely defending ourselves against a hostile take-over of Earthbaby for unauthorized military purposes. Their version demonizes us as perpetrators of the outrageous and unheard-of act of kidnapping the President of the United States and

Protectorates. Quickly and neatly they have taken us out of the pigeon-hole labelled 'dedicated space scientists' and put us into one designated 'subversive terrorists.' Such legerdemain now gives them the right to *search and destroy* with a clear conscience.

Irrational accusations, yes; nevertheless — as I well know — this kind of double-speak can have its effect and begin to erode one's own sense of reality. For Americans, there remains something mythical and sacred about the President's position itself, despite the fact very few holders of that office have been exemplary characters. Foreman has played on this by refusing to speak to any of us except through his lackey — the one with the broken leg — who refers to him constantly as "Mr. President."

As one counter-measure, I insisted on having the two separated, putting Foreman's lackey alone into what Grainger used to refer to as "the psycho-cell." It's a classic secure padded room in case one of us gets deranged with space-fever and needs to be locked away. I would have put Foreman in there, but the room has a convenient toilet the lackey can use rather than having to hobble painfully in and out of the chamber with its high threshold.

As another ploy to deconstruct the President image, I have made it a point to consistently refer to the bastard simply as "Foreman" — in fact as "that fucker Foreman." It makes him an ordinary man, separating him from all the political and social associations attached to his falsely-gained titles. I'm glad to see the others have picked up on it. Being isolated on Earthbaby so long, our crew's image of him is still fixed at the time before his election, another helpful fact.

What is needed is a direct confrontation between Foreman and the crew. Why did he come here? What is really going on down there on earth? Can we use him to negotiate something? About the first I'm beginning to get an idea. The Foreman people have been pretty close-mouthed about what they do (on orders I suspect), right after Gerhardt told me he was a weapons guidance expert. I have a suspicion, though, that this crew is pretty high-level all round, just from the way they disport themselves.

This Foreman issue needs to be resolved.... Then perhaps I can tackle the Regulator one....

*   *   *

Waking yesterday morning I re-read what I had written above and decided on a course of action.

Given my previous analysis of the shift in social dynamics among us, I waited for an opportune moment to get Alex alone, then suggested to her — thereby tacitly recognizing her new power — that we should have a formal "debriefing" of Foreman in front of all of us in Central (unaccompanied by his lackey of course).

"You and I know Foreman's a fake and a criminal, " I said. "I want to make sure Clarke and the rest aren't over-influenced by this Mr. President bit."

She was delighted with the idea. So delighted, in fact, it gave me a little shiver to realize how much she relished conducting a public display of her absolute power over someone of such importance.

"Let's do it right away," she said. "It'll help us decide what recompense is appropriate for persecuting our Regulator disciples."

By now I was getting used to this Regulator cant of hers, so I feigned a normal composure. As well as demystifying Foreman, my ulterior aim was to help Clarke re-establish some of his authority as our commander. Even if this Regulator epiphany turned out to be true, it struck me as unhealthy that Alex should become assume the role of cult high priestess — the *One-Who-Should-Be-Obeyed*. So I put it to her that it would be appropriate for Clarke to conduct the session. She went along with it.

When I approached Clarke, he seemed nervous about an immediate face-off with Foreman. I kept insisting to him that this was just a bunch of criminals we were dealing with, that their power was usurped, and probably temporary. It helped that I was able to bring some of his own observations back to him about how the old army had been far more principled and socially conscious before privatization and the Foreman take-over. What I was trying to do was put him in the position of being the restorer of justice to a corrupted system. In the short term, he would be our negotiator and fact-finder so we could make more rational decisions as to where we go from here.

Part of my scheme was to search out fatigues for Foreman that were either too small or too huge so he would look slightly ridiculous. In the stores, I found the latter. Then I had to ask Grainger to deliver them with a curt and dismissive order to Foreman to get dressed in readiness to present himself to the station commander.

There's a peculiar agony in having to continue normal relations with someone who's broken your heart. Grainger didn't seem overly affected though. If anything his manner was annoyingly gentle and concerned as if I were suffering from some illness.

Clarke looked splendid in his full-dress uniform which I insisted he wear along with all his medals — something he never did normally. I also admonished him to take charge of the meeting and conduct it as formally as possible. And so we marched in.

I decided to take notes — and I'm glad I did or this account wouldn't be so complete — to add an air of formality to the proceedings.

Clarke began strongly: "It would be entirely appropriate of me to conduct this as an ad hoc court martial, but your unauthorized presence here has led me to believe an Enquiry into the circumstances surrounding recent events might be more productive at this time." He then asked Foreman to explain why he had come on the shuttle to Earthbaby.

Foreman refused to answer. I had thought he might do that. It's a very effective way of maintaining your dignity by not deigning to recognize the person addressing you as having equal status. Clarke repeated the question as if Foreman hadn't heard it the first time. Again a long silence. Should I say something? Grainger and Adam looked non-plussed, following my example of folding my arms as if to say, we can wait here forever if that's the way you want it.

I looked over at Alex. At his refusal to speak and his arrogant demeanour, her face had grown highly coloured. All at once, she startled all of us by leaping to her feet. She rushed over to Foreman, pulled her devastator from her pocket and pointed it straight at him as if to eliminate him on the spot.

"You're a fake, aren't you?" she hissed. Such menace in her voice! "Some damned useless look-alike!"

The effect on Foreman was immediate. Alex had totally shaken him.

"I'm the President. I swear to you…I'm…"

"Order!" Clarke said. "Order please!"

Oh boy, talk about good cop, bad cop. Alex turned and sat down, cradling the gun on her knee.

"If what you say is true," Clarke said. "Then you will give us some explanation why, as supposed president of the United States and Protectorates, you came on this mission."

I looked at Alex. At first I thought — what an intelligent thing for her to do, how insightful. Then it dawned on me that she hadn't thought it through at all. She'd acted on pure whimsical instinct. She might indeed have pulled the trigger and done him in right away if Clarke hadn't called for order. And Foreman knew it. For one thing you don't get as high up the ladder as Foreman without having some pretty developed instincts about people and their degree of ruthlessness. I laughed to myself. God I wanted to see that bastard suffer.

The prick collected himself quite well — I've noticed this about highly self-involved people before. Unlike most of us whose boundaries of self tend to overlap with those of others, they have a very narrow single channel into which they direct all their resources.. Having broken silence he had lost round one. So now he was going to try for a tone of official authority.

"As President, and as your commanding officer, I am refusing to continue with this farcical Enquiry. I order you to release me and the rest of my men to occupy this facility as intended. You and your crew will return to NASA headquarters at the next opportunity, there to face appropriate charges."

This was the big one as far as Clarke was concerned. In normal circumstances having the President of the American Protectorates say those words to you would be pretty frightening. How would Clarke's long-standing conditioning to authority make him respond? I saw him swallow several times before answering. We were all looking at him, except Alex, I noticed, who was glowering directly at Foreman — a gaze he chose to ignore.

Before he answered, Clarke threw a look in my direction. I gave him an encouraging nod. I could see Foreman lean forward. In some sort of way he had divined where our weakest link might lie and, now, given Clarke's obvious hesitation, he thought he had made some kind of inroad there.

Then Clarke started up, shaky at first: "The moment I was seconded by the Lifeist army to be the Commander of this multi-partner enterprise, I ceased to be under its command. My duty immediately became the protection and welfare of the crew of this ship. It was in the spirit of that duty that I have given the orders and taken the course of action that I have. I perceive you and your escort to be a threat to the stated aims of the Earthbaby venture and a proven danger to the lives of my crew. I would remind you that you are ten light minutes away from your own command post. The law of space, like the law of the sea, is international. While you are here, you are under my direct supervision as Captain, do you understand?"

There was a solid silence. Foreman was the one swallowing now. I could tell he was really pissed off. It had been a long time since anyone had ever questioned his authority and he wasn't used to it.

"Answer Commander Clarke's question," Alex ordered him. Her eyes were narrow and her hand tightened on her weapon.

I was in two minds about her now. One part of me was approving. The other part was wishing she wouldn't be so blatant and threatening. It rather took away from Clarke's authority since he wasn't ordering her to do it. I am in charge here, she was saying in effect, so do what the man says before I plug you.

Her presence gave Foreman a chance to continue speaking without acceding he had been bested by Clarke in the authority contest.

Controlling himself with difficulty, he began, "Once again I insist you are acting illegally. Since I'm being threatened, I will answer you only because I do so under duress."

Taking his cue from Alex, Adam piped up, "Damn right you'll speak to us." I say "piped," because his voice was squeaky with indignation. "You owe us all an explanation. Months of valuable experimental work could have gone down the drain because of your ignorant stupidity."

This was more than Foreman could take. Red-faced, he growled, "I see I'm dealing with a bunch of egghead sympathizers with Ecomaniacs, Society and Regulator terrorists. Whoever you think you are, you could all get the chair for this!"

"All right," Clarke ordered. "Perhaps we can proceed without further interruption."

Foreman at last started in with a lot of crap about wanting to inspect for himself the new space facility and by his presence encourage these peace-keepers of the Lifeist army in their task of quelling the disruptive elements both inside and outside the American Protectorates who threatened its democratic institutions — and all that garbage.

I felt like doing the same sort of thing as Alex. I wanted to say — enough of all this piffle you murderous shit-head, I'm going to tear your balls off! I restrained myself. I felt it was up to Clarke to face him down.

As he continued to utter his bureaucrap, I was bitterly amused to see how he warmed to his task. Since no-one interrupted, he continued on as if he was actually getting somewhere, rather than revealing to us all his essentially manipulative insanity. How does anyone ever get inside someone like that? And if you do open the door, is anything ever there? And what is there in the human character that routinely allows aggressive neurotics, even psychotics, to rise to rule over us? I guess that's the bigger question, and the one asked by Ruth Benedict about the nature of human cultures a hundred years ago. In his earlier days, people had said Foreman was charismatic, but I had never seen anything in him but the most obvious egomania of that surly type of thuggy executive.

I did detect a slow blink rate, and what one would call in our trade a flat affect, indicating a high stimulus threshold and a very self-contained personality. I suppose some impressionable people would call him the strong silent type. Personally, I believe his kind of personality is so empty and vacuous it affords an opportunity for others to project any picture they want onto the blank canvas, so to speak, including their own unrealized fantasies about themselves. How else can you explain it?

Anyway, once he'd ended his disgusting platitudinous spiel, we started taking turns cross-examining him, hoping he would let slip some real information about the world down there. As luck would have it, Grainger, as an Agriminco man so to speak, pressed Foreman about why there had been no confirming directives concerning our replacement from President Powers as there had been surrounding the satellite incident.

Another angry flush arose in Foreman's face at the mention of Powers' name.

"Mr. Powers some time ago acceded decision-making on this project to the Pentagon and to NASA."

Well. Here was something new. We all looked at each other. NASA, of course, with Tremaine out of the way, simply meant Foreman and the Pentagon. So where did this put Grainger and Adam in particular?

"Acceded it," Grainger scoffed. "You mean you took it. In the same way as you cut out NASA by trying to eliminate Director Tremaine."

I could almost hear Foreman's brain thinking, "How the hell did they find out about that?" Suddenly things became clear to me — why none of the take-over shuttle crew had anything to do with space research, but were probably all high-level intelligence, communications, weapons guidance and strategy people.

"No honour among thieves," I cut in. "That's why you're here isn't it? You and Powers have split and it's become too hot for you. Two birds with one stone: get Earthbaby operational, and at the same time use it as a safe war room!"

The others all chimed in on what I'd said. Alex, oddly enough, sat there in a menacing silence. I had no idea how to read her at that moment.

"We know all about the warheads. We know your filthy game," Adam went on. "There's no-one in your crew capable of keeping this space garden going. You'd have let it all go to hell, wouldn't you? You and your kind have no appreciation of growing things. To you they're just a bunch of plants."

Adam and his garden. I could see Foreman's eyes glaze over.

I looked up through the dome. Against the utter darkness, we were all reflected on its inner surface as if we were far far away, floating like gods in an eerie black universe. This is a farce, I thought. In infinite time, whatever could possibly come to pass would come to pass. And this is why this is happening now, given the inestimable number of events and circumstances that have gone into making these moments be the way they are. I couldn't tear my eyes away from the picture above me. What it did was disembody me, like the first time I saw the Sistine Chapel ceiling and almost fainted. (I learned later it was known as the Stendahl syndrome, since he did the same thing.) Is this some kind of sudden religious epiphany, I wondered? Is this something to do with Alex and her Regulators? Are they about to manifest themselves?

"What Lilly says is true, isn't it?" Grainger went on, pulling my spirit back to the immediate living present. "So this puts a different light on things."

Foreman had not said a word. Now I was back, I was beginning to feel elated. I knew that this little exercise was now running under the heading of "the medium is the message." It didn't matter a hoot what anyone said or did from now on, the very act of having this Enquiry, by itself, had reconfirmed us as righteous and dedicated fighters for human justice.

Foreman knew he had lost this skirmish. I guess there were too many surprises in it for him to handle with his usual double-speak. I kept looking at that blank face for any trace of real emotion, seeking to make eye contact so that he could see how much I hated him. I knew Grainger was deliberately leaving the accusation of Jock's murder to me. He had a very serious tone in his voice now, one I hadn't heard before.

"I know it won't have any effect on you, but I want you to know the suffering you have caused just to the people on this station. For myself I will never get over being led to murder two innocent Eurosoviet astronauts. And to watch how dedicated people like those in this room with you, who never gave a single thought to hurting anyone, have had to fight for their lives, drawing on reserves of courage and comradeship you could never begin to imagine. I don't know what we'll do with you yet. But you better realize that as far as I'm concerned you don't even amount to the dirt under any one of my colleague's little fingernails."

I found myself almost in tears as he so passionately attacked Foreman for callously riding roughshod over real people with real dedication to serve humanity. For a moment I forgot about how my relationship with Grainger had been so brutally truncated.

I guess Alex and I were sitting there, feeding off the angry accusations being flung at our hated enemy, but unwilling, in some strange way, to vent our own feelings upon him, as though that would lessen his evilness by putting it into inadequate words.

Foreman was not through, though, the wily bastard. In a temporary lull, he spoke up.

"I'm not happy with what has happened here, but I realize now you people have been under considerable stress for some time. And I am taking all that into account. Certainly we have had a frank exchange of views here, though there are many wild and unfounded accusations that I would like to address."

"Do you deny murdering Jock MacDonald?" I suddenly cried out. "He knew about your smuggling the weapons onto Earthbaby didn't he? And you had to shut him up."

Foreman didn't even flinch at that one. He hadn't heard much from me except my revelation about the split with Powers.

"This is one of those wild accusations I thoroughly deny."

I could feel the whole crew were with me, now. If there had been more of us, there might have grown that critical mass which leads to mob violence.

Alex looked ready to explode. "Deny, deny, lie, lie. Always the same. And do you also deny instituting a campaign of oppression and murder against the Regulator disciples?"

By now she had put the devastator in her pocket, but her hand was resting over it. Foreman moved quickly to quell her rage.

"I beg of you. Don't believe everything you hear. You are not privy to all the information about these cases. You people have to understand there are issues of national security here. I have been shown top secret documents that, as President, I would be glad to release and make public, which I am sure would satisfy you all on many counts. And further I would happily answer any and all questions in a formal congressional hearing, duly constituted. Until that time, I'm not at liberty to discuss the issues you have raised any further. Already I may have spoken too much. And I am not excluding one or another of the personnel on this station. All may not be as it seems among you. I am sure if you knew the whole truth about certain people's terrorist connections and treasonous intentions you would have a different perspective on things. Everything that I have done both before and after my election as President has been to forestall terrorist elements from attempting to destabilize America."

Some part of me admired the way he could pull out all the paranoia stops and sow the seeds of doubt. No wonder he had got where he had.

But dear Clarke wasn't one bit fazed. That anyone should question the loyalty and motives of HIS crew, with whom he had bonded in life and death action...

"I think our perspective is quite clear," Clarke interrupted him. "It seems to me we might just have to keep you here for a few months and see what happens when the world realizes you're no longer in charge of your faction down there."

"Then we shall dispose of you as seems fit," Alex said icily.

As Alex was speaking I did catch Foreman's eye for a second. I know now what it reminded me of, and I shuddered with horror. It was like being regarded as potential prey, by a snowy owl, a stalking tiger, a vulture descending...

Once again I looked up, but by now an oblique dart of sunlight had blued and lightened the dome. Out little farcical tableau had all disappeared.

What a day. But my account is not finished yet...

And now I come to this evening past. It's had been five debilitating days and nights since the invasion. Over those days, the only comfort I had was Clarke as I watched Grainger and Alex cement themselves into the ideal pair bond I had once objectively rationalized as inevitable and productive — God that seems so long ago when the Eurosoviet astronauts died such a grisly death. Clarke could see what I was going through, and besides helping me tend the recovering prisoners, was as sweet and loving as anyone could be. So what just happened in retrospect, doesn't seem so out of place, especially since I feared Alex, now consolidated with Grainger and Adam, might well turn her attentions Clarke's way next.

We all went to bed early tonight. But again I couldn't sleep. Something drove me to go out into the corridor. We talk about counter-phobic behaviour. It consists of confronting your greatest fear and finding it is not as horrible in reality as it is in your imagination. So that's what I was doing: reconfirming that Grainger and Alex were spending the nights together. Sure enough, his cabin was open and tidy, hers was locked. I stood there, breathing in and out, in and out, telling myself the pain inside me was of my own invention, that the wound was to my ego only and not to my heart as it was when Jock was torn away from me. I grew calm and turned to leave when suddenly Clarke's door opened. Seeing me startled him a moment.

"I was just thinking about you, Lilly. I thought for a second you were an apparition."

"Maybe I am," I said, complimented he was thinking of me.

"Couldn't sleep thinking about everything that's happening lately. Thought I'd get a drink and a snack to settle down."

He stood there in a cuddly old dressing gown, belted around his waist. With his bare feet and legs and his hair askew, he seemed vulnerable and boyish in the dim light. I think now it was magical and significant he should appear at that moment when I was in such emotional turmoil. A safe, comforting harbour.

"You were magnificent today, Clarke. From beginning to end."

He seemed genuinely surprised.

"Well, you were the one with the wisdom to put it all together. And I guess we wouldn't be here at all if it wasn't for Alex and that regulator intervention business. Do you really think there's something more than just this existence, Lilly?"

I immediately understood he was thinking about his dead wife, and taking comfort from the notion that there might be more, rather than a dead end to things.

"Probably there is," I said. "But not necessarily the way Alex and the others believe. I have a lot to tell you about that, Clarke. Especially after Foreman let it slip he and Powers had split up today, I've become more convinced there's a lot of chaos down there. I personally believe it was possible Tremaine managed to re-establish the systems, not some organization of super beings. Alex has had that complex fantasy for some time, and now it's coming to fruition in her consciousness."

"You don't say? Well that puts a different light on it."

He sounded relieved there could be a simple explanation.

"There's a difference between a miracle and a lucky coincidence," I said. "I couldn't sleep either, trying to figure out how to proceed from here on in."

"Well, if I can be of any help. You know how much I admire what you're doing, Lilly."

We were very close by now. We had been whispering, but now were standing, silent, two against the world, in one of those vivid moments that are the real miracles. I don't know who reached out first, but his hand was fondling the hair on the nape of my neck and my fingers were combing white thatch on his chest. Then we were kissing, kissing again, leaning for support against Alex's cabin door, perhaps only a foot or two away from where she and Grainger were coupled up.

We went into his cabin and I spread myself out flagrantly on his bed, throwing open my magenta silk robe, conscious of how erected my nipples were and how full my breasts were getting. Despite my emotional turmoil (or because of it!), I recognized I had yearned for this release for some time. He gave me it wonderfully, tremendously sensitive, bringing me to blazing climaxes several times with his mouth. My God how wonderful it is to lie back and be done over like that for what seemed hours on end.

I did try to give him pleasure back of course, but it was his first time for a long time, he was greatly over-tired and his body at first refused to respond. I massaged his back and shoulders after a while and moved down to his legs. That got him to sleep, and I lay curled against him, slipping blissfully off myself.

A few hours later, he must have woken and turned. I woke up too, in a dreamy limbic state of sheer body happiness, not allowing any thoughts other than those coming from my nerve endings to register. I reached over and found him. Most men, I know, have a spontaneous early morning erection. So it was with Clarke. I caressed him gently and he moaned with relief and gratitude. I could feel he was soon close to climax, but I wanted him to have the emotional confidence from actually being able to penetrate me, so I stopped, turned him on his back, wet myself a little, moistened him with my mouth a few times.

Clarke, coming fully awake, reached up for my breasts and drove into me wildly. It was incredible to look into his eyes as he came. He didn't close them because I knew he wanted to see only my face. I don't know what he saw there, but I was completely ecstatic to see how astounded he was with himself. What wonderful power I felt dragging those cries out of him, his mouth babbling my praises as if I were a goddess. And Goddess I felt as my own ecstasy took me over.

I ended, though, in the aftermath, sobbing against him as he held me like a child. I'm sure he thought I was one of those weepers, one of those women who always burst into tears at orgasm. But of course I was already mourning the loss of Grainger as I welcomed this new-found consort.

I could tell Clarke was soon asleep. I slipped quietly out into my own cabin, happy and wide awake. Now I'm finishing this account, though, I feel a wave of tiredness. That's the way it's been this last week. No wonder.

As I reflect on this new situation, I find myself asking what future role, if any, is going to be available to me here on Earthbaby? And if ever I get to do it, what validity will there be to the social dynamics research report I will construct from this journal? I recognize how easily I could get drawn into and contribute to what may turn out to be merely a shared grand neurosis on Earthbaby. If only I knew as much about computers as I know about human behaviour! Attractive as this whole Regulator hypothesis is, I would always have a nagging doubt until I could return to earth and prove or disprove it.

Too much to think about. Like Clarke, I'm going to catch some sleep now. What did Shakespeare say? *Sleep that knits the raveled sleeve of care.* No-one knits any more. I sound like my Grandmother…. ᘯ

Since it's a fine clear day the pilot deliberately circles their plane around Manhattan. Tremaine hasn't set eyes on New York since he was a youngster. The sun angles on a high slant through the forest of massive obelisks, glinting on vast arrays of windows. It seems impossible the land could ever have borne the weight of it all, and that's the real reason it has sunk into the sea.

He points out to Lesley the older famous landmarks: copper-roofed Empire State, fanfare topped Chrysler Building, Battery Park, and finally the rebuilt twin towers of the World Trade Centre. How many people are old enough to remember all the turmoil over their destruction? And who could have seen what a galvanizing effect it would have on a dormant culture, turning the American dream rapidly into this current nightmare? As the plane descends, their viewing angle changes. Now they catch glimpses of boats, like confetti sprinkled on the flood-ways between shadowed canyons.

There's none of the old harbour left to speak of. The statue of Liberty, torch held high, floats bemused on a small square raft. High water has made it easy for vandals. They've picked clean some copper sheathing from her skeleton feet and flowing toga. Ghost bridges arch up like computer-generated sea serpents out of the waves, coming from nowhere and going to nowhere. Some are hung with comical rags of drying laundry. Those who lived under bridges now live on them.

Tremaine can see where last-minute dyke-works and diversions had begun from the higher levels of Staten through Ellis and the other outcrops. But they were started too late, and when the huge Ross ice-shelf broke off from Antarctica, that was the end — a rise of another six feet in less than a year.

"Strange to think," Leslie says, "that the world's centre of wealth and commerce allowed itself to get swallowed up like this, when the rest of the world managed the emergency pretty well. How could Venice survive, and New York go under?"

"You'd have to be born in the USA to understand why," Tremaine tells her. "The whole notion of big public works spending is anathema to American privateers. Except for water tunnel number three, New York didn't have a single large public works project after 1930. The subway, the bridges, the museums, Central Park, you name it, it all happened before that."

"Strikes me there was also a lot of denial and self-deception. I remember the corporate lobby hiring all these anti-ecology professors to run around the world telling everyone the sea-rise was just a natural fluctuation and would go down again in a couple of years."

"You're right," Tremaine agrees. "And what with business dematerialization, New York didn't fare so well economically after the millennium."

Indeed, from this height, you can see the pattern of it, Tremaine thinks. These great cubes of buildings were basically warehouses whose function was to store a host of filing cabinets. In turn, the overstuffed balky drawers of those units preserved folders and files which were tended and groomed by various levels of clerks and bureaucrats, all of whom needed a chair and a desk at a minimum, not to mention an office and a phone. All rapidly made electronically redundant by the info-net and the home-working movement. The stock exchange itself was first to go. You'd have thought that would have signaled a warning.

"With so many head offices leaving," Tremaine went on, "tax revenues declined and the city went broke."

"All those big houses with helipads. Isn't that Central Park Mansions? They look pretty dry."

"It's on somewhat higher ground. Once they realized the flooding was real, the surrounding big hotels went in with the private developers who'd bought the park from the city and they dyked it in. Having a big wall around it was in the original plans anyway because they wanted the development to be an upscale walled-in enclave to keep out the street people. My guess is a lot of those people living there now commute to those inhabited tower tops."

"Reminds me of when I did that Giza pyramid laser projection set-up in Egypt. The cemetery community, which inhabited the old tombs, had become over-populated. So all the new refugees fleeing from desertification into Cairo built mud-hut villages on top of the highrises. Hey look!. See how they've put bridges linking tops of buildings together? Just like they did there. And they've got gardens up there too. Is that a baseball diamond for God's sake?"

"Guess they don't care if someone's down below when they hit a home run. I see there's a hell of a lot of light copters around, too."

"*Top-downers*," comments a high-style older woman across the aisle from them. She could be Perlita's mother, Tremaine thinks, suddenly reminded of her.

"It's a lifestyle thing for rich squatters. Vintage Valentino suits, Cuban cigars, sipping single malt scotch, leggy blonde secretaries stretched out on leather couches... that sort of thing ... like in the corporate heyday. 'Top-downers' move in on the top few floors, walk up and down carrying briefcases. Weird eh? They play those old computer business games with each other, or Kung Fu video arcade stuff."

Leslie smiles at her, taken, as Tremaine also is, by her warm demeanour.

"I can see you really know your way around, here. You don't have the accent though," Leslie says.

"I'm visiting my daughter in New Jersey. Helping her move back to the Bahamas with me. Where you folks heading?"

"Just in transition," Leslie answers, emphasizing her English accent.

"From across the water? Guess a lot of people are heading there what with the recent troubles. Would you call this a civil war we're having?"

"Guess so in a way. It's hard to say."

"Don't understand what it's about, though do you? Not like the last one we had a hundred and seventy-five years ago. Things ain't like they used to be in our time."

"A hundred and seventy-five years ago, people had a good idea what the civil war was about because they didn't have television," Leslie comments.

Now they've banked out to sea again, coming round to the airport in New Jersey, Tremaine can see dark stains of drowned habitats. Battered and tilted, the Ferris wheel and roller coaster he rode fifty years ago are still somehow standing on what used to be Coney Island. No sign of the pier.

"If people use the tops — *top-downers* — does anybody use the bottoms?" Leslie asks the woman.

"O sure. Most buildings started to flood in the sub-basements. My daughter had her car parked under her building and one day when she went down in the elevator, the doors opened and let in a foot of water. A month later you could have held a regatta down there. At first they filled them with concrete. That helped stabilize them, so I heard. Then they did the same with the next floor. After that they gave up. Sewage drainage problems. Elevator troubles. Streets awash. No one could get in with the regular entrances blocked. Finally, the New York

288   *Earthbaby*

electric utility quit after the Canadian resistance movement cut off all power in the big blackout. That was the end. Those 'boat-people' down there are mostly Hispanics and Asians. The ones living on the lower floors are mostly from the old black ghetto."

"So what are they called?"

"Bottom-uppers."

Top-downers, bottom-uppers and boat-people. What you might call a stratified society, Tremaine thinks. But yes, you could easily disappear around here in the waterlogged ruins. Is that the Society's idea bringing them here? This is Foreman country for now. At least that crowd doesn't have a personal stake in him and Leslie like Powers does. And if the rumours are right — Powers dead and Foreman on Earthbaby, unless something drastic happens in the meantime, this whole mess will have to end soon.

"We're landing," Leslie reminds him.

Soon they are down. Tremaine has been trying not to be nervous about going through the airport. Going around the amazing washout of Manhattan has helped. But you're always vulnerable in these kinds of controlled circumstances. What's disturbing is not knowing exactly who the contact is. The whole thing's been put together pretty hastily. The story of his life lately. Just part of the general anarchy everywhere — he re-assures himself — nobody can be too definite about anything. That goes for Leslie too. Trust me, she has said. Very soon, I'll tell you everything.

And oh damn! They *are* doing ID checks, not usual on Protectorate flights. Leslie looks at him. He still has the Herman Pantone ID and Leslie has her Europass.

"Don't worry. They're just ripping people through. Probably some drug thing."

And that's how it does look, with a dog on random patrol sniffing through the crowd. The document officials are bored and rapidly dismissive. They'll soon be through. Tremaine keeps his head down. Don't catch anyone's eye unnecessarily. That's when he sees the woman from the plane reach into her bag, extract a kleenex, sniff into it and then discard it onto the floor with a quick flick of her wrist so it falls in front of them. It looks lumpy. He checks for the dog. It's still quartering the edge of the crowd to his right.

He pulls on Leslie's sleeve and moves her subtly to the left, as far away as he can without making too much of a disturbance. The woman, noticing, moves with them. Leslie, sensing something is wrong, whispers, "What's up?"

Tremaine nods towards the woman. "I think she did a drop."

He looks at the dog. Still quartering. The woman is quite close. He can smell frangipani perfume on her clothes. Should he say something? She looks at him and smiles. "Don't worry. You'll soon be on your way."

Before he can answer, the dog has raised his head, tail wagging, alert. A beeline for the lump of kleenex. His handler picks it up, looks towards the woman, towards them. The woman slips away. He comes over.

"Papers please?"

They hand them over and he inspects them.

"We didn't drop it. It's not…"

"No need to make a scene. It'll go much better if you don't. Bring your bags and come with me."

What else to do?

He takes them into a side office, hands the dog to another customs officer.

"Keep checking, Mike. I'll handle these."

Under the table top, Leslie is squeezing his hand tight. He watches the officer scribble on a pad. In the old days he could have read it off upside down at ten paces. Even his hand is a blur now. Zen out, he tells himself. Just try to Zen out.

"A couple of questions just to check your ID if you don't mind. What was the first name of the Eurosoviet reporter who did the special on you and Bill Edgely last year?"

Tremaine knows he's been caught off guard. It must be all over his face.

"Got you, didn't we?" the officer says, grinning. "Go ahead and tell me, then we can move on."

Tremaine looks at Leslie. What's the use?

"Rivka," he says wearily.

"Great! Just wanted to be super sure. See this address? This is where you go, O.K? Your lady friend was the pointer. Actually she runs a casino in Nassau. Good luck, guys."

He accompanies them to the exit door.

"All clean, Jack. Let them through."

Into a taxi still dumbfounded, and soon they are bowling along through green Jersey suburbs, only occasionally blighted here and there by ugly stacks of privacy modules.

"What a trip!" Tremaine sighs.

"This is our life, Buddy," Leslie cajoles him. "Better get used to it."

"At least we aren't going to be billeted on a sampan."

"In fact, this place looks pretty swish," Leslie remarks as they exit the taxi.

"A classic mid-twentieth century suburban ranch bungalow," Tremaine notes. "Even has the original aluminum siding, I bet."

"And look at that antique aluminum screen door with the flamingo on it."

Pushing that door open, a yell of greeting coming from his shining face, is Donald Grey. He hugs them close, almost in tears, saying, "You made it! Jesus this is amazing! You made it!"

Inside, more surprises, Beatta and one of her friends from the lesbian tent. They are welcoming, especially to Leslie, but very subdued, clinging together on the couch like frightened children. When he and Leslie follow Grey into the kitchen for drinks, he explains.

"Most of the tent were killed in the raid. Though I'm hoping some might have been captured and tended to afterwards. Beatta and Jennie were still outside when it happened. So they were able to get into the van."

Tremaine knows Leslie and Grey were very close to them. Speaking about it makes Grey tear up a little. Tremaine stands apart while Leslie hugs him and sorrows herself. After a while they break and Tremaine says, "That's rough. Really rough."

When they go back in with the drinks, Leslie commiserates with Beatta and Jennie. They sit in a huddle with their three foreheads touching, arms linked around each other's shoulders for several minutes in silence. Then they slowly break and clasp each other's hands, soft smiles beginning to light their faces.

The next few hours they spend eating, drinking and catching up with each other.

"The only thing I could think about," Grey recalls, "was whether the van's suspension would give out. We were so overloaded. We couldn't take the risk of going to the harbour. And how would we get in touch with Neil anyway? So we had to hide out for a few days in the jungle. Since we were off-track, it meant half the Euro team had to walk. The Euros were great. A couple of them would go off and quietly raid a tourist place for food and clothes and fuel. Finally they swiped a very fast boat moored in a small marina one night and we got over to Neil's. The Euros got orders to stay there if possible, and the rest of us lit out on the Bahamas route you came on."

Leslie tells them, "The Euros are still there. Got a lot of local support. Starting to clean out the Powers' people it seems. Those guys didn't make themselves popular ashing Neil's garage and Sonny's Frangipani. Made it easier for us."

"You and the Euros nearly shot us out of the sky. Did you know that?"

"Sorry about that. The boys said it was weird how the copter they shot at caused the other one to veer off, so we could get into the forest. Now I know. Thanks for that."

"Proved to be a bit of a useless exercise of course — trying to get out in the copter. Considering what's happened to me in those damn things, I don't think I ever want to be in one again."

"So you think it was James double-agenting?"

Leslie suddenly looks tired.

"Oh sorry," Grey says. "Shouldn't have brought it up. I guess it's like everything now. The days when you could wrap everything up neatly with a logical explanation have gone forever."

"So how did Bill get out?"

"More or less the same way you guys came in. Jocko — the dog man — handled getting him out. There's still an international megajet service. Tight security coming in; but not getting out. How long that service survives is anyone's guess these days."

"So where is he now?"

"St.Petersburg."

"With Rivka?" Tremaine asks.

Grey grins. "And Perlita."

"So why are you still around Grey? Besides helping refugees like us, that is."

Beatta answers for him: "He has a mission," she says.

"What's that?" Leslie asks.

"To find the rest who survived…. Like you and Andy did….

Leslie and Tremaine look at each other. Survived. Yes!

E vening of the same day. Lilly sits in her dispensary in a real quandary. All her instincts tell her this Regulator business is a big scam. But she's had quite a shock to her belief system once again. She's convinced what Alex told her a few hours ago is lies, all lies. But perhaps there's a tiny chance it isn't. Then what? Oh dear Jock, why aren't you here to help me at times like this? Yes, Clarke is wonderful, completely different from you of course, thank God for him too and his solid support of me. Still the terrible quandary. Where does Lilly find strength for her convictions? Perhaps because she knows her history. Didn't Christianity and Islam start the same way as the Regulators, with charismatic people claiming to be manifestations of higher powers? And didn't their early stages involve miracles (inter-ventions?) popularized by an elite corps of committed disciples to whom the divine ones had specially manifested themselves? Sound familiar? Now the Regulator movement is at the martyrdom stage of ultra-committed members sacrificing for the cause in the power-struggle against the old regime. Next comes infiltration of ruling class-es until Regulatorism (or whatever it gets called) is proclaimed the state religion by an Emperor or similar authority figure. Immediately afterwards will be the erection of a vast bureaucracy. Non-believers, naturally, will be made into outcasts or destroyed.

There are certain advantages to writing in the third person. Objectivity for one thing. Julius Caesar wrote of his own exploits that way.

Here, in my own little domain, it's very quiet. In some parts of the station, I've noticed there's ambient noise of undetermined origin caused by the station's systems. "Outside," in space itself of course, there's absolute quiet, not a trace of background noises despite all those old myths about the music of the spheres. The shuttle rockets, deafening on earth, make no sound when they depart, there being no medium through which sound waves can travel, or even begin to propagate. In space, the most awful destruction occurs without a whisper being heard — even the hugest nuclear explosions of dying stars cascade with reckless energy into utter silence. Over the black universe pinpricked with a scattering of solitary stars, presides a deaf god.

Heartening, isn't it? That's why I would so much like to believe in the meta-consciousness of the Regulators. Why couldn't it have been to me rather than to Alex they manifested themselves? Why is life such a struggle to make sense of? Don't you think after several million years it would have become perfectly clear to us, so we could pass it on to the next generation who would be free from doubt and worry? From what I have read of philosophy, particularly the late twentieth century variety, I think it would be very salutary for those aspiring to that branch of metaphysics to spend their time in graduate school on a space station such as this one. It might result in some pertinent answers to fundamental questions, rather than arcane and over-referenced obeisances to standardized notions promulgated by a tiny pantheon of institutionalized authorities. Okay, I guess I should stop messing around and tackle this head-on.

After I had completed my previous journal entry of yesterday morning, my catch-up doze was interrupted by Adam knocking at my door. Before falling asleep I'd only managed to wipe myself over with a wet towel since the shower produced only a lukewarm trickle. So I must have looked and smelled pretty slutty in my wrinkled silk robe, tousled hair and smeared eye-shadow when I opened the door.

He did do a little bug-eyed swallow before telling me: "NASA is coming through. Alex wants everybody in Central right away." He had the officious tone you find in the recently promoted.

I wanted to say, "Tell her to tell them to fuck off." But I merely said, "All in good time. They can always call back."

Even this little joke, I could see, was taken as a rebuff to his sense of urgency and importance.

I heard him deliver the same message to Clarke then leave. Obviously the three of them had been up and at 'em for some time. Would they guess Clarke and I were getting it on? I didn't care. Their *menage-a-trois* was pretty obvious.

In a few minutes Clarke came by. We didn't have a lot of time to talk, but we expressed our good feelings for each other with hugs, kisses and caresses. Too bad we couldn't have continued with things right then and there, but duty called.

"At least before I face the day, I'd like to have a coffee," I announced. So we went first to the food parlour. The machine took awhile, finally yielding a reluctant dribble.

"Tastes like hell," Clarke commented. "Hope it's not full of Adam's growth hormones or something."

"You've got as much as I can handle as it is," I joked, putting my hand at the appropriate place.

We went into a clinch again, said nice things, then parted, squaring our shoulders and marching off to do battle. Munching on the remains of the cup for a shot of energy, I felt alive and powerful as we got to Central. The three of them were there, looking impatient. I rather hoped Grainger, at least, would take us for a couple.

"I thought we'd be hearing from NASA," Clarke said. "Ever since you guys figured out the next shuttle departure window starts tomorrow and doesn't last more than a few days."

"And after that," Grainger added, "it'll be weeks before they can leave again."

"The problem is, our water shortage has grown quite critical," Adam said. "We won't be able to support the present number of personnel for much longer."

Having seen Adam's growing obsession with his garden, I wasn't convinced this water-shortage bit was absolutely necessary. I was suspicious Adam was putting plant health over human.

"We could cut down on the garden use, couldn't we?" I threw at him. "I mean now it's not absolutely crucial to produce all our air for us."

Rather than Adam leaping to defend the water rationing, the three of them looked tired and hopeless as experts often do when faced with a simple-minded questioner who hasn't the faintest idea, by God, of how incredibly complex the issue is. And even if you *did* take the time to explain it all, you know they *still* couldn't possibly understand, could they? I immediately regretted my ebullient mood had led me to utter such sacrilege. There was much significant looking back and forth among the triumvirate. I took this as a signal they were about to bring up one of their pre-arranged issues. And I wasn't wrong. I started to take notes for future reference since I would have no camera archive of this discussion.

Alex took the lead with it. "Adam's garden is a necessary component of our achieving the independence schedules. We are getting closer every day to being able to exist without the laser beam controls. Since the air and water cycles are closely linked in this respect, we have to use up the contingency reserves since the shuttle did not bring any safety margin of water cargo."

"I don't want to quibble with you experts," Clarke said. "But while we have Foreman here, NASA isn't likely to cut the beam. Can't we slow this down a little? You guys have been working day and night on it. I mean those independence schedules weren't meant to be completed until months from now."

"For one thing," I said, "how can you work on the deep navigation level of the station's orbit until we've had one complete revolution?"

"That is a problem," Grainger conceded. "Right now, if the beam were to be completely turned off, we would have to engage in crude over-rides which would use up all the orbital correction energy very quickly. To define and correct our orbit within inches as the laser now does, is possible because of the objective co-relatives achievable from an observational distance. To accurately define ourselves from ourselves, so to speak, is almost impossible unless we possess such an intricately rendered complete orbital baseline to work from."

At times like that, the only thing you can do is try to look intelligent as if you understand what the hell these techies are talking about. His conclusion was simpler.

"Once our orbital correction energy system runs dry, we would be prone to veer off into a grand solar orbit similar to a comet or random asteroid. There's no knowing where we would go, but the odds are in a few years we would travel too far from the sun to continue to exist, or most likely be dragged into an exponentially diminishing solar orbit and burn up."

Alex politely waited for him to finish.

"Grainger and I slightly disagree on this. My contention is we could manage it, especially if we found ways to use other motive energy sources."

She smiled at Grainger apologetically. I could see he would have loved to concur with her, if only to get her approval, but orbital mechanics was his specialty, and his professionalism couldn't quite allow him to do it.

"The fact remains, though, you aren't far enough along to go independent yet. We'd essentially be in the same state as we were before the invasion, isn't that right?" Clarke asked her.

"Well, I think we've begun to…"

"6including having to live in a completely self-sustaining ecology with all the inconveniences, and perhaps fatal consequences, that go along with it," Clarke concluded.

I could see Alex was getting ruffled by Clarke and his straightforwardness. Who would have expected at the start of this mission to see a leadership contest between these two unlikely candidates? Her two acolytes sat waiting to see how she would handle it.

"That contingency — having the beam cut off entirely — is why we have to concentrate as much of our resources as possible on the garden growth."

"It's the whole basis of our independent existence," Adam chimed in, swelling with self-importance.

"So there's no immediate hope in sight of a decent cup of coffee," Clarke grumbled.

I could tell the triumvirate had an agenda, but Clarke still had the authority of the station commander in dealing with NASA who recognized him as such; and I must admit, yesterday's performance with Foreman had, as I intended, confirmed that authority. The cards though were pretty well all on their side. They had the technical know-how and we didn't. And knowledge, as always, is power.

In the meanwhile, though, Clarke was still in charge.

"Well, before we connect with NASA, we'd better have a general agreement about what we want to do here. Does anyone have any idea what threat they could pull to bring us into line? Cutting the beam entirely as we've discussed, I suppose. But whatever they do to us, they do to Foreman; so I think that's unlikely."

"If the problem of getting good coffee is due to excess personnel as Adam says it is," I began, "then I think I can see a solution here. What we agree to do is let the shuttle return, with the excess personnel aboard...."

"...but we keep Foreman here, so they don't do anything dirty to us," Clarke finished for me.

We grinned at each other. I could see the three had already discussed this possibility amongst themselves. Alex, however, introduced a note of earnestness designed to quell our unseemly flippancy. She reminded us that a few weeks or so later on, we might be invaded again in a more sophisticated way — a nerve gas attack, for instance, introduced through the air system. Any number of things. After all, the shuttle crew had not been prepared for any resistance from us this time around.

"It might get you a better cup of coffee," Alex said, "but what we need is a long-term strategy."

I guess we had been put in our place. Silence again, until broken by Grainger.

"Still, at least it would give us a few weeks of grace, and God knows what could happen between now and then."

I was surprised Grainger felt he had to support me rather than acceding to Alex. But I guess that's his rather maverick nature, the bastard.

Adam, naturally, rushed to defend his mentor.

"Alex is right. I wish there was some other strategy that would guarantee our complete and long-range freedom from interference."

Alex did one of her "good-little-boy" smiles at him. Then she swiveled round, poised to operate the communication channel with NASA. How subtle she was in putting herself in the control seat.

"I don't think there's much point in discussing this further, until we know what NASA has to say."

"Just a moment," Clarke cut in, stopping her hand. "I just thought of it. Now the weapons-area hatch has been blasted open, why don't we simply get rid of the missiles? Then Earthbaby is no use to them."

For a moment I felt like cheering. The simplest answer is so often the right one, and here it was right in front of us. I turned to Grainger, playing it cool with an 'I'm-not-grieving-that-much-over-you-baby' attitude.

"How would we do that, Grainger? Would it be difficult to have them go into the kind of diminishing solar orbit you were describing and have them burn up?"

It felt good doing what I do best, pushing the group dynamics around like that. Grainger rose to my bait again, glad to display his expertise, attending to my question, rather putting Alex into the background for a moment.

"Very easy, in fact. Any kind of velocity you give them in the general direction of the sun, within quite a wide range of degrees, would see them accelerate into its gravitational field at an increasing rate. They'd melt long before they got there."

"All right. Let's do it, and so inform NASA," Clarke concluded.

I noticed the triumvirate looking at each other again. Alex signaled her decision by starting the communication sequence.

Blip, blip, beep, beep, buzz, buzz, ding-dong, chirp.... I caught Grainger's eye. When we were in daily contact with NASA he'd made that familiar computer hand-shaking mantra into a nonsense song to wake me after love-making. He looked away as the screen effloresced into life.

Doberman again, confident and dismissive, as if we were trash. Without any preliminaries he informed us that the laser-connection security over-rides had once more been activated. At any moment, NASA could again truncate the signal — all of it this time — and send us all to our eventual doom. He wanted to be quite clear about that. He then wanted confirmation that Foreman was still alive before saying anything further.

Everybody was angry and defensive about Doberman's attitude to us. I didn't say anything, but I worried there was more behind it than that outrageous bullying tone common to right-wing demagogues. Clarke couldn't see any problem with putting Foreman on, so he was hauled into Central before the cameras. Before we showed him to NASA, I suggested we get him to tell them we were going to immediately destroy the weapons.

Foreman wanted to appear with his jacket on, but I nixed the idea. You never know, they might edit and use this stuff for broadcast. After some harmless preliminary greetings in which he assured NASA he was still intact, he asked Clarke if he could deliver to NASA information concerning those who had not survived the attack. Again, Clarke, thinking that would be a good idea for humanitarian reasons, since these people may have families, let him go on about the dead "heroes" in a tiresomely platitudinous voice. We knew that would get an airing on the managed news. But these days, no matter whether they doctored it up or not, no-one really believed it. Then Foreman delivered the message about destroying the weapons.

I could see this had an effect on Doberman.

"All we want is to be left alone to do our jobs in peace," Alex put in, placing herself in front of Foreman. We then wheeled him into the background.

Doberman responded with a speech about how crucial Earthbaby and its weaponry was to anti-terrorist activity and world order. It was remarkably similar to the one Foreman had delivered the day before. The new twist was, however, that thousands of people were dying every day in a senseless civil war that threatened to destroy the American Protectorates. Clearly the Powers forces were in dire conflict with Foreman's, and I sensed this was a kind of message to Foreman that things were not going well.

When Doberman finished, Foreman indicated he would like to say a few words. Clarke nodded his permission.

"We all appreciate your concerns, Colonel. I have expressed the same sentiments to Commander Clarke and his crew in a recent discussion session. Unfortunately, we have not been able to come to a satisfactory agreement. Given the increasing urgency of the situation, I am going to suggest a last offer be made to the Earthbaby crew, which I wish you to record and to accede to. I am prepared to give a general pardon on mental health grounds of undue stress and isolation to all those involved in this unfortunate affair, if they return on the shuttle within the available time, leaving the station as it is in charge of myself and my crew. Will you give your word that my orders in this respect will be carried out?"

"Absolutely, Mr. President."

Foreman turned to us all. "There you have it, Ladies and Gentlemen. I can do no more. Take it or leave it."

"Take it or leave it?"

Oh, Oh. I'd been waiting for this, an Alex outburst. She'd been far too controlled as far as Foreman was concerned. Actually my blood rather thrilled as she got up and advanced towards him swiftly, drawing her weapon. Foreman jerked back, fear of her written all over him. She stuck it in his face then turned for NASA's benefit and said with a flat chill voice, "Understand this, you leave us entirely alone or your leader comes back to you wrapped as garbage."

Doberman kept a deadpan expression. Not a flicker. I thought, he's not that upset about the idea. I wonder what was in Foreman's mind.

"I don't see the value of such histrionics at this time," he said evenly. "We will await your answer. In the meantime, please do not underestimate our resolve in this matter."

Clarke, with a look at Alex, standing puzzled, I suspect, that her move hadn't elicited the response she hoped, asked her to terminate our communication with NASA until later. Still the take-charge guy, he told us very formally that he wanted us to consider all that had been said. To make sure no-one was being pressured, he would oversee a secret ballot poll. As everyone could have predicted, it was unanimously against accepting NASA's deal. Everyone concurred with the idea that none of us wanted Earthbaby to be the doomsday bomb in the sky, and even if we did want to get out, assurances from the likes of Foreman and Doberman were worth nothing.

We kept Foreman around for this discussion, Alex glowering at him occasionally in such a way he kept his mouth shut through it all, until the question of worthless assurances came up. He then gave it his best and last shot.

"Rather than demand I remain on board Earthbaby, I will offer to accompany you back to Earth in the shuttle as a hostage, to ensure your liberty will be protected on your return."

I chuckled inside, thinking of how Foreman's nightmare was to be stuck alone on Earthbaby at Alex's mercy.

Again Clarke took a secret ballot. Again it was unanimously against.

We decided not to contact NASA right away. I started a general movement to get rid of the weapons now we had the chance, feeling it would be a positive move to do something constructive together. But then Foreman put a damper on it.

"Let me just say," he began, with a rather wincing look in Alex's direction, "that there are more missiles available. I'm sure the next shuttle will transport them here to replace those you want to destroy. It would be to everyone's advantage, however, to keep the weapons already here readily available to prevent this terrible conflict that is tearing our nation apart. By this willful action, you merely create a small delay."

He was right, damn him.

"Let's do it, anyway," I said. "We'll all breath easier, and besides, who knows whether they can get neutron missiles as easily as they once could. These are not your every-day item."

But I wasn't successful. As Grainger pointed out, there were several problems with the project that had to be thought through. With the emergency bulkheads sealing off the breached area, access was only possible from outside via the space-buggy or a space-walk, both of which would use up cylinder air reserves. We also had no idea how the missiles were mounted; that meant taking out one or both of the weapons people who had come up with the shuttle. That could be a problem if we had to guard them during the operation. Who knows what might happen? It was something we could do, right enough, and should do, he conceded, being very polite and careful not to offend me. But if Earthbaby was subject to getting raided again, and the raid was successful, then re-arming was, as Foreman noted, no problem. Thus our efforts and resources would have been wasted.

So. There we were. We reconnected with NASA and told them our decision not to accept their offer, and also not to accept it even with Foreman accompanying us on the shuttle. Doberman didn't hesitate. Obviously other discussions had taken place in the meantime.

"You have twenty-four hours to accept this offer. The beam will then be entirely truncated."

I think everyone was shocked. We hadn't expected that, thinking we were in the power position with Foreman and the others as hostages.

"You realize you will be endangering the life of your President, and your colleagues," Clarke commented. (I noticed he said *your* President.)

"For the sake of our nation, that is a risk the Lifeist army has taken into account over the last few days of discussion."

I looked at Foreman. Surprised? He looked astounded, afraid. Of course he couldn't say anything. His hands clenched tight, sweat beaded along the wrinkles in his high forehead. Oh good. Suffer, you fucker. I'd suspected something was up when Doberman came on so full of himself. Goings on amongst the Lifeists themselves! No honour among thieves again. With half the army brass stuck on our station, this opened up unparalleled opportunities for promotion. I can see the meeting now, ambitious little Vice President Cadron presiding. You know, I maybe shouldn't put it this way, but isn't the army bigger than one guy? I mean, even if that guy IS the President?

The momentum of our initial resistance, and of our success, had kept us from really dealing with what might be our long-term future. In her own twisted way, Alex had been right. Now it had to be faced. And I knew what had to be done.

We took Foreman back to his quarters and then I insisted we begin discussions anew. Alex, Adam and, to a lesser extent, Grainger were loathe to tackle the issues any longer. They simply wanted to get going on the independence schedules to prepare as much as possible for the beam cut-off, in case NASA wasn't bluffing. I told everybody I was sure they weren't, and went over Foreman's reaction. Clarke, bless him, threw in that they should trust me on that, it was my area of expertise after all. From his army man's point of view, you never make idle threats in negotiations. If the Lifeists were prepared to risk terminating Foreman and his lackeys, then obviously they had contingency leadership plans. In short, things had probably become extremely critical down on earth, to the point where the leadership considered Foreman expendable. We therefore had little to bargain with.

I insisted our crew at least hear me out because I had an idea, shocking perhaps, but the only one I could see which offered a quick exit from all our dilemmas.

"Is this going to be the pattern of our lives," I asked, "scrambling along on minimal resources, all our efforts bent towards surviving on the edge, expecting one invasion after another? We all came up here for specific projects. Except for Adam, none of us has had the chance to really pursue them. Much as I hate to say it, given the Earth's present circumstances, the existence of any deep-space habitat like Earthbaby offers itself up as an opportunity to be used the way Foreman intended. Here's my suggestion. We all leave in the shuttle. But before we go we ensure that Earthbaby becomes entirely non-functional and uninhabitable. We then attempt to land in Euro-soviet territory. If we're lucky and succeed, we can put Foreman up for war-crimes trials."

It was a bombshell, all right.

I could see Clarke going for it. Adam looked stunned. Everything he'd said to Foreman he could now lay onto me. His dear garden he'd spent so much time on would be trashed. I looked closely at Grainger, whose initial reaction, I thought, was positive. His preference was for the active not the passive. But he quickly concentrated his gaze on Alex, prepared to take his cue from her.

"I can't believe I'm hearing this," she said. "How can we compare our petty little research projects to the key role we have to play in the construction of the solar computer? If we weren't an important part of the universal scheme of things, then why did the Regulators bless us with their intervention? We must do everything in our power to preserve this station. The Regulators will never abandon us. Lilly, how could you so casually think of destroying Jock's wonderful vision?"

I was shocked she would pull that one out of the bag. Damn Grainger for telling everyone about our relationship. I knew it would come back to me.

"Jock wouldn't have wanted Earthbaby to go on like this," I said hotly. "This isn't the kind of vision he had for it."

Her voice when she answered me was filled with a peculiar gentleness.

"Jock was the one who sponsored me as an Earthbaby crew member, Lilly. And for good reason."

What was that all about? My mind raced rapidly from thinking she meant they were lovers to some other obscure mystery about her.

"What do you mean, Alex?"

"Jock's vision for Earthbaby was the same as mine. Jock was a Regulator, Lilly. That's the main reason he was killed."

I'm still stunned by what she said. At the moment she told me, I believed her. It made such a lot of sense. The joy he had in living every moment. The boundless love and tolerance for other people and their foibles. The sheer creative energy and power of his work. His computer wizardry, of course. All that would make wonderful sense if he believed life had meaning and consciousness continued in a higher form. Yet, why oh why didn't I know? Why didn't he tell me? If all this was true, he must have told HER!

And she kept on.

"Jock wanted Earthbaby because the Regulators needed this deep space solar computer link. And I am the one he ordained to fullfil that dream."

I screamed out, "Then why the hell didn't they intervene to keep him alive! Why the hell don't they manifest themselves to me!"

"Have faith and they will, Lilly. Have faith!"

But by that time I couldn't see very clearly, I rushed out and flung myself into my cabin, sobbing my heart out. The whole idea of being stuck in space appalled me. Nothing was worth this insane existence. Oh God. I just wanted to get out of here, out of this nightmare, back to the tattered and diminished but real and solid world again.

In a few minutes, dear Clarke came to hold me and I calmed down after awhile. It was then the anger started.

"She's lying! I know she's lying, Clarke. Jock would have told me. He told me everything. She said it to get me on her side. She's ruthless, Clarke."

"It's okay. Lilly. It's all okay."

Moment by moment I came back to myself. No more dilly-dallying. It was clear what I had to do. Feeling the change in me as I lay against him, Clarke began talking to me.

"You know, Lilly, what you said about abandoning Earthbaby. It all makes sense. We're all useless up here, now. The time isn't ripe. In future years maybe. When the world has settled down some. As soon as you said it, I knew it was the right thing, Regulators or no Regulators."

Oh my God, How much I adored him at that moment.

"What are we going to do then, Clarke?"

"I don't know yet. But somehow I think you and I have to return in the shuttle, even if the others choose to stay. We'll do the last part of your plan and try to land in the Eurosoviet."

"Can you do it by yourself? Pilot the shuttle I mean?"

"Essentially. We don't have much time. While they're all busy I'm going to try and figure out getting ourselves onto the shuttle and un-docking."

"Bless you, Clarke."

And so here I am. Waiting for Clarke to return. Waiting in great calmness to make love again. Another pair-bond variation creates your classic three/two split.

End of social dynamics research project coming up! ∽

L eslie slides into his bed warm and magnetic against his back, her morning skin-smell like new-baked bread. So she's back. In the night he'd woken to an empty hollow beside him, still warm. He reaches behind him and pulls her close.

"Where have you been?"

She runs her fingers down his belly and squeezes him playfully.

"With Jennie and Beatta. Time to get up my darling. We must fly away again."

He keeps his eyes closed holding on to this lovely moment between wake and sleep, not wanting to move, just wanting to wear her on his back forever. Fly away? Where to? Why now? He stops bothering himself with it, begins to drift away again.

But she won't let him.

"Grey has heard from Bill, Perlita and Rivka. They're crazy about seeing us again and getting all the news. We should leave while the way is still open. Also, Janet gave Neil the shuttle radio frequency and he passed it on to them. You, of course, are pretty useless except to me. But you might be handy to have around when they monitor communications between the shuttle and NASA once it leaves."

No use trying to stop the flow of time. His consciousness is aroused now. He rolls away from her over the edge of the bed, breaking the electric field between them.

"So there's still no hard news about what's happened on Earthbaby?"

"All they know is the shuttle hasn't left yet — but it will have to within the next few days. Then there's this persistent rumour about Foreman being aboard Earthbaby."

"I worry we did the wrong thing with restoring the beam."

"It was the right thing. Please trust me."

"So this means our mission is over, so to speak."

"I'm taking you home to Europe with me. Now it's your turn to live in my part of the world for a while. Seriously, I have things to do there. Still trust me?"

"Why not? It's easy to just go along. So where are we going? St. Petersburg?"

"Close enough. I've told them to meet us in Helsinki. It's more peaceful there, and we'll also have access to Nordic Net's Communication Centre. I have an old friend I want to see there, Annina Mustonen, Head of their Experimentation division."

"I went through there as a young student in 2000. Helsinki was cultural capital of Europe. They only had a million back then; but boy, were they ahead of the pack."

Dressing automatically, Tremaine allows his dream-swept mind to re-experience hiking through Finland's coastal meadows, still rising inch by inch out of shallow waters since the glaciers departed. The sea-green flatlands made from silt, were embossed with rocky knobs, once islands, where Vikings had moored their high-prowed ships. Clambering up onto those timbered granite slabs, you could find here and there among the trees burial mounds of ancient nobles, made, some said, by funeral boats dragged inland, then overturned to cover them. Ah, but wouldn't a sea-rise have flooded those waist-high grass-lands again? And Europe's northward migrations have settled on those new-old islands, linked them with bridges, built over burial mounds…?

But one thing wouldn't have changed and those were Finland's long summer sunsets that turn without fading into long summer dawns. Hours of smoldering horizons when naked laughing bodies would run from sauna down sloping granite boulders into the frigid Baltic. That honey light on their dripping skins, on his own skin… this very part of it drawn tight over his round shoulder where a girl had laid her hand…is it possible for all this to have happened? How magical, how mystical, and yet how real that was, more real than anything before or since.

And isn't that the amazing reality of his own life this last little while? The long sunset of it brightening, then, when he expected it to falter and to fade into terminal darkness, not dwindling at all, but miraculously continuing to glow ….

He springs to his feet like a young man.

"Take me home, then, you beautiful witch. "

*   *   *

Through the taxi window, their last view of Grey: Jeannie one side, Beatta the other, his ape-like arms draped over their shoulders, walking across the tattered lawn and up the decaying concrete steps. A moment later, closing behind them, the aluminum screen door embossed with its extinct flamingo.

Hugging him, Leslie says, "I feel like I'm going on a honeymoon."

He puts his hand to her mouth.

"Don't say that. We're not there yet."

"I know you, Andrew. All the way to the airport you're going to be holding your breath."

"Somebody has to do the worrying. Somebody has to guard the treasure."

Step one: arrival at the airport. Accomplished. Step two: tickets ready at the counter. Step three: Jocko appears, escorts them through passport check. Step four: sitting with three hundred other passengers in the departure lounge.

He gets her a drink of water, trying to make sure she stays in sight.

"Thank you. But don't breathe yet, Andy. Wait till we're on the plane."

"No. Actually in the air."

There are many suspicious-looking people around him. He moves seats to see who might follow them. None do.

At last they stumble down the skid-proof ramp and over the threshold into the plane itself. The flight personnel are tall, well-dressed with symmetrical Baltic faces as perfect as androids. They find the seat. They buckle up and hold hands.

And then they are in the air.

In a few minutes they are beyond American Protectorate territorial waters.

He leads her up to the sky lounge where they celebrate with sweet, cheap Finnish champagne. A remembered taste.

"My God, Leslie. They still make this stuff."

In a couple of hours it grows darker; but they are flying the polar route.

Through one side of the roof, North West, the setting sun. Ahead of them, North East, a hint of dawn. The chink of glasses and bright stars between.

SOCIAL DYNAMICS PROJECT: EARTHBABY
JOURNAL OF LILLITH SHAWNADITHIT

E vents have moved at such a whirlwind pace I can hardly believe I now have several days — barring any accidents — to do practically nothing but lie here on this launch-couch trying to assess what has happened. I thought leaving Earthbaby would be a wrench. But uncertain as the future might be, I am experiencing only great relief.

The critical moment came with an urgent knock at my cabin door — some fifty hours ago. Clarke, I thought. But when I opened it, there was Grainger, ashen-faced.

"Let me in, Lilly. I have to talk to you."

I knew right away this was serious stuff. I closed the door and he sat on the edge of the bed. For the hell of it, in case I needed to go over it later, I hit the voice memo button on the cabin computer. What follows, then, is more or less a transcription.

"The guys in the aerobic chamber — they're all dead except Foreman!"

On the tape, I make no sound or reply. That's because my immediate thought was, the bastard killed them!

"No. I know what you're thinking. Foreman wasn't in the chamber at all. Last night Alex asked me to go down with her and take him out of there. I helped her secure him in the psycho-cell with his lackey."

"Dead? They're dead? How can that be?"

My own voice sounds appalled, whispery.

"I don't know. Maybe the air was turned off. I went to check on them this morning. I cranked the door open and said something like, "Have a good night, guys?" Then I saw them. They were gone. Fuck! It was horrible. Blue faces. Eyes wide one of them, half out of his bunk. It was just now, Lilly. I was just in there. I can't take it…. Alex…. She's crazy…. All this Regulator shit…."

"Alex?"

"I think she killed them."

"Why would she do that? I thought it was Foreman she…"

My voice trails off.

"She said Foreman should be in isolation to think over his sins against the Regulators. And then she said the others in there should be able to rest in peace without his evil influence."

Here Grainger pauses and catches his breath. It appeared to me he was hyperventilating a little, going into a panic attack. You can hear his gasping on the tape. His hands were visibly shaking. I'd never seen him so uncontrolled.

"Take it easy'" I say. "Do you want a drink, anything to calm you down?"

To my astonishment he burst into tears. On the tape there's this utterly devastated quiet sobbing. It's hard to hear the words clearly, especially since I am interjecting soothing sounds etcetera. It all sounds pretty confused, but the gist of it is Grainger says something to the effect Alex is a frightening witch who has had him in her power, mentally, physically — feeding his delusions of a blissful eternal paradise — sucking him into some crazy psycho-sexual cult. Then there's a lot of stuff about how wonderful and wise and understanding I am — how could he ever have fallen for it and so on.

Nothing like being proved right is there? I did put my arms around him, but in fact there was no huge rush of thankfulness and forgiveness inside me. It was more like a kind of annoyance at how fucking immature he had been and how insensitive and hurtful was the result of his childish behaviour. You have to remember this was just after the second great night of fucking I'd had with Clarke — towards whom I had redirected my considerable affectionate energies. So, flattered as my ego was on some level, I wasn't about to lay myself out for another go-round with Grainger thank you very much.

I hear myself on the tape starting to take control after a while.

"Look. Are you going to pull yourself together or am I going to have to stick a hypo in you?"

"Oh God. Please don't be rough on me Lilly. I'm just a wreck right now."

"I'm not being rough on you. But you have to understand I've suffered a lot through all this."

There's a pause. Then his voice, so surprisingly contrite, that re-listening to it I almost burst into laughter.

"I'm sorry," he says. Like some cute little boy.

"So how do you know Alex killed them? Did you see her do it?"

"No. Not directly. But it makes sense with what she did later."

Thinking back now to how I reacted, I must say how revealing it is, in hind-site, that somehow I couldn't quite bring myself to believe Alex could be so deranged...so cold-blooded.... Even with her attempt to make me believe Jock was a Regulator. But I held my thoughts back from Grainger. Whatever the case, I wanted him away from Alex, and safely back where he should be — with me.

"What did she do later to make you think that?"

Again Grainger pauses. I could see he was still in shock over the discovery.

"Put your head down for a minute," I say. I can hear myself getting up and trying to get water out of the tap. I got enough of a dribble to fill a disposable cup. He bent over, recovered himself, and started talking again.

"Well, once we had Foreman secure, she wanted to go back into the chamber. She said she had to talk to the boys alone about the Regulators. I went in with her at first because she said she wanted to have them strapped down just in case they decided to overpower her and hold her as hostage or something. That made sense to me, so she guarded me while I did it... Oh shit!"

"What's the matter?"

"My devastator. I don't have it! The witch. She didn't give it back to me."

"Oh great. Now she and Adam have got one each."

"Why didn't I ask her to give it back to me? Jesus, I'm so fucking dumb!"

"Calm down. There's still the ones we took from the shuttle crew. So what happened next?" (Dumb me. I later remembered Alex locking them up for safety somewhere in Adam's lab area.)

"I went out to get a coffee and wait. An hour, she said, then I could go back in and undo the straps. Well. The damn coffee machine wasn't working right. I know now it's to do with the water shortage. So I sat with the empty cup, broke it into pieces and ate it.

"Then I thought about your idea we should get rid of the missiles and how one of these days I should maybe go out in the space buggy to check the open hatch and drift around to see exactly what damage was done when Foreman's crowd blasted in from the weapons hold. Out of curiosity, I wandered down there, and as I was going past the aerobic chamber I noticed there wasn't any glow through the quartz porthole window. I couldn't see anything through it except a few vague shadows.

That made me uneasy. What if they'd somehow got free? Open the audio, I told myself. At least I can hear if she's okay. So I went to the control panel and pushed the button. Nothing at first. Then I nearly fell over. I could hear her screaming and moaning. I was about to go in there, when it dawned on me she wasn't in danger. She was just finishing off fucking one of these guys. He let out a real bellow and then another. I couldn't help it, I sat there aroused as hell thinking of them lying helpless while she did them both over. Alex is very into the Regulators as an ecstatic religion. Since the intervention she seems pretty insatiable, even with the two of us."

"Spare me the details…. Is that when you think she killed them, with your devastator? Right after she fucked them? That's the usual pathology here."

"No."

"Are you sure?"

"After she got through with the second guy, I heard her go back to the first one, who must have got aroused again listening to them. I think she jacked him off from the sound of it. Then she said stuff like, "There, can you sleep now, babies, can you sleep nice and quiet?' That kind of thing. And I heard them mumble back like they were dropping off. I realized she might be coming out, so I switched off and went down the hall, then came back whistling like I was just arriving.

"She was standing there with a plastic bag in her hand. I said, 'Want me to go in and unstrap them now?' It was hard keeping my voice straight. The look on her face was amazing. She was totally blissed out. 'No need,' she said to me. 'I already undid them. They were like little lost sheep.'

"Lambs to the slaughter," I couldn't help saying.

It's clear Grainger didn't really hear me. He goes right on like he's talking to himself.

"Yes. That's when she could have done it. In between the time I left and the time I came back down the hall."

A long pause.

"Is that the end?" I ask.

"No. There's more. I said to her, 'Want to go to bed now?' as if I had no idea what had been going on. She said she would love that, but first she had to go to the garden. I followed her along into there, my heart pounding every step. I remember thinking what a shock it was to go into the bright sunlight after being in the station's night-light programme. But then we went into one of the lab spaces and she opened one of the cryogenic fridges, took these two test tubes out of her plastic bag, put them on a rack and closed the door.

"I asked her what they were — though I guess I already knew. She didn't miss a beat. 'It's sperm.' Apparently, the Regulators want her to get pregnant, to start a real colony on Earthbaby. And they want Adam to do some in-vitro fertilization, then grow the embryos hydroponically in facsimile uterine tissue membranes. Rather than direct cloning. Seems they want a wider gene pool. Alex said she hoped you could contribute to it, if you've been on Menopause delay pills. You could still have some residual embryo cells left."

"So then what happened?" I asked, sounding — I must admit as I listen to myself — kind of dry and cynical (all right, jealous! damn it), because truth is I'm sure by now I'm completely non-reproductive no matter what technology you might want to apply to this old body. I go back to those tampon days where every month you dropped the remains of your uterine lining into waste bins, holding those things by their stringy tails like little bloody dead mice. Young as she is, I doubt whether Alex has ever even had more than her initial period to make sure she's ready for these modern-style hormone wipes.

No reply from Grainger on the tape. That's because he looked very sheepish, so I finished it for him. "You went to bed with her. Did she at least wash up and rinse her mouth out first? Guess not, what with our Adam and his garden-generated water shortage and all."

Still no reply. A long blank space, ambient breathing noises.

Then Grainger's choked voice. "She might have got up during the night and gone back there to kill them then. But when I woke up, she was still beside me, asleep. I've been pretty dazed lately, Lilly. I'm not making excuses. Just telling you how it's been."

I can hear how I'm now swinging my mood over to consoling him because I can tell he's getting to the trauma point again — of discovering the bodies.

"I understand."

"So I got up without disturbing her. I found myself walking right through the eating area — wasn't any coffee there any way. I wanted to just do a reality check by walking down to the chamber, maybe looking in to see what was up with the guys. I don't know. So I get there. No light on again. Still blissed out, asleep, I thought. For the hell of it, some kind of personal joke, I was going to wake them up. So I opened the door...."

The thought struck me. Whoever did this intended the bodies to be discovered, not by Grainger, but by me or Clarke, who were normally the ones to check on them. That way Grainger wouldn't have suffered this trauma quite so badly. Foreman she wanted to keep for a bargaining chip; until he proved worthless.

"If the air was cut off, Grainger, at least they didn't suffer. They'd have had no idea what was happening. They'd just gradually slip away."

Again on the tape there's this period of confusion and breakdown. Oh yes. She had done it to him this time. *Or had she?*

Oh my God, I said to myself. What if *Grainger* had flipped those air switches in some fit of deranged jealousy? Aren't they on the same panel as the audio? (If that *is* how they died, which seemed to me from his description of the bodies the most likely explanation.) Or, since there was no proof Alex had gone back there, maybe it was even Adam who had done it, knowing Alex would be collecting the sperm. Once he had that, the two bodies themselves were superfluous. *Superfluous!* That's right. According to Adam there's too many people on the station. Now there's two less.

Then I thought of Grainger's response to the lost Eurosoviet astronauts, how he'd held that painful death-watch over them. No. He couldn't possibly have done this. I looked closely at his face, swollen around his eyes from his distress. He had lost his youthful edge, and his hair was definitely thinner than when we first came aboard. I hadn't really noticed because until this recent break between us, I'd seen him every day — rather like the way we glance at ourselves every morning in the mirror and notice no aging for years on end until we get new contact lenses and gasp at the depth of our wrinkles. In everyone's life there's that notable date, different for everyone I suspect, which we thereafter call, 'the year I grew old.' This was it for Grainger — and for me.

"I know you're in shock right now, Grainger, but have you any idea of what you want to do about all this?"

"I want to get out of here. I want to do what you suggested yesterday: take the shuttle and disable Earthbaby."

"Then this makes three of us. Rest up for a bit," I soothed him. "I'm going to get Clarke in on this, bring him up to date."

Even as I stepped into Clarke's cabin an exultant rush swept through me. Tangled with the good fortune of Grainger's return to the fold and all that implied, was the lingering odour coming from Clarke's sheets of our recent love-making. I broke from his welcoming kiss, feeling quite triumphant and in control.

"Something important...just happened...Grainger...in my cabin..."

I stumbled it out. Clarke was stunned. Then he too saw the implications, saw himself as the commander closing down the mission with dignity and despatch, Grainger once again his co-pilot, both actively pitting their skill and experience to the task of traversing the deadly black wastes to bring us all safely home.

Clarke wanted to discuss strategy with Grainger right away. He'd checked things out yesterday, true. But there were a few problems with his doing things alone and in secret which now he wouldn't have to bother about with Grainger on hand.

"He's pretty shaken up. I left him to rest a while."

"God. This is wonderful news, Lilly. I knew the way Alex behaved yesterday something was going to crack. But what the hell are we going to do with her?"

"It could have been Adam who killed them; don't forget that."

Both Adam and Alex seemed psychically pre-conditioned to be equal candidates in this instance. What with everything that's been happening, I'm very aware how subject everyone is to erratic and unusual behaviour — even to a homicidal extent. I can't even exclude myself from this pattern when I think how better I would feel if Alex had killed Foreman and his lackey instead of the other two.

Such are the bizarre by-ways of our petty little psyches that living at this high level of intensity can numb one's cognitive processes and weaken ordinary behaviour controls. I'm ashamed to say it, but my session with Grainger had inflamed me. All Clarke had to do was slip his hand inside my robe and a rush like an opium haze overwhelmed me. Soundproofing or no soundproofing, how could Grainger next door have failed to hear my outrageous and prolonged come-scream? I went into a giggle fit afterwards wondering whether Grainger was comparing it to Alex's.

Afterwards I could barely function. Just thinking of it now, makes me pant. At this very moment I understand what living totally in the present means. I know I'm trying to write about how I got here, to being inside this shuttle hurtling earthward, so I have to deal with the past. But the future, even the immediate one, I can't think about — except I must leave this a moment and go forward to re-inject Foreman and his lackey so they'll remain semi-comatose for security purposes....

...Just finished re-reading the above after returning to my flight couch. Going through it, I edited out a few passages of flights of fancy and also what seemed to me on reflection some unnecessarily juicy sexual details. I did add one sentence, though, about including myself as being capable of homicide. Up until recently I've refused to come near Foreman, and so I found it breathtakingly strange to grab his actual flesh, bare his arm and push in the needle. Oh how easy it would have been to leave the hypo empty, to have squeezed a few centilitres of air into his veins and have him croak right in front of me from an embolism. Of course, my motivation for murder is far stronger than Alex's. Still, *let he who would cast the first stone....*

I was so shaken up I had to take a toilet break. Before taking up my position again, I floated up to the front where Clarke and Grainger were calmly handling things. They both turned and smiled at me and I said encouraging things in return. It was Grainger I was most worried about, but engaging himself like this is the best thing for him. Part of why I wrote what I did about living in the present, of course, involves how we three continue to function in the future as a team. I close my eyes and imagine how we are hurtling through black space, living bodies inside this graphoplaque skin, my two men, magnificent, guiding us.... And all this is my doing....

First things first. So the three of us jammed into my cabin in a conspiratorial huddle. Clarke was all for straightforwardly declaring to Alex and Adam that in his opinion things had gone out of control due to the unforeseen stresses we had been put under. That whimsically murdering people, whoever they might be, was not on. That the solution to our problems was as I had suggested yesterday, and therefore he was giving the order to immediately abandon ship. Grainger shook his head at that.

"We may be in the majority, but Alex won't let us do it. In her mind, she is going to carry out the Regulators' manifest destiny. Her plan was to keep the shuttle here so she can use its big thrusters for orbital corrections once NASA cuts off the guide beam. Of course, doing that means there's not enough energy to get the shuttle back to earth, as you know. The three of us have already been working on a five-year plan. My part was to do asteroid capture, both ice and mineral, to create future habitats. This sperm collecting and cloning she told me about is obviously all a part of it. Now it's plain they don't ever mean to go back."

I wondered whether Grainger's reluctance to go along with Clarke's idea of a direct approach was because he still had a lingering irrational terror of confronting Alex. In the same way we can never be totally objective in our dealings with our parents or our children.

"But if they don't go back with us," Clarke said, "how the hell are we going to disable Earthbaby?"

"Once they realize we're serious about that, surely they'll opt to come with us, won't they?" I asked.

Moot point. If they refused to come with us, did that mean we had to terminate them along with the station? We looked at each other. Could we bring ourselves to do that? Maybe in our imaginations. But to actually push the button? Maybe they would come with us. Maybe this was all hypothetical.

Well, as it turned out, it wasn't hypothetical. But more on that later. Clarke just turned to look back at me again from up front in the shuttle's pilot seat and waved me forward....

....Back again.

This time what Clarke had to say was something very important. "The beam's gone, Lilly. They just cut it."

So it had been no idle threat after all. Part of why I had felt little anxiety sitting here writing as we continued our mind-numbing rush through outer space was the fact the laser-beam, our guide rail back to Earth, had not been cut at NASA's deadline. Once NASA's deadline had passed, we had all cheered, assuming it had been a bluff and they'd keep it functioning. Since we locked out the shuttle's communication systems, NASA wouldn't even know we were speeding homeward. We wanted no deadly interference from them such as sending us into a spin crisis like last time. But now, without being able to ride the beam means navigating the shuttle turns into a no-rest situation for our four pilots. It has to be done on manual over-ride the whole rest of the way back — something never tried before.

Grainger suspects NASA must have tried to communicate with Earthbaby, but naturally got no reply. Keeping the beam alive for the last few hours was NASA just making sure there wasn't a malfunction in the communication system or beam alignment. (If it doesn't collide with something, I wonder how far a beam like that goes off into space before it dissipates?)

I look to see how Foreman has taken it, but like his lackey he's pretty dopey from the last shot I gave him and doesn't really get the significance. Once again I think, how much better to have flung him out into space as a sacrifice to Alex's regulators! Considering the trouble we went to getting him and his lackey on board, I am still hoping Foreman might be our insurance against those NASA bastards shooting us down once we get to Earth orbit, (if we ever make it that far!) or helping our escape using him as hostage.

I guess I'll never forget the look on Alex's face when she comprehended what we had done. It was Grainger's idea to pre-empt any expected resistance from Alex and Adam. While Alex and Adam still slept in their cabins, we went with him to his observatory where he quickly plotted an extreme orbital change for Earthbaby achievable by a uni-directional full blast of the orbital correction system. He fed the data into the system, over-rode the auto-security, and ignited the nozzles.

As we suspected, initial acceleration was so slow it was imperceptible. Overcoming the inertia of a large mass such as Earthbaby, with the forces to hand, is rather like a single person pushing off a very large boat in still water from the dock. But we knew the orbit had shifted when suddenly Earthbaby's various systems started to flicker out and the recently-established independence schedules began taking over. Earthbaby had severed itself from the laser umbilicous and was now alone, drifting further and further away from its lifeline at an accelerating rate.

Even though I had spent such a long time on Earthbaby and had become used to the dumbfounding idea that we were a mere particle adrift in a vast cold system, this irrevocable separation of the craft gave me a sensation of loneliness and horror. Now the structure we rode seemed incredibly flimsy and makeshift. From being an ocean liner steaming confidently to its destination, we had become a life-raft bobbing on an ocean, subject to whatever forces might sweep over us.

"They'll never find this place again," Grainger commented. "In an hour or so it will truly be lost in space."

I jumped to his words. All my instincts were to get out of there. Or be entombed forever.

Clarke had caught my feelings too, I could tell.

"We've got to get out of here, while we can still re-connect the shuttle to the beam out there," Clarke urged us. "If we don't have it for the initial trajectory it will be a hell of a bugger getting ourselves back to Earth."

"Let's start getting everybody on board," I said.

It was then I got the idea to trank up Foreman and his lackey so they could offer no resistance. Clarke and I did the job then hustled Foreman and his lackey through the docking lock and onto the shuttle. By the time we got there, they were pretty jelly-legged.

Risto and his co-pilot Tupac were playing three-D dominoes. Clarke had out his devastator, but it wasn't really needed. Once we told them about shifting Earthbaby off the beam, they had no choice but to go along with us. Besides which they were pretty sympatico to start with. Not being combat army types, they had no arms and Calrke and I quickly checked the lockers to see if they were clean as the two of them assured us they were.

Clarke and I headed back for the confrontation with Adam and Alex. I was worried about our fire-power being low if it came to a shoot-out and was anxious on Grainger's behalf, because he was unarmed.

When we got back to Central he wasn't there. Then I heard him coming down the corridor saying, "Keep moving Alex. You're coming with us."

Cunning devil. Somehow he'd got back his devastator.

"She was just getting dressed. I didn't let on to her what was happening until I had my hands on this thing."

"Why are you doing this to me, Grainger? What's happened to you?"

Grainger ignored her.

"I couldn't find her own weapon in there," he started to say, when Adam suddenly appeared behind him. I had no chance to shout a warning.

"That's because I've got it, traitor," he yelled. "Drop that damn thing or I'll blast you to hell!"

Grainger whirled around to face him, lowering his weapon as he did so, but Clarke had raised his.

"Hold fire, Adam! You're in my sights."

So there everybody was, at an impasse. Into this gridlock I

stepped forward and told Adam and Alex that Clarke had decided to order that the ship be abandoned. I added there was now no alternative, because we had taken the unilateral action of accelerating the station off the beam.

By now Alex had sidled her way next to Adam. She was bright. She knew the jig was up.

"Why did you betray us like this, Grainger?" There was all the fervour of the rejected lover in her voice, but also a strange note of resignation, almost martyrdom.

Grainger literally shook and his eyes watered as he looked at her.

"I found them dead, Alex. How could you do that?"

"It was necessary for everyone's survival, Grainger. It was a glorious sacrifice. Now they are manifested in Regulator consciousness. Had they remained oppositional, they would have been rejected."

I decided to cut through all the blather.

"So what are we going to do here? Shoot each other? Come with us, you two. There's no alternative and the longer we wait the less chance there is of getting back."

Then Adam, his weapon still pointed disconcertingly at Grainger, anxiety sweat beading on his brow, spoke up.

"We're staying. We have a job to do. The Regulators will help us."

"Yes," Alex continued, reaching out for his free hand, "they will intervene. Their will shall be done."

"You could be dead inside a year," Clarke told them. "Don't be nuts, Adam."

"The garden needs me. Alex needs me."

"And the regulators need us," Alex finished.

I could see persuading them was hopeless, and every minute we waited decreased our chances of re-locating the beam with the shuttle.

"We're leaving now," I said. "It's now or never."

In response, they turned dramatically and walked off towards the garden.

Grainger looked devastated.

"Alex!" he shouted after her, still holding his weapon.

She turned around and faced him. I held my breath.

"The orbital information is all saved in my computer in the observatory."

Alex stood silent, waiting for more from him. But that was it. Grainger was still with us.

Alex said nothing, just turned her back and took Adam's hand again as they walked off.

I thought I was strong and determined; so I was totally surprised when I found myself screaming her name, begging her a last time to come with us.

To no effect. I couldn't believe I would never see her again. It saddens me terribly now. What a dreadful life she has led, and how bravely and crazily she has tried to make her own sense out of it. But then I think: and how murderously.

Well, they are there, and we are here. Who knows if she might find some way to keep Earthbaby rolling around the solar system for ever and ever? She has Grainger's observatory, the new co-ordinates. Come to think of it, there's also the space buggy. And what might she be able to do with the rocket-power in those missiles?

As for us, with the beam gone, I know we are on the edge, almost entirely reliant on Grainger's orbital expertise and the others' ability to make fine touch adjustments to keep our craft matched with the navigation fiche overlays that Grainger is constantly providing. A curious thing, these operations, like video-games, with strange yet deadly exercises that threaten real not virtual destruction. So hard to relate to the actual physical reality of our hurtling across vast distances totally hostile to human life. Looking out the port is no help. Only when we get a visual of Earth framed there will it mean anything to me.

Meanwhile I am in this cabin, weightless, slightly too much blood going to my head and not quite enough to my feet, having some trouble with stomach regurgitation as I always do, my hair afloat, the couch-straps loosely fastened so I drift up and down an eerie inch or so above the mattress.

Grainger has turned things over to Risto now we've negotiated the second difficult parabola of our trajectory. It's straight ahead for a while. He's swimming back towards me along the roof of the cabin, looking utterly exhausted. I smile at him.

I will close this down now, then catch him in my arms and pull him down on top of me. That will surprise him.

Get us back, Grainger, and all is forgiven.... ❧

The building Annina has arranged for them to stay in is on one of the Jugendstil streets near Senate square. A Babylonian arch leads them into the central foyer, also circular and domed, decorated with Minoan columns and walls stencilled with old Greek key motifs. Spiral stone steps wind round the ancient open-cage elevator of shining brass which carries them up to the apartment itself.

"It's like a time capsule, isn't it?" Leslie murmurs, pulling blinds down over lofty casement windows with elaborate brass handles.

"Must have seemed very modern and up-to-date when Lenin slept here. When would that be, 1912 or so?"

"Must have been a lot colder in the winter back then," Leslie says, running her hand over a green tile stove, decorated art nouveau style with motifs of leaping salmon, which fills one corner almost to the ceiling.

How much the world has changed in little more than a very old person's lifetime. He imagines the time, over a hundred and twenty-five years ago, when, just like now, everything was up for grabs, in ceaseless turmoil. Yet somehow whole districts of beautiful buildings like this one rose out of the muck. At times like that all sorts of factions were coming and going, contending with each other, new movements being born and dying, just as they are doing now. It's rather like those short, chaotic periods of evolution during which new species proliferate right after some natural disaster which terminates long aeons of slow development.

She lies next to him, stroking his forehead. A swaying tree-branch outside the far window casts flickering shadows across the hardwood floor, up high walls and over laurel-wreath roundels on the decorated plaster ceiling. Lenin and his friend the chief of police, who should have arrested him and turned him over to the Russians, may have sat right there at that table, talking of revolution. And where did it all lead, after all? All gone: but this building and its ghosts remain.

A ring at their door. Suddenly the black wave of his jet-lag clears from his head. Bill and Perlita!

Perlita first, then Bill, almost speechless hugging him. He clings to their absolute physical presence, assuring himself they are here, they are real. Still holding hands together they discover in the kitchen coffee and cinnamon pullas, and a note from Annina to wait for her call.

"Annina and Nokia Net are keeping an eye on events as much as possible," Leslie tells them.

Perlita's communicator is in the middle of the table where, in exile, Lenin and his cronies planned their revolution. And now the four of them also sit round it, sharing their separate stories, so that in an hour or so Tremaine feels himself held together in common with them again. Will history also take note of this meeting? An odd thought. There's some strange fate, though, that the four of them, exiles from different places, should all meet up here, in this particular marked place. (A gathering contrived, don't forget, he tells himself, by Leslie and Annina!) When Leslie lets him in on all her secrets, will it turn out she is a secret charismatic leader of some new movement or another? He hopes not.

And what does being in exile actually mean? One's place of exile is another's native land. To the people out there in space, this whole world is home.

"If the shuttle doesn't take off in this window," Tremaine comments, "Earthbaby will be moving into apogee. It'll be months before the next chance."

No news yet. Occasionally Perlita's fingers run over her phone nervously. She's a lot improved, but not yet back to her serene and confident self. He remembers her triumphant stance, the set of her head as she emptied the bullets from her gun into the drawer after her election night mission. Her sexuality, yes, that's the thing most probably still damaged. Not to mention the destruction of her sense of place and community as she recovers from her trauma, in exile with the rest of them. When this is over, when she goes back, then let her be whole again he prays.

Bill, too, seems agitated.

"For an old anchorman, no news ain't good news!" Bill quips. "Sure would satisfy knowing what the hell's going on up there."

Perhaps because of Leslie's serene calm since they arrived, Tremaine doesn't completely share Bill and Perlita's anxiety.

"Must be hard on you, Bill," Leslie jokes, "not being the one who knows the news before anyone else."

Finally, Perlita's phone jingles a little musical riff.

"What?" Bill asks as she listens.

Leslie raises her eyebrows as if to say, See what I mean? But restrains herself.

"Here, Leslie. It's Annina for you."

Hand over the mouthpiece, Leslie relays the news to Bill as she hears it.

"They've been working with those laser-beam co-ordinates we gave them and sending out crunch-packet location signals to Earthbaby and the shuttle. Seems there's been some kind of detachment a while ago which they interpret as the shuttle leaving."

"Well, there you go," Tremaine exclaims.

"Annina wants us up there to go over the data with her," Leslie finishes, handing the phone back to Perlita.

"Did Annina say anything about auxiliary radio beam monitoring?" Bill asks.

"They've heard nothing on the channel at all."

"That's pretty scatty, Babe. Why wouldn't that shuttle crew beam down to NASA they were unlatched?"

"Depends who's in the shuttle, I would think," Leslie muses.

"Are you suggesting it may be our crew?" Tremaine asks her.

"Could be they pirated it," Bill concludes. "Why not?"

"They're all pretty damn resourceful," Tremaine says, picturing Lilly and Alex especially. And also that young Grainger who did so well during the spin crisis.

"But why fly it back to NASA?"

Perlita has a point there. She asks Tremaine whether the shuttle can ride the laser back without interference or communications from NASA.

"Sending signals from Earth takes too long. The shuttle's designed to follow the beam automatically, like a train riding a rail, except it's not a fixed rail. The beam is moving all the time in a trajectory determined mainly by Earth orbit and Earthbaby orbit. It's not like you're taking a straight shot back, though at any given moment the beam connects the two by the shortest distance in a straight line."

"Well," Bill says. "If communications remain closed, we might never find out anything at all."

"Nothing we can do about it," Tremaine says inanely.

"Well, let's get up there. I'm keen to see Annina again."

It's rush hour, and taxis are scarce. An antique green streetcar tackles the slope at the end of their street, so they jump it and ride the fifteen minutes up to Nokia Net.

Unlike New York, Helsinki has creatively transformed itself with verve and intelligence. Since the sea reclaimed much of the centuries of infill between its original granite islands, Helsinki has developed a Venetian air, very much in accord, Tremaine thinks, with its new Mediterranean climate. Strategically placed sea-locks and dykes maintain almost the same sea-level in the ponds and inlets of parks in the city centre. Unprotectable low-lying areas have become scenic waterways, with tourist boats visiting major buildings such as the Ateneum museum and the art deco railway station (converted into a market area) which have been elevated and re-foundationed.

Most of the old Jugendstil areas, such as the one where their guest house is located, were built on solid foundations high enough, for the most part, not to worry about. The white and gold Lutheran cathedral, of course, still presides over the ceaseless carnival parade of the low-rise city. It's become one huge outdoor café, Tremaine thinks. Stockmann's is still the centre of the known universe, the Esplanadi as fashionable as ever, and out in the bay the blue flag still flies over the fortress of Suomenlinna.. The old cobblestone waterfront market has gone — that's a big regret — but on the other hand, behind the statue of Mannerheim and the Modern Art Museum is a flooded glass monstrosity, comically afloat like an ice cube — an old newspaper monopoly head office from the turn of the century — scarcely built before abandoned.

Into Pasila and they jump off at Nokia Net, which inhabits the old radio and television station, a mass of post-modern tinted glass and echoing hallways. They are escorted right to the top and into the office of Annina Mustonen, Head of the Experimental Division, who embraces Leslie first, then all of them warmly.

"Tervetuloa. Welcome, welcome to Finland."

A fine-looking woman, Tremaine thinks. Except for the smile wrinkles around her mouth, her tight-skinned, high-cheekboned face conceals her late middle age, along with her boyish bobbed haircut, popular with Finnish women because it shows off their long necks. Tall and large boned, she moves with a country-lass awkwardness typical of her generation, but her opalescent blue eyes are small and lively over the perkiness of her ski-jump nose, and her low voice is strong and confident.

"Since we phoned you, we think something else has happened."

Her technical group bring over the data streams and spread them out for him and Leslie to look at. Thank God for Leslie's expertise, or he wouldn't know what they were talking about. It soon becomes clear, though.

"Well," he says to Perlita and Bill. "It's pretty certain, from what Annina and her team have gathered, that the laser guide beam has been entirely truncated. Those poor buggers on the shuttle, whoever they are, are entirely on their own."

SOCIAL DYNAMICS PROJECT: EARTHBABY
JOURNAL OF LILLITH SHAWNADITHIT

Awake again.

When I fell asleep, this little laptop suspended itself. I touch it…and it hums into action, as if nothing has happened, no time has passed. Still a little disoriented. Darkened quartz windows on the port side — sun must be at an acute angle — nothing to see except brassy iridescence. Through this near-side one — oh how lovely! — like a Faberge egg, Earth itself: blue, traced with emerald, gauze-wrapped…. My heart thumps with hopes of reaching it. What I want most? To hike along a wood's edge in soft rain breathing in smells of forest and wildflowers.

How encouraging to see it looming so large. Does this mean we are on track? How big does it have to appear before we can be sure we won't just whizz by it at an impossible speed without achieving orbit?

From the sublime to the ridiculous: I see it's time to knock out Foreman and his lackey again. I'd give them a bigger dose, but under these weightless artificial circumstances they might react badly. Since they proved useless to us, I wish we had left them on Earthbaby — to Adam and Alex's tender mercies. But as Grainger and Clarke have told me, how much better to bring Foreman back alive to face the world's loathing, a war criminal humiliated by the cowardly circumstances of his capture.

…back again. Every time I do this, it takes some while for me to calm down. My murderous impulses remain unabated. I try to flick off the touch of that bastard's flesh from my fingers.

And despite our visual contact with Earth, we are not out of the woods yet. How disembodied I felt floating about while Risto and Tupec slept, and Grainger and Clarke were calculating the thruster program to steer us through the next most difficult parabola. I'm worried about Grainger. Grey-faced, he's unable to eat despite my ministrations. While he was occupied alone creating fiches for the next sequence, I asked Clarke in whispers how he thought we were doing. He felt we might achieve orbit if we were lucky. But what about re-entry? "That's another question," he said. I said a few encouraging words to Grainger, and kissed him on the forehead.

As I gaze again at Earth (am I just convincing myself it seems larger than before?) it looks as if we could just aim ourselves straight at it. But of course Earth isn't the fixed point hovering in space it appears to be through this window. And neither is this shuttle. On Earth nature may be said to abhor a vacuum, in space it avoids a straight line. In order for these two objects speeding along their differently curved trajectories to intersect with each other in a precise enough way to produce an orbital relationship demands very complex navigating and precise adjustments of speed and direction. It's way beyond my ken. Only when I see the whole round world fill this window frame — as I remember it did a few hours after we left it so many months ago — will I know Clarke and Grainger's efforts have paid off.

How much has happened and how much has changed since Alex gently patted Adam and me like two helium balloons into position by this window to look back at that magnificent scene. I cried then and will cry when I see it again, I know; not just with relief, but for the failure of Jock and Tremaine's enterprise, and for those two we left behind.

Just a second. I hear Grainger's voice raised.

"Check it again, Clarke."

I look to see what they're doing. Clarke's using the virtual sextant program displayed on the monitor above his control seat.

"It's what I've got, Grainger. Definitely."

I see Grainger pour over his own screen, frowning.

"Shit! We must have been amplifying that damn micro-degree error for a couple of hours now. How do we get out of this?"

"I don't think we should try correcting just yet, Grainger. We entered the new parabolic shift phase about ten minutes ago. Changing to another plane angle could really screw us up. At least we have the error in only one dimension right now."

"Yes. But goddammit, waiting several hours to go through the shift program means a bigger correction and a longer burn time at the end of it."

"I know. You're worried about compounding our acceleration curve."

"Yes. And not having enough juice and time to countervail it sufficiently as we enter Earth field. Christ, Clarke! This leaves us with a choice between missing, or burning up."

"You've got a good point. My feeling is, though, our chances are better staying with what we've got. How about deliberately under-correcting at the end of it?"

"That'll see us with two anomalies."

"Better two half-problems, than one big one. What I'm saying is, we play along to the end, like a squeeze-play in bridge."

"Playing it by ear like that could be really hairy, Clarke."

"But that's what you're really good at," Clarke tells him.

Even from back here, I can tell Grainger is moved by Clarke's remarks.

"I'm not at my best, Clarke."

"You will be if you get some rest right now," I hear Clarke urge him. "I can take it through this phase, then hand it over to Risto and Tupec. By the time it gets crucial you'll be ready for it."

My aberrant mind flashes, where are you Alex when we really need you?

I have been thinking of Adam and Alex, doomed by their own insane choice to stay on Earthbaby, as already being dead. From what has just gone on between Clarke and Grainger, though, it seems all of us may be turned to cinders long before their consciousness finally flickers out.

I see Grainger accept Clarke's advice and recline his seat.

And so I continue to wait, willing that blue planet to grow larger…larger…

It's about two hours later….

Foreman woke up a while ago and started raving.

"No mercy for you, when we get back! I'll laser your eyes out! No fucking Regulators are going to drain my blood!" he kept screaming. That sort of craziness.

He managed to undo himself and careened around the cabin. I commandeered Risto and Tupec to help out. Once they had him strapped down, and I injected him again, they exchanged places with Clarke and Grainger, since they were awake now anyway. There were a few more hours to go to complete the turn cycle. I listened to hear whether Clarke and Grainger would fill them in on the gathering crisis, but I saw them give each other a look and nothing was said.

Does the world appear much larger? I can't honestly say. I trace my finger around its outline on the glass. So the deathwatch continues….

My Grandmother told me her very first memory was sitting in a coal cellar during a bombing raid in World War Two. In the darkness all she could see was the glitter of the cat's eyes sitting on the coal pile, and the smell of its shit it had tried to bury there. The cellar shook with the noise, she said, "like a piano falling downstairs over and over and over." Five hundred planes with four un-muffled piston engines on each — a continuous rolling doomsday thunderclap. Lofting upwards into this massive drone, desperate coughing of ack-ack and pom-pom anti-aircraft batteries created a crackling flak field, haunted by whining fighters.

At my urging, she was able to exactly reproduce all the different sound effects, including staccato stuttering machine guns, final death dives and, worst of all, the open-mouthed scream of bomb-lines tearing through the air then exploding in pounding bass-drum sequences of utter annihilation. Hands over her ears, eyes closed, she imagined herself having finished counting to ten and still being alive when she got there. Then she began counting, reached ten, and realized what she had imagined was true. She was still alive.

So she did it again. Hour after hour she began gaining confidence that what she imagined, if she imagined it hard enough, would actually come true. And so indeed she was passed over — the little row house suffering only blown-in windows and front door, someone's flying gas stove crashing through the upstairs wall, and a line of bullet-holes through her mother's maple wardrobe, her best dress miraculously untouched.

All my life I have been dreading the coming of my time to count to ten after imagining myself still alive at the end of it. Now I have a feeling.... ⌒⌣

"Our boys must've pirated the shuttle for NASA to screw them up like that," Bill says.

"What does cutting the guide beam actually mean for the shuttle?" Perlita asks.

"It still comes," Annina tells her, pointing to a stream of figures circled with a marker. "But there is more deviation than before."

"What Annina's saying," Leslie interprets, "is that the signals she and her colleagues are sending up from here — using tracking co-ordinates which we provided for NASA's laser beam — are still able to confirm the shuttle's presence; but their contact with it is not so consistent as it was before."

"Right," Tremaine agrees. "Now the laser's gone, it must be hell's own time for the shuttle crew to maintain the right trajectories using manual over-rides. They're probably bumping on and off course every few seconds."

"Obviously NASA doesn't care if it crashes. Like Bill says, it must be our people in there." Leslie concludes.

"No one has done such a long-distance trip on manual before, but I bet Clarke goes back to the old era before fully automatic guide beams, and maybe Grainger too," Tremaine tries to reassure them.

"What about communications?" Bill asks. "Isn't the auxiliary radio frequency still operative?"

"Yes. But Annina tells me the boys here have been monitoring that frequency and so far have heard nothing as before."

"That makes sense," Perlita says. "NASA wouldn't want to use it, and the people in the shuttle don't want to contact NASA either."

Tremaine ponders the situation.

"Even if they make it back to Earth and manage to slide into a reasonable orbit, there's a hell of a re-entry problem," he tells them. "One degree off the right attitude and they'll burn up."

Annina Mustonen has been listening to all this. She asks more questions

to make sure she has read the situation completely. "We need to connect with them somehow. The channel is still opened, not jammed. But as soon as we send a signal on it, it could be cut off."

"If they do make it to Earth orbit," Tremaine tells her, "then radio telemetry communication would be adequate to bring them through re-entry; but as you say, Annina, NASA could jam it at the crucial moment."

Annina reflects for a few moments, then seems to make a decision.

"I think we have to do something else. Let me speak with Leslie about this."

She takes Leslie aside and they excuse themselves while they go into her office. Tremaine can see them talking animatedly together. Then Annina calls on her communicator, talking rapidly in Finnish. A minute later, she and Leslie come out and Annina says, "Come with me. General Vehvilainen wants to meet with us."

They think they are going to another lab or office; but no. They go to the roof where they are met by the Finnish Eurosoviet General, Olli Vehvilainen, tall and impressive in full uniform. He speaks slowly in the old way, with a deep bass voice.

"I came right away from the reception. Welcome to Finland."

He shakes hands formally all round, but with a sweet eager smile lighting up his round cheerful face. Tremaine cannot help thinking how much he reminds him of a giant boy scout, the traditional Puukko in a leather sheath attached to his belt. Then he announces, with perfect timing, "Good luck in Lapland. Mustonen will go with you."

Before they can reply, the helicopter he has arrived in fires up, making speech impossible. They wave to the General and jump in.

"Not another ride in one of these things," Tremaine grumbles.

"At least you're not driving," Leslie says. "And look over there. The sun's coming up again."

"Only three hours and we are there," Annina reassures them.

At least this time he's a passenger. Following the rail lines, Helsinki has expanded out many times since he was here before, stretching into a flooded granite landscape of forests and farms. Here and there signs of denser habitation incise the dappled woods like shamanistic pictographs on lichen-covered boulders.

Then they are skimming over lakes of brass and forests of silver. So much water spilled by departing glaciers; and as dawn brightens he can see uncertain rivers questing serpentine through ribbon-bogs and low round hills to find blue sea. The fertile woodlands, made more fertile by each warming year, are crammed with birch trees, patched increasingly as they travel north with dark pine islands and yellow meadows.

Another hour and Annina points down.

"Rovanemi, on the Arctic Circle," she announces. "Now we are in Lapland."

Amazing the trees could still be so thick and tall so far north, Tremaine thinks. And even farms dotted about, hay from the look of it, to help feed huge reindeer herds which the warming trend has made it possible to sustain.

"Where are we landing?" he asks Annina.

"North of Rovanemi," Annina answers. "Sodankyla."

"What does that mean?" Perlita asks her.

"War village."

Leslie, clinging to his arm affectionately, squeezes the nape of his neck.

"So what dark secrets are you going to tell me?" he whispers to her.

He turns to look at her directly, then back to the window. Her face is still there reflected, smiling at him while skimming over the landscape. For a moment he is reminded of the copper room, the image of her working at the computer etched on the gleaming wall. In the beginning.

She leans forward onto his back so her chin is on his shoulder and she can look out with him. Now their two faces are reflected together in the window.

"Do you see that group of new town-sites down there?"

"Yes...?"

"Well, have you ever noticed, Andrew, with the way the streets and houses are arranged and interconnected, that they look exactly like circuit boards in a computer...?"

SOCIAL DYNAMICS PROJECT:EARTHBABY
JOURNAL OF LILLITH SHAWNADITHIT

An amazing thing has happened! I don't yet know what it's all about. I was dozing off again, thinking about counting to ten, vaguely aware of the Earth ball floating in velvet blackness, when suddenly the window was filled with blue light. It suffused the whole skin of the shuttle. I gave a sharp cry. Risto and Tupec had seen it too. Grainger and Clarke woke up, confused.

"What is it?" I asked.

"A beam. We must be in a beam." Clarke replied.

"Where from?" Grainger wanted to know. "I woke up thinking somehow it was coming from Alex and Earthbaby."

"Well at least it's not weaponry," Tupec said. "There'd be damage by now."

"Could be a target light to missile us when we get closer to home," Risto said.

Tupec took out the cabin lights and we all looked for a source. Unlike a searchlight on earth, any kind of light beam sifts invisibly through empty space since there's no reflective medium to pass through. So it wasn't as though the beam could actually be seen, only "known" as it hit us in the shuttle.

Tupec blasted out a radar pulse to see if the light was coming from any other object around us. Nothing.

But somewhere out there had to be the blue pinprick of the beam's source.

"You can see it's not coming from the sun side by the angle it makes coming through the viewports," Clarke demonstrated to everybody. "See. There's the shadow of my hand."

I guess I was the first to realize what was happening.

"It's coming from Earth," I said. "We can't see it because it's lost in the solar illumination of the atmosphere."

"She's right," Risto said. He'd picked up the control seat binoculars. "If you look very closely, now and again I think I can see the source dot and maybe even a little line as it passes through the atmosphere."

We passed the glasses around, but no one else seemed able to see it; but then Risto was using younger eyes. His idea it was an aiming laser bothered me. But then, as we were talking, the light began to flicker. It no longer came in the side ports. We could only see it through the front cabin windows playing on the nose of the shuttle's graphoplaque skin. If it was targeting us, it made no sense if it was drifting away.

Clarke expressed what I was thinking, "What else can it be but a guide beam?"

"But why put it in the visible spectrum?" I asked.

"So we'd notice," Grainger replied. "NASA would just turn on the laser again."

Now the blue light had shifted onto the forward fuselage of the shuttle. Only a thin edge of it still illuminated the cabin where we stood. The three of us were bouncing slowly up and down as we talked or gestured, swimming in the cabin air. The beautiful arrays of coloured lights from the control panel shone down on Risto and Tupec at their seats.

"Looks like we'll lose it soon, wherever it's coming from," Grainger warned.

He sounded very nervous. I knew from his conversation with Clarke that he felt very insecure about our chances of survival using manual over-rides. But would there be a happier conclusion should he somehow put his faith in this strange blue apparition? My own thinking was that maybe someone might be trying to help us. I looked at Grainger again.

Then the thought struck me. Maybe what Grainger had believed when he woke up — that the beam was somehow connected to Alex — wasn't so far off after all. For some moments I allowed myself the comfort of a simple explanation: this was another intervention by the Regulators!

"What do you think, Grainger?" Clarke wanted to know. "What should we do about this?"

Talk about a voice from God. I practically fainted from nervous shock because the next thing I heard were these words booming out of the auxiliary radio speakers: "Lock on the beam. Repeat. Lock on the...."

The rest of it was a harsh white noise of static.

Tupec wrestled with it, but to no avail.

At the same time we fell into darkness. The beam had slipped away from us.

"Clarke," Grainger said. "I don't know what this is, but I think we should take a chance on testing it out."

Clarke turned to me. "What do you say, Lilly?"

I drew a deep breath. So it was up to me was it? I was half-convinced it was the Regulators — but I didn't want to think about that, with all the confusion and maybe even guilt it could stir up in me. So I went to that part of my brain which instinctively deduced that since Earth was where we wanted to be, then anything coming from there, whatever its source, was something to cling on to.

"Go for it."

Clarke and Grainger got back into their control seats. Now they had to relocate the damn thing or we were back to square one again. Working on the visual angle of the beam's disappearance off the starboard side wing-stub, Grainger put in a tiny correction to our trajectory. We waited.

Perhaps the damn thing had been turned off. Tupec strained his eyes to catch another glimpse of it through the atmosphere swirling around the globe. No dice.

So here I am back here again on my launch couch, setting my belt slightly loose as before, fiddling once again with this stupid little device, staring out at that blue ball. If it's getting nearer then it's so minimal I can't discern it....

There's just been a cheer from up front! The beam is back!

"On the wing!" Grainger shouts. "Let it come right on to us."

And so it does. First through the forward view ports, then swinging round to my very own window again.

"Let's see what this thing is made of," Clarke mutters.

"Manual over-ride canceled," Grainger confirms.

I sit poised and ready over this keyboard. Is it going to be a go or no?

"Holding steady," Clarke announces.

One...two...

Grainger, watching the thruster array signal lights: "Rapid microcorrections on automatic mode, Clarke."

Four...five...

"Looks like we're riding on it, Grainger," Clarke responds. "Virtual sextant indicates partial correction of that incipient anomaly."

Seven...eight...

"They're guiding us in, Clarke. Still dicey on compounding our acceleration curve, but it looks like they're giving us the minimum possible for the correction. We couldn't possibly have done it like this on manual."

Ten.

All I can think of is *keep that blue light shining, keep that blue light shining on me...* Regulators or no Regulators....

And it is still shining several hours later as I take this up again. Not much to report except we are all still speculating about the beam's origin. All I care about right now is the world rushing up to meet my eager eyes, ever bigger, ever more beautiful. Oh Lord, one more river to cross, one more mountain to climb. I've always hated this next part, this part where you crash into the invisible, but oh-so-solid atmosphere.

Clarke and Grainger have been worrying whether the beam will carry re-entry information, or will it just take us into initial orbit. The damn auxiliary radio seems to be jammed in a wide spectrum, and this blue guide beam can't function as a communication wand like the complex laser to Earthbaby because it has no reciprocal hand-shaking termination station. On top of that, we're going faster than we should now we are in the Earth's field, and Grainger is again nervous about bringing it down at the right attitude if he has to do it himself. It seems to me, at the rate we are going, the deceleration G forces Grainger has calculated will likely black every one out. Not a healthy situation if we have to react to malfunctions.

Thinking about this, I have just suggested to every one that we should dress in our suits. That way we have a better chance of surviving excessive heat-rise, we are assured of a continuous oxygen supply, and God forbid it should happen, but we would also be protected against pressure blow-out.

Okay. So I am going to do that now....

Clarke just informed everyone we are about to enter orbit. And away we go. Now, as I look out the port, my visor up and my gloves off so I can still type, the world is right in our face. I don't think of us as moving any more. What it looks like, feels like, is some giant just started spinning the world at a rapid pace in front of us. The only way I know it is actually we in the shuttle who are moving is our rapid crossing of the twilight zone onto the night side.

"The beam's still with us!" Grainger shouts.

.

So they haven't disconnected after all. The light from it is intense against the blackness and the viewport darkens trying to average the light values.

"They might just be tracking us for an orbit or two," Clarke suggests. "We'll know if they mean to bring us down when they start changing our attitude."

"If they don't," Grainger says, "then we'll go to over-ride and fly this baby down ourselves."

Grainger going into his heroic role. At this moment I find it very endearing. I think of him and Clarke, and I have an overwhelming rush of love for them. Oh now, see this, it is almost comical: tears pouring down onto the backs of my hands threatening to destroy this keyboard....

"Attitude change!" Clarke yells.

"I'm checking it, Clarke. Seems a bit extreme to me. Do we trust this?"

"We have to. Port yaw, Grainger!"

Whew! I feel that one. My window is now pointing into space. I close my visor.

"Retro-ignition! We're going in, Grainger! Take it over!"

Holy shit! I must put on my gloves and shove this....

*   *   *

Vertigo. But still alive. Thanks Granny.

After all those months in space, it feels strange to have such a solid point of reference out there. Up, down, sideways. All meaningful terms once again. And the light! It's either dawn or beginning sunset out there, I can't yet tell which, but every object in creation is glowing as we float down, down like a snowflake over lovely dappled woods, a quietly meandering river, a shining eye of a reed-rimmed lake. There are meadows close by. And what is that? A rippling tide is flowing over the landscape as if some river had burst its banks and its silt-brown waters are churning, within them a jumble of torn-out trees, their branches tangled together.

Reindeer. I can't believe it. Are we in the land of Santa Klaus or in Regulator headquarters? What difference does it make? There are thousands of them, rumps heaving and antlers jostling: such profligate life. We fly right over them. It must have been our shadow which started them up. And now the landing strip.

We touch down, speed by everything in a blur as if we were those running reindeer ourselves. These fine moments of coming home. Running across the tarmac, ahead of everyone else, there's Andrew Tremaine. I should have suspected as much. Every one in the cabin is clapping and laughing.

We are here.

I think to myself, as I come to the end of this journey, and to the end of this academically useless journal, where is "here" anyway?

And I answer: Here *is* now *for ever and ever…*

Amen.

File/Save

Do you want to keep changes?

Yes ∾